HARCOURT'S
Mountain

Is love strong enough to save you from a broken past?

ELAINE DODGE

1867. It's Spring in British Columbia, Canada. Luke
Harcourt has made a mountain home for himself in the wild
forests. On a supply run to town he comes across the Bride
Ship. One of the women catches his eye. Although dirty, her
clothes speak of a gentle refinement, and her eyes of desperation. Luke knows he can't leave her there. He buys her on
a whim, compelled to save her from a life of prostitution
and slavery.

Hope Booker is terrified when she's sold, but Luke prom-
ises not to touch her. She's frightened and confused. Every
day she encounters new dangers on their mountain. As she
gets to know him, Hope is tempted to open her heart to
Luke. But she's afraid the biggest danger is falling in love
with her husband.

As Luke and Hope navigate their way to love, a string of
events arise, tearing them apart. Hope is left stranded on the
mountain in one of the worst winters in decades. She has no
idea where Luke is, or even if he's alive. Can Hope survive
a mountain winter alone? And will she ever see Luke again?

From the very first page, Harcourt's Mountain is a tale of
courage and love. Embrace this journey as you risk the wild
Canadian frontier with Hope and Luke. Follow their trials,
misfortunes, and the love they both deserve. Be part of this
epic love story.

PRAISE FOR HARCOURT'S MOUNTAIN

A brilliant achievement! 'Harcourt's Mountain' is a gripping, emotion-packed historical romance story with compelling characters, captivating adventures, and a most beautiful, epic love story. Dodge has a talent for painting vibrant scenes and stirring up strong emotions in readers. A well-crafted, immersive, and memorable story sure to appeal to fans of historical romance. 5 stars!

-Natasha Bentley — NY Literary Magazine

This is a masterfully woven tale that sweeps the reader away to another world where character overcomes tragedy in such breath-taking settings in a mountainous wilderness.

- Nick Read

Elaine Dodge paints a masterful canvas rich in authentic detail and replete with the gamut of human emotions in this tale about how the west was won for Luke Harcourt. A thrilling read from the very first page, this one gets five stars from me.

- Robert Groess

This book could be the cousin of the Outlander series if you ask me. LOVED it!

- JLC

Elaine Dodge has crafted a romance and a historical thriller novel that is ripe for those who thrive on adventures and evolving romance! Very nicely done, Ms. Dodge!

- *Viviane Crystal*

Beautifully written, page turning, Harcourt's Mountain by Elaine Dodge, will stay with you long after you have turned the last page.

- *Marian Phair*

You just don't read books like this anymore. It was a truly satisfying read in so many ways. A saga of drama, suspense, romance, and adventure. Touching, heart-wrenching at times, and beautiful. I loved the setting and I felt transported back into the time and culture. I was tense all the way, wanting the characters to win against almost insurmountable odds. I could not put this book down.

— *Kathy Bosman*

It's the best book of the genre that I've read.

— *Kevin McCloud, Best-selling author*

Elaine Dodge has a new style that keeps a reader turning the pages and wanting to know what is on that next page.

— *Shirl Deems*

I fear I am now suffering from withdrawal symptoms. This can't be the end; I have to know how their adventure continues.

— *D Piennar 5 Stars*

HARCOURT'S MOUNTAIN - *Elaine Dodge*

Published by Read ME Ink, Books for Everyone.

Author Copyright 2013 Elaine Dodge (http://elainedodge.com)

ALL RIGHTS RESERVED

Cover Art:
Potterton House / Read ME Ink Books / Kwarts Publishers
www.kwartspublishers.co.za

Photography: Carey Slade @careyslade_studio

Editor: Cindy Davis (http://www.fiction-doctor.com)

Formatting and Typesetting:
Read ME Ink Books / Kwarts Publishers
www.kwartspublishers.co.za

ISBN: 978-1-990929-03-8 (Print)
ISBN: 978-1-990929-02-1 (Ebook)

PUBLISHER'S NOTE

This is a work of fiction. Names, characters, places and incidents either are the product of the author's imagination or are used fictitiously, and any resemblance to actual persons, living or dead, events, or locals is entirely coincidental.

DEDICATION

*To my father and my brother
who have come to my rescue more times
than I can count.*

ACKNOWLEDGMENTS

Anthony Ehlers for encouraging me to write the book in the first place.

The western shooters of South Africa, specifically Robert Nothhaft, Brian Hoare and Garth Mackway-Wilson for all their advice on the guns of the era and also for teaching me how to use them. Any mistakes in the book are my own.

Phil Whitfield for so willingly sharing his wealth of knowledge about the landscape, animals and history of British Columbia and for his enthusiastic encouragement. Any mistakes in the book are my own.

Cindy Davis for her skilled editing and encouragement.

To all my family and friends for their encouragement and extreme patience - if I've left any one out, please forgive me: Geoff and Alice Dodge, Craig, Les and Rachel Dodge, Shirley Hardy, Bronwen and Josi Mackellar – thanks especially to Josi for the fabulous drawing of wolf. Jacques Erasmus, Denise Hamilton, Biddy Davey, Ulrika Hill, Julieanne Reid, Petro Van Dyk, everyone at Rosa – Romance Writers of South Africa, and last but not least - Henry.

HARCOURT'S
Mountain

CHAPTER ONE

1867

Silver Birch Landing, British Columbia, Canada

HE watched her sashay across the saloon of the Silver Forest Hotel, seduction written clearly on her face and in every curve of her body. Harcourt had to admit she was enticing. Big violet eyes, black hair twisted up in inviting curls, the knowing smile on her red lips, not to mention the tight, low-cut dress leaving little to the imagination. It all promised untold carnal delight.

Her perfume, a dark, satiny aroma eddied around him as she swayed to a stop in front of him, her hand on her tiny waist.

He smiled. "Miss Butler."

"Mr. Harcourt. I was watching you. You play well."

His smile deepened. He'd been very aware of her gaze during the game. As he'd left the poker table with the evening's takings, most of which had come out of Stephen Butler's pocket, he'd seen the calculating look on the man's face. A few minutes later, in the mirror above the bar, he'd watched Butler give the girl instructions. What kind of father would send his daughter to seduce a man? But here she was, and apparently, it didn't worry her in the least. In fact, she looked as if she were enjoying herself. This could be interesting.

"Would you like something to drink?" he offered.

"Some champagne would be nice."

He raised an eloquent eyebrow.

"We have to celebrate your winnings," she said, using her little girl voice. Did she always talk like that, or only when she was trying to entice a man?

"Of course," He nodded at the barman.

While the waiter was opening the bottle, a very expensive bottle, he noted, Harcourt looked Ida May Butler over, slowly. The fact that she wasn't insulted by it stirred his amused contempt.

He handed her the glass. Her fingers drifted over his as she took it. He was disappointed. She wasn't even original in her tactics. Mind you, she couldn't be more than seventeen under all that gloss. Taking the bottle and his glass, he followed her to the deep velvet sofa that stood in the alcove to the left of the bar - the one behind the potted plants and the artfully draped curtain.

She put her heart into the performance and Harcourt played along to see just how far she would go and exactly what she wanted. She coquetted outrageously for the length of time it took them to finish the bottle. When a waiter came to see if they wanted another, to Miss Butler's obvious disappointment, Harcourt shook his head. As the waiter left, she stretched out her hand towards the cord that held the curtain in place. Harcourt was quicker. He captured her hand saying, "Leave it. It might set tongues wagging."

She shot him a look, as if trying to read his face. Harcourt smiled, lifted her hand to his lips and kissed it. "We wouldn't want that," he said.

She fluttered her eyelashes. "Mr. Luke Harcourt. You don't mind if I call you Luke?"

Harcourt wondered if she seriously believed that half a bottle of champagne had made him more pliable. "Not at all, Miss Butler."

"You're a very good poker player, Luke. How much did you win tonight?" She moved closer, her knee touching his.

"Just over five hundred dollars, I believe."

"Don't you know for sure?" She laid her hand on his thigh.

He shrugged. "Counting the money while you play is a distraction."

"How wonderful to be able to play and not worry about how much you might be losing. That's awfully brave. You must be rich."

Harcourt gave a short laugh. "Not rich enough for you, Miss Butler."

"You could be very rich. My father says your mountain is a gold mine."

Ah. Of course. "Does he indeed?"

"Oh yes." Her fingers danced lightly on the muscle of his leg. "He says a man could be wealthy overnight with all that lumber and salmon. Not to mention the possibility of gold. Imagine how exciting it would be to discover gold!" Her hand tightened.

"Imagine."

"It must be awfully lonely living up there on your own." She gazed into his eyes, her hand drifting up his thigh. "I'd be terrified. It's so far away. No one there to keep you company. What if something bad happens? Indians or bears?" She took his hand, pressing his palm on her chest. "Here, you can feel my heart trying to leap out my body even thinking about it."

He let it lie on her white skin for a moment. It'd been a long time since he'd been with a woman. He felt a momentary flicker of disquiet. But looking into her eyes he caught a glimpse of her empty, amoral, little soul and knew he had no cause for concern. He moved his hand round until it cupped the soft weight of her breast. She breathed in.

"If you sold your mountain to my father," she murmured, "you would be very rich. You could move to town. We could get to know each other better." Her hand crept up his thigh. "I'd like to get to know you, Luke, very well."

He ran his thumb gently over her skin and bent towards her. She closed her eyes. Her red lips parted, softening in anticipation, her breath came quickly. He gave a soft laugh. He could feel her skin begin to warm under his fingers, her desire spreading through her like smoky whiskey, melting her in his hands. She seemed to have totally forgotten who was meant to be seducing whom.

"Luke," she purred.

"Miss Butler. Will you do something for me?"

His voice so latent with want she almost moaned in response. She could feel his breath on her face. She tilted her head back, shivering as his lips moved very gently on her neck, the tip of his tongue touching her. "Anything."

"Anything?" His voice was deep, intoxicating. She pressed herself into his hand.

"Yes."

"Good." His voice was normal, hard even. He released her and sat back, "Tell your father my land is not for sale."

She blinked. "What?"

"You heard me. Neither my land, nor my person for that matter, is for sale." He rose and put on his jacket.

"But why? I, I mean I don't know what..." She stared up at him. The shock of his rejection was swiftly replaced by outrage. She leaped to her feet. "Oh, how, how dare you! You were—"

"If you do want to get to know me better, Miss Butler, you can start with this - I'm not interested in little girls."

CHAPTER TWO

THE next day, Luke Harcourt was paying his bill at the Silver Forest Hotel. It was a surprisingly decent establishment, the interior green, plush and fairly luxurious, even the food was good. He heard a man's voice followed by a light, silvery laugh behind him and glanced over his shoulder. Stephen Butler and his beautiful, wilful daughter were walking out of the dining room surrounded by a small knot of men.

A slight smile twisting his lips, Harcourt turned back to the man behind the counter. He'd enjoyed walking away with the previous evening's takings. Now, he was paying for the privilege of sleeping in Stephen Butler's hotel and eating Stephen Butler's food with Stephen Butler's money.

He was well aware the man disliked him. He'd been a thorn in Butler's side ever since he'd arrived in town over a year ago. Butler had lost an important poker game to him then, so after losing again last night Butler must dislike him very much indeed. His daughter probably didn't like him much either. The look of disbelief on her face when he'd put a stop to the seduction she'd so artfully planned, had been as laughable as her father's attempts to play poker.

Harcourt hoped to leave the hotel without having to talk to either of them, even for politeness' sake. It turned out Ida May Butler had no intention of speaking to Luke Harcourt ever again. As he passed, she glanced up and saw him. With a slight smile, he touched the rim of his hat. His smile deepened as she tossed her head, put up her imperious little chin and turned away. He almost expected her to stamp her foot.

Then he grinned. She'd done that last night when he'd walked out on her.

The doors swung back behind him. Standing on the wooden sidewalk he took stock of what passed for a main street in Silver Birch Landing. It was a small, but growing frontier town on British Columbia's westernmost edge. It was trying hard; one had to give it that.

A sheltered port, it was becoming the start of many a man's journey. It had been two years since the American War between the States had ended, leaving men desperate, and homeless, drifting from one place to another. It was often gold that exerted the strongest pull on them. Even the rumour of a strike could entrap their minds, their souls, dragging them from one mountainside, one riverbed, to another.

But there were also men simply in search of a new life. Here in Silver Birch Landing, nothing stopped a man from leaving his past behind and, with luck, reinventing his future. Harcourt had been one of them.

Muddy streets separated the few shops from, on one side, the jail, the livery stables, the hotel and the brothel. On the other side of town was 'Johnson's Mercantile' - the general store, the Chinese 'Heavenly Spring Snow Laundry', and the Silver Birch Bank where Harcourt deposited nearly all his winnings.

The dockyards marked the ocean boundary of the town and, standing at the edge of the road leading to the barely explored interior, a church was being built. The lumber mill had been constructed miles out of town because of the noise, but Silver Birch Landing was still close enough for the lumbermen to think of it as their own.

Apart from the half-dozen whores and a small sprinkling of decent women, the population was comprised of men. Some were transients passing through without stopping, others came into town for supplies. Most came in to drink, buy time with the whores, and gamble. Nights in Silver Birch Landing could get rowdy, loud and liquored up. Men who came into town rich after back-breaking months on the gold claims woke the next day broke, with no memory of losing their fortunes to men who'd had the sense, or the cunning, to remain sober.

Either that or the whores had stolen it.

Harcourt strode along, weaving his way through the crowd. Was it his imagination or were there more men in town today? The women of the Bright Star Saloon must be doing a roaring trade, he thought. They'd probably be dead in six months from a dreadful disease, but at least they'd die rich.

He couldn't wait to get back to the mountain, away from this noise and stink. The throng of unwashed bodies made his nose twitch. He'd rather clean out the barn than endure more of this. One more purchase and then he could leave. He lengthened his stride in anticipation. It didn't last long. A muffled roar sounded from the docks. The small cannon on the balcony of the customs house had been fired. Its sound was a clarion call. Nearly all the men began to hurry towards the water. Lumber men, gold-panners, trappers - the numbers added up. Unwilling to get swept along in the crush, Harcourt stopped and leaned against a wooden pillar to wait it out. He watched the now-surging mob making its way down to the harbour. Across the road was the Bright Star Saloon. The prostitutes hung dispiritedly over the first-floor balcony of the brothel. They didn't look rich. They looked raddled, painted, tired and bored.

One woman stood as far back as possible from the railing. A heavy bruise darkened one side of her face. While the other women all wore bright, gaudy dresses barely hanging on their shoulders, she had on a dirty shift. A brute of a man came onto the balcony. She cringed into the shadows, but he'd seen her. He grabbed her arm and, grinning lewdly, dragged her back inside.

"Poor cow."

Harcourt turned. James Tyler, a short, neat man with a white moustache and goatee, bushy eyebrows and a doctor's bag in his hand stood beside him. He nodded at the whorehouse.

"That's another good woman ruined." He sighed.

"Good?" Harcourt raised an eyebrow. "I doubt a good woman would go near a place like that."

"That's a tad judgemental, Harcourt."

Luke shrugged.

"She most likely didn't get the choice," continued the doctor.

Harcourt snorted, shifting his shoulders against the pillar.

"You haven't been in town for quite a while, Harcourt," said Dr Tyler. "You know why these men are here today?"

"Apart from liquor, and them?" Harcourt nodded towards the brothel.

"The bride ship is coming in." The short man had a clipped way of speaking. Tidy, like himself.

"Bride ship?"

Tyler nodded. "It's the latest money finagling scheme our esteemed Mr. Butler has come up with. The whores up there are played out. Men want women and most will pay gold for them so Butler's bringing in new ones. Only this time he's calling them, 'brides'. He'd heard a similar scheme did well in other places, so he thought he'd try it here. But any one of these bastards will most likely toss his 'bride' aside when he's bored with her, or the minute she crosses him. Or simply kill her." He spat a short, neat stream of tobacco juice into the street, and wiped his mouth, almost delicately, with a handkerchief. "Why keep them when you can come back in a few months' time and buy a new one?"

"If no one buys them?" Harcourt asked, fairly sure he knew what the answer would be.

"If they don't get sold, they get sent to the brothel. Butler doesn't care. Either way, he makes a profit."

"So, either they marry one of these fine gentlemen," Harcourt nodded at the drunken miner who'd just thrown up in front of them, "and be his harlot for free, or join the ladies of the Bright Star and get paid for it."

"That's right. Except, those girls up there, they never see a dime. They're there for life. And if God is merciful, that won't be long." He touched his hat, gave a curt nod and in quick, sharp movements cut through the throng of men.

The mob had passed on, crowding their way to the harbour. Harcourt crossed the street and made his way towards the feed depot. He'd already bought the flour, sugar, coffee and beans. He'd splashed out this time and bought potatoes as well. As soon as he paid for the animal feed, he could fetch the wagon from the livery stable, collect his purchases and get out of here.

Unfortunately, the feed depot stood on the wharf, beyond the bride ship. Because of the crowd, he'd never get the wagon through to collect his purchases after he'd bought them. He realised he'd just have to wait. It had to end sometime.

To get out of the slightly drunken, malodorous press of men, Luke hoisted himself on to a large crate and made himself comfortable.

The mob was growing restless. The ship had docked a while ago with no sign of the women. Brogan, the brute from the whorehouse, appeared, roughly elbowing his way through the crowd, clearing a path. James Carter, the constable, followed behind him. The lawman didn't look happy. He clearly found the matter distasteful, but it wasn't illegal, as such, so he couldn't stop it. His presence, theoretically, should instil in the buyers a modicum of decency. He didn't look hopeful.

With a smile on his face and a small ledger in one hand, Stephen Butler sauntered along in his wake, a piratical swagger in every step. Cheering and applause broke out as he stepped up the gangplank. He turned at the top and took off his hat with a flourish. "Gentlemen! How good of you to come and welcome the new brides to our small town."

The mob cheered.

"Unfortunately, we cannot supply everyone here today with a new wife. Good women seem to be in short supply everywhere." The men laughed. "Now, just to be clear, I'm not selling the women. That would be illegal." There was a roar of delight from the mob. "But the expense of bringing them to you fine gentlemen needs to be repaid. However, as I said, there aren't enough of them to go 'round. So, this will be an auction. Each woman going to the man who bids the highest for her… for her expenses, I mean."

There was cheering, groans and a few angry shouts. Clearly the gold hadn't been good to some of the men this year.

"Shall we bring out the women?" Butler shouted.

The roar was deafening. Even the sight of a new woman was enough for men who either hadn't seen one in months or couldn't always afford the prices charged by Babette, the madam of the Bright Star.

The women were hauled from the hold into the bright sunlight until the deck was crowded with so-called brides blinking in the glare. What it must have been like below deck during the journey Harcourt shuddered to think. He'd captured a few slave ships during his time in the United States Navy. This one had the same lines. He wouldn't be surprised to learn it had been built as one. It would be perfect for this cargo. What were they after all, but another type of slave? It would also explain the smell that emanated from it. The stench soaked its way into the very fibre of the ship. You could never get rid of it completely, unless you burnt it. A fitting end for a foul vessel, as far as he was concerned.

With nothing else to do, he studied the women on deck. He couldn't believe any right-minded female would willingly put herself into this kind of situation. Their clothing was in various stages of disrepair, their hair bedraggled. They looked dirty, coarse and unkempt -even less attractive than the girls at the Bright Star, if that were possible.

It was obvious more than half were whores by profession already. In response to the catcalling and whistles they pulled down their tops and, shaking their shoulders, let their breasts wobble and bounce around. The men cheered, shoving to get to the front. The bidding was fast and aggressive.

The first woman off the ship disappeared into the mob. Harcourt doubted she'd make it through the day without being raped by at least a dozen men. The whole enterprise sickened him.

The auction took on a predictable rhythm. Harcourt leaned back against the wall, tipped his hat over his eyes, and dozed off. After a few hours, the crowd had thinned somewhat. Most of the women had been sold. Only a dozen or so were left. Harcourt stretched. He was just about to jump from his perch when a tall woman in a predictably dirty, once light grey dress, was brought forward. Perhaps it was the dress that caught his eye. It was silk, well cut and modest. It looked expensive.

Harcourt's eyes narrowed. This woman was no prostitute. She'd made an attempt to clean herself up and although her hair needed a wash and good brush, she had at least tried to bring some order to it. She looked intelligent and calm, despite the scared look in her eyes. Her hands were folded in front of her. She was clearly a lady. She made no attempt to catch the eye of any man in the crowd. Instead, she looked over their heads towards the mountains. Perhaps she liked what she saw for she took a deep breath, lifted her chin and squared her shoulders.

Instinctively, Harcourt knew she would be no man's whore. And, like the doctor had said, with the wrong man that would probably mean a killing. Harcourt glanced over at Butler. He was talking emphatically to the constable. He called over the big man from the whorehouse, indicated the woman and nodded, laughing at the obviously coarse joke he'd made. Harcourt realised no one had bid for her.

He stood up on his crate. "I'll take her."

Everyone turned to look at him, including the woman.

Butler stroked his thin moustache with his finger and thumb. He smiled. "Mr. Harcourt, you know the rules. You must bid for her. How much do you offer?"

"One hundred dollars, in gold."

There was a gasp from the men on the wharf. Even Harcourt was shocked. He'd spoken without thinking. It was the highest bid of the day, made more spectacular by the fact that it was totally uncontested.

"Sold to Mr. Harcourt!" shouted the constable before Butler, or anyone else, could respond.

A flash of annoyance crossed Butler's face. The lawman waved a hand, calling Harcourt on board.

A moment later, standing beside the woman on the greasy deck, Harcourt realised she was almost the same height as him. Slender with chestnut brown hair. He'd been right, she did have intelligent eyes. Apart from that, it was hard to tell what she'd look like cleaned up. One thing was obvious - she stank.

"Do you agree to this transaction in the full understanding of what it means and entails, and that it's legally binding as a marriage?" Constable Carter asked Harcourt.

"Yes," he replied.

Carter asked the woman the same question. She took a deep breath, "Absolutely not. I didn't ask to be brought here. I don't wish to marry any man. I do wish to be taken home." Her voice was pleasant, deeper than he'd expected. Tight with fear yet determined.

"Where is that?" Carter asked.

She looked scared. She covered her eyes with her hand. "I-I don't remember. I don't know how I got to be on this ship. I don't remember much before that."

"Do you know who you are?" Carter asked.

Her hand dropped away from her face. Harcourt thought she was about to faint and stepped a little closer, just in case. Her voice was anxious. "No."

Harcourt didn't like the smirk on Butler's face.

Taking the ledger out of Butler's hand, Carter pushed past him to the last of the women, who were leaning over the rails looking at their new home. He checked their names against the ledger.

Turning back to her, his finger pointing at a name on the list, he showed her the book. "It seems this could be your name?"

She reached out and touched the page gently. *Hope Booker*. Whoever had written it had been in a hurry. The name was slightly smudged, blurred. "That feels right," she whispered.

"Very well. Now ma'am, what do you want to do? Do you want to go with Mr. Harcourt?"

There was a strained pause.

"I tell you what," said Butler. "If you really want me to, I'll take you home." A wave of relief crossed her face.

"You simply pay off the debt I incurred getting you here, and what it will cost to take you back." He smiled. "A fine lady like you will be able to find the money easily enough, I should think."

An inexplicable flash of desperation stirred within Harcourt. He had to get this woman away from Butler.

He took her arm and yanked her around to face him. As abruptly and clearly as he could he said, "If you don't agree to come with me right now, Mr Butler will give you to this man," he pointed at the hulking brothel guard, "who will take you to the whorehouse where you will spend the rest of your life doing whatever these men want," he nodded at the crowd on the wharf, "whenever they want it and how they want it. Right now, you have a choice, but it might be the last choice you ever get to make. Believe me."

The little colour she had drained from her face. "You can't make me work in a place like that!"

"I won't. He will. After he's raped you and beaten you into submission," Harcourt said.

Brogan grinned at her. She looked at Harcourt in horror.

"I live in the mountains," he added. "It's not much yet, but I have an orchard, apples."

Butler snorted in derision.

"You'd have a home."

She looked at him, almost as if this were a choice that needed to be mulled over. He wanted to shake her.

Constable Carter shot a quick, emphatic jerk of his jaw at Harcourt, urging her on. "Make up your mind, lady," he growled. He didn't want another broken, ruined woman in his town. He was brutal, "Harcourt's right. There's only one job for an unmarried woman without money in this town at the moment, and that's on your back." His head twitched towards Butler, "In his brothel."

Butler gave a slight shrug and a smile.

She turned back to Harcourt. He didn't smile. He simply waited. There was that long, considering look of hers again. Turning to Constable Carter she asked, "Where do I sign?"

Harcourt handed over the gold. It was the remainder of the winnings from last night's poker game. The irony of the situation wasn't lost on him.

CHAPTER THREE

HOPE took the piece of paper the constable gave her and followed Harcourt down the gangplank. Hands tightly clenched to stop them from shaking, Hope kept her head down, her eyes fixed on Harcourt's boots. Ribald comments from the men on the wharf mocked her every step of the way. Hot tears sprang up. Could she feel any more degraded than this? Sold, like...

She took a deep breath, squeezed her eyes shut to force the tears back and set herself to focus on simply following the man in front of her. The man whose steady eyes had, for a moment, calmed the quivering in the pit of her stomach.

Harcourt stopped at the feed store. She stood quietly out of the way, while he negotiated and paid for the feed and, from there, they made their way to the livery stable.

The mules had been hitched to the front of the wagon and he tied his big black horse to the back. The deep quietness of the huge barn was a relief. Hope's hands slowly eased open again.

The dignified, grizzled, old, black man who ran the stables, turned courteously to her. "Would you be one of the new brides, ma'am?" he asked.

Hope couldn't help the painful humiliation from showing in her face. "I came in on the ship, yes."

"Well," he bowed slightly towards her, "welcome to our town. I do believe the good Lord has brought you here. Our Mr Harcourt has been alone too long." She felt as if his keen gaze saw right through her. "I suspect you have as well. I'm sure you two will do fine together. He's a good man and you look like a nice lady. Allow me."

Hope took his offered hand and scrambled up. Harcourt hoisted himself in and sat beside her.

"I will be praying for you both," the old man said. "Perhaps I shall see you again soon, ma'am. Take good care of her, Mr Harcourt. Those winter apples were a real treat, by the way. The horses and I thank you."

Harcourt touched his hat. "Goodbye, Mr Samson."

"Goodbye." Hope smiled gratefully at him. "Thank you."

"What a nice old man," she remarked as they drove away. It was the first thing she'd said to Harcourt since they'd left the ship.

"Yes, he is. He used to be a dresser for some famous actor back in New York. I sell a lot of apples to him."

"How big is your orchard?" She was intrigued; he didn't look like a farmer. A rancher maybe, but not an apple grower.

"Only about a hundred trees right now." He didn't elaborate.

They drove back down toward the wharf to collect his purchases. The last remaining stragglers from the auction were weaving their way towards the saloon. As Harcourt pulled up outside the feed store, Hope saw the whorehouse guard dragging a couple of women along the street. Neither seemed keen to go with him and wriggled in his grasp. He jerked one of them close, shoving his dirty face with its scraggly beard at her. Whatever he said did the trick. She cowered away from him, a look of shock on her face. He laughed and towed them along as he strode off once more.

The feed store boys had been keeping an eye out for Harcourt. His sacks were tossed on and stacked at the back of the wagon in a moment. His purchased bride looked across at the ship that had been her prison. The horror of that short time, which for now was the only memory Hope had, washed over her again and she began to shake. The sight of those two women in that brute's hands made her realise just how close she had come to being one of them.

She didn't know Mr Harcourt, didn't know what life with him would be like, but at least…well, she hoped, she would never have to endure what those poor souls would. She felt Harcourt's eyes on her. He hurried the boys along. As soon as the loading was finished, he climbed back up behind her. Slapping up the mules he put the wharf behind them as quickly as possible.

A moment later, they pulled up outside the general store, Johnson's Mercantile. Harcourt jumped down. "Wait here."

Hope felt very conspicuous perched up on the wagon. She longed for a bath. She knew she smelled appalling. The sweat and grime from the voyage seemed ingrained in her skin. Her hair was lank and greasy. She felt awful. She fingered her dress. It had obviously been a beautiful gown once. The sight of the stains on the skirt made bile rise in her throat. The fear and revulsion of the last few weeks would haunt her for a long time.

Hope took a deep shuddering breath and sat up straighter, concentrating on not breaking down.

Harcourt and a young man soon came out, hefting more sacks of flour, coffee, and sugar onto the wagon. The third trip brought a big bag of salt and a couple more of beans.

There was one more stop. The Chinese laundry. Harcourt once again climbed down and walked in alone.

While she waited, Hope realised she was still holding the document they'd all signed on the ship. She unfolded it. The words 'Bill of Sale' were printed across the top. Underneath that she read, 'Goods Purchased'. Her name was written next to it.

Seeing it like that brought back a shocking memory. It came so fast and with such force she clutched the side of the wagon feeling dizzy and ill. Closing her eyes, she saw a large, cool room with a high ceiling. Light curtains moved in the slight breeze drifting through the tall windows lining two walls. The scent of lilies wafted on the air. She was wearing the same dress, only clean and shiny. A beautiful, elegant woman, her mother, was sitting on a silk covered chaise lounge, one arm draped along its short back.

Hope's heart was pounding so hard it hurt. She remembered her mother saying icily, "You embarrassed me. You are clearly no daughter of mine. You never will be."

She tried as hard as she could to remember what she'd done to deserve the bitterness and contempt in her mother's voice, but she couldn't. She did remember the way her mother had smiled at her. *That* had hurt more than anything. The effort of trying to remember was making Hope's head ache.

She let go of the memory. It faded, leaving her with nothing but an overwhelming sense of abandonment.

Hope took a deep breath, steadied herself and looked again at the receipt. At the top was the date, '1st March, 1867', and the three signatures. There was his name - Luke Harcourt. It was an educated hand, a small measure of comfort. At least she hadn't been married to a complete barbarian.

Not married; sold. The reality of the situation bore down on her. The constable had said that this was a legally binding marriage certificate. But the receipt didn't mention that anywhere. It said she was simply purchased goods. Just like the sacks of flour and beans in the back of the wagon.

What did the man who'd bought her think? This Luke Harcourt? Did he see her as a wife or purchased goods? Was he expecting her to be a wife in the fullest sense of the word? She blushed even thinking about it. What would she do if he did? They weren't married, not really. Being his 'wife' would make her his mistress. His whore.

She took a deep breath and decided she would worry about that only if, or when, she had to. Maybe he just wanted a housekeeper. It was a small measure of comfort and she didn't put much faith in it, but she clung to it all the same.

He'd been gone about ten minutes when a white haired, plump, Chinese lady flew out the door and rushed over to Hope. She grabbed Hope's hands and tugged at her, all the time chattering away. Hope didn't understand a word.

An elderly Chinese man, clearly the lady's husband, hurried out of the shop behind her. He tried to get the old lady to let go of Hope's hands, but she refused. His eyes twinkling with affection, he turned to Hope. "Please, you will have to come inside. My wife will not be denied."

Hope climbed from the wagon and allowed herself to be whisked into a new and unexpected world.

The immense structure was filled with large wooden vats of boiling water, steam rising from them in great clouds. Clothes were either lying in large, dirty piles, being stirred around inside the vats, or being pulled out and hung up over lines that criss-crossed the shop in a bewildering fashion to dry. Felt-shod Chinese in plain, dark blue loose-fitting tops and trousers bustled around. In one section of the store young women ironed the clean clothes. Were all these people related, Hope wondered.

At the back of the warehouse, enormous fireplaces held large kettles of boiling water ready to replace the dirty water in the wooden vats when needed. The heat inside the building was enormous.

Perspiration ran down her face and back, making her feel more uncomfortable than ever. She wiped it off her forehead with the back of one hand. The old lady still had hold of her other one, still patting it and chattering away.

A young woman came up and spoke to the old lady who looked sharply at Hope. She nodded to the young woman. They both fingered Hope's dress, shaking their heads. Could this be more humiliating? They took hold of her arms and hustled her up a set of stairs. Hope was alarmed. What did they want?

"Do not worry," called the old man. "They take care of you. Go, go." He flapped his hands, shooing them away.

She looked back just in time to see the old man slap Harcourt on the back of the head. Surprised at the familiarity, she was even more surprised to see Harcourt simply flinch, rub the back of his head and shrug a question - then the corner and the stairs cut off her view.

In the upstairs room stood another smaller vat filled with hot water. After a lot of hand waving and pantomime, Hope realised they were offering her a bath. Without a moment's hesitation, she stripped off and climbed in. It felt like a miracle. Hope luxuriated in the hot water.

Scooping up her clothes the two women scurried out, leaving her alone to bathe. Hope breathed in the scent of the soap. It was the most wonderful thing she'd smelled in months! She picked up the scrubbing brush and set to work.

Much later, she climbed out feeling like a new woman. The nightmare journey receded slightly in her mind. Her skin, her hair, she was clean again and that awful musty odour of urine and grime was gone.

It was a passing pleasure though. She'd have to put that awful dress back on again. It was all she had to wear. That dirty, smelly, and revolting dress. What a joy it would be to burn it and never see it again. But she had no choice.

She had less choice than she imagined. The only garment in the room was a quilted dressing gown. At least, it looked like a dressing gown.

Harcourt sighed impatiently. He'd been sitting in the family's living quarters playing chess with his friend Lee-Chan for what felt like hours. He hadn't seen hide nor hair of the women since they'd disappeared upstairs.

The door opened, a young girl of about ten came in and laid out bowls of steaming rice, meat and vegetables on the table. Luke sighed. He knew he was here for a while longer.

Just then, the women came back into the room with Hope wrapped in a heavy, quilted dressing gown, her wet hair combed back from her head. She was pale, but at least she was clean. He hadn't noticed before, but now he could see that she had a fine bone structure. She certainly smelt better. It was about the only thing that reconciled him to the delay.

The old lady said something. Lee-Chan translated, "My wife would like now you introduce this lady to us."

Harcourt suddenly realised he didn't know her name. It hadn't been said out loud on the ship and he hadn't looked too carefully at the paper they'd signed. He paused awkwardly.

"My name is Hope, Hope Booker," she said, coming to his rescue.

"Hope," he repeated. It was a quiet name. It suited her. He cleared his throat. "Luke Harcourt." He didn't quite know what to do next. She smiled and stretched out her hand. He took it. Cool and slim it fitted into his as if it belonged there. There was a flicker of surprise in her eyes.

"How do you do, Mr Harcourt?"

"How do you do." They were both a little embarrassed. His strong hand held hers a fraction too long as he studied her. She pulled her hand away, flushing.

Shaking his head, Lee-Chan stepped in. "And I am Lee-Chan. This is my wife, Lee-Ming, my daughter, Sweet Jade We are very glad to meet you, Hope Booker." They bowed and bobbed to Hope.

"It's very nice to meet you Mr and Mrs Lee," said Hope bowing slightly in return.

"Now, we eat. Come, come sit down." Lee-Chan pulled out chairs for them. Lee-Ming passed Hope a bowl of food and some chopsticks. Hope had clearly never seen chopsticks before and didn't know what to do with them. She also couldn't let go of the front of the robe. It wouldn't stay closed.

Harcourt couldn't help but be amused at her dilemma. "Chan, have you got a fork? I don't think, um...Hope can use chopsticks."

Lee-Chan was immediately apologetic and hurried his wife from the room. She came back with a spoon. Hope flushed with embarrassment. She was the only one at the table eating with a spoon. Even Harcourt wielded the chopsticks as deftly as their hosts.

She wolfed down the delicious food, emptying the bowl in a few seconds. Shame flooded her face. Lee-Ming took the bowl and quickly filled it again. Hope ate more slowly this time.

At her deep sigh of satisfaction at the end of her third helping, Harcourt felt uncomfortable. She'd clearly been starving, and he hadn't even thought about offering her a meal - or the opportunity for a bath when they left the ship.

He turned to Lee-Chan. "We should leave. We need to make the top meadow before dark."

Lee-Chan spoke with his wife and shooed her out the door, into the depths of the laundry. Sweet Jade, took Hope's hand and hurried her back up the stairs.

Hanging over a chair was her shift and her grey dress. It had been washed and was now only slightly damp, smelling of hot steam where the laundry staff had tried to iron out the moisture. It would dry quickly in the sun. Hope sighed and picked it up. She had no choice; it was the only dress she had. Sweet Jade asked Lee-Ming a question. Lee-Ming nodded approval and clapped her hands, sending the younger one running out the room.

In the family room, Lee-Ming was helping Hope do up the buttons on the wrists of the grey dress when the Sweet Jade came in carrying a neatly wrapped parcel. She pushed it into Hope's hands, nodding and smiling. "For you," she said.

Lee-Ming bobbed her head up and down as well, a great big smile creasing her plump face.

Hope had no idea what the parcel contained but she was so touched at the generosity of these strangers her eyes filled with tears. Lee-Ming shoved another parcel into Harcourt's hands. It was a meal. He grinned and to her great delight, kissed her wrinkled cheek. She turned and wrapped her arms around Hope giving her a tight squeeze and while Lee-Chan beamed, nodding away, Hope thanked her for everything - the bath, the food and their hospitality.

Having finally gotten Hope into the wagon, Harcourt tried not to be rude to the Lees. With such a late start, it almost wasn't worth leaving town. They might as well spend the night at the hotel.

Harcourt wasn't sure if it was cowardice or not, but he had no intention of letting that happen. "Ming, Chan," he said. "We must go. I'm sorry. I'll be back in town again in about two months. I'll see you then."

Lee-Chan wrapped his arms about his wife's ample frame and pulled her away from the wagon. She was still trying to hold on to Hope's hands, patting them and chattering away in Mandarin. Lee-Chan remonstrated with his wife, but with a big, loving smile on his face.

"You go now, Luke, quick, before she's gets loose again."

Harcourt laughed, slapping the mules' rumps with the reins.

CHAPTER FOUR

A S the cart pulled away, Hope waved goodbye to the kindly old couple. She hadn't understood a word Lee-Ming had said but the warmth, love and joy she'd felt in their small steamy home above the laundry had been the kindest actions she'd encountered for a very long time. She blinked away the tears that had filled her eyes.

She wondered how hard it would be to learn their language. She sighed at the thought that she might not see them again. Mr. Harcourt hadn't mentioned bringing her back when he next returned to town. She gave herself a mental shake. Don't be a fool, Hope, you'll have enough to deal with, just living with Mr. Harcourt.

What was it about him that had made her agree to go with him? The truth was, to avoid being sold to the brothel she would have gone with anyone. No. Although that was a theory she'd never get to test; it had been the man himself who had made her sign that receipt.

She'd always imagined her ideal man would be taller than herself, with dark hair and brown eyes. She shuddered. That was a perfect description of the man on the ship, Stephen Butler.

Luke Harcourt had tawny hair and was only an inch or so over her own height. He wasn't exactly tall for a man, but somehow that wasn't an issue. From the way he spoke he appeared to be an intelligent, well-educated man. Was it the fact that he carried a gun, and knew how to use it?

She presumed he did. He looked like a man who would. But nearly all the men she'd seen here wore guns. Maybe it was the width of his shoulders, or the obvious strength in his forearms? His face had an arresting quality. He was the kind of man one looked at, twice. Yet on closer inspection he wasn't conventionally handsome. He looked like he'd been carved out of granite, with a blunt chisel, and chips of ice used for his eyes. His mouth wasn't symmetrical, it was almost crooked.

Feeling her gaze, he turned his head and caught her looking at him. She realised she'd been staring. She knew she was blushing.

"What?" he asked.

The heat in her cheeks grew deeper. She shook her head, unable to speak in embarrassment. Those intense, light blue eyes held her, then thankfully he looked away.

She breathed out and turned back to the town she didn't even know the name of. "Where are we?"

"Silver Birch Landing." He glanced at her. "British Columbia."

Hope stared at him for a moment, her eyes wide. She wanted to weep, but he was watching her. She swallowed hard and cleared her throat.

"You said you lived on a mountain, Mr Harcourt?" she continued in a stronger voice. An eyebrow rose in surprise as he nodded. "Is it far from here?

"My name's Luke," he said. "My place is about a week away, with the wagon." Their eyes met. Both looked away. He, to tend to the mules and she, to drink in the sights and sounds of the first town she had seen in weeks. A town so very different from…she still couldn't remember its name. Slowly images filled her mind; her family, her friends, her church, an old, established city, where ancient oak trees lined the streets and warm breezes drifted over lazy afternoons drenched with the perfume of lilacs, wisteria and magnolias.

She came close to tears as she remembered her stern, yet beloved English father. Images of Charlie, who was more like a twin than a younger brother, fluttered through her mind. She thought of her mother, that elegant beauty who somehow managed to captivate every man who met her. Hope was suddenly glad her mother would never meet Luke.

Her logical mind mocked her - then you'll never know if he'd be immune to her or not. And why should you care?

She forced the thought away. She didn't love him. He certainly didn't love her. They hadn't said more than a dozen words to each other. He hadn't even wanted to know her name until Lee-Ming had asked what it was.

She wondered again why he'd bought her.

As the busy street eddied around them, Luke's hands - strong and capable - worked the reins. An engraved signet ring on his right glinted in the sun. His hands made her feel safe.

An odd word, she thought. He was clearly a man who... well, he looked like a man to whom violence was no stranger. There was a sense of toughness, a cord of steel that seemed to run through him.

You're an idiot, Hope. Your imagination is running wild. You have no idea what this man is like. He could eat babies for breakfast for all you know. Her sense of the ridiculous reasserted itself. She forced herself to be plain and logical, as her father had taught her. Get the facts straight first.

And the fact was, she had no idea why this man made her feel safe, but he did. She knew deep inside her that this man would protect her. That he was strong enough for her. He also made her feel very feminine.

Harcourt was grateful she was quiet. He'd almost began describing the mountain when she'd asked earlier but had stopped just in time. Talking led to getting to know people.

Knowing people led to more pain than he was ever going to feel again.

He studied her face, wondering how young she was. Unlike Ida May Butler, she wasn't seventeen, thank God. But was it youth or inexperience he saw in her face? He let it lie. It made no difference anyway.

Despite the fact that he didn't like chatterbox women anyway, there was no room for further conversation at the moment. He had to concentrate on threading the wagon through the crowded street. Other wagons were also making their way out of town, some moving either towards the gold claims or the lumber mill. A few would be heading north. They would be the trappers. For a while they'd share the same road. Probably part company late on the second day.

The street was so crowded Harcourt couldn't get through. They came to a halt outside the brothel. With the bride ship in town it was a relatively quiet day for the girls of the Bright Star Saloon. They crowded the balcony watching the to-ings and fro-ings, calling out ribald remarks to men who had been customers only the night before.

A brightly coloured redhead spotted their wagon and, in a sing-song voice exclaimed, "Mr Harcourt has himself a bride. Heard you paid a lot of money for her, Luke."

"She doesn't look like a lot of fun, Luke," mocked a brassy blonde. "You could have had all of us for that amount of money, honey!"

"At the same time!" yelled the redhead. The girls screeched with laughter.

"Come on, Luke, ditch the stuck-up bride and come and have some fun with Babette and the girls!" The blonde wriggled her hips invitingly.

Harcourt felt a blush surge up. He wasn't sure if he was more embarrassed by the girls' attention or the flush in his face. He expected Hope to say something. It would be the predictable response. She shot a quick glance in his direction and then looked down at her hands but stayed silent. That was a surprise. Clearly, she'd decided discretion was the better part of valour. He tipped his hat to the blowzy girls.

"Afternoon ladies."

"Oooh," cooed the girls, giggling.

"Honey," the blonde one called, leaning as far over as she could, her straining bodice barely holding her ample self from tumbling out. Hope realised the girl was talking to her. "You going to let that new man of yours come by and visit with us next time he's in town? Or you going to keep him on a tight leash? We would hate to lose *touch* with a man we know so well."

The other whores roared with laughter at her emphasis on the word, 'touch'.

Luke grinned up at them. "Now ladies, you might know my name, but that's about all."

They immediately came up with a variety of ways they could get to know him.

"It all sounds very intriguing," he replied, "but I'm afraid I will have to decline, yet again."

The blonde leaned out even further. "We'll get you one day, Luke Harcourt."

The girls all laughed.

A space opened in front of them. He flicked the reins, tipped his hat again at the whores and the cart pulled away.

Glancing over at Hope he saw a small curve flicker across her lips. Although she was trying hard not to smile at all, her laughing eyes gave her away the relief she obviously felt. He wasn't sure why he'd wanted her to know he didn't visit the Bright Star. Even though they barely knew each other, Harcourt didn't want her thinking he was the type of man who visited prostitutes.

CHAPTER FIVE

VEHICLES and people jostled their way along the road. It was a fair distance to where it divided. When they reached the crossroad most of the wagons peeled off to the gold claims. More than half of those left, headed to the lumberyard. The remaining few continued straight, aiming for the far mountains. They would turn north tomorrow.

The noise and the dust made it almost impossible to hold a conversation. Hope spent most of her time just trying to hold on. They hit one particularly bad rut in the road. She lurched violently. The parcel from Lee-Ming slid off her lap. She flung out her hand and caught it just as the wagon hit a rock. She bounced hard and saw the ground rushing up towards her. A strong hand grabbed the back of her dress and jerked her unceremoniously back onto the seat.

"You all right?" asked Harcourt with a frown.

She was embarrassed. She must have looked like a hoyden scrambling for a parcel like that. "Yes, thank you."

She straightened her clothing, hoping no one else had seen her. No one had. Each wagon had their own troubles. She could see some of the other new 'wives' chattering away, despite the noise, to their so-called husbands, who already looked bored and irritated. One or two were arguing hotly with the men.

That didn't seem like a good way to start, in Hope's opinion. But then, she was no expert on being a 'bought bride'. Or a bride of any description when it came to that. One of the men snapped out an arm and hit the woman sitting next to him. Hope was horrified. She felt Harcourt shift on the seat. She was surprised to see how hard his face had become. He was almost a different man. What she saw in his eyes scared her.

He scowled, "No man has the right to hit a woman. I don't care who she is or what she's done." He turned back to the mules.

There wasn't anything profitable for her to say so she stayed silent. He didn't hit women. He didn't visit prostitutes. He made her feel protected. She wasn't getting her hopes up too soon, but perhaps things might not be as bleak as she had expected.

They travelled for what felt like another two hours. The only wagons left were Harcourt's and five others. Mr Cuthbert was a farmer in a valley two weeks further on from Harcourt's land. Mr Jefferson was hoping to set up a store in a new town on the other side of the far mountains. Two wagons belonged to the Harrison brothers— also farmers, and the last wagon belonged to a trapper who was going further north than anyone else.

Except for Mr Cuthbert, every man had a new bride inside his wagon.

They reached the top meadow just as the sun was setting. The wagon owners each chose a spot that seemed favourable to himself and set about preparing for the evening. Chores needed doing, there were mules to tend to, firewood to be collected and dinner needed to be started.

Hope quietly did what Harcourt told her, without fussing and without question. A hard slap rang out and a woman burst into tears. Startled, Hope swung round. Not far away stood a thin woman holding her face and sobbing. Hope moved to go to her. Harcourt's hand clamped down on her arm. His face wore that hard look again.

"Leave it," he said. "I hate it as well, but we won't be able to help her when the wagons separate. She'll be on her own with him then. She might as well get used to it now."

"But we can't—"

"Leave it." His voice was firm. "That's Tobias John. I heard he took a wife only a few months ago."

"How can he take another one then?" she asked.

"Guess the other one died. He's a trapper." As if that explained everything.

"He looks like an animal!" she exclaimed.

He nodded. "He is. We'll need more firewood. Stay close to the wagon though. I'll see to the mules."

Searching the area nearby for suitable wood, Hope couldn't help thinking about the poor woman. She was distraught at the thought of someone so frail being sold to a man like Tobias John. The woman was pale and had a harsh cough. She looked ill. She hadn't fared well on board the ship. Hope had never had a chance to talk to her during the voyage, but she remembered how the woman had battled seasickness the entire time. She'd hardly been able to keep down any of the meagre rations they'd been given and had grown weaker by the day.

Hope wished she could go over now and at least talk to her, but Tobias John was still there. The trapper terrified Hope. Her stomach churned at the thought of the man. Huge - well over six feet with long, black, shaggy hair tied back in an untidy ponytail, his clothes dishevelled. He was dirty and unwashed. Whenever he walked past her, which seemed to be more often than necessary, he bared his teeth at her. Once, he ran his thick tongue over his lips lasciviously and smacked them together. It made her skin crawl. He stank and his mouth was filled with black, rotting teeth. He looked evil.

Rusty traps hung from the sides of his wagon, unnameable bits of fur still stuck on them. No one would ever come across that wagon unexpectedly - it was an abattoir and it reeked like one. Even at this distance she could see a small cloud of flies buzzing malevolently in the air above it.

Harcourt walked round the side of the wagon. It was a relief to see him. The contrast he made with Tobias John was strong. She offered up a silent prayer of thanks that if she'd had to be sold that it was Luke - Mr Harcourt - who'd bought her. She could have ended up with someone like that monster across the field.

She felt sick as she remembered no one else had bid for her and she'd been on her way to the brothel. If Mr Harcourt hadn't taken her, she would have had to...with complete strangers. And they could have been just like Tobias John.

Hope sat down abruptly. She knew nothing about Luke Harcourt except that he seemed like an anchor in a very fragile world. Right now, she needed that more than anything else.

"Everything okay?"

She swallowed hard and nodded.

Across the field, the trapper was again yelling at the woman. Harcourt sighed. That woman wouldn't last a month living the way Tobias John did, even if he weren't hitting her.

He made up the fire and hung a pot over it. "Stir this," he said handing Hope a ladle.

She leaned over the pot and took a deep breath. The meal Lee Ming had given them was warming up inside and it smelled delicious. More fragrant than any meal she'd ever had before. While Harcourt got the coffee going, she stirred the food.

To take her mind off the miserable woman behind her, she tried to see if she could identify which herbs and spices Lee-Ming had used. Hope thought she could smell lemon but other than that she couldn't place anything else, and she wasn't even sure that was right.

Later, the fires died down and people climbed into the wagons for the night. Soon, there was raucous laughter and giggles from one of them.

Harcourt could see terror tighten Hope's face. Her eyes were huge, her skin as pale as chalk. What did she think he was going to do? Well, he conceded, that was fairly obvious considering what was starting in the other wagons.

What the hell have I done? I *bought* a woman! He cleared his throat. "Listen, I didn't go into town today to buy a wife. To be honest, I have no idea what to do with you. What I mean is, nothing's going to happen tonight, or any other night. I've never raped a woman in my life and I'm not about to start now. I'll never lay a hand on you."

He regretted saying that immediately. She was plain, but she was a woman, and a man could get mighty lonely in the mountains. He wasn't looking for love. He'd never do that again. He wasn't looking for meaningless sex either, but he couldn't help wondering. A muscle in his face twitched. "Unless you want me to. You have my word."

She didn't respond. He'd expected some kind of reaction. Most women don't like being told they're not wanted, even if they don't want the man saying it. But this woman hadn't flinched. She was frozen, staring at him. Her hands were gripping the coffee cup, her knuckles white. She clearly didn't believe what he'd said.

Harcourt sighed. "We'd better turn in for the night. I'm afraid the wagon's not very comfortable, but it's better than sleeping outside. It's big enough for both of us. I've made as much room as I can. Choose whichever side you want. I'll be a few minutes tidying up."

He stood up and took her cup from her. He almost had to pull it away.

"You're going to sleep in the wagon too?" Her voice was small.

He thought he'd made that clear. He had no intention of sleeping outside. He nodded over to Tobias John's wagon. "Would you feel safer on your own with him in the same camp?"

She climbed into the wagon without another word. By the light of the lantern he'd left on the seat outside, she saw that he'd moved the sacks so they formed two mattresses, one on each side, and were covered neatly with blankets. There was hardly a hand's breadth between them. Lee-Ming's parcel was on one. Hope wasn't sure what to do. She didn't want to take off her dress, but if she slept in it then it would be creased tomorrow. They hadn't covered eventualities like this at Mrs Mason's Finishing School for Young Ladies back home.

The memory surfaced easily. Well, perhaps they had.

She remembered Mademoiselle Florizette saying, "No matter what happens, girls, you must always, always remain calm, and never cease to behave like a lady." She heard Mr. Harcourt moving around. He'd want to come inside in a few minutes.

Although she felt safe with Mr. Harcourt, Hope realised she suddenly didn't feel safe from him. What if he expected her to sleep with him, tonight - here, surrounded by this company of strangers? He'd said he wouldn't, but would he change his mind? She didn't know him, let alone love him. She wasn't his wife. A frisson of panic rose inside her.

She pulled off her dress quickly, keeping on her shift, folding the dress neatly and putting it and Lee-Ming's parcel at the back of the wagon. She dived beneath the blanket and pulled it up to her chin. She turned on to her side facing the canvas wall and waited.

Ten minutes later, he knocked on the side of the wagon.

"May I come in?"

"Yes." Her voice was quiet and tight.

He climbed up, turned off the lamp and sat on the seat to pull off his boots, which he stored carefully inside. She heard him unbuckle his gun belt and strip off his jacket. He moved quietly into the wagon and settled on his side of it.

She made herself as small as she could so, hopefully, he couldn't touch her, even accidentally. The situation was unbearable. Once he was lying down, she heard him sigh and move slightly to get more comfortable. They both lay there silently for a while.

"Good night, Mr Harcourt," she said softly.

"Good night. And my name is Luke."

Just as she was beginning to relax a little, the laughter outside had ceased, and other sounds began. She heard a woman crying and the sounds of wood creaking. She was so embarrassed she wanted to die. It was clear what was happening in the other wagons. She tried to make herself even smaller, praying Luke - Mr Harcourt - wouldn't change his mind about her. Calling him Luke seemed too familiar, too personal. If she thought of him as Mr Harcourt it wasn't so bad. He stayed the stranger he was. She wanted him to stay that way, to keep his distance. Tears slid down her cheeks. She was so tense she thought she would literally snap into a million pieces.

The sounds from the other wagons never seemed to stop. Harcourt was irritated. As much as he didn't want to, those kinds of sounds, well, they affected a man. He glanced over at Hope. She didn't seem to be breathing. Even in the dark he could see every lineament of her body was rigid. He shifted, trying to find a better position but these damn sacks seemed to be filled with rocks. He shifted again, his arm touching her back. She gave a small mew of fear.

The groans and thumps from the other wagons were getting louder.

Harcourt felt stifled. How come he hadn't noticed how airless it was in here before? He couldn't bear it a second longer.

He sat up with a grunt and, pulling his jacket, his gun belt and his blanket with him, said, "I'll be outside."

Without waiting for a reply, he jumped down.

Soon the other wagons fell silent. Thankfully.

Hope waited. When it became clear that Mr Harcourt wasn't coming back, she slowly relaxed and even stretched out a little. He hadn't touched her. He'd kept his word, although she did wonder what happened to will-you-feel-safe-on-your-own? But not for long. He hadn't gone far away. Within minutes she was asleep.

Hours later, the quiet outside was profound. Hope woke with a start. A dark shape stood at the entrance to the wagon. At first, she thought it was Luke. Then the smell hit her. It was Tobias John. She lay as still as she could. She could smell the alcohol on him. Where was Luke, she thought frantically? Fear skittered through her on long, icy claws. Just as she was about to scream, she heard a metallic click.

The trapper heard it too and froze.

Harcourt's voice was quiet, "Going somewhere, Tobias?"

The trapper muttered something. He got down from the wagon and shambled away. Hope clutched the blanket to her and cautiously peered out.

The trapper stumbled to his own wagon. The man was as drunk as a bear on fermented honey.

"Go back to sleep," Harcourt said. "We have an early start tomorrow." He ducked back under the wagon and lay down, one arm behind his head. Although he put his Navy Colt back in its holster, the gun belt was within easy reach. Hope turned back into the wagon.

It was a while before she fell asleep again.

Harcourt felt like swearing long and viciously. He sighed. What the hell had he done? Why, in God's name had he bought this woman? It was the last thing he wanted. For five years his nights had drowned in the screams of dying men, thunderous cannon-fire, bloody, splintered remains of wood, bone and flesh ripping past him, slapping into him, never being able to breathe for the smoke and the vomit, the agony of knowing there was nothing he could do to stop it. Most of all, he was haunted by the darkness of discovering his own ability for violence. A violence that hadn't stopped when the war ended. The sight that tormented him the most was his wife, Tess - her broken body lying at his feet.

A year running from that memory followed, but no matter where he went all he found was violence, blood, greed and pain. The gold fields were another form of war. He hated them. He loathed the mass of men and their lust. The rape of the land was a sight which kept his own wounds raw and bleeding. To make matters worse, if they could be, violent men gravitated to him for some un-fathomable reason and, as naturally as flies follow a corpse, trouble followed.

He'd wanted to be left alone. He'd longed for quiet. His soul had begged for peace. When he'd arrived in these mountains, he'd felt this was a place he could hide. After a week in their solitude the nightmares had stopped.

So why had he thoughtlessly brought someone, this woman in particular, into his life? Into his sanctuary? He shifted his shoulders. The ground was as unyielding as iron, and as unforgiving. He hoped the fact that he wasn't spending the night in his own wagon wasn't a sign of things to come.

The next few days settled into a predictable rhythm. Rising at dawn, they would rekindle the fire. After a meal of hot porridge, they'd break camp and head out, winding their way higher into the foothills.

The women walked together for a few hours each day. Most of them had been on the boat, but things were different now.

Unconscious when she was dropped into the hold, Hope had woken when one of the sailors kicked her in the ribs. When one of the women told her she was on a bride ship bound for the men on the gold claims Hope had shouted frantically and banged on the underside of the hatch until she was hoarse and her hands sore. Exhausted, she'd slumped down and huddled in a corner. It was no use. The hatch was only lifted to toss down another woman or lower the food bucket. Bewildered, terrified and with large parts of her memory missing, Hope had kept to herself for the rest of the journey. Now, however, the women were grateful for each other's company and chatted endlessly about their possible futures, and the men they were with. Hope had no intention of discussing Luke with anyone. She only ever said that he appeared to be a good man. Even that brought enough crude jokes and laughter to make her blush.

Mrs Cuthbert seemed a homely soul with an honest, realistic and common-sense attitude. Whenever the other wives' conversation got too crude, she'd shake her head and drop back with Hope. She was a level-headed woman who did much to restore Hope's spirit.

The only one who never joined them was Tobias John's wife. Whenever Hope saw her, she had a new bruise.

At night, making sure they were as far away from the trapper as possible, Luke would park the wagon and unhitch the mules and the horse, settling them for the night. After sharing a quiet meal, Hope would clean up, say goodnight and climb into the wagon.

It had become a habit for Harcourt to stay outside drinking coffee and watching the fire die down. He'd let the sounds in the other wagons fade completely before retiring.

"I'm going to be sleeping in the wagon from now on," he said quietly one night, watching her over the rim of his coffee cup.

She simply nodded and poured herself another cup of coffee. Later, lying quietly in the dark, she waited. It was only the second night they'd shared the space. She was getting used to being around this man but somehow nights were different. And now he wanted to sleep in the wagon again. Why? Had he changed his mind about keeping his hands off her? Hope's nervousness increased when he climbed in.

But Luke Harcourt kept his word. He never touched her. Ever.

CHAPTER SIX

FIVE days from Silver Birch Landing they arrived at Thunder Creek. It wasn't a creek, but a wide, raging torrent that swept its way out of the mountain and roared down to the meadows where it finally slowed and quietly meandered to the sea. They followed it for quite a while, pulling up eventually at a wooden bridge, the only place where the river narrowed enough to build one.

The river's boisterousness was spectacular, alive and joyous. Hope's eyes shone. She grinned. It was the first time Harcourt had seen such joy in her face and it transformed her.

Hope noticed that one or two of the planks on the bridge were missing. "Is that safe?" she asked, pointing at the gaps.

"Should be," said Harcourt, turning his attention back to the task at hand. "It was like that when I crossed a few days ago." He leaned out to take a closer look. "Although the water's a lot higher now."

The bridge creaked alarmingly as the wagons swayed across one by one. The mules were not happy. It took a lot of lashing of reins and whips to get them to move. It was an unpleasant business. Their braying distress upset the women. After a while only Harcourt and Tobias John's wagons were left.

"Take these." Harcourt handed Hope the reins.

"What do I do?" She was clearly nervous.

"Just hold them. I'm going to lead the mules across." He jumped down and went to their heads. He spoke quietly rubbing their foreheads, then coaxed them forward a step at a time.

Things were going well until a rotten plank snapped beneath one of the wheels. The wagon lurched sickeningly. The mules took fright, reared up, pushing the wagon backwards.

Another plank broke. The wagon dropped deeper into the hole. It gave another sudden, awful stagger. Without warning, Hope was flung off the wagon.

"Hope!"

She was gone, tumbling over and over in the turbulent water, her heavy skirt pulling her down.

Abandoning the wagon, Luke leaped in after her. He managed to turn so his legs were facing downstream, trying to keep his head above the water as much as possible. He struggled for breath, battling against the force of the current.

He could see Hope flailing ahead of him. The river roared at Luke, tearing at his clothes, pounding him in the face, bellowing its fierce anger against him, beating at his body. It had no intention of giving Hope back to him. It flung her against a rock. She went limp and began to sink. Luke desperately tried to manoeuvre himself so the current would take him towards her. It worked. He grabbed her floating body as he went past. He turned her to keep her head above water, difficult in the turbulent water.

Going around a bend, they slammed into a tree that had capsized into the river. Some of its roots still clung to the bank. Instinctively, Luke grabbed it.

River water burned his eyes, his lungs dragged in air. Hope's head lolled on his shoulder. He didn't know if she was alive or not. He tried to figure out how to get her onto the bank. If he lost his hold on the tree they'd be swept downstream. His grip was slipping. He wouldn't be able to hold on much longer. The current was too strong. He had to get her onto dry land.

"Let go!" a voice shouted at him. He realised there were hands pulling at Hope. He looked up. It was Tobias John.

"Let go, I've got her," the trapper yelled.

Luke released his hold gratefully. Tobias John hauled Hope out of the river and dumped her on the bank. He turned back and heaved Luke out as well. Luke coughed, retching up river.

Quickly, he turned to Hope. How much water had she swallowed? She wasn't breathing. Had she drowned? He lifted her, cradling her against his chest and thumped her back. Nothing. He thumped again and again.

"Come on, Hope! Breathe! Breathe, dammit." He thumped her hard. Without warning she coughed out river water onto his shoulder. She was alive. She coughed a few more times, blinked, then pushed herself away, turned around and retched.

Thank God, thought Luke. She'd be fine.

"Drowned rats." Tobias John gave what Luke assumed was a laugh.

His voice was rusty and harsh, surprisingly high for a man of his size.

Luke stood up and shook the water out of his ears. "Thank you, Tobias." He held out his hand.

The big man just looked at it and then spat a thick, filthy stream of tobacco juice into the bushes on the side. "Your wagon's blocking the bridge. I ain't moving it on my own."

Whenever Tobias John went near the horse he'd raced down-river on, its head jerked up, ears pulled back, and smacked the ground with its big hooves. Luke moved quickly to Augustus Brown, stroking his big angular head to calm him. He saw the horse's sides were sticky with blood. Luke was furious; it was his horse, but he couldn't say anything, the trapper had just saved their lives. "Perhaps you should start back, Tobias," suggested Luke, trying to keep the anger out of his voice. "I think Hope needs a little while to catch her breath."

The trapper snorted contemptuously and strode off back towards the bridge, sending Augustus Brown jerking as he stomped past.

Luke waited a good quarter of an hour, giving both Hope and the horse time to rest and calm down. When he suggested Hope ride back, she point blank refused. There was no way she was getting on Augustus Brown. To be honest, the way the horse was behaving, Harcourt didn't blame her.

"I need to walk off the shakes," she said. He accepted her excuse without comment.

The two of them followed the river back to the bridge. After a while, they began to steam in the heat. It was a long, uncomfortable hike. When they arrived, they discovered that between them, the other men had rescued Luke's wagon, pulling it from the grip of the broken planks. Daylight was fading and everyone was tired. Everyone, except Tobias John, went about setting up camp. The trapper had chosen to keep going and whipping up his tired mules headed out.

Mrs Cuthbert waddled across to Luke's wagon. "Why don't the two of you come over for something to eat? We've got plenty and there's some good hot coffee brewing." She'd dug out a shift for Hope. "Take this, honey, and hang your stuff up to dry. I'll never get into it again so you might as well keep it. When you've changed, come over to us and I'll put some salve on your bruises. I reckon you must be pretty well covered in them."

Hope changed in the wagon. When she emerged, her face was strained with exhaustion. In fact, she looked shattered. She probably felt worse than he did, Luke thought. His body ached and all he wanted to do was sleep. She'd wrapped a blanket around herself. The lacy neck of the borrowed shift poked out at the top. It was clearly far too big for Hope.

Luke grinned when he saw the blanket. "Nice get-up. You could start a new fashion."

She flushed. "I feel almost naked," she whispered as she hung her sodden dress and shift over a bush.

Harcourt was amused. Unlike the other wives, who had no qualms about displaying themselves, Hope always made sure her dress was modestly done up and was as neat as she could be. Thankfully, tonight they didn't have to go far. The Cuthbert's wagon was right next door. Hope would have felt far too embarrassed to walk across the camp dressed only in Mrs Cuthbert's too-large shift and a blanket.

Both Hope and Luke were grateful for the filling, wholesome dinner Mrs Cuthbert had made. As she collected the plates afterwards, the plump, garrulous old lady was obviously keen for a good chat. Luke shot a glance at Hope. "Mr Cuthbert, Mrs Cuthbert, thank you for dinner. I think we'd better call it a night though. Hope is almost asleep," he said with a smile.

He walked Hope back to their campsite. He had to hold her arm, she was nearly sleepwalking. She curled up on her side of the wagon and was asleep as soon, if not before, she laid her head down.

Covering her with the blanket, he watched her for a moment. He'd been impressed by her fortitude. She hadn't complained or blamed anyone for the afternoon's almost disastrous adventure. But he could see she was rattled. She'd been on the verge of tears a few times tonight. A good night's rest and she'd probably be all right.

She might be, but that bridge wasn't. If it didn't get fixed now, there might not be a bridge when the rains came. A huge yawn overtook him. He hadn't realised how tired he was. He drifted off quickly.

Hope woke late the next day. She'd slept so soundly, she hadn't heard the other wagons leave at dawn. It was hunger that roused her. She groaned when she tried to move. Every muscle in her body ached. The bruises had begun to show.

There was a knock on the outside of the wagon.

"You awake?"

"Barely." She groaned again.

He laughed. "Breakfast's ready."

"Luke, would you mind passing me my dress please?"

She wrinkled her nose at it when he handed it in a moment later. It smelled muddy. But at least it was almost dry, only the remnants of early morning dew still clung to it.

"We're staying here till tomorrow," Luke said when she joined him at the fire. "I want to take a look at that bridge and see if I can fix it. There's plenty of driftwood around. I might be able to use that."

"All right." She took a long drink of the hot coffee and yawned. "Are you as tired and sore as I am?" she asked.

He nodded. "That was a pretty exciting ride yesterday."

"It was, but let's not do it again, at least for a while."

He laughed. "Not today anyway."

"If we're going to be here for the day, I think I'll wash my dress properly."

He nodded, tossed away the coffee dregs in his cup, dug some tools from the box under the wagon's seat and strode off towards the broken bridge.

Luke had expected her to bring him something to eat at noon, but she hadn't appeared. When he returned to the campsite, the fire was cold. Billowing in the breeze, her dress and shift were hanging over a rope she'd tied from one tree to another.

He found her on the other side of the wagon curled up on a blanket under a tree, wearing the shift Mrs Cuthbert had given her. Her long legs stuck out from the shift's flounce at the hem. The neckline had slipped, leaving her shoulder bare. Hope's chocolate brown hair gleamed in the afternoon sun. A soft tendril blew loosely around her face. She shivered as the sun went behind a small cloud and curled up a bit tighter. He went back to the bridge and carried on with the repairs. The sight of her sleeping like that, her shift falling off, her long slim legs, had been an attractive sight.

Not one he gave himself the luxury of dwelling on. He slept under the wagon again that night.

CHAPTER SEVEN

THEY turned off the trail two days later and, alone now, wound higher up the mountain, passing through meadows and parts of the forest. The tall pine spires stood quietly on the rocky slopes, the depths of the wood hidden behind ferns and underbrush. Pale shafts of sun glimmered softly down into the greenery, motes of dust wandering idly through the quiet, gold light. For a while Hope thought the forest was silent, but as they went further into its heart, she began to hear unseen birds calling to each other in muted tones and soft rustles in the undergrowth as the wagon passed by.

Hope, having never been in this type of forest before, discovered she liked it better than the often windblown, open spaces they'd travelled through to get here. It wasn't the same kind of forest that stood around...wherever it was she was from. She still couldn't recall the town's name.

That forest had been closer to a mangrove than anything else and much more humid. This one stood taller, reached higher, like pillars in a cathedral soaring to leafy, vaulted arches above. Its beauty was clean, the smell of the pines almost astringent. The ferns and underbrush softened its austerity; they brought gentleness to the forest. In places, the trees grew straight out of the rock.

It some ways, the forest reminded her of Luke. It made her feel secure. Before she'd found herself on the ship, she would never have said that one of her greatest needs was to feel safe. But since then, she realised, it was the one thing she craved the most. She was desperately afraid of finding out who'd put her in that stinking, dark, ship's hold. And why.

It was surprisingly hot for early spring, so the coolness of the forest was a welcome relief, even for the animals. Luke pulled up in a glade and set about preparing a meal. Later, sitting on a mossy rock, her empty plate on the ground at her feet, Hope lifted her face to the sun filtering slowly down through the trees, its softness lightly touching her skin. She closed her eyes and listened to the forest sounds. Filled with bird song, leaves whispering and laughing to each other in the breeze flitting through the tops of the branches, the comforting crackle of the small fire nestled among the circle of grey rocks...the sounds filled her soul. She sighed in contentment. It was so peaceful, she wished they could stay for longer than just this meal. She smiled at Luke.

"It's almost like church in here," she said.

Her face was glowing, her skin luminous. Her green eyes sparkled. He'd never noticed the colour of her eyes before. They were the same hue as the ferns that framed her. Big, dark rimmed eyes like that drew a man. His gaze lingered on her face. He hadn't really noticed before, but she had a lovely mouth. When she wasn't afraid or tense, her lips relaxed into soft curves, fuller and richer, slightly turned up at the corners as if she were about to smile. Like she was smiling at him now. He wondered what it would be like to kiss—

He frowned and without thinking reached for the coffee-pot. Instant white pain seared into one blistering moment of agony. He leapt up, dropping the pot with a yell, hot coffee flying everywhere as it hit the rocks. He swore mightily, shaking his hand, pacing up and down.

Hope raced for the wagon and dug out the salve Mrs Cuthbert had given her.

"Don't fuss, Hope. I'm fine," he growled. Dammit, it hurt like hell. Shit. What an idiot!

"Let me see."

He wanted to cradle his hand against himself, but she was standing in front of him. He'd look childish if he refused.

She took his hand carefully. She must have hurt him, his hand jerked when she touched him. A wide, angry scorch mark crossed his palm. As she smoothed on the salve he hissed in pain. She glanced up anxiously.

"It's fine," he said.

Hope tore a piece off the end of her shift and carefully wrapped it round his palm. She was standing close to him. Her hands were gentle and cool. When she lifted her face, those green eyes were filled with concern.

"Does that feel a bit better?" she asked, "I'm sorry if I hurt you."

"You didn't. Thank you."

She was still holding his hand, standing close to him.

He stepped round her. "We might as well get going. I'd like to make it through the forest today. Then tomorrow we'll be at the cabin."

That night, they camped in the fringe of the forest. Luke had been abrupt all afternoon and now, lying side by side in the wagon with Hope, he was restless and grumpy.

Before the sun came up, he was awake and making coffee. They broke camp and were on the move straight after breakfast. Hope was sorry to leave the forest behind. It had a music that brought her peace.

The way curved up even higher. At noon, they crested a rise and there before them lay a valley. Luke's valley. Long and narrow with foothills and mountains on either side - it was a beautiful sight. A tree-lined river flowed through it with apple trees planted in neat, orderly rows on this side of the river. Past the orchard, a meadow stretched towards the far mountains.

Beyond the river stood a cabin and to the left of that a large barn painted a dull, dark red. A smaller wooden building stood nearby. Hope was pleased to see how close the forest stood to the cabin, sheltering it, a defensive wall at its back and how it lay thick on the mountain behind it.

With the end of their journey in sight, the mules were keen to keep moving. They trotted along the trail that followed the river. Here the water was slow and calm. It meandered round large boulders, formed pools beneath the overhanging willow branches, gurgled over rocks and through reeds. Ferns grew along its banks and Hope thought she saw the blue flash of a kingfisher darting through the trees. The willows occasionally hid the cabin and barns from view.

"It looks like you have a visitor."

Luke glanced across the river. A small shaggy pony was tied to the railing of the cabin's porch. "Daniel. He looks after the animals while I'm away."

"Does he live here? At the cabin, I mean?"

"No. The other side of the mountain. I live alone."

That hurt. Surprisingly. Hope looked away. Why did he buy her? He was such a self-contained man. She was obviously an unwelcome intrusion. Whoever had put her on the ship, clearly hadn't wanted her. Was this 'marriage' going to work or would she be just as unwanted here?

She sat up straighter. She couldn't think like that. Take one day at a time. That's what her father had always said.

The afternoon was fading as they came to a narrow stretch of river where the clear water tumbled through a rocky crevice to a pool below. They clattered across the narrow wooden bridge stretched across the boulders and drove up to the red barn.

Pulling up, Luke jumped down and gave his hand to Hope. With a smile of thanks, she took it. As she stepped down, she thought she saw the barn door close.

"I'll unpack the wagon. Why don't you take these things inside?" Luke asked. He loaded her up with Lee-Ming's parcel as well as other smaller packages. "The cabin door sticks occasionally, just give it a hard push." He climbed in to the back of the wagon to start unloading the sacks.

Arms full, Hope went across to the rustic dwelling. A porch encircled the cabin like a narrow moat. Taking up one side, as high as the overhang of the porch roof was a large pile of neatly stacked wood. Beside the front door, an old wooden chair rested contentedly against the wall near a small pile of logs, which lay quietly, slowly growing a soft blanket of moss. A few pale dried-up curls of wood shavings lay at the feet of the chair.

So, Luke liked to sit out here and whittle. He didn't strike her as the whittling type. Not old or ornery enough. Glancing back at him her gaze was captured by the vision across the valley. From the porch, the end of the apple orchard was visible. It was filled with light, an almost otherworldly, glowing yellow. Behind the blue-grey mountains in the far distance, the sky was alive with colour, pale purple shot through with orange, green and pink. High up in the darker indigo vault of heaven, a sprinkling of the brightest stars were already shining.

It was a view of which only the hardest, dullest person would ever tire. To see that every day she'd take up whittling too.

She pushed open the cabin door. Once her eyes had adjusted to the darkness, she could make out the furniture. Hope found the shutters and opened them wide, letting in the last of the daylight, and took stock of the cabin that was now her home. Larger inside than she expected, it was clean, tidy and neat as a pin, with a big fireplace. A rifle and shotgun hung above it. There were two more hooks for another, shorter gun. Two armchairs sat in front of the fireplace and, which she hadn't expected, a tall bookcase crammed with books stood to its right.

Putting the parcels on the table, she went to investigate. Shakespeare, the Bible, nautical books, books on geography, history, a smattering of almanacs and works by Charles Dickens. There was even a copy of Jane Eyre! She was delighted. Reading was one of her greatest pleasures. It also meant Luke was probably the educated man she'd thought. Well, that she'd assumed he was. Maybe he just liked the look of books. But it was a long way to bring books only to have them sit on his shelves.

She turned back to the room. There was a dresser against the wall, and on the far side of the other window, a cupboard. A large cedar chest had initials intricately carved into the lid. They weren't Luke's. She ran her fingers over them. A curly T intertwined with a G, both surrounded by ivy leaves and birds. It was a beautiful piece of furniture. It stood at the base of the bed. The only bed in the room.

Her heart dropped. Now they were back at the cabin how would things change between them? He'd given his word, but this was his cabin. Would he expect her to sleep here in this bed, with him? After all, he'd thought he was buying a wife. That's what the auction was all about. Men buying wives.

But they weren't married. She kept thinking about the receipt. 'Goods Purchased'. No matter how you looked at it, that wasn't a marriage certificate.

Hearing voices outside, Hope tore her eyes, and her thoughts away from the only piece of furniture in the room that made her heart stand still. Luke and...oh, yes, Daniel would probably want dinner soon. She'd better see what she could find.

She spotted a door just to the right of the fireplace. As much as she didn't want to, her mind was still pondering the sleeping arrangements. Perhaps this was another bedroom? She opened the door. Instead of a solution to her problem it was a storeroom, a larder. Quite a large one, but still only a larder.

How foolish, what else would it be? Why would a man living alone need two bedrooms? Inside, a large tin bath hung on a nail on the back wall. A broom and a butter churn sat tucked beside it. Two wide shelves on each side ran the length of the larder. Beneath them stood a pail and some very depleted sacks of coffee, sugar, flour and beans. There was also a large crate packed with old, wrinkly apples.

Stacked on one shelf, sat a neat pile of crockery. Hope ran her fingers over the edge of a plate. It wasn't the finest of china but on the other hand it wasn't tin either. Knives, forks, spoons and a couple of long handled ladles jutted out of a tall white jug. Earthenware dishes, with their lids settled on top, rested beside it.

On the other shelf squatted black, heavy pots and pans. A scurrying spider caught Hope's eye as it skittered into the shadowy corner and disappeared behind a few tall bottles of whiskey.

Please don't let him drink. To be with alone with a man who drank could be - would be awful.

She pulled herself together. The bottles were full and covered in dust. The spider had commandeered them as a base for its web. Hope was so relieved she decided the spider could stay for as long it wanted.

The larder was neatly laid out and although a little musty and dark, was clean. A trap door in the floor led, she discovered, to an empty root cellar.

Luke carried a large sack of beans into the larder as she lowered the cellar door back into place. He dropped it onto the floor with a thump.

"Put this away. I'll get the rest." He unstrapped his gun belt and hung it over the back of a chair. Hope tried to pick up the sack. It didn't budge. She gave another heave, and a grunt. Luke smiled and as he walked out the door, she was attempting to drag the sack across the larder floor.

Luke returned and dropped a second sack on the floor. He saw she'd persevered and now the first hessian bag was under the shelf. She'd put the nearly empty one of beans on top of the new sack and was dusting off her hands and her dress.

Six or so more trips and there was one full sack under each nearly empty one.

"Is Daniel joining us for dinner?" she asked as he pushed the last bag under the shelf.

"No. He went home a while ago." Luke gave the sack another shove. "If you get the fire going, I'll start toting water so you can have a bath."

"Perhaps I should tote the water," replied Hope. "I have no idea how to start a fire, I'm afraid."

"Really?" Luke was astounded, then felt foolish. Before he'd come west most of the women he'd known wouldn't know how to light a fire.

"Don't worry, the water's heavy. I'll do it for you today. Why don't you unpack those parcels and get down the tin bath from the larder? You can set it in front of the fireplace and the water will warm up a little."

He knelt and started laying a fire. Hearing Hope gasp he twisted around. She'd opened Lee-Ming's parcel. Inside there was a skirt and a shirt.

"How kind of Lee-Ming!" She held the clothes up against herself. The sleeves of the crisp white shirt were a little short, but nothing to signify. The pale blue skirt was just the right length.

The clothes were simple, well-made linen garments. And although not exactly perfect for everyday wear here in the mountains, they were at least a change of clothing. "What's that?" Luke pointed at the small pile still in the open wrapper. Hope laid aside the skirt and held up the foamy, white stuff. It was a flouncy petticoat and fancy undergarments, all lace and silk. Hope blushed a deep red, and hurriedly put it away.

"Oh. I think, um, where can I put my clothes?" She tried not to look at Luke.

"There should be room in the closet, just push my stuff to one side." He turned back to the fire, his face split with a grin. Those were very fancy undergarments. He couldn't help but wonder what she'd look like wearing them.

The fire was going; it was time he fetched the water.

The bath was half full. Hope decided that was enough or he'd be toting water all night. "Take your time. I've got chores to do in the barn," he said.

"Thank you for the water. A bath is just what I need."

He nodded and walked out, shutting the cabin door behind him.

While the water warmed up, Hope opened the closet to pack away her new clothes. It held a few surprises. A heavy, dark coat with a wide collar hung at the back. She rubbed the fabric of another jacket between her fingers. Luke had some excellent quality clothes, the kind her brother and father wore. These fragments of memory confused Hope. She still wasn't sure if she wanted to remember everything. She couldn't imagine an apple farmer ever having an occasion to wear clothes like this. But then, what did she know about apple farmers? Luke - she'd unconsciously stopped thinking of him as Mr. Harcourt - was the first one she'd ever met, and it seemed he read Shakespeare.

There would be more than enough room for her one skirt and a shirt in the closet.

Hope found an empty shelf for the fancy underwear. She was too embarrassed to just leave it lying on the shelf, Luke would see it every time he went into the closet, so she carefully wrapped it up again in the brown paper before putting it as far back on the shelf as she could. The water must be warm by now. She'd better not take too long. Luke could be back at any minute.

Hope had found lamps in the larder while Luke was toting the water. She'd watched carefully when Luke had lit the wagon lamp each night on their trip from town and now she managed to get these house lamps going without too much of a struggle. She was quite pleased with herself. The lamps gave off a lovely light, nice and bright, albeit a bit smelly. She closed the shutters and stripped off.

The bath, although not as warm as she'd hoped, was wonderful. She washed her hair first. It always made her feel better to have clean hair. After the bath, she washed her dress and her shift. She would have to try and mend the tear in the bottom of the shift. She'd never sewn anything in her life, except samplers and tapestries, which couldn't really be considered sewing. She wondered if Luke even had needles and thread.

She'd realised, that first night off the ship, that although Luke had said he didn't want a wife, he certainly wasn't going to wait on her hand and foot. She'd have to learn to be a homemaker as quickly as possible, if only to pull her weight.

Housekeeper, not homemaker. Homes were where families - husbands, wives and children - lived.

She felt like a different person when she put on her new clothes. Everything except the lacy underwear. She wasn't that brave, and it occurred to her that it should be kept for a special occasion, although what that occasion could be she had no idea.

The memory of Luke's face earlier in the day suddenly came back to her. They'd crested the rise and the valley lay before them. Unconsciously, he had sighed deeply. Expecting him to say something, she'd caught instead the look a man wears when he comes home; deep, peaceful and full of satisfied joy. A joy that comes from knowing everything is going to be all right, now that he's back where he belongs.

Luke rubbed down the mules and the horse. Augustus Brown's sides were healing. He fed and watered all the other animals and cleaned out their stalls, laying fresh, sweet smelling hay, even though Daniel had done it that morning. It took a while, but it was good to do something physical after sitting for so long on the wagon.

His hand still hurt. Perhaps Hope would put some more of that salve on if he asked. Too late to haul more water for a bath for himself. It was easier just to go down to the river and bathe there. Chilly, but at least he'd be clean. Better get some clean clothes to take with. Hope would die of fright if he wandered around in nothing more than a towel. He grinned and closed the barn door, dropping the bar into place.

On his way back to the cabin, Luke saw her dress and shift hanging on the line. She must have washed them and changed into that new outfit Lee-Ming had given her. Had she put on the fancy underwear?

The cabin was ablaze with light. The door and every window stood open, light streaming out. She must have lit every lamp he owned!

Luke was relieved to discover she hadn't, only two, which was one too many. He turned them down. Burning so high, they were smoking. They'd be out of fuel in a month at that rate.

Although she'd never complained on the trip out from town, it had become obvious to Luke that she'd probably grown up in a fairly pampered home. Now, Hope had a pot on the fire and was stirring something inside it. He hoped it was edible. Women who led the kind of life he thought she may have, generally didn't know how to cook. Taking clean clothes out of the closet he spotted the brown paper parcel on the shelf. So, not the fancy underwear then.

When he came back to the cabin, dinner was ready. He watched her as she dished up the food. She moved easily and with unconscious charm. Everything she did was graceful. Living with her might not be that hard after all. Dinner, to his surprise, was tasty and filling.

Hold on. He took another bite. Ah. It was the reheated remains of the meal they'd had at noon and he'd made it to start with. He did make a good rabbit stew. Hope had warmed it up and added beans and apples. It was a nice touch.

"I found some honey. Would you like some toast as dessert?" she asked, clearing away the dinner plates.

"Sounds good. I'll get the coffee going."

A short while later, they were slathering the crunchy toast with butter and thick dribbles of the honey she'd discovered in a stone jar in the larder. It went down well with the good coffee Luke made.

While they were drinking the coffee, Luke yawned and stretched. "It's been a long day. I'm ready for bed."

The colour drained from Hope's face. Her eyes went wide and she sat very still.

Luke frowned. Hope shot a quick, almost involuntary glance, over at the bed and then down at her coffee cup, blushing hotly. Luke followed her gaze across the room. He sighed. Of course.

Hope, the colour still high in her cheeks, said, "Please don't worry," as if he had been. "This is your cabin. If I can have a blanket and perhaps a pillow, I'll be more than happy to sleep in the barn."

Luke snorted. Did she think he'd begrudge her a blanket and a pillow? And did she honestly think he'd let her sleep in the barn? Perhaps she was merely being polite. But she was right, someone had to sleep there. He should have seen this coming.

"This cabin's always needed another room. I'll get started on that as soon as I can. In the meantime, I'll sleep in the barn."

"But I—"

"Lady, no woman sleeps in my barn when there's a perfectly good bed. Thank you for dinner." He got up and went across to the closet.

"But that's not right, this is your cabin. Honestly, I'm quite happy to sleep in—"

"Don't argue, Hope." He cut her short with a frown. "As you say, it's my cabin. It's also my barn, and if I choose to sleep there, I will."

He gathered up the blanket and the quilt he'd pulled off the top of the closet. "Good night."

Opening the cabin door, he turned, "You might want to keep the shutters half closed. Just in case a bear pays a visit."

"Bears!" Her hand flew to her throat as he walked out. He grinned. It was a cheap revenge for having to sleep in the barn, but it was worth it to see the look on her face.

He drifted to sleep thinking of plans for the new room.

CHAPTER EIGHT

HER life at the cabin had a peace about it that helped Hope find her feet and settle in easily. She did the chores Luke assigned to her willingly and without complaint. Luke found a sewing kit in the cedar chest and she fixed her torn shift.

Although curious about that chest, Hope instinctively stayed away from it.

Her chores were relatively simple, keep the cabin clean and tidy, do the washing, the cooking and milk the cow. Of course, that meant making butter and cheese as well. She didn't have a clue how to milk the cow, let alone churn butter.

The day after their arrival, it was barely sunrise when Hope had woken with a start. Luke was knocking loudly on the cabin door. "Time to get up, Hope. You need to milk the cow before breakfast," he called through the door.

She scrambled into her clothes as fast as she could. Her hair was a rat's nest. She'd spotted a hairbrush on one of the shelves in the cupboard as she had packed away the items Lee-Ming had given her. Hoping Luke wouldn't mind her using it, she dragged it ruthlessly through her hair, plaited it as quickly as she could and ran outside.

This early in the morning it was still cool in the mountains. The sun was only just tinting the tips of the mountains across the valley. She shivered, wishing she had a shawl.

Luke was waiting outside and together they headed across the yard.

It was warmer in the barn, much to her relief. She saw the makeshift bed Luke had made in the hay. Hope turned away from the quilt folded neatly below the pillow. It seemed an invasion of his privacy. It made her feel uncomfortable to see where he had slept, when he should have been by all rights, and perhaps expectation, sleeping in his own bed.

Luke didn't notice her discomfort. "There's the two pails you need for milking. The wooden one for water and the metal one for milk. Don't confuse them or the milk spoils. And now, Hope meet Pinkerton. Pinkerton, Hope."

She laughed. "Not the usual Bessie or Daisy?"

"Too predictable. Everyone calls their cow that kind of name. Besides, she looks like a Pinkerton, don't you think?"

The small cow, munching on some new hay, turned her head and blinked her gentle, long lashed, brown eyes at Hope. A young calf lay in the straw at her feet.

"Hello Pinkerton," said Hope with a smile. "It's so very nice to meet you. What's your baby's name?"

"Don't name the animals you plan to sell," said Luke, "Makes it easier when they go."

She saw his point of view. She also saw a tenderness of heart she hadn't expected, or even hoped for.

"You may as well be formally introduced to the other animals as well." Luke led her deeper into the barn to the other stalls. The large, black horse stuck its very Roman nose over the stable door and into his hand, snorting a soft welcome.

"This here, as you know, is Augustus Brown." He rubbed the horse's nose. Hope bowed her head politely but kept a discreet distance away. She was afraid of horses, mules, ponies, anything that big with four legs, lots of teeth and a tail. She was a bit nervous of Pinkerton, but it wasn't the same somehow. Pinkerton had such gentle eyes. And one never heard of cows rearing up and lashing out with huge hooves. Augustus Brown terrified her. He loomed over Luke.

Despite her fear, she could still appreciate the horse's magnificence: the proud arch to his neck, his completely black, glossy coat gleaming like wet ink.

"He's majestic. Imperial almost," she said.

"He certainly is a little arrogant. People thought I was crazy when I bought him. I got him for almost nothing."

"Why? He looks expensive."

"He was a hellion. Unrideable, angry and vicious."

Hope's nervousness swelled. "And now?"

"A little gentleness and a few quiet conversations and he's an old softie."

Looking anything but, the horse rolled a large, liquid eye at Hope. She was sure it'd taken a lot more than a few quiet chats to tame him.

"I wouldn't use spurs on him though," Luke said. "They turn him back into a demon." He gave the horse's nose another rub and fed him an apple from a crate standing against a wooden pillar.

"Charles Dickens and William Shakespeare, you've also already met." Smelling the apple Luke had given Augustus Brown, the two mules who'd pulled the wagon from Silver Birch Landing popped their heads over their own stable doors in anticipation. Luke gave one to each of them, rubbing their foreheads and talking quietly to them.

Watching him, Hope remembered her father commenting once that one could generally judge how a man would treat a woman, or a child, by the way he treated his animals. He'd said it the day they saw a young man, with hopes of courting her cousin, beat his dog for a minor infraction. She'd married someone else, to their great relief.

The recollection brought tears to Hope's eyes. Her memory had begun to return not long after Luke had paid for her. Slowly, each day she remembered more, sometimes in chunks, sometimes simply one conversation. Perhaps, one day, she'd remember everything. Her heart tightened at the thought. Did she want to? Was it safe?

She walked further into the barn so Luke wouldn't see her tears and discovered a white goat. Long hair hung in little twisted spirals over its eyes. It tilted its head in a considering way at Hope, then trotted over and rammed the stall door.

"Hello you," said Hope, reaching over and scratching the goat's head.

"Careful."

Hope jumped. She hadn't heard Luke come up behind her. Did he have to move so silently? Never extravagant in his movements or gestures, his quietness gave him an air of power, of strength, a man who knew exactly what he was capable of, with no need to prove it. Perhaps it was that which made her feel protected? "Franklin will eat your skirt right off you if you let her."

"Franklin, for a girl goat?" Hope laughed.

Luke grinned. "I know. I couldn't help myself. She seems to like it." He got back to business. "If you could milk Pinkerton every day and turn all the animals out into the paddock behind the barn, I'll clean out their stalls and feed them." He opened the large barn doors.

Cool air billowed in along with the sharp, fresh scent of the new morning. Long golden fingers of sunlight stretched themselves across the thick, dewy grass of the large field outside. Spider webs glistened between the pale fence railings. Twitterings and bursts of song from the forest greeted the sunrise. In the distance, the lavender mountains looked freshly painted.

Hope heard the animals stir. Her mind jolted back to the barn. She didn't think she could do this. She'd never be able to get close enough to the horse and the mules. She didn't know what to do even if she could. Luke opened the stall doors for the mules that trotted out, heads held high. As they passed, Hope pressed herself against the goat's stall. She saw Luke going to the horse. Moving as quickly as she could, without actually breaking into a run, she made sure she was on the other side of the stalls before he got the stable door open.

The horse seemed even larger than before. He was a powerful, quiet animal, just like his master. Augustus Brown swung his big head and stared at Hope before turning and sauntering outside. He walked with a well-muscled swagger.

The goat simply leaped the low fence around her stall and trotted after him.

Pinkerton was feeling ignored and lowed in protest. She needed to be milked and had a hankering for some fresh air and green grass as well. Smacking her with affection on the rump, Luke plonked the milking stool next to the cow and set about showing Hope how to milk her.

"You must wipe off her udder first or anything sticking to it might fall into the milk." He dipped his hand in the wooden water pail and cleaned the cow. She twitched and stomped her back foot at the shock of the icy water. "Make sure the milk pail is clean as well." He pulled at the teats and quickly a bluish-white stream squirted out, ringing as it hit the metal pail.

"Your turn." He stood up and made way for her. Hope sat on the tiny stool, feeling very vulnerable and tried to do exactly as he said. It was hopeless.

"I don't think she likes me," said Hope tugging away fruitlessly at the teats.

Luke laughed. "Here, let me show you." He crouched next to her and put his hands over hers. His touch shocked her. His skin was warm, his hands strong, hands that worked for a living. An expression she'd never encountered before rose in those blue eyes of his. She felt flustered.

"Hold your hands like this," he said, turning back to the cow.

Perhaps she'd imagined what she'd seen in his face. She shifted on the stool and concentrated on the lesson. Once she had the rhythm correct and the pail was slowly filling with milk, Luke took his hands away and left her to carry on by herself.

The reaction he'd felt when he touched her had been a complete surprise. He had no intention of anything happening with this woman, but when he'd covered her hands with his he'd suddenly been very alive to how close, and how feminine she was.

He hoped she hadn't seen his awareness. There was a strong possibility she had. He thought he'd covered his mistake well enough. As soon as he looked away, she'd settled almost immediately and quickly got the hang of milking, a frown of concentration creasing her forehead. Taking the water pail and a hard-bristled broom leaning against the barn wall, Luke went out into the paddock to make sure the water troughs were clean and full.

The calf could smell the milk. He climbed, rather ungainly, to his feet and came to investigate. Hope giggled as he tried to suckle her hand. His tongue was rough, wet and ticklish. She pushed him away, but he was determined. He didn't take kindly to being refused access to his mother. He tried to push in and drink out of the pail. Hope's three-legged stool wasn't the most stable piece of furniture and its height, or rather lack of height, made her an easy pushover for the calf. As she tumbled into the straw, her foot caught against the pail. Milk went everywhere!

Luke hadn't gone far and came running as soon as he heard the clatter of the pail and Hope's startled exclamation. He grinned at the sight of her sprawled in the hay, the calf licking at her face and the overturned milk pail. He pushed the calf away and helped Hope to her feet. The front of her new skirt was damp, sticky with spilt milk.

"You all right?" he asked.

She laughed, trying to brush off the straw sticking to her. "Oh yes. Bother! My skirt's going to smell awful now."

"Wait here." He disappeared from the barn, returning in a moment with a moist cloth to wipe her skirt and a large, snowy white, beautifully embroidered apron. An odd garment for a man to have, it looked like part of a bride's trousseau. Did it come out of that cedar chest? She hadn't found one anywhere else in the cabin. She mopped herself up and tied on the garment. This was much better. It was a lovely apron. It almost seemed a shame to use it.

"Thank you."

"When you're done with the milking, put the pail in the root cellar. You'll find a pile of cheesecloths down there in a bag. Cover the milk pail with one. It needs to cool down before you can make the butter and cheese." He smiled at the consternation in her face. "Don't worry, I'll show you how." He left the barn to go see to those water troughs.

CHAPTER NINE

THEY'D been at the cabin four days. After the early morning chores were done, Luke went to the orchard leaving Hope sweeping the cabin. She was creating more clouds of dust than anything else, but she was enjoying herself and, when she wasn't sneezing, singing softly. He'd noticed she always sang as she worked, hymns usually. She had a pleasant voice. If he was looking for her, all he had to do was stand still and listen. Her quiet singing was unobtrusive; it belonged here as much as the wind, the bees and the soft gurgle of the river.

It was a balmy day. A good one to do some washing. Perhaps the sheets. They needed an airing. Might as well wash them. She dragged the tin bath outside under the shade of the old oak that stood next to the red barn and set to work.

As she hung the sheets on the line, she thought she heard a horse harrumph and stamp its foot. Assuming it was Augustus Brown she thought no more about it. It happened again. She looked over at the paddock stretching out from behind the barn. Augustus Brown and the mules were on the far side, eating the sweet grass that grew under the trees, too far away for her to hear them.

The sound came again. She looked towards the forest. There, in a line watching her, stood a dozen Indians, all on ponies. She'd never seen Indians, she'd only read about them, how they attacked homesteads, killing and scalping everyone, even children. She panicked. She was alone. Her heart fought to get out of her chest. Her lungs squeezed tight. She couldn't catch her breath. She ran for the cabin, praying she'd make it before they fired arrows into her.

She grabbed Luke's shotgun from where it hung above the fireplace and ran back outside. She practically fell into the yard. She'd never fired a gun in her life, let alone a shotgun. That much was obvious to the men who sat on their ponies watching her. Looks passed between the men as she struggled to wield the long gun.

"Who are you?" called Hope, her voice cracking with fear. "What do you want? Go away. I'll shoot!"

One of the men nudged his horse forward. Another one started forward. It was too much for Hope and she swung the shotgun up. It went off before she was ready.

The gun slammed into her, knocking her to the ground.

Luke was on his way back from the orchard when he heard the shot. His head jerked up at the sound and he began to run. He tore into the yard to see Hope climb to her feet, pick up the gun and start waving it at the line of men whom, he could see, were struggling not to laugh.

The shotgun pellets had gone wide. An abstract pattern of neat holes now adorned the sheets on the washing line. Luke strode up to Hope and snatched the gun out of her hands. "Hope, these men are my friends. I'd appreciate it if you didn't kill them."

Fear, shock and surprise were written all over her face. Putting his hand in the small of her back he propelled her forward. He could feel her pulling back. He scowled. Her behaviour was appalling. He could see the fear deepening in her eyes. If he forced her to move it would only highlight her behaviour. He stopped and greeted the riders in Nlaka'pamuxtsn. He apologised for what had happened. The men shrugged it off. If she'd hit any of them, it would have been a miracle. No one was hurt. Except for the sheets. They found the incident more amusing than anything else.

Luke switched to English for Hope's sake. "Adam White Knife, gentlemen, allow me to introduce you to Hope. Hope, this is Adam White Knife and some of the men from the Nlaka'pamux tribe from the other side of the mountain." He nodded towards a young man at the end. "Daniel." The young man nodded back.

"Hello," she said quietly, embarrassed. "I'm sorry for the misunderstanding."

The man called Adam White Knife shrugged ever so slightly. "It is a pleasure to meet you, Hope. You are Luke's new wife?"

New? He'd been married before? The chest with the initials and the ivy leaves. Had that belonged to his first wife? How many times had he been married? Where was his wife now?

"Yes, something like that," replied Luke. He gave her a quick frown. What was the matter with her?

Adam White Knife nudged his horse closer. Hope stepped slightly behind Luke, who felt another flash of irritation. They were going to have words if she kept this up.

"We have come to tell you about the men we have seen, Luke." Adam White Knife switched back to his own language.

While they talked, Hope studied the riders. Adam was probably the oldest of the group. They all had long black hair either hanging straight down over their shoulders or tied up in rather startling ways. All were dressed in light buckskins painted in strong designs or decorated with beadwork and shells. Long fringes ran the length of their trouser legs and sleeves. Some had glossy feathers tied into their hair, and riding bareback, all sat their horses as if they were part of them.

She wasn't so afraid of the men anymore, but she felt them watching her. Especially Daniel. She recognized the shaggy pony he rode. How could she have been so stupid?

Luke invited the Nlaka'pamux to stay for a meal. To Hope's relief they politely declined. Apart from telling Luke about the men they'd seen on the mountain, they'd also come to invite Luke, and now Hope, to attend the *Oolichan* Run, before going further down the valley to invite the neighbouring village as well. If Luke wished, he and Hope could ride along with them on their return journey.

After they'd gone, Luke turned to Hope. "Why the hell were you waving the shotgun around like a demented hen?"

"I didn't know they were your friends!" she retorted. "I thought they were attacking us."

"By sitting quietly on their horses? You were the one shooting at them!" His irritation was overflowing.

"I panicked!"

A deep frown cut down his storm-laden forehead.

She took a deep breath; she wasn't backing down on this. "I was trying to protect you! I mean the—"

"Protect me? I wasn't even here, and I don't need you to protect me! And that's not the point," he growled. "You were rude to them even after I told you they're my friends."

"How?" she asked indignantly.

"You made it obvious you didn't want to be anywhere near them!"

She didn't know what to say. She couldn't tell him she was afraid of horses. He might think she was trying to get out of doing her morning chores. "It wasn't that."

His look told her he didn't believe her.

"I promise. I honestly thought they were attacking us. I didn't know what to do. I didn't know they spoke English. I didn't know where you were." Her voice grew quieter.

He took a deep breath. She didn't kill anyone, so no harm done, he supposed. But bloody hell, she could have. "Fine.

Just don't touch my shotgun again." He stomped back to the cabin leaving her standing there.

Later that afternoon, Luke was packing the wagon with a few supplies and some bedding. To make amends, Hope was trying to be as helpful as she could, but it seemed to irritate him even more. Eventually he snapped. "We're going to be three or four nights at the Nlaka'pamux village, make sure you have whatever you'll need, then get in the wagon and stay there."

A swift retort rose to her lips. Even though she hated fights - they often made her feel physically ill - she also had a quick temper she'd struggled her whole life to control. Now her anger flared. She hated to be spoken to as if she were a child. But she'd brought it on herself. Taking a deep breath, she chose the least confrontational option. She shut her lips firmly and strode off to quickly gather her few things.

Sitting quietly on the wagon seat a short while later she remembered something her father had once said. She'd no recollection of when he'd said it, but it was as if he was sitting next to her, "Look for the humour in any situation. If you can't find it, look harder."

Closing her eyes, she thought back over the arrival of the Indians and tried to picture what she must have looked like from their point of view. A soft laugh gurgled out of her.

Luke looked up in surprise. She smiled down at him. "Adam White Knife will be regaling his family with tales of the crazy white lady shooting the sheets for ages," she chuckled.

The frown eased out of his forehead. The corners of his mouth twitched.

"What's oolich...oolijan..." she asked.

"*Oolichan?* Fish."

"Don't we need your fishing pole then?" She moved to jump down and fetch it.

"Not that kind of fishing."

A short while later Hope asked, "What about the other animals? Will Daniel be staying to look after them?"

"No. I've put down enough food and water for them."

"What about the milking?"

"The calf will take care of it. In fact, he'll feast. We'll only be gone a short time. If you look in the barn, in the large trunk under the stairs, you'll find some large burlap sacks. Bring a couple of them. You can use them as aprons at the run."

He was hitching up the mules when the Nlaka'pamux rode back in. Adam White Knife was surprised to see the wagon. He said something to Luke who jerked his head in Hope's direction as he answered.

She realised Luke was only taking the wagon for her. She sighed. Luke would simply have saddled Augustus Brown and taken nothing more than a bedroll. It appeared she was being a nuisance just because she was there. A brief fear that he would come to regret buying her nibbled at the edges of her mind.

A few minutes later, they were following the Indians out of the yard. They didn't turn up into the forest like she expected, but instead followed a trail that led around the mountain, but the path they traced soon wound through the trees.

As they came around a bend they broke out into the sunlight, the path was right on the edge of a cliff. It was a dizzying drop to the narrow valley hundreds of feet lower than the orchard. On either side, the dark blue rock flowed into the almost black green of the pines that crowded the steep, heavily wooded cliffs. Cutting through the mountain was a rushing torrent of a river. that appeared to come out of the rock itself. She leaned out as far as she could to try and see where it leaped free of the rock. A hand grabbed the back of her skirt. She got such a fright she nearly fell out of the wagon. She was yanked roughly back onto the seat.

"What are you trying to do?" asked Luke. "Throw yourself off the cliff?"

"I was trying to see where the river came out," she replied.

"If you wait a little while, I'll show you."

She assumed an air of complete docility, sighing heavily and folding her hands in her lap.

Luke's mouth twisted as he tried to suppress a smile.

"Be patient."

Thank goodness. He didn't seem angry anymore. That was a relief. His annoyance earlier had been very uncomfortable. And worrying.

A few miles further on, in the middle of the path a massive flat boulder lay over a narrow rocky chasm, a stone bridge under which clear water flowed like molten glass.

"Adam! Hold up," Luke called. The Nlaka'pamux came to a halt.

"Come on." Luke jumped from the wagon and came around to help her out. She followed him down the slope. It was a beautiful part of the forest. Tall, dark pine trees towered over them, strong sunlight speared down into the thick, lush, knee-high carpet of ferns. Small, pale pink, purple and white flowers popped their heads through the greenery in delicate surprise, and moss lay in emerald blankets over fallen logs and stones.

The slope became steeper. The undergrowth patchier. Luke took Hope's hand to help her over the rockier parts. Then the trees stopped abruptly, so did the mountain and in front of them was the plunging drop to the valley below.

"Wait here." Luke went to the edge of the cliff. A square, smooth rock jutted out into fresh air. Stepping out on to it carefully he bounced a little. It should hold. To be safe, he kept one foot on the mountain. He held out his hand to Hope. Her heart started to flutter madly. That was a very small ledge. Would it hold both of them?

With her heart in her mouth, she took his hand and stepped towards him. She was too terrified to put her foot on the rock. Luke turned her around and put his arm around her waist, holding her firmly against him. Her heart pounded, leaping in fear at the void before them.

"Look down there." He pointed to just beyond the cliff face.

Hope leaned out against his arm to look over the edge of the rock. The water in the narrow chasm burst from beneath the rock under their feet, escaping gloriously in thunderous delight as it left earth, shooting out into space, twisting and shouting as it leapt to a small pool below, then fell further on down the cliff in a raging torrent of white water, ricocheting off rocks, bounding over barriers, laughing all the way to the valley and the quiet water that lay beyond.

"That's where we're going." Luke pointed to where the river headed off towards the sea. In the distance, Hope could see what looked like low tents stretching nearly fifty feet in length, with thin spirals of smoke lazily lifting into the afternoon sky from the fires built between them. The tents were set in a long curve a fair distance from the river. People moved about, horses grazed, and children ran around.

"It doesn't look real somehow, more like a painting," she whispered, gazing on the beauty below her.

Luke could feel her breathing against his arm. Quick, tremulous. It had been a long time since he'd been this close to a woman. His cold, deliberate flirtation with Ida May didn't count. Hope was different.

"We'd better get going."

Gripping Luke's hand Hope stepped back onto the mountain slope. He helped her get her footing then dropped her hand. Together they climbed back towards the path.

The pine needles littering the floor were slick. There was hardly any purchase at all. Not more than sixty feet up the slope Hope slipped. She began to slither towards the edge.

"Luke!"

Quick as lightning, Luke swung round and grabbed her out-flung arm, but she was going too fast. He slid as well. They were moving fast. They had only a few feet before the edge. He gave a tremendous heave, pulled her up to him, shifting her sideways. They slammed into a tree; Hope crushed beneath him, her hands wound tightly in his shirt. Fright made her eyes wide. They stood for a moment, breathing hard against each other.

Luke's reaction to Hope's soft, trembling body beneath him was immediate. He pushed himself away.

What the hell? But he knew exactly what. He killed the thought. If he entertained it, it made it real. He didn't need real. Not that kind of real anyway. He took her hand in his. She clutched it as he led her safely back to the wagon. They were barely seated when the Nlaka'pamux moved off, following the trail once more.

Luke could see she was shaky and trying not to cry. He was edgy himself. He tried to persuade himself it was simply reaction to the shock of how fast and how close they had come to the edge of the cliff and not the remembered feel of her pressed against him. He forced himself to concentrate on driving the mules.

CHAPTER TEN

THE sun was sinking behind the mountain as they arrived at the fishing camp. Luke stopped the wagon on the camp's outskirts and unhitched the mules. Hope tried to get a fire going for dinner. She wasn't making a very good job of it. While she struggled, Adam White Knife brought his family over to introduce them. Seeing Hope's dismal attempts at fire-making he set two of his young sons to the task. Hope flushed, neither boy was over ten. She was grateful for the distraction of the small girl whose hand Adam had been holding, coming over and standing before her. She had a solemn little face, and a slight, endearing squint. Hope crouched down to get to her eye level.

"Hello," she said. "My name's Hope, who are you?"

The little girl tentatively stretched out her small hands and laid them on either side of Hope's face. Then, as if coming to a decision, she nodded once, put her arms around Hope's neck and hugged her.

"I see you have met my daughter, Esther," said a warm voice. A beautiful, finely boned, Nkala'pamux woman about her own age stood in front of Hope, a baby in her arms. She stood with the almost arrogant pride that seemed to characterise the Nlaka'pamux, but her eyes were warm and kindly.

"Yes. She's very sweet." Hope smiled. "My name's Hope. I'm..." she faltered. She didn't want to lie, but she also didn't want these people to think she was living with Luke without being married to him. She rose, uncertain what to say.

"Hope is my wife," said Luke joining them. A slight frown twitched on his face.

"You are very welcome, Hope. I am Rachel, Adam White Knife's woman. These are our children."

"All of them?" Hope asked in astonishment. There seemed to be a small tribe running around them.

Rachel laughed. "No, just these five." She did a quick round of names. "Thomas and Jude are making the fire, Peter's seeing to your mules. Esther, of course, and this is Ruth, our baby."

"They're beautiful children," said Hope.

Little Esther leaned back against her. Hope smiled. She was such a sweet, quiet thing with a very self-possessed air. Her heart warmed to the small child. How could it not? A surge of indefinable protective longing welled up inside Hope. Did Luke want children? He was talking to Adam. His eyes met and held hers for a heartbeat. Hope realised she wasn't breathing. Esther tugged on Hope's hand to get her attention. Hope tore her eyes from Luke and let the little girl lead her to one of the nearby tents.

It wasn't what Hope expected, but then she'd never really thought about it either. It was fairly makeshift, certainly not a permanent dwelling, but was low, warm, homely and comforting. Clearly more than one family slept in here. Esther tugged her hand again and led her across the tent to kneel in front of a wide, low rimmed, wicker basket. A dog of a very nondescript breed drowsed inside it. Eight or so fat, sleepy puppies, their eyes barely open, snuggled up with soft mewls against her. The bitch lifted her head. Seeing Esther, she thumped her tail gently. Esther's dark brown eyes were lit with joy, a small chubby finger laid against her lips.

"Shh," she whispered. "Sleeping. Must be quiet."

Hope nodded. Esther patted the dog very gently on its side. The tail thumped again. With exaggerated care Esther pushed herself up and, taking Hope's hand, led her back out-side.

The next day dawned crisp and clear. The whole village rose before the sun had slipped over the tops of the mountains. Hope scrambled to get breakfast ready for herself and Luke. The camp was filled with a tense, crackling excitement.

"I know this probably sounds very ignorant," said Hope to Luke, "but how come they - Adam, Rachel and their children speak such good English? And have biblical names?"

"There's a Catholic Mission further inland, set up by a Father Pandosy. Adam and his family have a lot of contact with him. I've only met him once. Seemed like a nice enough man. If they're Christian, Indians use their baptismal names for us white folk." He shrugged. "Sometimes they just use white names anyway."

"Wouldn't it be more polite for us to use their Indian names?"

"Most whites can't pronounce them, if they'll even tell us what they are, which they seldom do."

"Do you know Adam's real name?"

"No." He poured himself another cup of coffee and changed the subject. "There's a few apple trees up at the Catholic mission. The ones in our orchard come from there."

Hope wondered if he realised he'd said 'our orchard'.

It seemed the Nlaka'pamux couldn't wait to start the day.

"Is everyone going fishing?" asked Hope bewildered at the number of people making their way to the river.

"It's a big job, it takes every hand available. There's probably two or three villages here for this."

"I thought only the men would go."

"There's lots to do besides catching the fish. They have to be gutted and smoked as well." His eyes caught hers over the coffee cup. "You don't work, you don't eat."

He'd said it so bluntly Hope was shocked. Did he think she wouldn't work? Hadn't she been pulling her weight back at the cabin? Before she could ask, Esther ran up and threw her arms around Hope's neck and nestled into her lap. Adam and Rachel strolled up after her.

"Good morning." Hope smiled.

Adam nodded at her, then spoke to Luke in Nlaka'pamuxtsn. Hope saw that Rachel had the baby tightly wrapped up and tied on her back in a sort of a long, narrow basket.

Luke tossed the remainder of his coffee away. "I'll see you later." He strolled off with Adam towards the river, leaving the women to make their own way. Each person had a particular job assigned to them, depending on their age. The men would fish, the old men and women gut the catch and prepare it for smoking. Hope tied the burlap sacks over her dress, ready for anything Rachel asked her to do.

Across the river was a weir, a trellis made of willow staves. It stood at an angle in the water supported by long, stronger poles dug into the riverbed. Running the length of the weir was a narrow platform. Luke took his place on it with the other men. A knee-high rush basket stood near him, and a long pole with a net at one end was handed across.

The river writhed against the weir wall with thousands of small, silvery, blue and brown fish trying to escape the trap of the trellis. The men scooped the fish up with the long poles and emptied the nets into the baskets. When the baskets were full, they were passed down the line to the waiting women on the shore.

Hope's job was to collect the baskets of fish and take them to the women who gutted the catch. From there, the fish would be strung up on long thin poles tied to upright frames to dry over the smoky coals beneath them.

The day settled into a hard-working rhythm. Whenever Luke stopped for a brief rest, he found himself looking for Hope. She was always walking either to the river with an empty basket or up the gentle slope with a heavy basket of fish. He hadn't seen her rest once. Despite the load, she moved with grace, almost elegance. His eyes strayed over the sway of her hips, his mind going back to the waterfall. He remembered the feel of her body beneath his, the soft expression on her face when she'd met little, squint-eyed Esther and the way she'd turned towards him. It had aroused some instinct in him he wasn't prepared to explore.

Rachel was skilfully gutting fish after fish. Luke saw her point at the fish with her knife and Hope hold up her hands and laugh. She backed away, picked up an empty basket and made her way back to the weir.

A young Indian fell into step with her, nodding at her with a shy smile. Daniel. Luke's eyes narrowed slightly. This wasn't the first time the young man had sought out her company. The boy stepped onto the platform and edged past the other men to a spot not far from Luke. He was a good-looking young man, strongly built with a ready laugh. He greeted Luke with a smiling nod. Hope had exchanged the empty basket for a full one and was already making her way back up the incline. Luke saw the young man staring after her. Annoyed, Luke thrust his netting pole deep into the boiling mass of fish. He worked steadily until early evening, refusing to take a break unless Daniel did, which he didn't.

The young man matched Luke easily, basket for basket, which irritated Luke even more.

The next day followed the same pattern. Hope was up before he was, preparing their breakfast. She worked steadily, only stopping when it became too dark to work. Even then, he had to make her sit down. Her face was growing pale with exhaustion. There were light purple smudges under her eyes.

That evening, everyone was tired. It had been a good two day's fishing. The smell in the camp was atrocious. The fish guts had been burnt outside the camp during the day to keep unwanted guests, like bears and wolves, at bay. The fish hung up to dry weren't a pleasant odour either.

The Nlaka'pamux were content. A few more days fishing like this and soon enough stores would be laid up till next spring.

Rachel, Hope, the other women and the children went up stream to bathe and wash the stink away. The other women laughed at Hope, teasing her mercilessly when she refused to take off her shift. She'd change later in the privacy of the wagon.

The main bonfire that night was a large one. Singing and raucous laughter echoed around the camp. Luke was standing with Adam and some of the other men on one side of the fire. Hope was sitting with Rachel, a few of the other women and the children, most of whom were either asleep or fading fast. Luke found the sight of Hope with little Esther on her lap compelling, drawing and holding him. He didn't want a wife. That was his past. He didn't want the emotional destruction that came with sharing his life again.

But seeing Hope with Esther, he couldn't help but wonder what having a family - with her - would be like.

Hope yawned deeply and shook her head. Rachel laughed. "I think we should put both you and the children to bed."

Hope nodded, yawning again. The two of them collected the kids and disappeared into the lodge not far behind them.

They didn't come out again for ages. Luke began to think Hope was going to stay there all night. She'd better not. He'd brought the wagon for her. She should sleep there, with him.

The canvas flap lifted, and Rachel and Hope stepped out. Daniel sauntered toward the women. Luke was too far away to hear what they were saying to each other, but Hope laughed. Luke's eyes narrowed. As the trio walked back to the fire, Hope stumbled. The young man caught and steadied her, his hands lingering on her arms. Luke growled under his breath. Adam looked at him in surprise. Before Adam could stop him, Luke strode towards them.

He wrenched the young man away from Hope and punched him, hard, in the face. The astonished youngster staggered under the blow. He recovered quickly, and was just about to launch himself at Luke, who was only too willing to mill him down, when Adam stepped in. A curt command brought the young man to a frustrated halt.

"You are tired, Luke, you forget where you are." Adam motioned to Daniel to leave. Reluctantly, the boy obeyed, rubbing his face and scowling at Luke. Hope took his arm as he went by. "I'm so sorry," she said.

"Don't you dare apologise!" snapped Luke. His face was dark with rage barely under control.

"Well, someone has to," she retorted. "What were you thinking?"

"We're leaving." He turned to walk away.

Hope didn't move. "Luke, wait, please, we can't be so rude. You just punched a boy for no reason at all!"

Luke stopped and turned around. His eyes blazing. "Either stay or come with me, it's your choice." He stalked off towards the darkness beyond the fire.

Adam's cold voice rang out. He spoke in his own language. Luke spun around and in a few ferocious strides came as close to punching his friend as he ever had. Adam didn't flinch; his gaze remained unblinking. Luke's fist had clenched so hard his knuckles turned white.

"Luke," begged Hope in a whisper. His eyes slid over to her. The frightened look on Hope's face stopped him cold. His shoulders sagged. His arm lowered, his fist slowly uncurled. Hope took a tentative step forward. Luke's bleak eyes turned from her and met Adam's hard ones.

"We should go. I've ruined your evening." His voice was quiet. He hesitated. "I apologise and—"

"You are a friend, Harcourt," Adam interrupted. "Friends make mistakes and are forgiven. I will make it right with Daniel. You are always welcome here, you know that, you and Hope. And not just because of the land."

Luke noted that Adam didn't ask them to stay. It made sense; he'd brought that on himself, and Hope. He sighed and shook hands with his friend. Adam gave a curt nod, the incident done with.

Turning to Hope, Luke said in a low voice, "Will you come back with me?"

As soon as the mules were hitched, they drove out silently into the night.

The cool night air eventually doused the remnants of Luke's temper. It brought with it a cold realization that the violence he thought he'd left behind, had still been inside him all the time. He pushed the thought deep into the recesses of his soul and smothered it. But the unfortunate events played over and over in his mind. Hope's voice saying in shocked accents, 'You punched a boy for no reason.' echoed in his head. No reason. Did he have a reason? An excuse? Nothing that made sense - except - she was his wife, dammit.

The wagon's seat seemed uncomfortably hard. He'd behaved like a jealous— how could he be, he'd have to have feelings for Hope in order to be jealous. He remembered the softness of her skin, the colour of her eyes - a gentle green like the moss that covered the rocks in the forest. This was ridiculous. He'd been alone too long, that was all. He was tired from the two days of intense fishing. Besides, Hope wasn't the kind of woman men fought over. He snapped the reins and the mules broke into a trot.

For a while, Hope had wondered what Adam White Knife had meant about the land. But as they drove deeper into the dark, Hope had struggled to stay awake, dozing off, then jerking awake. Her back and neck ached. Her eyes burned. The night was well advanced by the time they arrived home.

"If you could get the fire going, I'll see to the animals," said Luke jumping from the seat. Hope covered a huge yawn with her hand and drifted into the cabin. She was tempted to sit, only for a moment, in one of the soft armchairs, but knew she'd fall asleep immediately if she did that.

Luke had mentioned something about a fire. She laid it mechanically. With a snap and a hissing crackle, the dry kindling caught alight quickly. She sat back and resting her arms on her knees, she put her head down with a deep sigh.

"Hope!"

Luke's yell jerked her back. He was kneeling in front of her, beating at her feet. There was smoke in her dress. "What's wrong?"

"You're on fire, you silly woman!"

"What?" She gave a small, panicked scream as she tried to stand.

"Sit still, dammit." He gave the skirt of her dress a shake. "There. It's out now."

He shook his head. "What were you thinking?"

"I didn't set myself on fire. I don't know how it happened." She was too tired to think clearly.

"Let's have something to eat and call it a night," he said. "It'll be dawn in a couple of hours."

She tried to get some kind of meal together while Luke cleaned up the burnt remnants of her dress. She was so shaken and exhausted she was getting in the way. She could barely hold anything and was hardly making any sense; her words were almost slurred. Luke pushed her gently into one of the armchairs.

"Sit here." He wasn't sure if she'd even heard him.

He made some coffee and quickly toasted a few thick slices of bread, spreading them generously with butter and honey. It wasn't much, but at least it was something. She munched slowly, too tired even to eat.

Her fingers played forlornly with the damaged hem of her dress, but her eyes were unfocused. She'd never been so exhausted in her life. Her mind was cotton wool. Everything seemed hazy and far away. After a few sips of coffee, she leaned her head back against the chair and in seconds was asleep.

It was a good thing he'd only given her half a cup. It tilted at a precarious angle as she relaxed. Luke reached over and took it carefully out of her loose hand.

Everything he'd been telling himself on the drive home melted away like a mist, unnoticed and forgotten. He realised he'd stopped thinking of her as plain. Her intelligent eyes, that sweet mouth, those calm hands, the graceful way she walked, her laugh—

Putting the cups on the table, he went across and lifted her out of the chair. She felt good in his arms. Warm, living...female. She wrapped her hands around his neck and snuggled her head into his shoulder, murmuring quietly. His heart began a slow, deep pounding. He carried her to the bed and laid her down. She whispered his name, one hand taking hold of his shirt. His pulse leapt. Her face was so close to his, her eyes closed.

She was asleep. He could smell the perfume of her, overlaid by the smell of the fire. He breathed it in, his skin warming in response. The beat of a soft pulse moved under the creamy velvet of her throat. He wanted to touch it, feel it against the tips of his fingers.

Not tonight.

He took her hand and eased it off his shirt.

She moved, turning her head, murmuring. Her lips were now just a breath away from his. Open, soft lips. It was barely a conscious thought, simply the impulse of the moment and as swiftly carried out. He kissed her. His lips barely touching hers. She gave a quiet sigh and stirred.

Luke pulled back quickly, stepping to the end of the bed. He unlaced and eased off her thin, lavender shoes as gently as he could. The last one thumped a little on the floor as he dropped it. She stirred again, turned on her side and curled up. He twitched the end of the blanket so it flopped over her.

He shouldn't have let her work so hard. He'd forgotten she wasn't used to it. It would take some time for her to recover from the effects of the horrific voyage on that ship. When he'd asked, Hope had told him just enough for him to know it'd been as terrible as he'd imagined.

It was his fault she'd come so close to being badly burned, that her one and only dress was damaged. Thank goodness she had Lee-Ming's skirt to wear. Closing the shutters halfway and turning out the lamps, he made sure the fire was safe for the night and then took himself off to the barn.

That kiss was a mistake. It should never have happened. Idiot. What the hell were you thinking? He needed to pull himself together. Despite his determination not to, he fell asleep thinking about how soft and warm her lips were. He could still feel them against his own.

His last waking thought was that kissing her simply complicated matters.

He didn't need complications.

But complications were what made life interesting. Living almost demanded them.

CHAPTER ELEVEN

WITH the shutters almost closed, the inside of the cabin was dark, and Hope slept till nearly mid-morning. For breakfast, Luke ate a couple of apples he'd stored in the barn for the animals. If he went into the cabin, he'd wake her. He was also feeling a bit foolish over the fight and, if he was honest, for kissing her. He was happy to have a bit of time on his own.

When she did finally wake, she was still groggy and couldn't stop yawning and dropping things. Eventually, Luke took her down to the river and gave her a fishing pole. After showing her how to use it, he settled her under a tree and told her not to come back until she had enough fish for their supper.

When he returned half an hour later, he found her fast asleep again.

Needless to say, she didn't catch anything. When Luke checked on her in the afternoon, the fishing pole was leaning against a rock and she was paddling in the river. She looked rested and happy, so he refrained from pointing out she was probably scaring the fish away. He'd brought some bread, cheese and apples down with him and they sat on the riverbank and munched in companionable silence. He was grateful she didn't mention what happened at the Nlaka'pamux village. Most women would have.

It was pleasant sitting under the willows with Hope, watching the river slide by. Luke was reluctant to go back to work in the orchard. The end of her fishing pole twitched.

"Pass me the pole."

She handed it across. "I don't think there are any fish in this river," she said. Luke gave the pole a quick jerk. "I've been here for hours and I haven't seen—"

A wet, wriggly fish flew through the air and landed in her lap. It thumped onto the riverbank a second later. She leapt to her feet with a scream. The unlucky fish gave a few more twists and then lay still.

"Ugh!"

Luke laughed. "Want to see if you can catch the next one?" He held out the pole.

"Perhaps you should do it. You obviously have the knack. They just ignore me."

That seemed to be true. Within a very short space of time Luke landed three more fish. When he took out his knife to gut them Hope retreated, carrying the remainder of the bread and cheese back to the cabin. She enjoyed eating trout but watching them being gutted would spoil her appetite. She'd had enough of that at the *oolichon* hunt. In fact, having eaten fish for breakfast, lunch and supper for two days in a row, she wasn't sure she wanted fish for dinner now.

Luke set to work and gutted all four quickly and efficiently. They'd be delicious roasted over the fire. Just the thought of them made his mouth water.

By the time Luke returned, Hope had laid the table for an early dinner. She'd found some sorrel at the edge of the forest and turned it into a delicious sauce for the fish. She wished she had pepper and nutmeg. The sorrel leaves she didn't use she put, with tender fern curls and wildflowers, into an empty jar on the centre of the table. When the sauce was ready, she put it aside to keep warm and started peeling and slicing potatoes into an earthenware pot. She covered them with thick cream from the root cellar and putting the lid on, set it amongst the coals to bake.

It was a beautiful evening. With all the shutters open and the door standing wide, the view across the valley to the mountains was breath-taking. The sun lingered, reluctant to leave such a beautiful day. It would be a few hours still before it was dark.

Hope sighed in contentment as she chewed. "This was a good meal," she said. "I was wondering, could we plant a vegetable garden?"

Luke frowned. Was she saying he didn't provide for them?

"Just think, we could have carrots, spinach, cabbage, maybe even some sweet potatoes!"

"I've got enough to do with the orchard and the animals. I don't have time for vegetables. Besides, we don't need a vegetable garden. We eat well enough."

Hope was stung by his instant refusal. "No, we don't." Perhaps it was the remnants of yesterday's tiredness, but it was out before she thought about it. "All we eat is beans, potatoes and deer. It would be nice to have something differ-ent. We need more variety. Just for once I'd like not to have beans for every meal."

"You didn't have beans tonight or last night or even the night before. Then you had *oolichon* for heaven's sake. Tonight, you've eaten trout!" Luke was getting angry. "And you didn't have beans down at the river today either."

"No, we had apples! Again! I'm sick of wrinkly, old apples."

"Really! I suppose you want pineapples!"

"It would make a nice change!" They were both yell-ing now.

"Feel free not to eat my beans or my apples then."

"I don't need your permission for that!" Hope sat back and folded her arms, a dark look on her face. She was sick of beans. She wanted a vegetable garden. She was prepared to fight this out till she got her way. She didn't get the chance. Luke was incensed. He stood up so fast he knocked his chair over. Grabbing his hat, he stormed out, muttering under his breath, slamming the door behind him.

Hope immediately felt terrible. In fact, she felt rather ill. She shouldn't have argued with Luke like that. Her wicked tongue! How could she have been so rude? It wasn't as if they were starving. Luke made sure they always had more than enough food.

Still, even in her remorse, she was too honest not to admit she was bored with the same menu all the time. She didn't think her request for a vegetable garden was so bad, but she could have asked nicely, instead of throwing a fit like a petulant child. What on earth had come over her?

She needed to find Luke and apologise as soon as she could.

Luke strode furiously up the trail into the forest. His annoyance was all the greater because he knew she was right. Only when she'd said it had he realised he was also weary of the same food every day. And he'd been eating it for over a year! A vegetable garden was a good idea. But he was damned if he was going to tell her that! He climbed deeper into the forest.

It was a hot evening and soon he was sweating. He came to a small pool in the worn basin of a large rock at the edge of a clearing. Taking off his hat, he splashed his face with the cold water and took a deep breath. He felt foolish. What a ridiculous argument to have. He sighed and rubbed his eyes.

Then he saw them. In the clearing was a thick cluster of mushrooms. He loved mushrooms, especially the way the Silver Forest Hotel did them—cream, port, a nice thick sauce poured generously over a juicy steak. He only had whiskey in the cabin. Maybe that'd work just as well. He picked enough to fill his hat to overflowing.

Might be a good peace offering, he thought.

He was on his way back down, when he heard the awful sound of a steel trap being sprung and the agonized yelp that came after. He followed the sound of the desperate whining until he came upon the trap and its victim.

A young wolf, still in its leggy, cub phase had been caught in the rusty teeth of a trap Luke had never set. He hated traps. It was a cruel way to kill an animal. Apart from that, whoever put the infernal device in these woods was trespassing. He wondered if it'd been Tobias John.

The wolf couldn't make up its mind what course of action to take when it saw the man. It alternated between growls and whines of fear. Luke put his hat down and moved carefully towards the animal. Its hind leg was caught in the trap's teeth.

Luke hunted for a stout stick, one that wouldn't break too easily. Finding one, he knelt with caution, staying as far from the fang end of the wolf as possible.

The wolf still wasn't sure what to do. Although it seemed to understand the man was trying to help, the pain was unbearable and every now and then it lashed out at Luke, trying to sink its teeth into whatever it could grab a hold of. The desperate lunges only made the pain worse and the trap bite deeper.

Soon, the animal lay still and watched the man's face intently, its black lips pulled tightly back, teeth bared, a low growl hovered in the air between them.

Hope decided to take the bull by the horns and go find Luke. She hunted around outside the cabin, but he'd vanished. He couldn't have gone far. He'd left his gun behind. Perhaps he'd gone into the forest.

Although she'd never admit it, she was too nervous to stray far from the cabin on her own when the sun was going down. They'd heard wolves howling last night as they'd wound their way back along the trail. Although she'd loved the sound, she didn't know what she'd do if she came face to face with one of the creatures.

She took Luke's Colt out of the holster he'd draped over a chair and went in search of him.

After what had happened the day she took his shotgun, she knew she probably shouldn't take this gun, but she wasn't going into the forest without it. Not with wolves around.

She could always hide it in her apron pocket when she found him.

Among the cool pines and ferns, Hope breathed deeply of the scented air. She loved it here. For a while she almost forgot she was looking for Luke. Then, she thought she heard his voice. Who was he talking to? She heard a dog whining. That was odd. What would a stray dog be doing all the way out here? She climbed towards the sound.

There. Luke was crouching over a dog. It seemed to be injured. She took a step towards them and realised Luke was bending over a wolf.

CHAPTER TWELVE

LUKE managed to get the stick into the right place in the trap mechanism and gave a heave. A hard metal twang cracked through the air, an anguished yowl, an angry snarl, a leap and Luke was rolling in the dirt trying to keep the wolf's teeth from his throat. Luke had his hands buried in the animal's fur trying to find his throat, but the coat was too thick. He dug his hands in to it and pulled back as hard as he could.

The young wolf was strong and the pain had maddened him.

"Luke!" he heard Hope scream. He twisted his head just in time to see her raise his gun, point it at him.

"No! *Hope!*"

Too late. The bullet tore past his arm and into the wolf. A brief yelp and the creature collapsed on top of him.

Luke lay there for a moment catching his breath. He glanced across at Hope. She was white and shaking. He pushed the wolf off and trod a little unsteadily towards Hope through the thick, slippery pine needles that covered the forest floor, keeping a wary eye on her hands. They were shaking, clutching the gun tightly, still pointing it at him.

"Give me the gun, Hope."

"It was attacking you! Are you all right? You're bleeding!" She took a step towards him, the gun wavered dangerously.

His hands closed quickly on hers and he took the weapon carefully away from her.

"Oh no!" she gasped. He glanced down and saw the scorch mark on his shirt. The wound was bleeding sluggishly. It was also burning like crazy.

"Well, you did shoot me."

She went white. "I did that? Oh, Luke, I'm so sorry. I thought it was going to kill you. Oh, Luke, I shot you!" Her eyes filled with tears. She was horrified to think she'd actually put a bullet into Luke.

"It's just a graze. But I think the wolf might need some help." He removed the bullets from the gun and put them in his pocket. "Hold this." He gave her back the gun.

As he walked to the wolf, he took out his handkerchief and using his teeth, tied it round his arm to stop the bleeding. The wolf lay unconscious, its long tongue hanging out its slack jaws. Running his hand down the wolf's side Luke assessed the damage. The bullet hadn't gone in that deep, and although the leg wound was nasty, the animal would wake up soon.

"Hope," he called over his shoulder, "let me have your apron."

She quickly untied it and handed it to him. Her hands were still shaking. "What are you going to do?"

"Get that bullet out, see if I can fix up that leg. It's in a pretty bad way. It's going to need time to mend. Doesn't look like it's eaten for a while either." He laid down the apron and rolled the wolf into it, wrapping it up tightly, like a swaddling blanket.

"You're going to keep it? In the cabin?"

He couldn't tell—was she was afraid or disgusted? He hefted the wolf into his arms and cradled it against his chest. "No, I'll keep it in the barn."

"Poor thing," Hope said. "She looks so young."

Luke's mouth twisted as he tried not to smile. One minute she's trying to shoot the animal and then next, almost crying over its wounds. "It's a he," Luke said. "Bring my hat, would you? It's over there. I, ah, found us something to make breakfast a little more interesting."

She picked up his hat and went red with shame when she saw the mushrooms. "Luke, I'm so sorry about what I said, before, at dinner."

"Forget it. Let's get him back to the barn before he wakes up again."

Luke managed to clean the wolf's foot, dig out the bullet, wash and bandage the wounds before it regained consciousness. He'd found an old horse blanket and laid the animal down in the barn as far away from the other animals as possible. Just the smell of him frightened them.

Luke took the time to calm each one down, starting with the cow. They didn't need her scared dry.

He packed some hay bales around the injured animal to keep him out of sight, and out of harm's way. Hope probably wasn't happy about the wolf, but she'd accepted it without further demur and did all she could to help. He expected her to get squeamish over the blood, but she was her usual calm, quiet self.

With a wound in both shoulder and back leg, the wolf was going to be around for some time. It also meant he'd be easier to handle when he woke up.

Hope put a little meat into a bowl, warmed some milk in another and took them across to the barn. Luke was sitting with his back against a hay bale watching the wolf sleep. He'd most likely keep watch all night. It pleased her that he was the kind of man who would do that. Other men may not have tried to save the wolf from the trap in the first place. They may not have left him to suffer, but their choice of help would have been a bullet.

Putting the food and the milk where the wolf could reach it when he woke up, she went back to the cabin, only to return a short time later with a fresh basin of hot water, some clean cloths and a shirt for Luke. She set it down and, to Luke's surprise, knelt next to him.

"Your arm." She pointed at it.

In sorting out the wolf he'd forgotten all about it. As she untied the handkerchief, a small dark trickle of blood flowed out.

"Apart from shooting you," she said ruefully. "I've ruined your shirt as well."

In one easy move, he pulled it over his head and stuck his fingers through the hole. "That's easy to fix," he said. She didn't say anything.

Hope was so embarrassed she didn't know what to do. She'd never been this close to a man with his shirt off before. Luke was golden brown and nothing about him was soft. Like his face, his chest and arms seemed hacked out of rock. The sculptured muscle sat tightly beneath his skin. A long white scar ran across his chest. She had an overpowering desire to touch him. To see what he felt like.

That shocked her more than anything else.

Luke's eyebrow shot up in surprise at the deep blush filling her face. A slow grin spread across his own.

"I think I'm bleeding to death," Luke said when she didn't move. The grin fought for control of his mouth.

Hope set about cleaning his wound, keeping her gaze fixed on his arm. He couldn't help but tease her. He winced when she touched him, just to get a reaction. Which he did.

She was trying so hard to be gentle. He overdid it though when she tied the knot in the bandage. She glanced up and caught him grinning at her.

"Oh, you!" She smacked his shoulder. He faked an agonised groan. "Just for that I hope you do bleed to death." She rose quickly to her feet.

He grabbed the edge of her skirt. "Wait, Hope, I'm sorry. You didn't hurt me. Please don't go. I think the wolf's waking up and I may need you to protect me," he said, laughing.

She whisked her skirt out of his grasp, but a smile hovered around her mouth.

"Hmm. I'll stay, but I think you should put a shirt on. You'll catch a cold like that."

His mouth twisted as he suppressed another smile. A cold was the last thing she was worried about.

The wolf stirred a short time later. Luke, with a clean shirt on, held out a piece of meat from the bowl. The wolf growled, his teeth bared. Luke just sat there quietly. Soon hunger overcame fear and the wolf sniffed the meat. He snatched it with a snap.

By the time the bowl was empty he was calmly taking the food from Luke's hand. Hope went for a refill and when she came back Luke made her feed the wolf.

He took her hand and held it out to the animal, who sniffed it cautiously. When he recognized Luke's smell there as well he took the meat out of her fingers without concern. Luke took his hand away and sat back. Hope felt a twinge of disappointment mingled with embarrassment. She was very aware of him.

Slowly, she fed the wolf the rest of the food. When the bowl was clean, she reached out to pat him. A very low growl sounded in his throat. She drew her hand away.

"Should I get him some more?" she asked.

"Yes, if you wouldn't mind. I'll give it to him later though. I think he's had enough for now."

Besides the fact that she felt so guilty about the food fight and shooting both the wolf and Luke, watching Luke's gentleness with the scared and injured animal and helping him to care for it, had made Hope feel closer to Luke than before. He was a good man.

Even though she believed that, she still felt a little safer when he'd put another shirt on. Maybe not safer. Maybe that was the wrong word. Perhaps, just a little less...distracted.

The barn was quiet, the other animals had settled and were dozing. The wolf lay still, watching Luke through half closed eyes. Luke turned down the lamp and was unrolling his blanket and the quilt when Hope returned with the other bowl of food. As she gave him the bowl, Luke's fingers brushed her hand. In the warm, intimate glow cast by the lamp it felt almost like a caress.

"How's your arm?" She seemed a little less nervous.

"It's all right." His voice was quiet. "Perhaps you could loosen the bandage just a little?" It was the only thing he could think of. Being with her this evening, looking after the wolf had changed something. He wasn't sure what, but he didn't want her to go back to the cabin just yet.

She nodded. "If you roll up your sleeve—"

Luke had already stripped his shirt off, again. He could see the flush rising once more in her face. She finished up quickly.

"There you are. How does that feel?" she asked, patting his arm.

"Much better, thanks." He stretched out a hand but she stepped back quickly, turning away and pretended not see it.

She picked up the water bowl and bloody cloths. "Good night then," she said and almost before he could reply she was gone, shutting the barn door after her.

Luke sighed. What the hell was he doing? He'd told her when he bought her that he didn't want a wife. And he didn't. Not after Tess. So, what was it he was starting to feel for her? Was it just lust? She wasn't really the kind of woman he liked. He'd always preferred small, blonde haired women. Like Tess. Tess had glittered like a diamond. Hope was different in every way. Despite their fight earlier, Hope was like the calm of the forest, the quiet after a storm. He was starting to crave her company. He'd found himself lingering over dinner, putting off the time he'd have to go the barn for the night. When he touched her, even accidentally, he found he wanted to linger there as well.

He needed to stop behaving like this. He'd never love her. And he wouldn't use her simply to satisfy his own physical needs. He wouldn't use any woman that way. He'd never sought out another woman after Tess, not even briefly. It would have been easy to do, the lights and the girls of the Bright Star told him that every time he passed the brothel.

But the thought of a whore, the thought of paying for something— He wasn't that kind of a man. One woman. His woman. A woman whom he loved and who loved him, exclusively, that was the only kind he wanted.

At Tess' funeral he'd vowed he'd never love anyone again. But when he put out the lamp, it wasn't Tess' face he saw in the dark.

Between the two of them, Luke and Hope cared for the wolf for over a week before he tried to get to his feet. When he did, he'd hobble a few steps and then lie down again. With the resilience that youth and all wild creatures enjoyed, the wolf soon recovered. He still slept in the barn occasionally, but on most nights stayed in the cabin with Hope. He was obedient to Luke but clearly besotted with Hope. Unless Luke called him away, the wolf followed her around all day, often getting under her feet.

Both Luke and Hope expected him to leave once he was healed and go back to his pack. He often wandered off and each time they thought they'd seen the last of him. But invariably he came back, just in time for dinner.

One night, the wolves on the mountain began to howl. They sounded like they were calling from deep in the forest.

Lying in front of the fireplace the young wolf raised his head, tilting it to one side. He rose and went to the door.

"I guess this is goodbye." Luke opened the cabin door. The wolf went out and stood there listening. He trotted off the porch without a backward glance. Leaving the door open, Luke sat down and they finished their dinner in silence. Both were disappointed. It had been good to have a 'dog' around the place.

Sometime later, Luke was pouring the coffee. It was always his job to make the coffee; his always tasted so much better than Hope's, for some reason. They heard the clicking of nails on the porch and the young wolf trotted back in. He went straight to Hope and lay next to her chair. Putting his head on his paws, he sighed deeply and closed his eyes.

Luke smiled. "I think he likes you."

Hope scratched the top of the wolf's head. "That's good, because I like him." She smiled at Luke. "Very much."

The lightest tingle went through Luke. Was she still talking about the wolf? He knew then he'd have to stay away from Hope. No matter how she was making him feel, he didn't want her. He had to just keep telling himself that.

"Do you think he's here to stay?" She was delighted the wolf had come back.

"For now, at least," replied Luke. "It's entirely up to him. As long as we keep feeding him, I guess he will."

"What do you want to call him?" After the names the other animals had been given, she expected something interesting from Luke now.

"You don't name animals that are leaving, remember?"

"Well, while he's here we can't not call him anything. He might decide to stay forever."

"Wolf." The animal looked up at Luke. "There you go, his name's Wolf."

Hope rolled her eyes. "Fine. Wolf it is then."

The animal sighed gustily and that ended the matter.

CHAPTER THIRTEEN

I T occurred to Hope that life had become a series of adventures since Luke had rescued her. One thing she could say for sure was that life had definitely become more interesting than she had ever imagined it could be. She knew a lot more about farm life now than she thought possible, for one thing. On the day of the Indians and the sheets she realised she hadn't thought of her old home, that still nameless place, in a while.

Luke was in the barn cleaning and reloading his guns a few days later while Hope hung the washing. The breeze was billowing the sheets on the line into high arching sails. The young wolf, convinced this was a new game invented just for him was leaping, snapping at the ends as they whipped past him. He was still very much a cub at heart. He never caught anything, so Hope let him play, laughing at his antics. He was so easily distracted that in the middle of a lunge for a sheet he would veer off and chase a bug wandering past.

The breeze carried the scents of hay from the barn, rich earth and sunshine. It was a good day.

Hope pulled another sheet out of the basket and stood up. The hairs on the back of her neck lifted. She suddenly felt cold. Another scent had infected the breeze. The scent of death. Putrid and dark. Only once before had she ever smelled something like that. She turned around slowly. Tobias John was crossing the bridge and coming towards the cabin. He sat his morose horse like a bag of filthy rags.

"Luke," Hope called. "Come quickly."

"Be there in a minute," he yelled back.

Wolf stopped playing to watch the man and horse approach. A low growl rumbled in his throat. Tobias John pulled up in front of Hope and leered down at her. "How do ma'am. Fine day isn't it. Your man around?"

She nodded.

"Get him." He spat a filthy stream of tobacco juice onto the ground.

Hope's stubborn streak instantly asserted itself. She raised her chin, trying hard not to show her fear. "What do you want, Tobias John?"

"Nothing to do with you, woman. Do as I tell you." His high voice was at odds with the attitude he affected.

"You don't have the right to order me around in my own home, so please don't speak to me that way." Where is Luke?

Wolf growled again. His head dropped, his back arched, all the hair along his spine stood up. He took a stiff legged stance in front of Hope.

Tobias John whipped up his carbine, pointing it straight at the animal.

"No!" cried Hope, trying to stand in front of Wolf but he pushed past her.

"It's a good day to shoot wolves," snarled the trapper.

"Go ahead," Luke's voice was hard and measured. "But that's my wolf. You pull that trigger; you'll be dead before he is."

Luke had been on his way out the barn when he saw Tobias John ride into the yard. He went back inside and strapped on his gun belt. He slipped out the barn's back door and crept up unseen behind the trapper.

Over his shoulder, Tobias John saw the gun levelled at him and laughed. He lifted his carbine. "My apologies. I didn't know you liked wolves."

"There's wolves and there's wolves. Put the gun away."

The trapper shrugged and slipped the gun back into the saddle holster.

"What do you want, Tobias?" Luke asked as he came around to stand in front of Hope. He holstered his gun but left his hand casually resting on top of it.

"Going into town, get me a new wife. You gonna ask me to get down and sit a spell, maybe give me a meal? Be real neighbourly if you did."

"No," said Luke. "What happened to the woman you bought less than two months ago?"

"Stupid bitch died on me." He spat out more tobacco juice.

Hope's heart lurched in pity for the poor woman.

"I'm sorry to hear that." Luke nodded his head towards the water trough under the oak tree. "You can water your horse over there, but then you ride out."

The trapper sniffed. He ran his eyes over Hope, then turned back to Luke. "Your place, your rules. But it ain't kindness. I'm a grieving man and I'm out of food."

"Go get some food, Hope. We can spare what's left of that leg of venison."

Hope took hold of Wolf's ruff. As she dragged him away, she heard the trapper, with no attempt at hiding his lust, ask Luke, "You wanna sell her to me? Got gold. Reckon she'd last longer than the others." Luke didn't bother replying.

"You're not much one for talking, are you?" Tobias John scoffed.

"Depends who I'm talking to."

The silence filled with a stench that rose like a miasma from the trapper. His horse didn't even bother to shake off the flies that crawled over its eyes.

Hope hurried out of the cabin with a parcel, shutting the door on Wolf. She'd wrapped the food in an old piece of cheesecloth. She handed it up to Tobias John, who grabbed her hand, leaning down to kiss it. She forced herself to stand as still as she could, but her skin crawled and vomit rose in her throat at his smell. She couldn't help the revulsion she felt from showing plainly on her face. When he stuck out his tongue to lick her hand she panicked and tried to snatch it away, but the trapper held it tight and jerked it back.

Luke stepped in. He grabbed a handful of the trapper's long, greasy hair and wrenched his head back as hard as he could, forcing the trapper to grab for his saddle or he would crash to the ground. It gave Luke immense satisfaction to hear him squeal like a girl.

"Go inside, Hope." His voice was quiet, flat.

She didn't hesitate. She ran.

Luke twisted the trapper's head hard and painfully. "When you talk to my wife, be polite." He let go of the trapper's hair and stepped back.

He been expecting it so when the trapper whipped out a vicious looking butchering knife, Luke's reaction was fast. Stepping in and sideways, he had the trapper's wrist before he'd even raised the weapon. Luke twisted the man's arm backwards and pulled down hard on his elbow. If he gave a strong enough tug he could snap it. Probably break his elbow and cripple him for life. The temptation was strong. He twisted harder until the trapper dropped the knife.

"We've given you food and fair warning. Now get off my land." He stepped back.

Tobias John cradled his injured arm and scowled at Luke.

"I need my knife," he growled.

Luke, almost casually took out his gun. "More than you need to live?"

Tobias John looked at him, then tried to call his bluff. No one said the man was clever. "You know what they say about you? That you're a man of honour." He said it like it was a dirty secret. "You wouldn't shoot me."

"You're right," said Luke.

A flicker of surprise showed in Tobias John's eyes.

Luke drew back the hammer on his gun and lifted it. "It is a good day to shoot wolves."

His eyes were ice cold. There was no compromise, no second chance in them. Tobias John believed what he saw - he either rode out or he'd die right here, right now. The trapper's face darkened with hate. Without another word, he turned his horse and trotted out the yard. Luke didn't move until Tobias John crossed the bridge and set the horse into an easy canter in the direction of Silver Birch Landing.

CHAPTER FOURTEEN

HOPE was fidgety for the rest of the day. She felt dirty and uncomfortable. Eventually, she decided the cabin needed a spring clean.

Luke collected the scythe and a burlap sack and calling Wolf, went down to the orchard. He would spend the afternoon harvesting some of the alfalfa he grew around the apple trees for the horse and mules. He'd keep some aside for tea. He was quite partial to alfalfa tea.

Hope carried some water from the river and set to work. She washed everything she could, whether it needed it or not. She wielded her cloth with vigour and determination. Small clouds of dust rose everywhere, making her sneeze. She didn't feel like singing anymore. She hung the rugs over the washing line and walloped them till her arms hurt. She'd need a bath herself later on.

As she was repacking the larder, she thought she smelled a dead rat. She hadn't seen one. Was it behind one of the sacks? She hoped it wasn't *in* one of the sacks! She heard a footstep. Perhaps Luke could smell it and help her find it. It was a good time for a break and a pot of tea anyway. She stepped out of the larder wiping her hands on her apron.

She froze. It wasn't Luke.

It was Tobias John.

Complete terror constricted her heart, filled her mind and stopped her breathing. She instinctively knew what was going to happen. She'd never get away from him this time. She was on her own. His thick purple lips split in the travesty of a smile. The man was filthy. Black dirt was ingrained in his skin and caked under his ragged, long fingernails. Old bloodstains were smeared across the backs of his hands and arms. Unnameable horrors had stained his clothing. At the sight of his green, rotten teeth, vomit surged into Hope's throat.

"I've come for my knife," he said. "But as I'm here, I think I'll take you as well. You weren't very friendly the last time."

She tried to speak, but nothing came out. What could she say anyway? He feigned a lunge at her. She jerked away. He laughed and lunged again. She forced herself to stand still and think. If she could get back into the larder and shut the door… but he was faster. His ape-like arms grabbed her. He shoved her face first into the cabin wall, pressing himself against her. He seized a handful of her hair and pulled her head back, viciously.

"I've been told to be polite," he sneered. "I'll be sure to say thank you when I'm done."

*

Luke swung away with the scythe. He'd set up an easy rhythm and was enjoying himself. He always liked harvesting alfalfa. Wolf was chasing field mice. He'd lie low and then leap straight up in the air and pounce, his long tongue lolling out. He seldom caught anything. Luke didn't think he was really trying to; it was more a case of pouncing for the fun of it. He could swear the mutt was grinning.

The grin vanished. Wolf stood still, rigid, staring at Luke. He dropped his head. All the hair on his back stood up and a deep, low growl started in his throat.

Luke glanced over his shoulder. There was nobody there. Wolf had gone from cute, leggy cub to killer in a second, for no apparent reason.

The animal started a stiff-legged walk, his growl more menacing than before, black lips drawn back over long, sharp vicious teeth. An angry wolf was not something to be taken lightly. Luke stood very still, the scythe held loosely in his hands, watching him carefully. Wolf took a step and then, as if he was on a spring, leapt into a run, streaked past Luke, heading for the cabin.

Hope!

*

Tobias John's obvious delight in her fear grew with every twist of her body and every cry Hope uttered. He had her on the floor, his big, heavy body on top of hers. He'd pulled her skirt up, his knee thrust hard between her legs, one hand twisting the soft flesh on the inside of her thighs, digging his nails in hard. She struggled desperately which only made him laugh even more. She tried to scream.

He wouldn't let her. With a giggle, he clamped his other hand on her mouth. The smell of him made Hope's stomach heave. She was afraid she was going to choke to death on the bile that filled her mouth.

"When I'm done," he growled. "Harcourt will never be able to touch you again, 'cause every time he looks at you, you'll know what it felt like, what it smelled like to have a real man inside you. You ain't never gonna forget Tobias John." He gripped her face tighter and tighter until Hope thought he'd crack the bones. "I like to leave a mark on my women, but your man took my knife." He giggled. "I see the fire's not out. Never branded a woman before, that oughta be fun. Maybe we could put my mark right across here." He smeared his hand hard across her face as if trying to obliterate her features.

Hope sobbed in terror, stretching as far away from him as she could.

Tobias John took her neck in his hand, squeezed hard, leaning in close. "You want me, bitch? I think you do." He ran his thick tongue up her face slowly and laughed as she squirmed, trying to get away.

"I think you're so wet for me now you can't stand it." His hand twisted her breast. Pain ripped through her. She arched herself against him, trying to push him off. He hiccupped with pleasure. She hit him wherever she could, her fists beating at him. It made no difference. Against him she was powerless.

"You prissy ones are all the same," he sneered. "Think you're so clean and superior. Think you're too good for Tobias John, don't you?" He ground his knee hard up against her. She cried out, the sound muffled against his hand clamped across her face. "But I know, deep down, the finer the lady, the more she enjoys a bit of rough. Well, Tobias is gonna give you rough." He took hold of her shirt and ripped it open, his nails leaving long red marks on her chest. His filthy mouth came down on her breast and bit hard.

Wolf flew through the cabin door. He landed on top of the trapper and sank his long teeth deep into the man's neck. Tobias John screamed. He wrenched himself off Hope, trying to reach round to the vengeance tearing his neck apart.

Hope scrambled out of the way and crawled into the larder, cowering behind the sacks, trying to find safety in the dark, trying to hide, trying to pull her skirt down and her torn shirt closed. Tears and sobbing whimpers of fear and pain forced their way out of her.

The horrendous sounds of man and wolf fighting drove her deeper into the dark.

Wolf had only one agenda, to kill. Tobias John lunged across the room, knocking over the table and chairs, but he couldn't shake Wolf. Only Wolf's inexperience saved the trapper's life.

Luke was at the door. One look was enough. The violence that lived in Luke, that he'd run so far to escape, that he thought he'd tamed, raised its head and smiled. Its cold breath filled his soul and a dark, blood-red mist flooded his mind. Taking hold of Tobias John, Luke threw him outside.

Wolf let go of the man. As the trapper hit the ground he pounced again, stretching his neck, angling to get a better grip, eyes demonic, savagery rippling through every linea-ment, thick blood dripping from his fangs.

"Wolf! Find Hope," Luke commanded. He had to say it twice before it penetrated the killing lust. The look on Wolf's face changed when Luke said Hope's name again. He went back inside immediately.

"That damn wolf's ripped me up. I'm dying," Tobias whined.

"Not yet. Get up."

Tobias struggled to his feet, holding the back of his neck. It was a mess. He glanced at Luke but all he saw was a fist barrelling towards his face. The beating was hard. Luke was merciless. Tobias tried to fight back. He had a height and weight advantage and landed some solid punches. He was also a dirty fighter. Gouging and kicking whenever he could.

Luke had the advantage of sheer rage and self-control. A long time ago, Luke had learned the hard way not to let rage dominate the fight, but to use it to hone the intent, to concentrate the pain where his punches landed and to sharpen the anticipation of where retaliation would come from. As soon as he realised he was enjoying it, he pulled himself back, stopping short of killing the man, but despite that, Tobias John was a bloody pulp.

Apart from the mess Wolf had made of his neck, his face was ruined beyond recognition. His jaw was cracked; two ribs, and an arm were broken. It would be touch and go if he kept the use of his left eye. He lay face down, coughing blood into the dirt.

Luke walked the trapper's mangy, thin horse over. "I don't want my land tainted by dead men's blood. Get on your horse. Go die somewhere else."

The trapper dragged himself up, every movement agony, battling to stay conscious. Luke held the horse still while Tobias John struggled into the saddle.

"You should have killed me, Harcourt," he mumbled through split and swollen lips. "'Cause I'm gonna kill you." The horse moved off and carried Tobias John slowly away.

As soon as the trapper was out of sight, Luke went to find Hope. Wolf was lying with his nose on his paws, staring into the larder. He glanced up briefly when Luke came in and whimpered, his attention on the storeroom. Luke gave him a brief pat and stepped over him.

"Hope?" Luke crouched and saw her hiding in the dark, twisted tightly into herself. She was shaking all over, her arms covered in marks that tomorrow would be dark purple, dirt smeared across her face. She was holding tightly to her shirt. He didn't know if Tobias John had actually raped her, and he wasn't sure how to ask.

"He's gone, Hope. He won't be coming back. You're safe now." He kept his voice quiet, calm and low. He moved slowly, holding out a hand. She whimpered. He stopped, his hand still outstretched. "He's gone, I promise. You're safe."

There was a silence broken only by her soft hiccups and shuddering breath. "He hurt me," she whispered.

Luke felt ill.

"He hit me. He bit me and he tore my shirt."

Luke had to know; he didn't know how to help her, if he could, unless he knew. "Did he, did he—" Perhaps the best way to ask was straight out. "Hope, did he rape you?"

She shook her head. The relief he felt was overwhelming. He breathed out slowly.

"He's gone, Hope. You're safe now." He'd keep saying it till she believed it.

She turned her stricken eyes towards him. Anger welled up again inside him at the sight of her; rage and pity flooded his heart. The bastard had punched her hard, a number of times. One side of her face was swollen and already turning blue, her eye was almost closed. Tears had left streaks down her face. He knew if he'd seen her first, he would have killed Tobias John.

"Hope," he whispered.

She reached out and took his hand. Coaxing her gently out from behind the sacks, he led her to the bed, moving with care. She was more than fragile. She was breakable. He didn't want to be left with only shards of the woman he was coming to know. He wanted her whole.

"Lie down and rest for a while. I'll get a hot bath ready for you."

"No." She clutched at him, "Don't leave me. Please. Stay with me." She shuddered again, her eyes large with terror. When he lay down next to her, she turned to him, clutching his shirt tightly in her hand. He carefully put his arms around her. She moved in as close to him as she could get, trying to burrow into him. Luke held her, trying not to hurt her. If that's what her face looked like, her body was probably just as damaged. He gave up a silent prayer of thanks that he'd gotten there in time to prevent her rape.

Hope knew she was safe now, but the smell of the trapper was still on her. It invaded her mind. She drifted into an uneasy doze for a while, then her body would shudder, and she'd whimper. Eventually though, Luke's deep, calm breathing, the slow rise and fall of his chest and comfort of his strong arms slowly calmed her and she fell deeply asleep.

His hands grazed and aching abominably from the beating he'd dealt out, Luke lay there holding her. He'd hold her as long as she needed him. Wolf lay on the rug next to the bed. She woke in a panic a couple of times, crying out in sudden fear. Wolf gazed up in concern and whimpered. Luke spoke quietly, telling her over and over that she was safe, and slowly the darkness in Hope's mind faded and she fell asleep in his arms again and Wolf's head sank back onto his paws.

CHAPTER FIFTEEN

THE aroma of freshly brewed coffee filtered through the mists of sleep. Hope cracked open her eyes. Or at least tried to, only one would open and it throbbed in protest. Her body felt the same way. Hope could hardly move. She bit back a cry.

"Take it slowly," said Luke. "I've got a hot bath ready for you. Would you like a cup of coffee?"

She nodded.

"I'll leave it on the chair for you by the bath. I'll be right outside if you need me. Take your time." He poured the coffee and then, taking Wolf, left the cabin, shutting the door.

She heard the chair on the porch creak as it took his weight. Hope desperately wanted to bathe. The smell of Tobias John was everywhere. For the second time in her life burning her clothes was something she desperately wanted to do. Perhaps this time she would.

Luke must have woken early. He'd bathed, probably in the river. He'd righted the furniture, started the fire and carried water up to the cabin so a hot bath would be ready when she awoke. No one would ever know what had happened in the cabin the day before. Perhaps it was only the comforting smell of the coffee which made her think that.

On a chair near the bath, Luke had put a clean towel, Mrs Cuthbert's comfrey salve and her clean dress. On the table a jug was stuffed with wildflowers. Some of them were only weeds, but they looked pretty. Her eyes teared up again. Luke was not only kind, but thoughtful as well. Hope's heart was a deep well of gratitude towards him.

Every movement hurt so it took a while to undress. Eventually, she eased herself into the hot water and lay back carefully, sinking down until the water covered her head. Hope held her breath for as long as she could. Arms aching, she washed her hair about four times, digging deep into her scalp. She was covered in bruises and scratches. Long red gashes on the inside of her thighs marked where his nails had dug in her flesh. Teeth marks made purple, ragged circles on her breasts. She sat up at long last, took the brush and set about scrubbing every inch of her body as hard as she could bear, over and over again.

Much later, she cracked open the cabin door. Luke had said Tobias John was gone, but her fear still lingered.

Luke stood up when she peered out. Her hair was tangled and damp, the contusions standing out harshly against her pale skin. She looked dreadful, but at least she'd lost a fraction of that devastated look. "Would you like some?" He pointed to the coffee pot. "I've got cream and sugar out here for you as well."

She nodded, opened the door wider and stepped outside. He helped her into the chair and went inside to get her cup. He brought another chair out with him when he came back. They sat quietly together, sipping the hot coffee, looking out over the yard, neither saying anything for a time.

Hope put down her cup and asked quietly, "Would you brush my hair for me? It hurts to lift my arms right now."

"Of course, where's your hairbrush?"

"I hope you don't mind, but I've been using yours," she said.

It wasn't his. It had belonged to Tess. Luke felt terrible. Hope had nothing. Not even her own hairbrush. He hadn't given it any thought when he'd brought her home from the ship.

He was very gentle, working out the knots as carefully as he could. It took a long time and her hair was almost dry by the time he was finished. Its dark, chocolate waves were like silk. He had a sudden impulse to twine it round his fingers, hold it up to his face and breathe in its scent. Brushing her hair was the most intimate thing he'd done with her. Holding her last night didn't count. She'd been through so much and he hadn't been there to protect her. He felt unbelievably guilty.

Her eyes were closed and her head tilted back a little. She looked so vulnerable, so trusting. That was a mistake. Tess was evidence of that. He stopped brushing. Hope opened her eyes. Large green pools of—

"There you are." He handed her the brush. "I'd better see to the animals. I'll leave Wolf with you. I'll be in the barn. Will you be all right?"

She nodded. He stepped off the porch and walked away.

Hope watched him go. If it hadn't been for Luke, Tobias John would have raped and probably killed her. Luke had rescued her. Luke had found her. Luke made the dark go away. Just like he had the day he took her off the ship. Being in his arms last night, held with such gentleness and concern, hearing that strong heart beat steadily and calmly, his care for her this morning— she realised it wasn't the cabin that was now her home.

It was Luke.

CHAPTER SIXTEEN

L UKE slept in the cabin for a while. He was thankful he'd gone to the trouble of bringing those armchairs all the way up the mountain. He wouldn't be able to sleep too many nights in them, but for a short while, for her, he'd survive.

The first night Hope woke screaming hysterically, fighting Luke. He simply held her and let her hit him, reassuring her in a calm, low voice until eventually she quietened again. The nightmares continued over the next few nights, but Luke was always there. As long as he held her, she slept.

Luke insisted Hope take it easy for a while. She could barely move for the first three days anyway. Each morning he took her on short, gentle walks down to the river or into the forest. He wasn't sure if she had a cracked rib or not. Often, when she moved, she drew in a sharp breath, but when he asked, she assured him she was fine, just a little sore, and she always insisted she was feeling much better than before.

He could see she wasn't. She had dark rings under her eyes, and her skin and hair had lost their lustre. He was convinced that though she slept, she wasn't sleeping well. Sudden noises or movement scared her. She panicked if he was away from her side too long. She was constantly tense, tightly wound up. It wouldn't take much for her to snap.

Hope was clearly haunted by the fear of Tobias John coming back. If Luke had been away for longer than he'd intended, the relief in her eyes when he returned was frightening. At times, for no reason at all she'd start to shake, and Luke would catch her eyes darting towards the larder. The need to crawl back under the larder shelf and hide behind the sacks was overwhelming. He didn't like the way she was turning in on herself, that her terror was pulling her into the dark. He didn't want that to happen, but he wasn't sure how to stop it. She was disappearing before his eyes.

Ten days after Tobias John had left, a badly damaged heap of a man only held up by the bag of bones vaguely resembling a horse, Luke put the animals back in the barn and set up a row of cans on top of the fence railing.

Hope was sitting in one of the armchairs, mending a tear in one of Luke's shirts but her eyes kept blurring with tears. She heard Luke coming into the cabin. He always called her name before he stepped on the porch so she would know it was him. It was sweet of him. He didn't need to do that; she knew the sound of his walk, the sound of his breathing, the way he always wiped his feet on the mat at the door. She quickly rubbed her eyes.

Luke took down his shotgun and the rifle. He pulled a couple of boxes of cartridges out of the dresser drawer. Her heart thumped as if it were a wild thing trying to escape her chest. He only wanted his rifle if he was going hunting. He might be gone all day.

"There's something I need to show you," he said. "Come outside."

She put down her sewing and followed him. "What is it?" Her voice had grown quieter each day. Sometimes he could hardly hear her. Not that she was saying much. She'd nearly stopped talking altogether.

"I thought I'd better teach you how to shoot, as you can't seem to leave my guns alone." He smiled. He put the rifle on the ground. "Here." He swung the shotgun closed and gave it to her. "Be careful, it's loaded. Don't put your finger on the trigger until I tell you."

She gingerly took the gun. She'd forgotten how heavy it was.

"Put your left hand here on the barrel, and your right here. Tuck the stock into your shoulder like this. Higher. Yes, that's right. If you don't make sure it's tucked in well, when you pull the trigger, you'll get hurt...or knocked over."

She flicked a glance at him and saw his grin. A small knot of tension eased, had he forgiven her for shooting at Adam White Knife? He stood close behind her and put his hands over hers on the gun. She stiffened, her heart beating a quick double time, then it stilled. This was Luke, not Tobias.

"Now, aim at the first can on the left there. When you've got it lined up on the sight on the front here and the one back here, then put your finger on the back trigger. See, there's two of them. One for each barrel. Good, now don't pull at it, squeeze it."

She tried, but she was nervous. She dropped the stock a little and jerked the trigger. The gun roared and bucked. It went off frighteningly fast, much quicker than she'd expected. She was so startled she jumped. Luke swiftly took her arms to steady her.

"You all right?" he asked.

She nodded. She'd missed the can. The gun felt unwieldy and awkward in her hands.

"I missed the first time as well," said Luke.

She didn't believe that for a second. She could hear the smile in his voice, and she appreciated the encouragement.

"Let's try again," he said, dropping his hands. "Now, use the front trigger."

This time, she was prepared. The front trigger was more comfortable; it didn't go off so fast. She needed to remember that. The bullet still didn't hit the can.

Luke reloaded the gun and gave it back to her. "Try again."

After a few more attempts he said, "Let's try the rifle now." He took the shotgun away and gave her his Spencer rifle instead.

"Careful, it's also loaded. You hold it the same way."

This gun was much lighter. It felt better to hold as well. It sat well, tucked against the hollow of her shoulder. Her aim was off as she was expecting the same reaction from this gun as the other one when it fired.

"Don't worry," said Luke. "We'll keep practising. It's important you know how to use them. Then you'll feel much safer."

How could she tell Luke that the only time she really felt safe was in his arms? But he couldn't be with her all the time. She'd have to learn how to shoot this damn gun if she wanted to stay here, with him. She lifted the gun and tried again, tucking the stock well into her shoulder, leaning forward a little. This time, she imagined Tobias John's face on the can. Hope fired. It gave her a lot of satisfaction to see the can leap off the fence.

"Well done. Let me show you how to reload."

He took her through the steps, handed back the rifle and moved away. She would have to do this one on her own.

She swung the gun up and took aim at the next can. She was handling the weapon a little easier now. Something had changed.

She seemed to have lost some of that worried look, but now he saw a different expression and what he saw gave him something new to be concerned about. This was suddenly a woman with a purpose. He knew what that purpose was: she wanted to kill Tobias John.

It was understandable. He'd almost killed the trapper himself. But he wasn't teaching Hope to kill. He only wanted her to feel safe, to be able to protect herself. Hope didn't know it now and he hoped she never would, but killing a man, it changed you. And what it changed wasn't pretty.

No matter how justified you were in the killing, part of you went cold, hard. It vanished and never came back.

The can jumped and disappeared into the long grass. He took the gun away from her. "I should have told you this before. Never pick up a gun unless you plan to use it. Never aim a gun at anyone unless you plan to pull the trigger, and never pull the trigger unless you're prepared to kill, because you will have to live with that death the rest of your life. Do you understand me?" His voice was harsh. She nodded. He doubted if she did. You only really understood after you watched a man die with a bullet in his gut. A bullet you'd put there. It was a slow death, a horrible way to die.

"Show me how to load it again."

He gave her a long look. "Tomorrow. That's enough for today." He picked up the shotgun and took the weapons back to the cabin. He could feel her watching him as he crossed the yard.

CHAPTER SEVENTEEN

L UKE gave her a lesson every day for about a week. She was determined to learn and learn fast. By the time they were finished, she could strip, clean and put a gun back together, fire, reload and fire again almost as fast as Luke. But most impressively of all, once she'd knocked her first can off the top of the fence, she never missed another. Luke, although still concerned that her motives were wrong, knew he had to keep teaching her how to use the guns. Whatever her reasons, the lessons were exactly what she needed. Her confidence was returning.

But it was when Luke heard her singing again that he moved back to the barn.

They both lay awake a long time that night.

Hope curled up under the quilt, missing Luke's presence in the cabin; even Wolf had gone to the barn tonight. She knew a measure of peace now that she could shoot, and she was quite proud of the fact that for six days in a row she had hit every single can. But what if the trapper came back? If she allowed herself to think about that day she started to shake. She tried forcing herself to relax, but that just seemed to make it worse. Eventually, she remembered what her grandmother had once said: Live the faith, not the fear. God will make a way, she'd said. Believe that, live it out.

It was such a hot night Hope opened the shutters to let in some fresh air. The moon was a sliver of silver hanging like an upturned bowl out of which the stars had spilled, thick across the dark indigo sky. Hope spent a long time looking up at them, drinking in the beauty spread out above. She breathed in deeply as a light breeze carried the warm scent of the pines past her. She sighed out a silent prayer, almost wordless and let the quiet of the night fill her soul.

She climbed back into bed and for the first time since that awful day, Hope slept alone, deep, peaceful and dreamless, waking the next morning refreshed and clean.

In the barn, Luke, although grateful he wasn't sleeping in the chair anymore, kept wanting to go check on her and make sure she wasn't having a nightmare. He smiled ruefully when he finally admitted if he did check on her he hoped she would be caught in a wave of terror and need him to hold her again. It was good to feel needed, to be someone's protector. It made him feel, well...like a man again.

Be honest, it simply felt good to hold her. If he needed anything to remind him he was a man, that was it. He sighed, rubbing his eyes. What a fool. Carelessly making a stupid, thoughtless promise never to touch her. A promise that would be difficult, if not impossible to keep.

One morning, as Luke stepped out of the barn, he was surprised to encounter the delicious aroma of baking bread. The cabin door stood open, the scent curled invitingly out. He walked in to discover four beautiful loaves of bread on the table. Hope must have started baking before sun-up.

"Morning. Those look good. I didn't know you could bake bread," he said.

She grinned, which surprised him. She seemed totally recovered from her ordeal now.

"One of my very few, real housekeeping skills, I'm afraid. My grandmother taught us. She said the one thing everyone should know is how to make bread. As soon as it came out of the oven, we cut thick slices and buttered them. We couldn't wait for them to cool off. Then we'd put chunks of cheese on. That, with a cold glass of milk was one of our favourite things. My brother was better at it than I was. His loaves were scrumptious."

"I didn't know you had a brother," said Luke. He noticed one of the loaves was already missing one end.

"Yes. Charlie. He was younger than me."

"Was?"

"I mean is."

Why had she said "was" like that, Luke wondered. Did she consider her family lost to her? "I take it your memory's returned?"

"Some of it," she replied.

For some reason that worried him. He realised she'd been here for over two months and he still knew almost nothing about her. Almost nothing, except that he liked having her in his arms at night. He tried not to think about that. It seemed wrong for him to have liked holding her - she'd only been there for comfort, to chase away the nightmares. Nothing else. He'd begun to know her spirit, the way she wasn't afraid to tackle hard work, her sense of humour, her courage, her compassion, her modesty. He'd seen her accept her situation without complaint, well, almost none - if he didn't count the vegetable plot discussion. But her family, her history, her hopes and dreams; these were things he knew nothing about.

"Why were you on that ship?" he asked bluntly. "You don't strike me as the kind of woman that would even think of selling herself like that."

"I don't know." She cut and buttered a thick slice of hot bread then laid a generous slice of cheese on top, put it on a plate and handed it to him. "I haven't remembered that." She didn't meet his eyes.

"Or who put you there?"

She shook her head, poured two glasses of milk, handed him one and sat down. "The last thing I remember before that was being at a church picnic. My mother had one of her bad headaches, so my father stayed behind with her. Charlie was studying. He wants to be a doctor. Gabriel had offered to escort me. My mother insisted I go with him."

"Who's Gabriel?" Luke felt a very faint, odd stir of jealousy in his stomach.

"Gabriel Hunter. His father was— is the Episcopalian bishop. He had something to do with the railroad as well. I'm not sure what. Our families weren't really friends, but we all moved in the same circles, so we knew each other socially."

"Do you remember where you're from?"

"No. I remember the place, but not its name." She took a sip of milk.

"You were telling me about Gabriel," he prompted.

"Yes, my mother thought he was perfect. She was always inviting him over to the house and encouraging me to spend time with him. So, when he said he'd take me to the picnic, she practically forced me to go with him."

"What's your mother like?" he asked.

"Beautiful. Men adore her." She took a sip of milk.

That was it? No more to say about her mother? Hope hadn't looked at him when she'd said it. That was interesting. Luke moved on. "And your father?"

She smiled. "He has quite a gruff look to him. He's always frowning over some problem he's trying to work out, so people think he's always cross. But he wasn't. He was just lost in thought. He could be very abrupt, which didn't help."

She'd switched back to the past tense again, as if he were dead. "He was an English Quaker and a naturalist. He'd come to our town to study the plant life of the swamps. He met my mother at church, her parents were also Quakers. My mother refused to go back with him to England. He agreed to stay and they were married. He always had his nose buried in a book or writing his papers or wandering through the swamps collecting specimens and forgetting the time. I used to go with him whenever I could." Her eyes glittered with unshed tears as the memories became clearer.

It wasn't hard to guess which parent Hope had been closest to. Her mother clearly hadn't been the mother Hope needed. It didn't surprise him. Most of the exceptionally beautiful women Luke had met were often bad mothers to their daughters. He'd had enough daughters thrown at him to know. A few mothers as well. Women like that either produced cookie-cutter copies of themselves, only shallower versions, or they didn't want the competition, so they brought up their daughters to believe they were worthless. Is that what Hope's mother had done? Was that why she hadn't been offended when he said he didn't want her? Is that what she'd expected? Is that why she didn't try to flirt with him? He wasn't what most women would call handsome. It never bothered him. Women always seemed to put themselves in his way, on the flimsiest of excuses. Hope didn't. She moved gracefully, which was attractive, but she never moved provocatively. He didn't know how she felt about him. He couldn't tell if her blushes were shyness or desire.

"What happened at the picnic?" he asked.

"All I remember is that it was a sweltering day." Her face took on an abstracted look with the effort of trying to remember. "So hot I thought at one stage I was going to faint. Gabriel took me for a walk by the river. It was cooler under the trees. I remember he said he wanted to ask me something."

Luke knew what was coming. This Gabriel - whom he'd decided he didn't like - would've asked Hope to marry him. Perhaps that's why Hope hadn't minded when he said he didn't want her. She was in love with someone else. Luke found himself tensing up.

"Did you say yes?"

Hope looked startled. "How did you know what he asked me?"

"Educated guess. Did you? Say yes?"

"I can't remember. That's odd, isn't it? I only remember the day clouded over."

"You weren't in love with him?" It didn't sound like it, but for some reason he needed to hear her say it.

"No. I wasn't. I do know that. But I think I was supposed to be. Does that make sense?"

Luke felt a whisper of relief. "What else do you remember?"

She paused as if deciding what to say next. "Well, there's nothing but this vague memory of it getting dark and that we seemed to be lost. But that's all. I don't remember anything else. When I woke up on the ship, I had a terrible headache. I must have fainted or something and hit my head. I had a lump on the back of my head the size of an egg and it'd been bleeding. I don't know what happened to Gabriel. He wasn't there. I seem to remember a train and then being on a different ship, the one that went to Silver Birch Landing. But it's patchy, so I may be wrong."

Luke knew exactly what'd happened. His fist clenched as she'd been talking. Someone had hit her over the head and knocked her out. They must have hit her very hard for her to have lost so much memory. Had it been this Gabriel character? Why would he do that? Because she'd refused him? Seemed a bit drastic.

From what she said, she'd probably been taken by ship to the Panama Railroad. The women would have been transported across the narrow stretch of land, then put onto the slaver he'd bought her off, taken to Silver Birch Landing via to San Francisco.

"Would you like some more cheese and bread?" asked Hope.

"Yes. It's good."

She smiled as if he'd given her a gift. "Thank you. That's very kind." She handed him another slice.

"Kindness has nothing to do with it. It's the truth. Your grandmother taught you well."

"I always liked spending time with her. She was very grandmotherly, all soft lap, silver hair and smelling of cinnamon."

"I know the type. Mine was the same. Did yours wear blue most of the time?"

"Yes," she laughed. "Yours?"

He nodded, his mouth full of hot bread, melting butter and cheese.

"Blue eyes as well?"

"Yes. Just like mine."

Their eyes met, his with a smile in them. There was a pause. She felt a heat lightly touch her cheeks. His eyes might be the same colour as his grandmother's, but she was sure the old lady never had the same effect on other people with them as he did. They could be as deep as a well, hard as rock or cold as ice. Either way, despite the reserve that lingered at the back of them, an expression that held her away, Hope's heart always did a double beat when he looked at her.

From the moment she'd realised she was in love with Luke - the day he brushed her hair - she'd found herself blushing when their eyes met, her heart tripping over itself if he touched her. And he only ever did that accidentally. After he'd moved back into the barn, he'd never held her again.

Luke drained his glass. "Shall I make some coffee? Might go well with this bread, and some honey?"

Thankful for the change in subject Hope nodded and went to the larder. She came back with the honey jar.

"We're out of honey. I'm sorry, I don't seem to be as good at this as I thought. Housekeeping, I mean. There's nothing left," Hope said in a troubled voice. Luke's eyes twinkled, but she didn't see it. She was looking into the empty jar as if she might discover a little bit of honey somewhere in its depths.

Sighing dramatically, he replied, "You know I can't go to town for another month." As if he got his honey from a store in town! Now she looked nervous, perhaps he'd overdone it.

He relented and with mock severity said, "It's a good thing I know where we can find some wild honey. Try not to use it all at once."

CHAPTER EIGHTEEN

ONCE they'd finished early morning chores, Luke came to find Hope. He was carrying a can with a lid tied on it, a bucket and some heavy gloves. "Come on, let's go get that honey. Take this."

Giving her the can, which was heavier, and smellier than she expected, he led the way into a section of the forest she hadn't been in before. Wolf trotted along beside them, when he wasn't making small forays into the undergrowth.

After a short while, Luke stopped ten feet away from a ruined tree. It had been hit by lightning at some stage. The tall, blackened stump was hollow – the ideal place for bees. Sure enough, a small number flew busily in and out of the tree. Luke pulled on the heavy gloves, took the can from Hope and untied the lid. Inside was a handful of dried cow dung. Hope wrinkled her nose as Luke lit it and worked with it till it was smoking.

"What's that for?" she asked.

"The smoke keeps the bees quiet," Luke replied. "You put the can inside and then wait a short while. Then you can take the honey without getting stung too much."

"Won't the honey taste like smoke?"

"Doesn't seem to. I've always thought it tasted a bit like apples, but then maybe I'm just around apples too much."

"They probably get their nectar from the apple blossoms," said Hope.

Of course. Why hadn't he thought of that? It gave him an idea. He'd need to put more thought into it.

He put the smoking can into the base of the tree and then sat down to wait. Hope sat near him and waited. He'd noticed that although she was always within reach, she was careful never to touch him.

The smelly smoke drifted out from the top of the stump. The bees grew quieter.

"Do the bees go to sleep?" she asked after a while.

"No, they just get groggy."

"How long does it last? The grogginess."

"I don't know. Never stayed around to watch. Probably not long. Bring the bucket," he said getting up. Reaching into the tree he gave a yank and pulled out a thick, sticky, dripping honeycomb and dropped it into the bucket. He reached in again and pulled out another one.

"That'll do. The honey jar won't hold any more than that. If you ever do this, don't take it all. Leave some for the bees."

She nodded. The smoke seemed to be fading. Half a dozen bees hummed sluggishly around. One, it turned out, was a little more alert than its fellow workers. It landed on Wolf's nose and took its revenge. Wolf yelped and jumped back. He put his head down and rubbed at his snout with his paws. Luke laughed, reached into the tree again and lifted out the can.

"Let's go before they all come 'round."

Once they were back at the cabin, Luke sauntered off to the orchard. If the bees were taking took the nectar from the apple trees, why not make it easy for them? He wondered how much honey he'd get if he put some hives into the or-chard? Would it be enough for him to sell? It might be worth trying. He'd have to find out how to make a hive, and how to separate the honey from the combs.

He told Hope about his idea when they ate their midday meal together.

"That's a wonderful idea. Apart from the honey, we could make beeswax candles with the combs," she said excitedly. "They smell so good and last for a long time. If we have enough, we might be able to sell them as well." Every cent would help.

"Whoa, hang on. One thing at a time." Luke laughed. "Let's see if the hives in the orchard work first. Still, it's not a bad idea."

He went to the cedar chest and pulled out a small box - it was shaped just like the big chest - and opened it. Hope saw that it held documents. It looked like the corners of share certificates poking out. Lying on top of all of them was a small, black leather notebook. Luke took it out. He rummaged around in a drawer in the dresser until he found a pencil. When he opened the notebook a folded piece of paper slid out onto the floor and fell open. Hope leaned down from her chair to pick it up. It was the bill of sale – the one with her name on. Her day suddenly went flat. Wordlessly, she handed it to Luke, who put it back in the box without even glancing at it. Completely focused on the new idea, he started a few drawings.

Muttering under his breath, he wrote out a list of notes and questions he would need answers to on another page.

Hope made a pot of tea. She would love to sit and help him with this idea, but he'd become absorbed in it and shut her out. She was used to that. Her father had been the same. She might as well get on with the chores.

Today was washday. She hated washdays. She always ended up wet and hot. She really needed to wash the clothes she was wearing; she stank of cow dung smoke and there were sticky honey patches where the combs had dripped as she was fitting them into the jar. She sighed. Her only skirt was already dirty. She had nothing else to change into. Everything was in the wash pile.

Luke put the notebook back into the small chest. "I think I'll keep this in the barn. That way I can scribble down any ideas or solutions I come up with in the middle of the night before I forget them."

Hope watched him stride back out of the barn and head off towards the orchard. He had that same look her father used to wear - the lost-in-thought look. She sighed; she missed her father and Charlie. She longed to see them again. Her hands stilled. What would she do -if she ever remembered where home was - if she ever had the choice? Would she go? It meant leaving Luke. In a way, she hoped she would never have to make that decision. Even if Luke never loved her, she would rather be his housekeeper than be without him.

She had to distract herself from thinking about her father and Charlie. And Luke. Hard work was the best way. Time to do the washing. She really wanted to get out of these clothes but needed something else to wear instead. Although she'd kept a tight rein on her curiosity and never looked inside that big, carved chest standing at the end of the bed, it was still a temptation. Now she had a legitimate excuse. Besides, there was probably time before Luke came back. She knelt in front of it and heaved the heavy lid back.

Not sure what to expect, she didn't know how to react to what was inside. It was full of women's clothes. Dresses, undergarments, a velvet opera cloak, skirts and blouses, all of the finest quality. They were some of the most feminine garments she'd ever seen. She lifted the cloak and held it to her face. The feel and smell of the fabric immediately brought her mother's image to mind. Whoever these clothes belonged to obviously used the same perfume.

Hope held up one of the skirts. Its owner was clearly a tiny woman. Too tall to have ever been called petite, even at fourteen Hope had been the same height as most full-grown women. Folding the skirt again she felt as if she was being watched.

Tobias! She turned swiftly, cold with fear. It was only Luke.

But there was nothing 'only' in his face. He was white with rage, terrifying to look at. Hope swallowed, tried to say something, but the words wouldn't come out. Luke silently eased the skirt out of her hands and put it back in the chest and closed the lid. He moved carefully, but there was no mistaking his intent. "Get out."

It was said quietly. Hope didn't linger. Wanting to apologize but appalled, frightened by the look in his eyes, she turned and fled the cabin.

Back home she would have gone to the big tree that grew in the swamp and climbed into its strong branches, staying there till it was safe to come down. But here—Luke had been that safe place. How appallingly stupid to have looked in that chest! She'd known instinctively it was a forbidden place.

Had Luke looked like that when he'd beaten Tobias John? Would she be taken back to town and left there? Being un-wanted wasn't anything new but still, nausea rose swiftly, burning her throat. There would be no begging or pleading with Luke. She'd face whatever he doled out, even if that meant— well, he hadn't wanted her in the first place. This might just be the excuse he needed to get rid of her. Her fragile heart splintered.

With no money, going home, wherever that was, especially thinking what she did about her mother, wasn't an option. The desolation of knowing that cool beauty had never liked, certainly never loved - what was her mother's part in her abduction? Hope couldn't go back there. And now, now she was going to see that look, the one that flitted across her mother's face so often, the expression that said *not good enough, your fault* on the face of the man she loved.

Perhaps Lee-Ming would have a vacant place in the laundry. How long would it take to save enough to go… somewhere? Working at the laundry was a future that didn't include Luke, which made her want to weep, but at least it was a plan.

Did he expect her to apologise? She would anyway but... she wouldn't whine about it. She'd had a perfectly good reason for— No, she didn't. She could try and justify it as much as she liked, but she'd had no business looking in that trunk.

CHAPTER NINETEEN

LUKE opened the chest. The interior was lined with blue velvet with pockets sewn into the sides. He drew out a photograph and ran his fingers over it. Tess Harcourt smiled back at him, one of those extremely beautiful women Luke had known.

Would she have been a good mother? Unlikely, considering... It was stupid to have kept the clothes. He'd almost forgotten they were there; it had been so long since he last looked at them. The chest had become just another piece of furniture.

Even when taking out that apron for Hope, the thought of Tess had been momentary. The apron had been right on top, maybe that was why. What he didn't know was why Hope had been looking inside it. When he'd walked in and seen her going through the chest, then holding the skirt against herself, his reaction had been inexplicable, even to himself. It had felt like a desecration. As if muddy boots were trampling over Tess's memory. Tess, beautiful, glittering Tess, the woman he'd loved so passionately. The wife he'd killed. Her memory wasn't held in this chest, it was twisted deep inside him.

Now, looking at the clothes again, he saw them for what they really were – just things. Things he'd almost forgotten. After looking at the picture for a long time, he tucked it back into the side pocket and closed the lid.

Hope was standing by the paddock. He owed her an apology... or at least an explanation. Not sure what to say, he stood in silence for a while, leaning on the top rail of the fence.

"I'm sorry Luke, I—"

"Don't." His voice was harsh, but it was the quietness of it that was frightening. "Those clothes belonged to my wife." He breathed in, then let it out slowly. "We were married for a little over two years. She died."

"Oh, I'm so sorry Luke. How did..." She faltered.

"I killed her."

Hope's eyes went wide with shock, she blinked and then, after a heartbeat, her eyes gentled again. "What happened?" Hope asked quietly.

He could hear the compassion in her voice and hated it. Compassion was the last thing he deserved. He sighed. He'd begun so he might as well finish it. Let her know the worst about him now, even if it meant she—

Skipping school whenever he could to haunt the docks, scrambling over the ships, getting in the sailors' way. Ten years old, his first berth, cabin boy, on his uncle's ship. Working his way up quickly through the ranks. The outbreak of Civil War. Captain of his own ship. Three years of unmitigated hell. The splintered shard of wood slicing through the air, deep across his chest. Sent home to recuperate.

"I met Tess at a dinner my uncle held. She was the daughter of one of the Jamaican planters. She'd come to Boston to stay with her aunt for a while. We were married within a month. I had to rejoin my ship almost immediately afterwards."

Paris. We'll go to Paris. As soon as the war's over. Have your things packed and ready. I'll come for you as soon as I dock.

"I disembarked from the Navy ship, had my uncle's cargo, which was waiting in the warehouse, loaded onto his ship, and went to fetch her. We would set off on the very next tide. I hadn't seen her in two years."

The front door standing open. Straight in, past an astonished footman. Pausing only long enough to ask where she is and order a sailor to take her chest from the hallway to the ship. Bursting into the morning room.

He paused, took a deep breath, then sighed heavily. "A man was there. I didn't recognise him. She was in his arms. She'd been crying. When they saw me, he laughed. Tess said she didn't want to go to Paris with me anymore. She wanted to stay in Boston, with her...friends."

What will I do in Paris? I know no one there. Oh, you, well yes. But when we leave? I'll be alone on your ship. I'll be bored. Don't be angry. I can't bear it.

The man smiling, coaxing her on.

Are you lovers?

Luke, don't be like that.

ARE YOU?

You've been gone so long. I hardly know you.

He stopped. He'd never told anyone the full story. Now he knew why, it was cutting deep into him and the darkness of that time was flooding back in through the wound.

Hope stood quietly and waited. He needed to tell this in his own way. Luke straightened up, his hands unconsciously gripping the fence railing.

"I needed to get away before I— I didn't say anything. I just turned and walked out. I heard her calling my name. I had to get away from her as fast as I could. He laughed. I wanted to kill him, whoever he was. I wanted to kill her. I heard her running after me and calling. I couldn't bear to look at her. All I could see was her, my wife, in the arms of a man who thought adultery was amusing."

He paused again. His voice grew quieter. "She caught up with me."

Wait! Luke! Wait! Don't leave like this. Please.

Clutching my arm. Her tear streaked face.

Get off me! I came for you! I loved you! And you—you're with another man?

Wait! Luke, I'm so sorry.

GET AWAY FROM ME!

"I pushed her away, hard."

The horses whinnying. Her scream. The thump of the carriage as it hit her. The noise, the shouts.

"It was going too fast to stop in time. It dragged her down the street. She was caught up in the traces and the wheels. She dropped and it ran over her. By the time I got to her, she was already dead.

The man was her cousin. I don't know if he was her lover. No one volunteered the information and it wasn't the kind of question I wanted to ask, in case I was right. But if I hadn't been in such a rage— if I hadn't— but I did and she's dead."

Hope stepped closer and put her hand on his arm. He glanced at her, but she was looking out at the field and the mountains beyond. Without knowing it, she'd done exactly the right thing. There'd been no judgment, no turning away. Nor had she done the predictable thing, making it maudlin and saying it wasn't his fault. With her quiet touch and calm, silent presence, he felt the darkness move away again.

They stood like that for a short space of time. Her hand warm on his arm. Augustus Brown ambled over and nodded his head at Luke. Luke scratched the horse's forehead.

Hope stepped back. "I'll leave you two gentlemen to commune. I need to get that washing done or it won't dry before sunset."

CHAPTER TWENTY

FIVE minutes later, Luke called to her. "I'm going down to the bottom meadow. Augustus Brown needs a good gallop," called Luke from the back of the big black.

"All right, I'll see you at dinner." She waved as he trotted out of the yard.

He came back in the middle of the afternoon to find her taking the washing off the line. In his clothes. He didn't say anything, he simply raised an astonished eyebrow. It quickly changed to amusement at the absolute mortification on her face. He knew he should be shocked, but he was more surprised than anything else and, to be honest, she looked good. His shirt was loose on her and gaped a little at the front.

She obviously didn't realise that from Augustus Brown's back he could see more than just that long slim throat of hers. But he wasn't going to tell her. Not that he could see much more, but it was enough. He laughed as she grabbed the washing basket and ran inside, shutting the cabin door quickly behind her. Why on earth was she wearing his clothes?

He was rubbing the horse down when it hit him. How could he have been so stupid?

She'd changed quickly and was just shutting the closet door when Luke knocked and walked into the cabin.

"I'm going into town tomorrow," he said. "Make a list of everything you need."

"All right. I thought you were only going back in three months' time."

"I need to get Augustus Brown re-shod." He didn't, the horse had been shod the day he bought Hope, but he couldn't think of anything else. They didn't need supplies. Not even honey. His mouth twisted in amusement.

"Give me the list at dinner. I'm going to the river to bathe. I need to get the smell of that cow dung smoke off me." He reached into the closet and took out the trousers and shirt she'd been wearing.

"Are you finished with these?" he asked with a grin. Her blush was instant and deep.

Later, at dinner, Hope gave him the list. It wasn't that long. Cinnamon, nutmeg, ginger, lemons, tea, coffee, sugar and pepper, if he could find any. Apart from coffee and sugar he'd never bought any of these things. The fact that Silver Birch Landing was a frontier town so it was unlikely the general store would stock them, was something she probably hadn't thought of. But now that he saw them written down, he wanted them himself. If her bread was anything to go by, what she could make with these things would be amazing.

"This list is only supplies," he said. "Isn't there anything you want for yourself?" He'd expected a list of personal items, like clothes, rather than this list.

"No, but thank you." She turned away. She always did that when she wasn't being truly honest. It was her 'tell'.

He'd seen how she fingered the velvet of Tess's opera cloak and the look of longing when she'd held the skirt. Now she'd probably never wear anything she found inside the chest. Not after what he'd told her. It probably wouldn't fit anyway. Tess had been a lot shorter than Hope. She'd been wearing the same dress he'd bought her in every day for two months. Well, that and the one skirt Lee-Ming had given her. If he had to go without sugar for a year, he'd buy her a few dresses at least. Maybe even a tortoise shell comb for her hair, some perfume - but that might mean no coffee - he wasn't sure his generosity extended that far.

"Will you be taking the wagon?" Hope asked.

"No, it'll be quicker if I ride. And I don't need a wagon to haul these few things."

"If you see Lee-Ming please tell her I say hello. And Lee-Chan of course. And Mr. Samson. Oh, and if you see Mrs Cuthbert, please ask her if she can give you the recipe for that salve of hers?"

He heard the disappointment in her voice and was tempted to change his mind and take her with him. There was no reason why he shouldn't, except that it would spoil the surprise.

He hadn't planned on surprising her, but as soon as the idea occurred to him, he realised that's exactly what he wanted to do. He was looking forward to it. He'd leave as soon as it was light.

Hope struggled to get to sleep that night. Her heart wept for Luke. He was carrying a burden that would have crippled most men. Telling him it wasn't his fault would have been a waste of time. He knew it was an accident, but until he chose to believe that, he'd carry the memory, the guilt as his punishment. Standing so close, her hand on his arm, she'd tried to pour as much comfort into the touch as possible. His eyes had been so empty, so full of pain.

It had been the memory of his eyes that had given her the idea. She was almost the same height as Luke. She had figured if she worked quickly, she might just get away with it. And it had been a hot day so her dress, or a skirt at least, should have dried quickly. Wearing Luke's shirt she could possibly get away with, but his trousers? Even thinking of wearing them was scandalous. And now he'd caught her in them! He'd probably think she was a hoyden - or worse.

CHAPTER TWENTY-ONE

LUKE arrived in Silver Birch Landing soon after midday two days later. It'd only been three hours, but it felt like he'd been there a week. The place was growing all the time, with new buildings going up and more people around.

After visiting the Lees, he left Augustus Brown with Mr Samson and made his way to the general store. It was quite a large establishment, selling everything from food supplies, gold panning equipment, tents, to saddles and everything in between. Including honey, Luke noticed. There was a small display standing on a barrel.

"Morning Mr Johnson. Ma'am," Luke greeted the couple behind the counter.

"Mr Harcourt! How nice to see you. We didn't expect you for another two..." Johnson looked at his wife for confirmation. She nodded. Her small, sad eyes looked exhausted. "Yes, another two months. I'm not sure we have your regular supplies in stock right now."

"How is your new wife, Mr Harcourt? Hope, I believe is her name?" asked Mrs Johnson. Her voice was so tired Luke was surprised she ever used it.

"She's fine, thank you." He turned back to her husband. "I don't need the usual list. I have a new one." He handed it over. Mr Johnson adjusted his glasses. He read it through, then glanced up at Luke, surprised. He cleared his throat.

"Well now, Mr Harcourt. I do have two-dozen loose lemons. The trees won't grow here you know, too cold. But, and I don't know if you're interested, I do have a couple of pear trees in stock. Mr Jefferson ordered them, I presume for the new store he's setting up. I don't suppose it matters which store sells them, does it? Which would you like?"

"I'll take everything," Luke was feeling extravagant.

"Thomas!" Mr Johnson called across to a young man who was sweeping the floor nearby. "Thomas, please can you bring both those pear trees that came in yesterday, and the loose lemons as well?" The young man stood his broom against the honey barrel and disappeared into the depths of the store. "Now, how much cinnamon would you like?"

"I have no idea." Luke suspected he was going to be taken for a bit of a ride but that was all right. The sooner he was finished the sooner he could get back.

The Johnsons had almost everything on the list. As it was being packed up for him, Luke's eyes fell on a small narrow box lying on the broad, dark wooden counter. It was packed tightly with envelopes of seeds. He pulled it towards himself and flicked through them. "Mr Johnson, I'm going to need some of these as well."

Mr Johnson did an almost admirable job of hiding his surprise. In the end, Luke bought tomato, onions, lettuce, spinach, cabbage, runner bean seeds, and some more coffee.

"I see you have honey." Luke pointed to the display.

"Yes. Shall I add some to the parcel?" sighed Mrs Johnson. Luke gritted his teeth. Her voice made him want a stiff drink.

"Do you sell a lot of it?" he asked.

"Oh yes. We never have enough in stock," Mr Johnson said.

"Would you be interested in a new supplier?"

"Are you thinking of keeping bees, Mr Harcourt?" Johnson was intrigued.

"Just making it easier for the bees that already live near my place. You don't have any hives in the store, do you?"

"No, but I can get some for you. How many would you like?"

"Let's start with say...four?"

Johnson made a note. "They should be here in about two months. Will that suffice?"

"I'm sure the bees will cope. They're living in a tree at the moment." he smiled.

"Will there be anything else Mr Harcourt?" whined Mrs Johnson.

Luke hesitated. "I'm not sure if you stock any of this."

He took another list out of his waistcoat pocket and stood there holding it. The shopkeeper and his wife exchanged glances. They had a fair idea of what the list contained. Luke wasn't the only man recently to have come into their store looking to buy supplies for their new wives. The Johnsons preferred it when the women came with them; they made more money that way. Luke cleared his throat and put the list down. Mrs Johnson picked it up and read,

Dresses

Shirts

Shoes

Brush and comb

Toothbrush

Coat

Hat

Nightgown

Luke had covered the basics, but he'd run out of courage before he'd written down anything else. Mrs Johnson gave a dry smile. "What size shoes does Mrs Harcourt wear?"

For a moment, Luke didn't know who she was talking about. "Hope? Oh, I'm not sure."

"Does she have small feet?"

"Yes, I think so."

"Well, does she have small hands or large ones?"

"Small."

"And how tall is she?"

At last, a question he could answer. "She's almost my height." At that moment, Thomas returned with the trees. Mr Johnson sent him back to look for a pair of shoes he thought would fit Hope.

"Will she be making her own clothes, or are you looking to buy ready-made dresses?" asked Mrs Johnson as the young man disappeared once again.

"Oh." That was a question. He'd seen Hope mend his shirts, but he had no idea if she could make clothes. He knew women did, but he'd never personally known any who could, or would have dreamt of doing so. If she could bake bread she could probably sew. But how long did it take to make a dress? And what if she couldn't? Hope needed clothes immediately.

"For now, I think I'd better buy ready-made ones," he said.

"Well, we have some nice skirts in stock. Let me show you." She took him across the store to where the skirts were kept. Luke wasn't sure he would have called them 'nice', but they were good quality, of the hard-working type. Material that would last a long time. All in dull colours that wouldn't show the dirt too easily. Luke sighed. He knew she needed clothes like this but...well, it wasn't quite what he wanted. He realised his purchases also needed to be practical, so he bought two, a grey and a dark blue serge. When Mrs Johnson showed him the shirts he rebelled. He wanted to get Hope something pretty, not these utilitarian, ugly, shapeless garments.

"Don't you have anything more..." The shopkeeper's wife already looked insulted. He took a deep breath and ploughed on. "More feminine? Maybe something with flowers on it?"

Mr Johnson came to his rescue. "I know exactly what you mean, Mr Harcourt. Ladies do like flowers."

His wife, in her tightly buttoned up, dung coloured dress, frowned.

"There's a new shop in town. It's just opened up near the church. It's called Miss Sylvie's. I think you'll find what you're looking for there."

Mrs Johnson sniffed.

Thomas came back with the shoes. Very practical, sturdy ankle length brown boots. They'd probably last longer than Hope. They brought Luke's mother forcibly to his mind. He imagined that very refined lady, who had more shoes than she could possibly wear, instantly bursting into tears simply at the sight of this functional footwear.

"Thank you. How much do I owe you?"

Mr Johnson tallied it all up and Luke handed over the money.

"Can you pack it for me? I'm not in the wagon today. I'm going to need to be able to carry it all on the horse." He was already regretting not having the wagon. Those pear trees would be a problem. And he still had more purchases to get. "Could I pick it up after I've been to Miss Sylvie's?"

"We will have it ready and waiting when you come back."

"Thanks." He turned to go when another thought struck him. "Do you have any call for beeswax candles?"

Another customer came into the store and Mrs Johnson moved off to serve him.

"We don't usually stock them. They tend to be too expensive for our customers, but if you supply them, we can see how they sell?"

"Fair enough."

Mr Johnson looked around to see where his wife was and then said in a lower tone, "Say hello to Miss Sylvie for me, won't you? It's important that we shopkeepers stick together. So much better than competing against each other."

Luke's lips twitched. "I'll do that. Near the church?"

"Yes, that's right."

Luke walked out with a grin.

CHAPTER TWENTY-TWO

L UKE found the place easily. A neat, smart shop painted a very pale, almost lavender blue, it was one of the few buildings that did have a coat of paint. The sign was a work of art. Luke wondered if Mr Samson had done it. He painted nearly all the signs in town, except those of the brothel and the saloon. He'd politely, but firmly declined when asked.

When Luke walked in to 'Miss Sylvie's Haberdashery and Ladies Emporium', as it was called, a small bell rang above the door. The scent of roses and tea wafted through the room. A large Persian rug lay on the floor. Dresses were tastefully arrayed on mannequins. Displays of ribbons and hats graced one counter, and on another, a pair of shoes his mother would have declared 'perfectly delightful', but which wouldn't last two days on the mountain.

He heard someone moving around in the small room that led off the main room. "Hello?" called Luke.

A head popped through the doorway. A small, bird-like woman with large bright eyes and almost blue-black hair piled high with cascading ringlets followed immediately afterwards. She was wearing a tight, pale pink, floral gown with a number of flounces on the bottom and a small bustle on the back. The dress showed off a decidedly hourglass shaped figure to perfection.

"I'm so sorry to have kept you waiting. I'm Miss Sylvie. How may I help you?" She was very feminine. Her voice was as tinkly as the bell above her door. It had a very slight French accent about whose authenticity Luke had some doubts, but it added to her charm. She gave an impression of enthusiasm held in lady-like check, but only just, with a sparkle of mirth bubbling just below the surface. Luke smiled. Mrs Johnson had better watch out.

For some reason, Luke didn't feel at all embarrassed about his mission here. Perhaps it was the utter femininity of the store and its owner. Perhaps it was that improbable French accent.

"My wife needs some clothes," he said.

"I see, and will she be joining us?" the little lady asked brightly.

"No."

Miss Sylvie tilted her head at him.

All of a sudden, Luke wanted to talk about Hope, "Perhaps I'd better explain."

"Wait!" She held up her hand imperiously. "I sense a story and for that we need tea." She slipped, as quickly as she'd appeared, back into the room beyond.

A few moments later, she re-emerged carrying a laden silver tray. Luke took it from her and set it down on the small table between two chairs that stood on one side of the shop.

"Sit, sit," she commanded.

Luke eased himself down on to one of the fragile gilded chairs. They were almost exactly the same chairs his mother had in her dressing room in Boston, only hers, the last time he'd seen them, were covered in pink satin, whereas these were in pale blue velvet. Miss Sylvie poured the tea into delicate china teacups and handed him one. It was very good tea. He was impressed, but then looking round the shop he realised he should have expected it. This was not a cheaply priced general store. His purchases here were going to be costly.

"So, now. Tell me about your wife."

Luke tried to keep it simple, but he found Miss Sylvie very engaging and soon they were laughing over Hope wearing his clothes. Mrs Johnson was in more trouble than she realised.

"So," Miss Sylvie said, "your Hope is in need of clothes, and some other things I imagine. What sort of figure is she?"

Luke stood up. "She's about my height, a little shorter but not much, and she's slim but not thin." His hands moved in the air trying to draw her shape before him.

Miss Sylvie tried not to smile.

"Come with me." She tucked her tiny hand into Luke's arm took him over to the window. "Now, who can you see that most resembles your Hope?"

Luke looked out onto the street. "There, that lady in the blue. Hope is sort of that shape only not quite so..." His hands moved out from his chest. Miss Sylvie giggled. A deep flush swept up from under Luke's collar.

"Not so blessed?" Miss Sylvie smiled mischievously.

He looked at her with a grin. "Hope is blessed with a shape that suits me better." He realised that was true.

What was it about this woman that he could talk so freely to her like this? She was going to make a huge success of her business. He wondered why she'd chosen Silver Birch Landing. She could have set up shop in Boston, New York, London even, and become rich and famous overnight.

"I know just what you mean." She laughed. "And what colour skin, hair and eyes has she?"

"Light, chocolate brown and green."

"Now, Mr Harcourt," she clapped her hands and became business-like in a flash. "If you would sit down and enjoy your tea, I will put together a selection."

She flitted around. Soon piles of clothing lay strewn over the counter. Luke began to worry. This was going to cost a fortune. Besides, he couldn't carry it all, plus the supplies and two pear trees, albeit small ones, on Augustus Brown. But he didn't need to be concerned. To his relief, she went through the pile again, tossing garments she'd changed her mind about onto a chair.

Finally, she turned back to Luke.

"You have bought a grey and a blue serge skirt from the charming Mr Johnson. All of these blouses will go with both of those skirts. Tell me which ones you like the most." She held them up against her one by one. They were all lovely. Luke chose three.

"Those are all practical, yet very pretty. I think your Hope will be pleased."

He liked the way she called her 'your Hope'.

"I have made up a parcel of undergarments I think you will like."

That he'd like? Luke tried not to grin. The chances of him seeing them on Hope were less than small, but he appreciated the sentiment.

"Here are some dresses. Which do you prefer?" She held them up for him to see. He liked all of them but decided on only one. It was a pale yellow with small blue flowers scattered over it.

"Good," chirped Miss Sylvie. "Now, the hat - for Sunday or every day?"

"Every day."

She took down a wide brimmed straw hat encircled with a yellow ribbon. It wasn't quite as practical as it should have been, but it would do the job.

"I have put some green ribbons in the parcel. To match her eyes, you understand?"

He nodded. He was thoroughly enjoying himself. "Nightgowns?" he asked.

Miss Sylvie raised one extremely elegant eyebrow and ran her eyes over him. She clearly saw nothing she could fault. He could feel himself blushing. Again.

"These she needs?" He nodded. She narrowed her eyes. "Hmm. If you insist." She went across to a shelf and took down two of the most exquisite nightgowns he'd ever seen. Not even Tess had owned anything like these. He felt a warm stirring inside him. It occurred to him that he'd like to see Hope wearing these flimsy, almost not-there robes.

"Hope will want something a little less... revealing. Something more modest."

"Like this?" She draped the filmy robes over the chair and shook out a white, lightly embroidered long sleeved, high-necked gown.

"Yes, I'm afraid so." He realised how that sounded and cleared his throat. "It does get cold on the mountain, so that's far more practical."

"Practical!" The little woman gave a lady-like snort. "She has you to keep her warm. She doesn't need this farmer's wife's nightgown."

Luke grinned. "Well, I am a farmer so..." Despite the charm of this lady, he felt no need to explain the sleeping arrangements at the cabin.

Miss Sylvie tossed her head. She clearly had very little opinion of farmers. "Does your Hope need a shawl?"

He nodded. "Better give me a couple. Do you have coats?"

"Practical as well?" Miss Sylvie asked, an ever so slight hint of sarcasm in her voice.

He nodded. She sighed and raised her eyes heavenward but bustled into the back room. She came back with two: a lovely pale blue and a dark brown. Luke sighed. He knew what he'd rather buy and what he should.

"The brown."

Miss Sylvie said nothing except, "Have another cup of tea. I shall wrap these for you." Her imperious tone was back.

He settled the bill, which was just as steep as he'd expected, picked up the fairly bulky parcel and the hatbox. Putting on his hat, he said, "Good day Miss Sylvie. It's been a pleasure."

The doorbell tinkled as she shut it after him.

CHAPTER TWENTY-THREE

WHEN Luke went back to the livery stable to collect Augustus Brown, Mr Samson asked if he wouldn't mind waiting for a few minutes and keeping an eye on things while he went across the road briefly. While he waited, Luke sat down on a hay bale and tallied up his day's purchases. It seemed like a lot of money, but he'd had a good time spending it. He looked forward to seeing Hope's face when she opened the parcel.

The hairs on the back of his neck stood up and a cold feeling swept over him. It was a sensation he'd learned never to ignore. Very carefully he put the two packages out of harm's way and stood up. He took his hat off and put it on top of the parcel. He turned around, his hands hanging loosely at his sides. Leaning against the paddock doorway was Brogan, the brothel guard, an ugly smirk twisting his features.

"Mr Butler wants to talk to you, Harcourt."

"What about?"

"That mountain of yours."

"There's nothing to say. It's still not for sale."

"He ain't gonna be pleased. He wants that land."

Luke gave a slight shrug. Brogan spat, hitched up his trousers and grinned around the butt of the cheap cigar sticking out the corner of his mouth.

"How's the bride, Mr Harcourt? Tired of her yet?"

Luke wasn't going to waste words on this oaf. He could smell the liquor on him from where he stood. The man swaggered towards him till he stood no more than six inches away, towering over Luke.

"I was sorry to see her get bought. She was a prize, a payment of debt you might say, and Mr Butler wasn't pleased when you bought her off him like that."

A debt? Luke put that thought aside swiftly. He'd think about it later.

"She any good?" Brogan asked. "Those quiet ones are often the best whores once they've been broken in. I was looking forward to riding the filly myself. So, what's she like? She a screamer?"

The man reminded him of Tobias John, the kind who liked knives and would probably carry two. Knowing where they were might be important. There was one visible, stuck in his belt. The other would either be in his boot or stuck in his belt at the back. Luke guessed the boot.

Brogan laughed coarsely. "You have ridden her, haven't you? Does she—" He choked; his voice cut short by the agonizing pain that exploded between his legs. He didn't have any time to think about it. Luke slammed his head against the wooden pillar, kneed him in the gut and drove a ferociously hard right into his face. Almost immediately an equally hard left slammed his head against the pillar again. Brogan went down on his knees, his face bleeding. Luke kicked out as hard as he could. But Brogan moved, caught Luke's foot and yanked. Luke hit the ground hard. It drove the breath from his body. Brogan lunged. Luke rolled out of the way just in time. Brogan's fist hit the ground where Luke's head had been a split second before. Luke punched Brogan in the side as hard as he could.

Both men were seasoned fighters. They fought hard and with intent. The horses shifted nervously in the stalls. Luke knew he was in trouble. It usually took three or four men to bring the big man down. Brogan punched Luke hard in the face, sending him spinning into an empty stall. This was worse. The stall gave Brogan the advantage, keeping out of his way would be harder here than out in the open. Luke landed face down. He shook his head. He was dazed. His vision blurred.

Brogan laughed and walked into the stall. He bent, reaching for Luke. Luke twisted and Brogan found himself face to face with Luke's long barrelled Colt. Luke slowly pulled the hammer back, hoping his vision would clear quickly.

"Now, you don't want to do that, Harcourt," Brogan said. "You'd end up in jail, and then who'd take care of your little whore?"

"Not you, sir," said a voice behind him. Brogan turned his head only to have it beaten into oblivion from the stock end of Mr Samson's rifle. Brogan collapsed unconscious on top of Luke.

"I apologise for taking so long, Mr Harcourt. Are you all right?"

Luke pushed Brogan off and gratefully took hold of the hand Mr Samson held out. He was whole, but a little shaky. "I'm glad you came when you did."

"Sit here."

Luke perched on the hay bale.

"Drink this." Mr Samson handed him a bottle of brandy. Luke took a swig. It tasted expensive.

"I didn't know you drank, Mr Samson," he said.

"I keep it only for medicinal purposes, Mr Harcourt, purely medicinal." A brief smile twitched his lips.

Luke grinned. "Like now."

"Exactly. Please, have some more. I believe it will do you good."

"No doubt about that. What are we going to do about him?" He nodded back towards the stall.

"If you would hold this on him, in case he wakes up, I will endeavour to find the constable. He may possibly offer the gentleman accommodation for the night."

Luke gave a short laugh. He enjoyed the donnish way the old man spoke. He took the shotgun out of his hands. The old black man bowed courteously and strode from the barn. Luke took another swig of the expensive brandy and rested his back against the wooden pillar.

The sun was starting to set, and its long golden rays slanted in through the open doors. It wasn't long before Mr Samson returned with the constable and the two deputies.

"Evening Harcourt," the constable said.

"Evening Carter."

"You fall down?"

"A number of times."

"You should be more careful."

"I'll do my best."

The constable squatted and had a look at the supine Brogan. "Seems he's been falling a fair bit as well."

"Not as much as me, unfortunately."

"Maybe, but he has a longer way to fall, which would account for the mess his face is in."

Luke took another pull at the brandy. Carter gave a soft snort and pushed himself to his feet. "Take him boys."

The two men who'd come with Carter dragged Brogan out none too gently.

"'Night, Harcourt. Mr Samson." The constable tipped his hat and followed the men out.

Luke had drunk a fair amount of the brandy. His head was a bit fuzzy. He handed the bottle back to Mr Samson. He'd buy him another one before he left town.

"If you would be so good as to sit here where the light is better, I will see to your face, Mr Harcourt. That's a nasty split you have over that eye." Luke moved to the chair Mr Samson set for him.

"Now," continued the elderly man. "If you don't mind my asking, what was that all about?"

"He insulted Hope." Luke didn't really want to discuss it. Besides, his face hurt.

"How is Mrs Harcourt?" asked the old man. He'd taken out a small box with lint, cotton wool and a bottle of iodine in it. He filled a basin with some water from the bucket and began cleaning up Luke's face.

"She's fine."

"Is she settling in to life on the mountain?"

"She's trying to."

"How are you two getting on?"

Luke was annoyed. It was none of the old man's business. He didn't say anything for a while. Perhaps it was the brandy, Mr Samson's calm courtesy, the settling of the day into night, or the fact Mr Samson had just saved his life, and wasn't the kind of man who would blab to anyone else, but the quiet stable somehow took on the air of a confessional.

"She's had a rough time," he finally said. "She was attacked and almost raped by Tobias John. She almost set herself on fire and she's had to deal with Indians and wolves since she's been there."

Mr Samson looked shocked at the news about Tobias John. "I do trust that she is fully recovered from her ordeal?"

"Yes, she is now. She's a good woman."

"I thought so the moment I met her. This may sting a little." Mr Samson applied the iodine. It did sting. "I'm glad you like her."

"Well, yes, I haven't thought about it."

"Yes, you have," he said.

Luke's eyebrows snapped together. He shot him a look.

"You may not realise it Mr Harcourt, but it is obvious that you have some of the more tender feelings a man enjoys towards Mrs Harcourt. Does she feel the same way about you?"

Luke couldn't believe he was having this conversation. "I don't know. She doesn't...I don't know." It occurred to him that it was more than some tender feelings. The thought lifted his spirit one second and then made his heart constrict. Was he falling in love? Was he already in love with Hope? He'd been determined that it was something he'd never do again.

"Why don't you ask her?" said Mr Samson matter-of-factly.

The question shocked Luke. How could he ask her when he'd made it clear he wasn't interested in her as a wife? She might get the wrong idea entirely. Although, she did blush when he looked at her. That meant nothing - she might simply be shy. And another thing - if he did ask and she felt nothing for him it would make living together very uncomfortable. But the seed had been sown. What did Hope feel for him, how was he going to find out, and what was he going to do about it?

Luke stayed the night at the hotel. Sleeping in a comfortable bed once again— he hadn't realised how much he'd missed it. The moment his head hit the pillow he was unconscious.

When he woke, the sun was just rising, its long rays slipped over the windowsill and slanted across the bed. He was almost about to roll over and go back to sleep when he remembered Mr Samson's question from the night before - does she feel the same way about you?

Although he still wasn't perfectly sure how he felt about Hope, he thought about Mr Samson's question. He thought about Hope. He tried to define what it was that he liked about her.

She was taller than most women. A lot of men would find that intimidating. She was quieter, calmer and smarter than most of them as well. He'd stopped thinking of her as plain, but he hadn't thought further than that.

Well, apart from those mesmerising green eyes that he could feel himself drowning in every time he looked into them... that thick chocolate hair he wanted to sink his hands into... and the creamiest skin he'd ever seen.

She apologised quicker and easier than any woman he'd ever met. She was shy, modest, hard-working. There had to be something...she could be stubborn, well, so could nearly everyone he knew. Including himself.

Yes, he knew what annoyed him - she expected nothing. The list was a good example. She was ready to accept or agree to whatever he wanted. But probably not a change in the sleeping arrangements. She seldom did anything she wanted. She demanded nothing. It did annoy him. He wanted her to fight back, stamp her feet - although there had been the 'discussion' about the vegetable garden.

He threw back the blanket. It was time to go home.

He collected Augustus Brown and picked up his purchases at the general store. Thomas had rigged together a sling that worked the same as saddlebags to hold the small trees. The hatbox was a nuisance. The other bulky parcels weren't much better. Luke made double sure they were strapped on well. He hoped he didn't look as much like an itinerant peddler as he felt. He wasn't the only one. Augustus Brown was fairly insulted that he'd been turned into a pack animal, but a handful of carrots persuaded him. They made a nice change from apples.

As they wound their way through town Augustus Brown suddenly stopped and refused to go any further. Nothing Luke did would make him go on. He kept shaking his head and pulling on the reins, trying to get his head down. Perhaps one of the parcels was slipping. Luke dismounted to check. The parcels were fine. He was just about to remount when he saw Augustus Brown nosing something in front of him. He looked again. It was a tiny ball of fluff. Luke went 'round to have a closer look.

A minute kitten was patting at the huge horse's nose. Luke was amazed. It was fearless in the presence of Augustus Brown. He picked up the kitten. It was completely one shade of dark grey with no variation anywhere.

He was never sure why he did it. Perhaps it was because the kitten had the same colour eyes as Hope, but he tucked it into his waistcoat. It wriggled 'round till its head was poking out and then seemed to settle down. He could have sworn it even sighed contentedly. The kitten now safe, Augustus Brown moved off as soon as Luke was back in the saddle.

It was an interesting journey home. That night, as he sat in front of the fire, Luke watched in amusement as the kitten attacked the ends of Augustus Brown's tail switching back and forwards. Luke stretched out on his blankets and tipped his hat over his eyes. That seemed to be the kitten's cue. She jumped onto Luke's stomach and batted the brim of his hat. Luke flicked her paw with a finger.

"No. Go to sleep, Harriet."

The newly christened Harriet curled up on Luke's stomach and yawned. Her own belly was fat and round, stuffed almost to exploding point with meat from Luke's dinner. Luke only moved her when the little thing started to dream. Her paws twitched, digging needle sharp little claws into his stomach. Moving her barely woke her. She rolled over, curled up even tighter, covered her face with her paws and went straight back to sleep with a sigh.

During the day, when she wasn't asleep inside his waistcoat, Harriet rode sitting on the saddle in front of Luke, behind him perched on the hat box, or on his shoulder, making Luke feel more like an eccentric salesman than ever. All he needed was striped gaiters and a long peacock feather sticking out of an old top hat.

The first time Harriet tried to climb onto his shoulder it was a painful experience for both of them. But the next time, she simply leapt gracefully up and sat there looking back the way they had come, her tail twitching against Luke's jaw every now and then.

"You're a nuisance Harriet, you know that?" Luke complained once.

The kitten turned her head and chirped in Luke's ear, her long whiskers tickling his face. When she was tired, Harriet climbed back into Luke's waistcoat and dozed. It was fine for now, as she was so little and it was the safest place for her to sleep while they were on the horse, but Luke hoped she would grow out of this habit. He wasn't having some large fully-grown cat trying to get in there.

CHAPTER TWENTY-FOUR

H E'D been gone a week. Hope had always scoffed when young wives complained when their men were absent, leaving them alone for even two nights, but now she found herself in the same situation.

At first, her concern was simply being alone. After Tobias John, she could hardly bear to let Luke out of her sight. Now, when he wasn't around, her fears surfaced again. She kept Wolf close by all the time. For the first two days, when she left the cabin, she stayed in the yard. She went outside only when she absolutely needed to do the chores. Hope had to do Luke's as well as her own. The only one she'd thought would be a problem was getting the mules back into the barn at night. Thankfully, they simply followed the goat. Franklin had taken a shine to Hope. It didn't take much to get her to come into the barn.

Hope was also running short of wood. She imagined Luke would be back soon, but she decided to pick up the axe and do the job herself. After all, it couldn't be that hard. She found the axe in the barn. Its length and weight surprised her. Once outside at the stump, she tried to remember what Luke did. She realised that when she'd watched him chopping wood, she'd been watching him and not the task in hand.

She laid the log she was going to split on the stump, and with a grunt swung the axe, completely missing the stump, never mind the log. Her next attempt was better; at least she hit the stump. But now she couldn't get the axe out again.

She yanked and pulled but it wouldn't move. She put her foot against the stump and heaved. Her hands slipped and she fell on her backside with a thump. She sighed. Now she'd broken Luke's axe.

Wonderful. He'd be so pleased.

There must be some way to get it out of that stump. She got up and dusted her hands off. She took hold of the axe handle one more time and gave a yank. It didn't move.

She was so focused on what she was doing that she didn't notice Adam White Knife nudge his horse out of the forest and walk it towards her, until he spoke.

"Good morning, Hope."

She whirled round. "Oh goodness. You gave me such a fright! Hello, Adam White Knife. How are you?"

He dipped his head in acknowledgement.

"I'm afraid Luke's not here. He should be back any day though." She wiped her forehead.

"A deer." He gestured at the dead animal draped over his horse. "I'll put it there." Long sentences were in short supply with the Nlaka'pamux.

He nudged the horse toward the smokehouse. Hope tried again to pull the stubborn axe out of the stump. It wouldn't budge. She sighed. When Adam White Knife returned, he took hold of the axe handle, gave it a wiggle and it came free. Hope harrumphed, which made him smile slightly. He put the log the right way up on the stump, swung the axe and split the log.

He put another log on and gave the axe back to Hope. Wrapping her hands around the handle she took a step closer to the stump. Just as she was about to lift it, Adam stopped her, rearranged her hands and pulled her arms further back.

"Up here, then down," he said.

This time, she actually hit the log, which stuck to the axe. Adam took the axe from her and thumped it down to split the log all the way through. He put another in its place and handed the axe back to her. "Harder."

It worked. The log split the first time. He nodded. "Again."

He made her do it a few more times to ensure she had it before he mounted his horse, nodded goodbye and made his way into the forest.

Hope was delighted with her new skill and split logs all afternoon, until she could barely lift the axe anymore. By the time she'd stacked the wood and toted water for a hot bath, her shoulders were burning. She lay back in the water. After a few minutes of quiet soaking, the water soothing her tired body and mind, she fell asleep.

The next day she'd realised she couldn't let fear rule her or she'd become one of those awful, clinging-ivy type women. And she didn't have anyone to cling to. Luke wasn't her husband and he didn't love her. She would have to face her fears. She would have to go beyond the yard. If she didn't, Tobias John had won.

That thought alone had been enough to make her get up early and go outside. She forced herself to go to the orchard and stay there all day, cutting alfalfa for the animals.

By mid-afternoon, she had a heat-induced headache and went to the river to lie back in the cool water and try to think of something else except the possibility of Tobias John returning.

She thought about Luke. It wasn't so much thinking about Luke, as letting his face, the image of him, hang in the air in front of her. It was clearer when she closed her eyes. She felt again the way her skin grew hot when his hands touched her. She tried not to think about how he went out of his way not to touch her. Then, all she could think of were his hands, how strong they were and yet so gentle when he'd brushed her hair. She remembered his eyes when he'd coaxed her out from under the shelf in the larder.

ELAINE DODGE

The thing she remembered most about that time, after
Tobias John, was the comfort of falling asleep in Luke arms.

Hope's headache faded after the cool bathe in the river
and a few long, cool glasses of spring water. She strolled
back to the cabin to change. Wolf was getting in her way
this afternoon, constantly underfoot. Perhaps he was missing Luke as much as she was. She put the wildflowers she'd
picked near the river into a jug and turned to Wolf. She gave
him a hug and a good rub and scratch behind his ears. He
pushed his head against her hand, giving little whines of
delight. Pushing him out of the way she shut the cabin door
and pulled off her damp shift, putting on her clean skirt and
shirt instead.

Despite her gratitude to Lee-Ming for the clothes, she
longed for something more feminine to wear.

She longed for Luke to come back.

Wolf jumped up and ran to the door wagging his tail.
He looked back at Hope and whined, sniffing at the door,
scratching at it, his tail wagging.

"Oh no, Wolf," she sighed. "It's too hot for a walk, even
in the forest."

Wolf scratched at the door again. Hope's heart gave a
skip. Luke! She felt breathless. She almost ran to the door
and wrenched it open. There was no one there.

She felt literally ill with disappointment. Hope stood still,
hoping the nausea would go soon. She closed her eyes and
took a few very slow shallow breaths, then a deeper one.
Wolf cannoned into her, almost knocking her over. He leapt
up at her again and raced off. She watched him go and that's
when she saw Augustus Brown coming across the yard, with
Luke sitting on top of the large horse. Her heart banged
against her ribs. She'd forgotten how just the sight of him
made her heart dance. She wanted to fling her arms around
his neck, then she saw his face.

He'd been in a fight. The bruises were fading, and the cuts were healing but it looked like it'd been a nasty battle.

Luke had seen her long before she'd looked up. Just the sight of her standing at the cabin door and he knew he'd come home. The delight on her face made his heart beat faster. He nudged the horse into a faster gait. He had a sudden urge to leap off, sweep her up in his arms and kiss her. He tipped his hat at her and grinned.

But then, her smile faded, and a frown crinkled her forehead. What was the problem? Whatever it was, there wasn't going to be any leaping off the horse and grand gestures of welcome. Luke rode the horse into the shade of the oak, dismounted and began untying the parcels. Wolf was yelping and leaping up at him.

Luke had one parcel free by the time Hope walked over. The frown had vanished, but her eyes were filled with concern. She tentatively lifted a hand and touched his face. He stood very still. It was the first time she'd ever deliberately reached out to touch him. He hadn't shaved that morning and the bristle rasped against her fingers.

"You're hurt."

He'd forgotten the fight, the few remaining bruises and the cut over his eye. He wondered how bad it looked. "It's nothing," he said.

For a moment, her fingers rested lightly on his cheek, then she pulled her hand away quickly. Her gentle touch left a cool place on his skin.

"Hello, Hope," he said, he couldn't help a smile breaking out as he handed her the hatbox from Miss Sylvie.

"Welcome home, Luke." Hope smiled back at him. The expression on his face confused her; she looked away hurriedly. Her eyes fell on the pear trees. "You have trees." She felt foolish. Of course he did, there they were, as large as life.

"Yes. I thought we could plant them on either side of the cabin door."

"How lovely."

He frowned at her. "Is that where you want them? I'll plant them anywhere you like."

She was a bit taken aback. "On each side of the door is perfect." It would be handy when they started producing fruit, the breeze would blow their scent into the cabin and they'd provide some shade when they got bigger.

His frown deepened. She tilted her head, her eyebrows twitching slightly together. "Don't you want to put them there?"

"Where do *you* want them, Hope?"

"I think on either side of the door is a good place."

"Are you sure?"

"Yes." She couldn't figure out why was this so important. "The more I think about it, the more I like the idea. But..."

"But what?"

"Well..."

"Spit it out, Hope."

"It's your home, I don't want— I mean, it's your home so you must put them wherever you'd be happiest with them."

His eyes narrowed. "It's your home as well, Hope, so where do you want the pear trees?" His voice had an edge.

She swallowed. This wasn't the homecoming she'd dreamed of. "The front door."

He turned back to the horse. "Fine. Here," he said giving her the other parcels. "Can you manage these as well? I'll see to Augustus Brown." Luke led the horse to the barn, Wolf still jumping up at him.

CHAPTER TWENTY-FIVE

HOPE dropped the parcels on the table. She quickly made some coffee and put a generous slice of freshly made apple pie and cream on a plate for Luke. She wasn't sure what she'd said wrong, but Luke clearly wasn't happy. She didn't want him to think she was taking him, or his home, for granted.

She was very aware that without Luke she would be in dire straits. Actually, without Luke, she'd be one of the girls at the Bright Star! But having a safe home wasn't the only reason she was here. Even if Luke had nothing, she knew she wouldn't want to be anywhere without him. Not unless he threw her out.

Perhaps she was reading too much into this.

Hope made a conscious effort to put the matter out of her mind and think about something else. The hatbox and the two brown paper parcels looked very interesting. Hope was almost beside herself with curiosity. The corner of one parcel had a small tear in it. It beckoned her. She gently lifted the tear and looked closer. Luke came into the cabin and caught her. She leaped away from the table.

"How was your trip?" she asked, almost stuttering with embarrassment as Luke hung his hat up, unstrapped his gun belt, and sat at the table running his hands through his hair with a sigh. She put the pie and a cup of coffee in front of him.

"Good. It was good." He dug into the pie and chewed. He groaned with pleasure. "This is great pie." He took another huge mouthful.

"Did Augustus Brown behave himself?"

Luke hesitated, unsure what she meant.

"At the farriers? When you had him re-shod?" she added.

"Oh, yes. As always. Wolf, down." This last to the inquisitive mutt that kept nosing at him. The wolf thumped his backside on the floor, his eyes fixed on Luke.

"Did you see the Lees? How is Mr Samson?" Hope asked.

"The Lees and Mr Samson send their regards. So does Constable Carter, by the way." He picked up the coffee cup and took a hefty gulp. He choked, spluttering and coughing.

"Is it still bad?" She bit her bottom lip anxiously. "I've been practising. I'd hoped I was better at it."

He laughed, wiping his mouth with the back of his hand. "Tell you what, you stick to apple pie and I'll keep making the coffee." He manoeuvred another piece of pie onto his fork. "Why don't you open the parcels?"

She turned to the nearest one, untied the string and pulled open the brown paper. It was the general store parcel. She drew out the boots first.

"I hope they fit," Luke said.

"They're for me?"

"They're not quite my style so I guess you better have them." He grinned. "I know they're not very elegant, but I figured you needed something a little sturdier for up here than the shoes you have."

Hope tried them on. They were almost her size. A little big but no matter. She gave a quick prayer of thankfulness. Her own thin shoes were fast falling apart. In fact, she would have been barefoot in a few weeks. "Thank you so much, Luke."

"I hope the rest of the stuff fits as well as they do."

She found the skirts. Taking the blue one out she held it up against herself. "I think they'll be fine," she said, removing the other one and laying them down carefully on the bed. She was amazed at the gifts, but a twinge of disappointment tugged at her. These were good, practical clothes and would last a long time. A *long* time. She was grateful for them, but, oh, how much she longed for something pretty. She gave a small sigh. With something else to wear she need never wear Luke's clothes again just to do the washing.

Of course, she'd never admit to sleeping in one of his shirts. It had brought a measure of comfort, his scent in the material was a reminder of those dark times when she'd fallen asleep in his arms, when only his voice had driven away the nightmares. Coming back to the table, she sat down, hands folded in her lap.

He recognized the signs. She was going to say something serious. His lips twitched.

"Thank you, Luke. That was very thoughtful and kind. I'm very grateful."

So, she's 'grateful' but not excited by the practical clothes. He didn't mind; he hadn't expected her to be. He hadn't been that impressed with them either. He really wanted to see her open the other parcel.

She glanced up, and then laughed, which surprised him. "Who have you got there?"

He'd gotten so used to the small wriggles of the kitten, he'd completely forgotten Harriet was inside his waistcoat. No wonder Wolf had been so interested in him since he got back. The talking had wakened Harriet and she'd popped her head out and was blinking at Hope with huge green eyes. She yawned and then struggled to free herself. Luke pulled her out, handing her across to Hope. The little cat stretched her neck and sniffed at Hope, reaching out a small paw to pat her face. Hope laughed.

"Hello, little one," she said delightedly. "Who are you and where did you come from?"

"Her name's Harriet. I'm not sure if Augustus Brown found her or if she accosted him, but he refused to leave without her." Luke entertained her with the story of how they'd nearly ridden over Harriet, how the tiny feline wasn't afraid of large horses or heights and how she enjoyed riding on his shoulder. The kitten wandered across the table and was investigating the jug of cream, which was taller than she was.

"Oh, no you don't, madam," said Hope and was about to put her on the floor when Wolf stood up. He'd been staring at the small creature the entire time. Hope looked anxiously at Luke, who shrugged.

"Only one way to find out," he said, but he laid his hand on Wolf's ruff anyway, and nodded to Hope. She'd have to do it, but she really didn't want to. She put the tiny kitten on the floor and held her breath. Wolf stretched out his neck and sniffed at her. The kitten's hair shot up all over her little body. Arching her back, she hissed, spitting violently, swiping sharp talons across Wolf's nose. Wolf got such a fright he yelped, leaped back, scattering a chair, almost turning a somersault in his desire to escape. He raced out of the cabin. The kitten's fur slowly laid back down, she began to clean her paw as if scaring wolves was something she did every day.

"Well, now we know. Our Wolf is a coward." Luke laughed. He stood up. "I'm going to the river to bathe. After that, I'll see what I can get us for dinner."

"Oh, you don't have to," Hope said. "Adam White Knife came by a few days ago, with a deer. It's hanging in the smokehouse."

"Really? That was good of him."

"He also taught me how to chop wood."

"He did?" He was annoyed at the quick twist of jealousy he felt. If there was anyone he could trust, it would be Adam White Knife.

183

She laughed. "I think he had the same opinion of my wood chopping skills as my shooting skills."

"Then he obviously hasn't seen you shoot lately. Why don't you pack the rest of that stuff away?"

"Is this parcel the supplies?" she asked.

"Yes. Something like that." He took out some clean clothes went down to the river.

Hope put down a saucer of milk for Harriet and then, unable to restrain herself any longer, opened the other parcels. Inside the smaller one were the spices and seed packets. This man was so kind. After she'd been so rude he'd still bought seeds for a vegetable garden. She vowed never to complain again.

There was also a toothbrush, hairbrush and comb. Luke lived in a cabin, and although it was better furnished than she ever expected a cabin to be - if she'd ever thought about it - he didn't live like a wealthy man, most likely every cent mattered and here he was spending it on her. A wave of guilt for not being generously thankful for the boots and the skirts lapped at her conscience.

She opened the other parcel and abruptly sat down. It was filled with beautiful fabrics, delicate, feminine clothes. Everything was perfect, exactly the right size, in colours that couldn't have suited her better if she'd chosen them herself. Overwhelmed with his generosity she knew she'd done nothing to deserve this.

Luke had been right, Hope loved the nightgown, with the gossamer lace edging and the delicate embroidery around the cuffs and the neckline, it already felt like a friend.

The blouses were definitely not shirts, but delightful, pretty tops that would make her feel like a woman again. Especially the blue one. Once on, it moulded itself to her. She quickly redid her hair, brushing it till it shone and sweeping it into a soft pile on the top of her head. Soft curls escaped, framing her face. It felt good not to have it all pulled back into the usual practical knot on the back of her neck.

Picking up the dress and holding it against herself, she wished there was a mirror to see what it looked like. She'd save it for a special occasion. Having no idea when that would be it might be a waste to wait, so she decided that it would be Sundays. Yes, they never worked then, it being the Sabbath, and if not loafing around the cabin reading, they went instead for walks in the forest, sometimes hunting for mushrooms or nuts. She would wear it then.

The hat was a complete surprise. It's sweeping brim and wide yellow ribbon, which exactly matched the dress, was the most romantic hat she'd ever seen. She put it on and twirled around the room in it, feeling delicious. It made her think of the afternoon tea parties on wide green lawns under the oaks and the delicate china teacups they'd used at home. She wouldn't have dreamed of wearing those ugly boots then, or in fact ever, but Luke was right, up here in the mountains they were definitely required footwear.

She put the hat carefully back into the box, first taking out the kitten who'd climbed in to explore the heavenly depths of the tissue paper inside.

There was one last parcel left. The brown paper crackled under her fingers. She gave a soft gasp. There, beneath her hands, lay undergarments that eclipsed even the beautiful pieces Lee-Ming had given her. These were never meant to be purely practical. She was covered with embarrassment. She'd never had garments like these, ever! Had Luke chosen them for her? Just the thought of Luke touching them made her blush. Her mind leapt unbidden to the thought of her wearing them, Luke's hand on them. The room seemed too hot, airless. She carefully re-wrapped the parcel and laid it on the shelf with the one from Lee-Ming.

Hope was laying the table for dinner when Luke returned. She thought she'd recovered her composure, but, thanks to the smile in his eyes, she knew she was blushing again.

"I'll do that," he took the plates from her, his hands accidentally brushing hers. Startled, she turned back to the fireplace in confusion, her fingers lifted to the top buttons on her blouse. Hope was so aware of Luke she could barely breathe. Her mind was still full of the lacy underwear and the possibility of Luke having chosen it that when his hands had touched hers the shock was startling.

"That blouse looks nice. I'm glad it fits. It suits you." He was startled to realise that she was, in fact, quite pretty. That light, indigo blue turned her eyes a deeper shade of green and made her hair look richer. He liked the different way she'd done it as well. He preferred this to that tight bun she always wore it in. He wanted to reach out and loosen it, let it fall. His eyes lingered on her long, slender neck. He wondered what it would taste like.

He needed to get a grip on himself.

As he laid the table, Luke saw that all the parcels had been packed away, including, maybe especially, the one with the undergarments from Miss Sylvie. He wondered if Hope was wearing any of it. Was that why she was blushing? What exactly had Miss Sylvie put in that parcel?

Thanks to Tess, he had a fairly good knowledge of expensive and lacy female apparel and he grinned to himself. He felt a slight regret at being a gentleman with a code of behaviour which, knowing what was wrapped in the brown paper, meant a trip to the river rather than staying to watch her open it.

CHAPTER TWENTY-SIX

SUPPER was over. Luke helped to clear the table, said goodnight and was on his way out to the barn.

"Luke?" Hope came out onto the porch, trying to meet his eyes but failing. His mouth twisted in amusement.

"Thank you so much for all those clothes. I didn't expect— I mean, you didn't have to...I—"

"Yes, I did. You needed them. If they fit you and you like them, then good. I take it you do like them?" There was a note of rough anxiety in his voice now.

"Yes, yes, I do. They're beautiful. They fit perfectly. Thank you. I'm very grateful."

"My pleasure." He turned away.

"Luke?" She put her hand on his arm to stop him. She hesitated and then quickly placed a soft kiss on his cheek. "Thank you." Hope whirled away and went swiftly back into the cabin, shutting the door.

He stood, staring at the closed door. He could still feel her lips on his cheek and smell the light perfume of her hair. He took a step towards the door, his hand on the latch. He hesitated, then turned and walked swiftly to the barn.

*

It was very early the next morning when Luke went down to the river before dawn. He hadn't slept well. Hope was just coming out of the barn, having milked Pinkerton and was carrying the full, heavy milk pail, when he walked in. They collided at the barn door.

"I'm sorry." Luke took hold of Hope's arms to steady her. She looked tired. There were soft lavender smudges under her eyes. Her lips curved in a shy smile. The temptation was too great. He leaned in, but she pulled away quickly. He stepped back at once.

"I'm sorry, this pail is heavy, I need to—"

"Let me." Luke took it from her and moved aside to let her pass through the door. They started to walk back to the cabin.

"I thought I'd make pancakes for breakfast," Hope said, filling the awkward silence.

"Sounds good."

The silence stretched again.

"Would you like them with cinnamon and honey or..."

"Sure," he replied.

Had he been going to kiss her or was that just her imagination? She felt so foolish and clumsy around Luke. Even more so as she fell deeper in love with him. Had Tess ever been as silly or awkward as she was? She'd probably been sophisticated, assured and confident, as well as beautiful, which is why Luke had loved her. Hope took a deep breath.

The only men Hope had ever really spent time with had been her father and brother. She'd never really learned how to behave around other men. She was shy of them. She expected the same kind of relationship with them as she'd known with her father and Charlie. Sometimes it frightened her to know that other men wanted more. And now, so did she. The force of her feelings for Luke scared her. Even though she couldn't really define or wouldn't let herself define them.

A memory surfaced abruptly, like a slap in the face.

Her cousin's wedding celebration.

A handsome young lieutenant who made her laugh.

After the ceremony, they spent the afternoon chatting and walking through the gardens together. He brought her a small glass of champagne and a plate of sandwiches. They sat on the lawn, making up highly unlikely stories about the other guests also enjoying the sun-drenched afternoon. It was innocent and hardly flirtatious at all.

When he said goodbye at the large, white fountain, joyously bursting, cascading exuberantly with water in the centre of the park, he bent over her hand and kissed it, giving it a slight squeeze.

"Thank you, Miss Booker, for a thoroughly enjoyable afternoon. Will you be at the ball this evening? If you are, perhaps you would do me the honour of dancing with me?"

She dressed with care, putting on her most feminine gown and a very small amount of perfume. She was on her way downstairs when her mother called her into her bedroom. The scent of lilies suffocated the silver and yellow room.

Without preamble her mother asked quietly, "Why was that young man talking to you all afternoon?"

Hope began to feel shaky. She always did when her mother questioned her. "What do you mean?"

"Was he drunk?"

"What? No."

"So, it was you?"

"I only had half a glass of champagne!" she cried.

"Don't be so melodramatic, Hope. I don't think you were drunk," said her mother looking at her own flawless reflection in the mirror. "I do think though, that if he wasn't drunk, then you must have behaved in a most unladylike manner. Quite like a whore in fact to have encouraged him like that."

Hope felt sick and faint. The best day of her life was ruined. Without another word she turned around and went quietly back to her room and shut the door.

Now, walking beside him, she was more aware of Luke than ever. *Oh God, I shouldn't have kissed him!* How could she have been so stupid, so forward, so sluttish?

They'd reached the cabin and Luke stood back to let Hope go in ahead of him. Her face had lost its colour. "Are you all right?" he asked. She didn't answer. She just stood there, her thoughts a million miles away. "Hope?"

She looked up. "Oh, I'm sorry, I was daydreaming. What did you say?"

Daydreaming? He'd always thought daydreams were supposed to be happy. Whatever she'd been thinking about certainly wasn't giving her much joy.

"I was just asking if you were feeling all right. You look a little pale."

"Oh, no, I'm fine. I probably just need some breakfast," she said with a slight smile. She stood up a little straighter, "I'll get started on that right away." She stepped through the door ahead of him.

He frowned, he didn't like that lost look trying to hide at the back of her eyes.

*

They were finishing breakfast when Harriet jumped onto the table. Luke picked her up and put her back on the floor. The kitten sat there staring unblinkingly up at him and then leapt onto his knee. She mewed and rubbed herself against Luke. She stood up, her front paws against Luke's chest, stretched to pat his face and mewed again.

Luke smiled and poured out a saucer of milk, putting both the dish and the kitten on the floor. Harriet rubbed herself against Luke's leg before going to lap her fill of the fresh, warm milk.

"You would have gone with anyone just to get a roof over your head and food handed out to you, wouldn't you? And you'll flirt with me just to keep it all, you little trollop."

He scratched the kitten's head. Straightening up, he saw Hope staring at him. Her eyes were huge, her face white. She turned away quickly but what he'd seen in her expression had rocked him. Why was she so upset?

"Hope?"

He saw her take a deep breath. "Is that what you think?" Her voice was small. "That I—" she stopped.

Luke frowned. "What? I was talking to the cat, Hope. Not you."

She nodded, but he could see the rigidity in her back. He pushed himself away from the table and swung her around to face him. "Hope. No one could ever think of you as a, a trollop. In any way. Look at me."

Her eyes were swimming in tears. "I certainly don't," he continued. She sniffed. "It's the first thing I saw in you. The fact that you're a lady."

A small smile flickered bravely at the corners of her mouth. He wanted to wipe away the tears. He wanted to kiss— he dropped his hands. "I want to get the vegetable garden in today. Will you give me a hand?"

She nodded, wiping her eyes with the edge of her apron, and squared her shoulders. Luke smothered a grin.

"How big do you want it?" he asked.

"Um, how about ten feet by twenty feet?"

He cocked an eyebrow at her. "You sure?"

"We can always make it bigger, or smaller, later."

"True." He liked the 'we'.

Her smile didn't reach her eyes yet, but it looked a smudge healthier. Perhaps this would work. Give her something else to think about.

"Right, let's get to work." He rubbed his hands together. "I'll get the spade." He strode out of the cabin, clapping his hat on his head as he went. Even though her hands were still shaking a little, his enthusiasm was contagious. She dug the seed packets out of the dresser drawer.

By mid-afternoon the bed was dug, Luke had turned in some manure from the animals' stalls and they'd planted nearly all the seeds. They were sitting under the shade of the tree near the barn having a late lunch.

Almost without thinking Luke said, "I know it hasn't been easy. It's probably not what you expected...a marriage to be. It's not what either of us wanted, but I'm glad you're here."

He smiled at her, hoisted himself to his feet, collected the tools and went to start digging the holes for the pear trees.

Hope sighed. He was glad she was here. That was something. It was better than what he'd said earlier.

To the cat. What he'd said to the cat.

Would she ever hear him say what her heart craved?

CHAPTER TWENTY-SEVEN

LITTLE green shoots sprouted quickly and soon became sturdy plants. The beans and peas began their climb towards the sun, twining their delicate hooks around the sticks Luke had put in to support them, clinging to each other as if they couldn't bear to be apart. The tomatoes blushed in the sun, lettuce frilled their way along the rows. A very narrow band of rue planted around the vegetable garden kept the insects and even the birds at bay.

It wasn't long before Hope gathered her first early harvest. Luke decided to give her a hand. It made a nice change from the orchard.

Although he'd finally admitted to himself that he liked her, he still wasn't sure how she felt about him. He found reasons to spend more time around her. Working together in the garden, listening to her humming gently and talking to the plants, gave him a measure of comfort he hadn't felt for many years. Her sense of the ridiculous delighted him. She was a bright woman and although not really a chatty female, she occasionally initiated conversations on subjects that surprised him and showed a clever mind at work behind that lovely face.

She was lovely, with those high cheekbones, green eyes, and chocolate brown hair that always smelled like an early morning. He frowned and yanked out a weed that had taken root amongst the cabbages spraying dirt everywhere. A splutter of laughter from Hope didn't improve matters.

The day had started out cool, but as the sun rose it burned away the softness and replaced it with a blistering oven-like heat. After a few hours, it became knee-cracking work bending over in the garden. There wasn't even a breeze. At least in the orchard he could work under the shade of the apple trees. The sweat made his shirt stick to his back. Under her broad brimmed hat Hope still looked cool. How did she manage to do it? A flicker of annoyance licked at his mind. She'd planted far too many seeds; they'd never eat all this before it went off. What a waste.

"Do you think that the same people who buy your apples, and hopefully soon the honey, would also buy eggs?" she asked.

"Yes, I suppose so. Why? Do you want chickens now?"

She was so wrapped up in her thoughts about the eggs she missed the slight grumpiness in his voice. "Do you think we'd be able to transport them to town without breaking them?"

Hmm. She'd clearly been thinking about this. He didn't want to get railroaded into something till he'd had a chance to mull it over.

"We'd need a fair amount of chickens to make it viable," he said discouragingly, "and a lot more trips into town to sell them." This was a bad idea. Going to town more often was not high on his list of priorities.

"Maybe if we packed them in hay, we wouldn't lose too many."

Was she even listening to him? It sounded like she'd made up her mind already.

"How many chickens were you thinking of?" he asked.

"A hundred?"

"A hundred! Are you insane?"

He saw her back stiffen. He stiffened in retaliation; this was shaping up to becoming a fight. He didn't want chickens. "I'm not having a hundred chickens running around the place."

"Why not?"

"We'd lose all of them in a week."

"Why?"

"Wolves, for one thing."

"We could build a coop for them."

We? *We* wouldn't do anything of the kind. He would have to. And he wasn't going to. It would be a huge coop. One hundred chickens. The woman was off her rocker.

"I was thinking we could put it over there," she continued.

"No."

"Isn't that a good spot?"

"We're not getting a hundred chickens, Hope."

"How many do you think we'd need? If we're going to make any money—"

"We're not making money off eggs. We don't need it."

Now, she was cross. He wasn't listening. Why couldn't he see what a good plan this was? "I'll look after them, you won't have to do a thing," she said crossly.

"Yeah, right. Except build a massive coop, deal with the chickens that die, and they will, or wring their necks when you want to cook them, and I'll be the one that has to take the eggs to town!" His look said it all. "We're not getting them!" They were almost shouting at each other.

"Why?"

"Because I said so!" He could tell straight away that was the wrong thing to say. Her face grew stormy. She planted her hands on her hips and glared at him. "For one thing, that many chickens would stink, Hope!"

"It's not that many..."

"I said *no!* That's the end of it!" he yelled, throwing down his spade. He turned on his heel and stormed off.

He could feel her eyes boring into his back and although he couldn't hear the words was well aware she was muttering angrily and heard the splat of an unfortunate tomato as it hit the ground.

Luke slapped the saddle onto Augustus Brown, viciously pulling the girth too tight. The horse swung his head and nipped at Luke's shoulder. When Luke didn't respond the big black stepped into him and pushed him away. The strap slipped in Luke's hand.

"Don't you start," growled Luke. Mounting, he headed into the forest and wound his way up the mountain until he reached the end of the track. Tethering the horse, Luke began to climb.

The exercise did him good. By the time he'd reached the lookout ledge his annoyance had eased. He sat down, rested his head against the rock behind him and closed his eyes.

Up here the breeze was cool.

He rolled his shoulders and tried not to think about Hope.

Ten seconds later, he tried not to think about Hope again.

Ten seconds after that, he realised it was hard not to think about Hope. Even when she enraged him, he was thinking about her. Wondering what she would say if he kissed her or ran his hands through her hair. For a man who valued quiet, he was always wanting to know what she was thinking. He enjoyed listening to her voice, even when they were yelling at each other. He was inordinately glad she didn't have one of those breathy, little girl voices.

Or the tired, whiny voice Mr Johnson's wife had. Or Mrs Stuart's voice – the screechy, grating sound that could peel paint off the barn door. How Stuart could bear it he had no idea. Luke wanted to murder the woman after just a few minutes and he'd only seen her three or four times last year.

But Hope - Hope's voice was calm, quiet, deeper than most women, especially when she laughed. A man didn't hear Hope's laugh, he felt it. Luke shifted on the rock. This wasn't helping. What was that fight about anyway? Chickens? He sighed. Perhaps he could build her a chicken coop. Maybe if he bought a dozen birds, well, maybe eight or so, she'd be happy. It was a compromise. Eight wasn't so many, but it might be enough. The thought of fresh eggs for breakfast everyday sounded mighty good.

The mountain, the breeze, the soft sighing of the pines, all worked their magic. He'd go down and apologise.

Hmm. He'd go down and tell her she could have half a dozen chickens.

Closing his eyes, he slowly drifted to sleep.

*

As Luke rode out, Hope stood there, fuming, hands on her hips. How could that man be so stubborn! Why shouldn't they try and sell apples and eggs in town? She'd take care of the chickens. It wasn't like she was asking him to. All that was needed was a chicken coop. If she knew how to make one, she would!

She spun on her heel, tripped over Wolf who'd sat behind her and fell sprawling to the ground, knocking over the pail at the same time. Dirty water splashed out. She could have screamed with annoyance.

Wolf began to lick her face, tail wagging, delighted with this new game. She pushed him away. His ears drooped and his shoulders sagged. Poor thing, her bad temper wasn't his fault. When she stretched out her hand to pat him on the head, he moved away. She was horrified. Was she really so awful? Bursting into tears, she buried her head in her hands. What was wrong with her?

The young wolf immediately came and slobbered all over her, whining softly. Forgiveness was so easy for animals. She wrapped her arms around him and gave him a hug. "Come on boy, let's do the washing, shall we?" She wiped her face with the back of her hand adding a new smear of mud to the one already there.

She gathered up all the dirty washing in the cabin, plonked it in the tub and dragged it outside. It was hot, heavy work and her temper didn't improve. It wasn't long before Hope was crying again. The clothes she was wearing were now saturated with sweat and dirty water.

Once the washing was hung on the line to dry, she took one of her new skirts and blouses out of the closet, grabbed the bar of soap and a towel and headed down to the river. Luke wasn't back yet and she desperately needed a bath. She didn't have the energy to carry more water back up to the cabin. It was just too hot.

She chose a quiet spot hidden behind some willow trees and pulled off her dirty shirt and skirt. She didn't have the courage to strip completely. What if he came back and saw her? She could bathe quite easily in her shift and wash it at the same time.

After a good scrub, Hope washed her hair as well. It felt good to erase the dirt, and her temper. Ruefully, she admitted her temper might need more time. She laid out the skirt and shirt on the tree branches to dry and pushed herself back into the river. Soapy trails slid off and slowly meandered their way down stream.

Clearly bored, Wolf wandered off.

The water was delightfully cool, and Hope felt herself relaxing. She lay back and floated, watching the sunlight flicker through the long, drooping strands of willow branches caressing the surface of the water. The sky was so soft, so light that it seemed not to have any colour at all. There were no clouds. The vault of heaven seemed so high that she had the strangest feeling she was looking into eternity. That seemed important. Chickens would be nice, but they weren't important.

She'd have to apologise. She sighed, closed her eyes and let herself become as light as the sky. Her mind cleared and the sensation of cool water was all she was aware of. Small sounds were distorted beneath the surface. Hope let her imagination drift - the river was talking to her. She tried to hear what it was saying, but not very hard. She soon gave up and simply floated.

*

When Luke rode back in, Wolf pranced with delight. As he unsaddled and rubbed down the horse, Wolf pulled at Augustus Brown's loosely draped rein. The horse pulled back good naturedly. Both animals enjoyed the tug of war. Whenever Luke spoke to him, Wolf yelped, almost grinning, his long tongue hanging out. His greatest joy was always a tummy rub and Luke indulged him, guiltily aware that he was putting off the moment he'd see Hope again.

"Come on you," he said to the wolf, "where is she? Let's get this apology over with."

The washing was hanging on the line and Wolf snapped at it as they went past. Luke called him to order. So, she'd been busy - not sulking in the cabin. No. That wasn't fair. He'd never seen Hope sulk. He went outside again, looked around but couldn't see her anywhere. Perhaps she was getting water from the river. He'd stroll down and carry the bucket back for her.

As he approached, he saw the shirt and skirt hanging in the tree. He stopped and was just about to turn around when a movement caught his eye. She was lying back in the water, dark hair fanned out behind, eyes closed, her hands waving gently against the slow current.

At first, he thought she was naked. He should leave. He knew that but was rooted to the spot. She sat up slowly, lifting her arms to keep the long hair back off her face. Water cascaded down. She was still in her shift. If that was for modesty's sake, and knowing Hope it would be, it made no difference. The material moulded itself to her body. Wet, it was almost transparent.

Luke stopped breathing. She was...beautiful. He swallowed hard. Heat surged through him. Then she stood up, and he knew he was in even deeper trouble. The force of his reaction was shocking. Her slim body had curves that would make a man weep - perfect breasts, created to fill a man's hand exactly, the small mound of her belly, the curve of her hips. He wanted to dive into the water. Put his hands on her damp body. Taste her skin. Take her—Wolf bounded past him and crashed into the river. Water went everywhere. Luke stepped behind a tree, trying to stay out of sight. Thankfully, all her attention was on Wolf, laughing and scolding at the same time.

"Wolf! Wolf! Stop," she cried. "Wait. Silly animal. Do you want a bath as well, huh? Do you? Do you? I think you do. Come here, Wolf. Come on, you'll love it, I promise. You need it. You'll be so nice and clean. You'll smell better too. Come on, stand still."

She hadn't seen him. Thank goodness. Luke turned and walked quietly away. Things were going to be different now. A lot different. And he wasn't sure what to do about it.

Much later, he stripped off his sweat-sodden shirt, tossing it aside. Splashing his face with cold water from the bucket didn't help. His mind drifted back to the river. To be honest, he hadn't stopped thinking about it. About her. Coming across her like that so unexpectedly, the image was branded into his imagination. The way the wet shift clung as she rose out of the cool water. The sunlight sparkling on her damp skin. Soft, velvet skin. He burned to touch her. Damn, why hadn't he seen it before? How had he ever thought she was plain, or even pretty? She was beautiful.

And he wanted her.

What he felt was deeper than lust. He was falling deeply, irrevocably in love. But right now, all Luke could think of was her body in that wet shift, the image seared into his mind. He'd forced himself to walk away, back to the cabin and had spent the afternoon chopping wood - ferociously. He grabbed the bucket and emptied it over himself. Rubbing his wet head vigorously, he sighed.

He'd just have to chop more wood.

*

Hope watched him swing the long, heavy axe, strong arms raising and dropping the blade rhythmically. She could barely lift the thing, but Luke made it look like the axe was an extension of his arm. They really didn't need more wood. She watched the powerful muscles working beneath the tanned skin. He was sweating in the late afternoon sun. Something stirred within her. Almost without thinking she picked up the juice pitcher and a glass and walked outside. Was he still angry with her? Would he take this as a peace offering? She planned to apologise, but not yet.

Perhaps at dinner.

Feed him first. That was a good idea.

As she approached, Luke stopped swinging the axe and watched the sway of her hips. Hope suddenly felt very self-conscious. As she drew closer, Luke's eyes darkened. Was he still so angry? It didn't feel like anger, but it did feel just as dangerous. She became flustered, nerves leaping all over the place. Concentrate, she told herself, but the word dissolved in her mind. Those blue eyes held her. She stopped, confused.

To distract herself, she began to pour the apple juice, but her hands were shaking so much it spilled everywhere. His hands covered hers and steadied them. Strong firm hands. Her pulse jumped. He was smiling gently at her, but it was the look in his eyes that made her panic. She jerked her hands away, nearly dropping the jug and almost ran back to the cabin leaving him holding an overflowing, sticky glass of juice, a crooked, bemused twist on his lips.

CHAPTER TWENTY-EIGHT

THE next few days had a constraint to them, which hadn't been there before. Luke couldn't help but see her in the river each time he looked at her. The memory made him breathless, his heart pound and his mouth dry, as if his skin would burst into flame if they touched. Perhaps it was the hot weather.

Luke knew exactly why he felt the way he did. He'd fallen in love and wanted her, badly. His promise had become an iron collar and the constricting weight of it was more than he could bear. He tried not to let the need show. He wasn't succeeding very well.

At night, during dinner, Hope would suddenly look like a startled deer and, realizing he'd let his gaze rest on her, allowing his thoughts to go places they had no right to, he'd abruptly finish eating and leave the table and the cabin. Perhaps they should eat outside while this hot weather lasted.

He tried to find things to do away from the cabin. Things that would physically exhaust him. It didn't work. Because of the heat, he'd opened the upper loading bay door in the barn and lay there night after night, listening to small rustles in the hay, watching the stars, thinking of her.

Towards the end of the week, he was working in the orchard, digging around the bases of the apple trees so he could mix some of Augustus Brown's manure into the soil. Once that was done, he was planning to scatter some of the rue he'd harvested from the vegetable garden around each apple tree. It had worked so well keeping the bugs and birds away from the vegetables, Luke was hoping to get the same result in the orchard.

Wolf was chasing small rodents in the undergrowth. His head came up, ears pricked, his tail wagging and he yelped delightedly, bounding off. Hope had arrived, carrying a basket and a jug. It looked heavy and having a young, leggy wolf leaping up at her wasn't helping.

Luke called Wolf to order, rested the spade against the tree trunk and, pulling on his shirt, went to take the jug from her.

"I've brought you water and something to eat," she said, her eyes barely meeting his, a slow flush creeping into her cheeks. He smiled, doing up the buttons on the shirt. Her shy awareness of his body brought a measure of hope that she wouldn't be averse to him. He just didn't know how to approach the subject. If he said or did the wrong thing, she'd bolt.

He wanted her in his bed, not just for the pleasure of sleeping with her – he wanted her as his wife. Whatever he did, it had to be the right thing. He only hoped he could figure it out before his desire broke out of control and did something else.

It was a good meal with cold meat and, he had to admit, thanks to her vegetable garden, crisp beans, summer tomatoes and lettuce. They finished off with apple pie and cream, washed down with cold water. They ate in silence under the budding apple trees, sitting in the long grass, bees and butterflies dancing over the meadow flowers swaying in the breeze around them. A short distance away stood the open wagon, filled with manure, the pile of rue at its side keeping the flies at bay. Augustus Brown cropped a particularly delicious patch of alfalfa close by.

"That was nice," Luke said, dusting off his hands. "Thank you."

"My pleasure." She smiled back at him. She yawned, quickly covering her mouth with her hand. "Heavens." An even bigger yawn stretched out of her.

Luke laughed. "Why don't you take a nap? It's too nice a day to be inside anyway. Lie down here."

"Mmm, good idea."

Luke walked back to where he'd left his spade and began working again. Smothering yet another yawn, Hope packed the basket and lay down on her back, closing her eyes.

The day drowsed on as Luke dug around the trees and Hope slept. Luke stood up and wiped his arm across his sweaty forehead and watched Augustus Brown cropping near Hope. Too near. She twitched, then shot to a sitting position. The horse's head was right by her face. He harrumphed, stepped closer and ruffled her hair with his velvet nose.

Luke's laugh at her surprise was cut short. She was white, her whole body rigid with terror. He tossed the spade aside and strode over swiftly, took hold of the bridle and pulled Augustus Brown away. The sight of those huge hooves so close was Hope's breaking point. She scrambled to her feet and ran.

In a few long strides Luke was beside her, pulling her into his arms. "It's all right. He won't hurt you." She was shaking violently and trying hard not to cry, gasping deeply for breath, struggling against him.

"Slow down. Take a deep breath. It's all right."

Once her breathing slowed she gave a quick, tremulous, little sigh and stepped back. "Sorry." Her voice was still shaky, her hands twisting together. She must be scared; they were usually the calmest thing about her.

"Don't apologise. You had a fright. Why didn't you tell me you're afraid of horses?"

She shrugged slightly.

"A lot of people are." He paused. "If you would like, I can teach you not to be."

"No. No, I can't."

Her eyes were still fixed on the ground. He knew this was a totally irrational fear, yet for her it was very real. But out here, it was a fear she couldn't afford.

"Hope, there may come a time when you will have to ride either Augustus Brown or one of the mules."

She backed away, shaking her head. "No. I can't," she whispered.

"What if I'm not around? What if you have to get help?" She was trembling again. He pushed on. "What if something has happened to me? I'm sick, injured, been eaten by a bear." That was just ridiculous; if he'd been eaten by a bear, he'd be dead.

She didn't notice.

"You'd have to get help. You'd have to ride."

She grew even paler.

"Sit down." He took her arm, steered her to a fallen log and pushed her down. He waited until she'd stopped trembling before he spoke. "I'm sorry, Hope, but you're going have to conquer this. You do need to know how to ride. We live too far away from anyone else for you to get there on foot, in a hurry. It would take you nearly two weeks to walk to town, if not longer. If I was the one in trouble, I'd be dead before you got back."

She blinked. "All right," she whispered.

Luke smiled. "Good girl. Let's start now."

She swallowed hard, shaking her head.

"We'll take it slowly. I won't make you ride him today."

He snapped off a handful of alfalfa, took Hope by the hand and pulled her up. "You stand behind me," he said, "and hold onto me."

Hesitantly, she put her hands on his waist. If she wasn't so scared, she would have been too shy to be this near to him. He took her left hand and wrapped it round his chest pulling her against him. He tried not to breathe. Her soft body moulded against his back was playing havoc with his emotions. He took her right hand and turned it so that her palm lay face up in his. He put the alfalfa inside it.

"Keep your hand flat," he said. He whistled for the horse, who walked over, his big head swinging. Luke felt Hope stiffen, pulling back a little, her hand shook slightly, her breathing quickened.

"I've got you," he said. "You're safe behind me. Just stand still."

Augustus Brown stopped in front of Luke and whiffled at the alfalfa. His hot breath and long, whiskery nose tickled her fingers. She jumped, instinctively trying to snatch her hand away, but Luke's fingers closed around her wrist. He felt her pulse flutter.

Neatly, the horse took the alfalfa and crunched it with his strong, yellow teeth. The sound was surprisingly loud. Luke turned Hope's hand and laid it gently on the horse's forehead. Thankfully, the horse stood still.

Luke couldn't resist, he rubbed his thumb softly against the back of Hope's wrist. She moved her hand and, tentatively, stroked Augustus Brown's forehead. He pushed his soft square nose into her palm and blew. She gave a little shiver; a small giggle broke out. The horse tossed his head and walked away to carry on cropping the grass under the trees.

"That wasn't so bad?"

"No," breathed Hope. "Not so bad." They were still standing with Hope's arms around him, her body pressed against him.

Luke moved first. "We'll do some more tomorrow. I'd better finish up these trees." He walked away, picked up the spade and went deeper into the orchard. He needed to put some space between them, fast, or he'd probably scare her even more. For a completely different reason.

Each day he took her near the horse and, holding her close, or letting her stand behind him, slowly got her to relax around Augustus Brown. That was the plan anyway. He grinned, while she learned to trust the horse, she was becoming used to him at the same time. He wasn't complaining.

Luke dragged out the sessions. Once she knew how to ride there wouldn't be an excuse for having her in his arms anymore. She might be getting used to him, but unless they were working with the horse, she still jumped when he touched her, even accidentally.

A few days later, Luke took Augustus Brown out for a long hard ride. He wanted the horse tired when he put Hope on his back. Returning, he found Hope in the yard, taking the washing off the line. He walked the horse over to her and dismounted. "Time for a riding lesson," he said.

"Now?"

"Good a time as any."

"Oh. Yes, I suppose so." She'd come a long way and he'd been impressed with her courage, but this was a big step for her. Would she back out? She wiped her hands on her apron. "What do I do?" Her voice was a little shaky.

"Good girl."

He walked the horse over to the stump. He pulled the axe out of it and gave her his hand. "Stand on the stump." Hitching up her skirt a little, Hope stepped up gracefully. Luke turned the horse so it was closer to her.

"Take hold of the pommel and swing your right leg over the saddle." Her hand was shaking. This was her moment of truth. She squared her shoulders, gripped the pommel with one hand and pulled herself onto the saddle. Augustus Brown shifted under her weight. She grabbed the pommel with both hands. Luke laughed. "You all right?" She nodded.

"Put your feet in the stirrups. Good. Now all you have to do is sit there and hold on. I'm going to lead him around the yard."

They walked across the yard and back again. Hope seemed to be coping, so Luke did the trip a few more times. When she dismounted onto the stump, her face was pale, but pleased.

"I did it," she said.

"Yes, you did. Well, done. We'll do a little more each day. I'd better get him back in the barn."

As he walked the horse away, he heard Hope give a happy, frightened, surprised, little sigh, and he smiled.

CHAPTER TWENTY-NINE

A T the end of the week, Hope was trotting gently round the field while Luke held the long training lead. Her fear was subsiding, and she was beginning to enjoy it.

The next day, she was standing in the yard looking out to the mountain, her hand shielding her eyes from the afternoon sun when Luke rode in.

"Hope!" he called. "Do you trust me?"

"Why?" She was instantly suspicious.

"Hold out your arm."

"Why?" she asked again.

The word was barely out of her mouth when Luke and the big black horse thundered towards her. She was horrified. It was only the wild grin of delight on Luke's face that kept her from fleeing to the safety of the cabin. She stuck out her arm and squeezed her eyes shut. As the black galloped past her Luke grabbed her arm and swung her up behind him. With her arms wrapped tightly around him, they whirled round and raced off to the river. Hope's heart pounded as hard in her chest as the horse's hooves beneath them. She clung desperately to Luke. The horse seemed to be going faster. The beating power of the animal's body beneath her was terrifying. She could hardly breathe.

Their path led along the river to the bridge. They clattered across it at a trot. Augustus Brown took off again as soon as his hooves left the bridge. Pressed against Luke's hard, muscular back, Hope soon relaxed and began to enjoy the wild, intoxicating ride. The wind pulled her hair loose. It streamed out behind her like a dark banner. When Hope laughed, Luke relaxed and urged the horse on even faster.

He took her out to the edge of the meadow where he reined in. To the left, they could see the ocean. To the right, the valley stretched away, blue in the distance where it folded up into the misty grey mountains. He showed her where one river started in a long, slender waterfall, became a tumbling roughness of white as it hit the rapids, then turned to a deep blue as it meandered through the valley in slow oxbows and flowed past their cabin on its way down to the sea.

The colours below them were brilliant; the dark green of the forest was almost black in places. It contrasted sharply with the river's diamond shades. The valley was a shimmering meld of emerald and light green, whose edge was cut by the sandy ribbon of the trail heading north.

No wonder God had declared his creation was good. This untamed vision, this wild, vast land swept Hope up until felt like she was on the edge of heaven looking down on the earth, and all she could see was boundless, frightening beauty. Hope could feel Luke breathing under her hands. She could feel the warmth and strength of him. The anchor she felt being near him was settling deeper and deeper into her spirit. Each day, she was falling more and more in love with him. If that were possible.

The sun was slowly setting over the ocean, the sky was purple and turquoise, shot through with orange when Luke turned the horse, and they wound their way slowly back to the cabin, the long grass shushing softly as they moved through it, the wild flowers dancing around Augustus Brown's knees. Neither of them said a word.

They arrived back at the cabin as twilight was fading into night. Luke dismounted and held up his arms to help her dismount. She swung her leg over the horse's neck, reached for his shoulders and slid down. They stood, unmoving, their hands resting on each other. Thanks to Luke, she'd lost her fear of Augustus Brown. But the feel of Luke's body against hers still made her tremble. It was the power of him, the masculine hardness that made her pulse race, and her skin hot.

"Thank you for teaching me to ride," she said, a quiet, yet shy smile in her eyes. "You were very patient. I'm grateful. I'd better get dinner ready."

Beneath Luke's hands was that feminine body he'd seen in the river, that narrow waist with its easy curves. And only a few heartbeats away was that soft mouth he so badly wanted to kiss. His hands tightened on her waist. He breathed in the scent of her, the warmth of her body against his. It made it difficult to think straight.

She stepped away from him. He reluctantly let her go and she walked away. He ran his hand through his hair. He couldn't do this much longer. He could still feel her body pressed against his in the wild excitement of the ride, her hands resting lightly on his hips as Augustus Brown had carried them slowly home. She'd never been that relaxed that close to him before.

It gave him an idea.

The next day, Luke disappeared, along with some of the kitchen supplies. He only rode back in towards evening, just as Hope was about to start dinner. He swept into the cabin saying, "Don't worry about that."

He took the knife out of her hand, tossing it onto the table. "I want to show you something. Bring a couple of quilts." And walked quickly out of the cabin again. As soon as she came outside, he took and laid the quilts over Augustus Brown's saddle and tossed Hope up. In one smooth move he swung himself up behind her, collected the reins and set off, his arms cradling her loosely.

Making their way into the forest, Luke turned left at the old honey tree and followed a narrow track that wound its way high up the mountain between the pines. At a small stream Luke turned the horse, heading even further up the track.

An hour or so later, he pulled Augustus Brown to a halt at the side of a long thin waterfall and dismounted. Helping Hope down, he hobbled the horse.

"It's this way." He walked towards the waterfall that hung over the rocky cliff face. Luke stepped carefully over the wet rocks. "Come on!" he called as he went through the mist.

Hope climbed carefully over the slippery rocks. Behind the pale sheet of water was the entrance to a small dark cave. As soon as she appeared, his fingers closed over hers.

"Follow me." He led her deeper into the cave, lighting their way with a flaming torch. The ground sloped upwards, the cave grew narrower, until it was no more than a passage twisting through the mountain. He could feel Hope's grip on his hand tighten. "There's a crack in the wall over here. Are you afraid of small spaces?"

"A little."

"It's only as deep as a doorway, you'll be through in a moment."

"Alright, but don't let go of my hand."

He grinned. "I won't." He turned sideways and slipped into a shadow on the cave wall pulling Hope after him. It was a very small space. When he pulled her through, he saw she'd squeezed her eyes shut. As if that would keep the dark at bay. "Open your eyes."

She gasped in amazement. The view from the cave was magical. Framed by the ancient rock, far below them was a long, narrow chasm filled with dark pine trees, a thin, silver, knife-like river glinted along the valley floor.

"Look up."

The cave was filled with fantastical paintings, all glittering in the glow of Luke's torch. In the flickering light, red, yellow, ochre and black figures of men and beasts leapt and danced across the cave walls. "It's incredible. Who made them?"

"No one really knows, they're ancient. Adam White Knife thinks it may have been the original Nlaka'pamux. His tribe have been using these caves in their rituals for as long as anyone can remember."

"It's absolutely beautiful," she whispered, entranced. It was clear she'd forgotten he was still holding her hand. "What kind of rituals?" she asked.

"Seeking visions mostly, as far as I know. It's a very spiritual place for them."

"How many caves are there like this?" She stepped closer to the wall, her fingers trailing lightly over the painted figures.

"I've no idea. Adam might, but he's only ever shown me this one. They tend to keep this kind of thing secret."

"Are we allowed to be here? Won't Adam be angry you've shown them to me?"

"Well, Adam showed them to me, so I figure he won't mind me showing them to you." He looked out over the dark valley. "I've never brought anyone else here." Their voices had become low, intimate. All that could be heard in the quietness of the cave was the hissing crackle of the torch. She laid her hand on the rock.

"What do you think this one is? It looks like the biggest moose that ever lived," she laughed. It echoed through the cavern. Luke stepped closer to her, bending his head to have a look. His breath stirred the loose tendrils of hair that lay on her neck. He gave an odd laugh and stepped back, releasing her hand.

"I don't know much about moose, but you're right, if it is, it's a very large one!"

They spent an enjoyable time trying to decipher the paintings.

"Feeling hungry yet?" he asked.

"Starving! But I don't want to leave yet."

"I'll come back and get you in a few minutes then. I need to...check on the horse." She was so absorbed in the paintings she barely noticed when he handed her the torch and slipped out of the cave.

True to his word it was only a few minutes later when he stuck his head back into the painted cave. "Ready?"

They pushed their way back through the crack into the outer cave. When they stepped out from behind the waterfall, Augustus Brown was nowhere to be seen. Luke took her hand again and struck off down a path that led into the forest. They walked silently together in the dark until they entered a small glade.

It was almost as beautiful as the painted cave. High pines stretched up into the night. Moonlight filtered down through the branches. In the dark, the forest had a different quality. The peace was profound. Augustus Brown was quietly nibbling the grass on the other side of the glade. A small fire flickered. Two trout were spitting and roasting gently over its flames and the coffee pot was bubbling away on the rocks around it. The quilts had been laid out on the grass. Hope gently pulled her hand out of his.

"Some dinner, my lady?" Luke said, smiling at her.

"Why, thank you, kind sir, that would be most acceptable."

It was a delightful meal. As the sparks from the fire burst and drifted to the sky, they came up with all sorts of fantastical notions about the cave and what the paintings meant that kept them laughing as they ate.

He'd been right. Getting Hope away from the cabin was a good idea. She clearly loved the forest and she was much less conscious of their self-imposed constraints here in the shelter of the trees.

Time slipped away like a mist into the forest around them.

The meal was over. Luke took her plate, scraped it into the hissing fire and put it aside. As they sipped coffee in silence, the quietness of the night lay down around them. After a while, Hope glanced nervously at Luke. He saw a pulse jump in her neck.

"Are we going back now?" she said in almost a whisper.

"No, it's too far to make it back tonight. We'll sleep here." Although his voice was low and quiet, his blood was racing.

Her eyes widened. Was his desire that obvious? She looked as if she wasn't sure whether to move towards him or run. He took her coffee cup away and put it on the rocks around the fire. His gaze drank her in. He tucked a long, loose tress of her hair behind her ear. His fingers lingered on the back of her neck. The feel of her skin ignited a longing in his own. A smile tugged at the corner of his mouth. She stared at him, her eyes huge, making her look even more feminine. It made him feel strong...and very male.

The tips of his fingers drifted around her neck and traced the curve of it up to her jaw. The sensation of her skin seemed to be all that existed. He ran the back of his hand across her cheek, a finger over the sculpture of her lips.

Slowly, he leaned towards her.

Wolf burst between them. He was overjoyed. Wet and exhausted, his unbounded delight at having found them slobbered itself all over them. His muddy paws went everywhere at once. His long, hot tongue licking every surface of their faces and hands he could reach. It took a long time to calm him down, feed him and give him some water, which he clearly desperately needed. Once he'd drunk his fill he bounded over and flopped down in the middle of the quilt, put his head on his paws, sighed gustily and began to snore.

Luke growled in frustration, which made Hope laugh. He frowned at her, lay on the quilt, wrapped an arm over his eyes and muttered a sullen good night.

He got up early the next morning and had the coffee and trout cooking over the fire by the time she woke. Wolf was staring at them, quivering, salivating at the smell of them. Luke, a cup of coffee in one hand, was trying to push him away.

"Get lost, Wolf, go on. These fish are not for you. Go hunt something. That's what wolves do. Go away!"

"He doesn't seem the worse for his adventure," laughed Hope as Wolf deftly moved out of reach of Luke's boot and sat down again, staring at the fish, willing them to cook faster.

"No, he doesn't, does he." Luke was more than grumpy. He was bloody annoyed. His carefully laid plans were ruined by that stupid animal. He'd wanted their first time together as man and wife, to be special. The journey to the cave, the magic of the paintings and making love there in the glade should have been perfect. Damn animal. He tried to banish the memory of how soft and warm her skin had felt under his fingers. Or how large and green her eyes had been as he'd leaned in. There was no doubt in his mind about what would have happened if Wolf hadn't appeared when he did.

She pushed off the quilt Luke had covered her with last night and came over to the fire for breakfast. He'd forgotten all about this other quilt. If he'd remembered perhaps...

No point in thinking about it now.

Luke was grumpy all the way back to the cabin. As soon as they arrived, he disappeared. He always stayed away when he was out of sorts. He was doing that a lot lately.

CHAPTER THIRTY

A FEW days later, early in the morning, Hope was sweeping the porch.

"Hope? Could you come into the barn?" Luke called.

He was standing at the horse stall when she came in. Luke caught his breath. She seemed to bring the sunshine in with her. He couldn't believe he'd thought she was plain the first day he'd seen her. Had he been blind? She was most the breath-taking woman he'd ever seen.

"Hello, Augustus Brown." She stroked the horse's Roman nose.

"Today you're going to learn how to saddle a horse," Luke said, laughing as her face crinkled with concern. "It's easy. The saddle's a bit heavy, but that's about all." He took the bridle and showed her how to put it on. It seemed easy enough. Taking it off again he handed it to her. "Your turn."

Nervously she lifted the bridle towards that strong jaw, those big teeth. The horse snorted and nodded his head.

"Behave horse!" said Luke, "Try again, don't let him see you're afraid. If you do, you'll never get it on."

This time, thankfully, the horse stood still. The metal rattled against his teeth as he took the bit into his mouth.

"Good. Now the saddle. After you." He held the stall door open. He could feel her stiffen a little as she stepped past. With both of them inside the stall, the horse seemed large even to Luke. He was aware of how narrow the stall was with Hope standing beside him.

"First put the blanket on." He threw it over and smoothed it down. "Then the saddle." He showed her how to fold the stirrups over the saddle first. She lifted it up, surprised at its weight. She grunted as she hefted the saddle in her arms to get a better grip, then tossed it up. Luke showed her how to tighten the girth, how the horse always took a breath to try and keep it loose and how to adjust for that. Augustus Brown shifted, side stepping and nodding his head.

"Well done."

Hope smiled joyously at him and ran her hand along the horse's shoulder.

The barn was warm, filled with a golden glow and the scent of fresh hay. She was so close to him. Luke saw the horse's skin quiver under her gently caressing hand. His blood stirred, he took a breath, it was now or never. No matter what she said, he had to tell her how he felt.

"Hope," he began.

She turned her head, her lips curving with that soft invitation it unconsciously carried. The horse moved abruptly and banged into Luke, throwing him against her. They crashed into the wooden side of the stall, his hands on the panelling on either side of her face, his body pressed up against hers. He eased back slightly and looked into her eyes. His heart started that slow, deep, hot pounding it always did when he was close to her.

Very, very slowly he leant towards her and kissed her, his lips barely grazing hers. He heard her take a small, quick breath, her lips quivered under his. He kissed her again, letting his mouth press softly against hers. She sighed and then went still.

She didn't move.

There was no more response from her. None at all.

Had he made a mistake?

He pulled away and looked into her eyes. He wasn't sure what he saw there. Was it fear? Her face was almost blank.

She wasn't even looking at him. Her gaze was fixed some-where over his shoulder.

A small frown creased his forehead. A trickle of fear ran down his spine. He'd thought she was over what had hap-pened with Tobias John. Was he wrong? Had the trapper damaged her worse than he thought?

"Hope?"

Augustus Brown was restless; he moved and pushed Luke again. It wouldn't take much for Hope's new-found confidence in the horse to splinter. Taking the bridle, Luke led the animal out of the barn. Augustus Brown tugged at the reign, dancing around, tossing his head. Bloody Hell, this is the wrong time to misbehave, you stupid animal. He looked back at Hope.

"Hope?" He didn't know what to say. "He's going to tear the place up. I've got to ride the fidgets out of him. I'm— all right horse!" The animal was jerking his head up and down, trying to wrench the reins out of Luke's hand.

Hope hadn't moved. Before Augustus Brown could tear his arm out of its socket, Luke mounted and rode away.

＊

Hope blinked, put a hand to her throat, a deep sob broke out. She stifled it immediately. Her knees felt weak. She slid down the partition. Her lips could still feel the touch of his. The feel of his body against hers had taken her breath away. As he'd moved towards her she had remembered Tobias John. A shiver of fear had run through her. But the thought was fleeting. Luke wasn't Tobias.

She'd been about to close her eyes and return his kiss when a sharp, harsh glint blinded her. The sun bounced off the metal hinges on the small chest standing on the shelf in Augustus Brown's stall. The small chest that held the receipt, the bill of sale Constable Carter had given her on the ship.

She'd gone numb inside. No matter how much she wanted Luke, it couldn't happen. She wasn't his wife and wouldn't be his whore. Tears rolled slowly down her face. She wanted him to love her. She wanted his arms around her. She wanted him to kiss her. She wanted to run her hand through his hair and to kiss the hollow at the base of his neck. She wanted to feel his hands on her skin.

Hope stood up abruptly, if a little unsteadily. She had to stop thinking like this, stop thinking about his mouth and the way it twisted when he was deliberating or trying not to smile. She had to stop thinking about the way his eyes gleamed when he laughed. She straightened her back. If she put her mind to it, she could do this.

She had to.

She spent the rest of the day digging and weeding in the vegetable garden hoping to work herself into exhaustion. It didn't help. When Luke still hadn't come back at sunset, she'd taken a quick bath in the river and gone to bed without dinner. She couldn't face food.

*

Luke had let the dancing, restless horse gallop its fidgets away. A deep frown gouged its way down his forehead. He couldn't figure her out. He could have sworn she did feel something for him. He was convinced he'd seen love, even shy desire, in her eyes lately. Her pulse had raced under his fingers, and now, when his mouth had claimed hers, her lips softened under his. He'd sensed the heat from her skin, the sigh in her quickly drawn breath. She'd wanted that kiss as much as he did. He was sure of it. So, what happened? Why did she suddenly go so cold? So....blank?

It had to be Tobias John.

Luke wasn't sure what he should do. He knew what he wanted to do; throw her on the ground, rip her clothes off and make passionate love to her.

He gave a scornful laugh. Yeah, that would help. He needed to think. Chopping wood wasn't the answer anymore. He rode into the forest and climbed up to his lookout point, only coming back much later that night. The cabin was dark and quiet. Hope had gone to bed.

When she heard him ride into the yard it was nearly midnight. Would he come into the cabin? Part of her wanted him to; the other part knew he wouldn't. She heard the barn door open, close and then, silence. Hope cried herself to sleep.

*

The next day they tried to act as if nothing had happened. The day was a nightmare. At dinner, Luke pushed his plate away saying he wasn't hungry. He didn't even suggest coffee. Scraping his chair back, he strode off to the barn as soon as he could.

The night deepened into indigo. Wolves howled high up on the mountain. Hope sat staring into, but not really seeing, the warm, flickering flames in the fireplace. It was so cosy here in the cabin. She wondered what it was like to sleep in the barn. Was it cold? Her mind shied away immediately from the thought of him with her in the cabin. Sleeping in the cabin.

Did he have enough blankets to stay warm? The hay was probably prickly. He might appreciate another blanket or a quilt. After all, it was his bed she was—

She gathered a quilt from the closet and ran quickly across the yard.

Pulling open the door she slipped inside. The barn was surprisingly warm. Heat flooded her body when she saw him. His shirt lay tossed over the ladder to the loft. A bowl of soapy water stood on a hay bale. He was drying himself with a towel and in the warm glow of the lantern he was... disturbing. She wanted to run her hands over his back. The sight of his golden, muscular body did more than stir her, it confused her. She realised she'd been holding her breath. It escaped in a ragged sigh.

He turned. A look of surprise crossed his face.

She swallowed convulsively. "I've brought you a quilt - another quilt," she stammered. "I thought you might be cold." He looked anything but cold. His face softened. His eyes glowed.

"Thank you." He tossed the towel aside and walked towards her. Instinctively she took a step backwards, clutching the quilt. The slow smile that took her breath away crept across his face. He held out his hands. Why was he smiling at her like that?

"What?" she whispered.

His smile deepened. Her heart turned over with a frightened lurch. He could probably hear it thumping like a drum in her chest.

"The quilt?"

"Oh, oh yes, here you are." She shoved it at him, without even looking at it he tossed it onto the bed of straw against the wall. She could see the imprint on the straw his body had made, the dent in the pillow where his head had lain. The thought of him lying there— she had to leave. She turned away, only to be roughly pulled back, into his arms.

"Don't go. Not yet." he said quietly, his face only inches away from hers. He drew her even closer.

Her hands pushed against his chest; her eyes wide. His body was strong, warm, very male. It was the only place she wanted to be, and she was drowning.

"Hope," he murmured.

She gave a gasp as his mouth - that crooked, incredibly kissable mouth she had dreamed of touching - came down on her lips.

When he lifted his head, she was breathless. She couldn't think straight. He kissed her again, gently, an almost feather-light softness, a caress. Instinctively, she leaned into him and the kiss deepened. He drew her down onto his makeshift bed, his kisses growing more passionate, the heat of his hands searing her skin through her clothes.

"Hope" he whispered, mouthing softly at her neck. "Hope."

His hand slipped under her shirt. Fire followed in its wake. Her breath came quickly, quivering as he touched her. She clung to his strong shoulders. His mouth was hot, urgent against hers, against the soft skin of her neck. She was melting in his arms. Desire burned through her body as he murmured her name. They were sinking into that place where all thought vanishes, and only sensation remains.

A loud clank. The horse had knocked over his metal food pail. It might as well have been cold water. Hope gave a gasp and frantically pushed Luke away.

"What have I done?" she whispered. She scrambled to her feet.

His hand shot out and took her arm. "Hope? What's wrong?"

She wrenched herself free and stood up, away from the straw bed and tried to pull her shirt straight. She was trying hard to keep tears from falling. "I can't." It was a harsh, broken whisper. "I won't be your mistress."

"Mistress?" He stood up, reaching for her but she pulled away. "You're my wife."

"No, I'm not." Her eyes were huge. She was trembling.

"What?" Seeing her very real distress he smiled and tried to say as lightly as he could, "You are my wife, Hope. I have the documents to prove it."

"No, you don't." She cried, her hands shook as she tried desperately to do up her buttons. "A bill of sale isn't a marriage certificate. You didn't marry me, you bought me. You went to town for supplies. You bought coffee, flour and me." She clutched her shirt closed, turned and fled from the barn.

*

He was stunned. Was that really what she thought? The document they'd signed - it was a marriage certificate. Carter had said— in a few steps he was inside Augustus Brown's stall. He pushed the big horse aside, took the small chest off the shelf. Going through it he found the bill of sale.

He ran his hand through his hair. Damn. She was right.

It might be a binding marriage document according to the law, but there was no denying it was a receipt. Just a receipt. For bought goods. And for a woman like Hope, that wasn't enough.

His mouth twisted in wry acknowledgement. It wasn't enough for him either.

He was kept awake formulating and discarding plan after plan to try fix this. Convinced he hadn't misread her response he was now sure she loved him and wanted him as much as he did her. That soft look in her eyes, the way her lips parted when he kissed her, the heat of desire he'd felt in her skin.

He knew what he needed to do. Once he'd decided how to accomplish that, the memory of how she'd felt in his arms, the trembling of her body and echo of her soft sighs made the rest of his night a torment.

*

Hope tossed and turned, tangled in the sheets. Perhaps it would be best if she left him. But she had nowhere to else to go. And he'd paid so much money for her. She had nothing; how could she pay him back? If she left, she would have to. It was only right.

But she didn't want to leave him. She wanted more than anything else to be near him, to be with him.

She would have to stay out of his reach. She would have to stop seeking him out. She would have to stop thinking about him. Stop remembering the feel of his lips against her skin, the hard muscle of his back under her hands, the weight of him. Exhausted from crying, when she finally did sleep her dreams were troubled and her rest uneasy.

CHAPTER THIRTY-ONE

THE sun had barely broken over the tips of mountains across the valley and mist still curled over the yard when Luke put his plan into action. It would probably wake Hope, but he wanted to get an early start.

When she came out of the cabin a little later, he was sawing away at a piece of timber using the stump as a base. She brought him a cup of hot coffee. She was clearly nervous; it seemed as if she were jumping out of her skin. Would she say anything about last night? He hoped not.

He took the cup, watching her over the rim as he drank. For once he didn't notice how bitter it was. She couldn't meet his eyes. Her eyes were red, her face pale. She'd been crying. She probably didn't get much sleep either. His heart twisted. She didn't deserve this. He tossed back the scalding liquid, set the cup down and picked up the saw. For the plan Luke had concocted the night before to work, he needed an excuse for going into town. Building the chicken coop would solve a number of problems.

"Hold that end." He pointed to the plank of wood balanced over the stump.

Hope practically had to sit on it to keep it steady.

"I'm going to have to sharpen this," he remarked looking at the teeth on the blade.

In a rush she said, "Luke, I'm sorry—"

"Take hold of that end again," he interrupted. He worked his way through the planks until he had the sizes he needed.

Then he stepped back and dusted off his hands. "Good. Is there any breakfast?" he asked, knowing full well there wasn't.

Hope's face fell. "I haven't even started it."

"Didn't think you had. Why don't you get that going and I'll wash up?" He smiled as she almost ran back to the cabin.

A while later, when he sat at the table and took the hot plate from her hands, it was mounded with more beans, deer steak and toast than he could ever eat. Wolf was going to feast on leftovers. He was already drooling at the delicious smell.

"You know what would go well with this?" His eyes twinkled. "Eggs."

She burst into tears. Her face buried in her hands. His eyes widened in surprise. That wasn't the reaction he'd expected. He didn't know what to do.

"Hope? What's wrong? I thought you wanted eggs – chickens, I mean."

"I did, but I was so nasty about it and why should we make money off anything else? You do such a good job of providing for us. Your apples are wonderful, even when they're wrinkly and old, and you work so hard, and you're right, we don't need to clutter the yard with thousands of dirty, smelly chickens that you don't want and..." Here she started to become inextricably entangled.

He wanted to laugh. His eyes danced with delight. He loved this woman.

"Hope. Take a deep breath." He watched as she struggled for composure. "You were right, chickens are a good idea. However," he kept his mouth and his tone prim, "I don't feel we can supply the entire town. I do think we can meet our own needs. So, I have, with your very valuable help, begun building a chicken coop. As soon as it's done, I will go into town and get us a dozen chickens. Please let me know your preference regarding colour of bird as soon as is convenient for you." With a small bow, he went back to eating the over-load of beans and toast.

She burst into tears again.

"I thought you'd be pleased!" he exclaimed.

"I am," she sobbed, and with that, ran from the cabin.

He rolled his eyes. Women! Wolf had gone to the door and was whining, looking out to where she had run.

"Go on, Wolf. Go see if she's all right."

He bounded out after her.

*

It took half an hour, but eventually, she made her way back to the cabin. When she came out to where he was hammer-ing away, she'd mopped herself up and tied on the heavy sacks she's used as an apron at the *oolichon* hunt. Squaring her shoulders, she said, "I'm sorry I was so foolish," she said. "Thank you for the chicken coop. What can I do to help?"

He handed her a jar of different sized nails. "You can stop apologising to start with, then you can sort these for me. I need as many of this size as you can find." He held out a sample nail. His mouth twisted with amusement at the busi-ness-like way she took the nail, put it carefully aside, poured the nails from the jar into her lap and picked through them.

Harriet arrived. She was bored and looking for compan-ionship. She'd found a large feather by the barn door and was dragging it around trying to decide what to do with it. It was at least twice, if not three times, her size. It became her mission to wrestle that feather into submission. Luke was pleased to see most of the trouble that clouded Hope's eyes lifting as she watched the kitten's hilarious antics.

By the end of the day, the coop, sturdy, strong and big enough for a dozen chickens to live a life of luxury, was finished.

"I'll start early tomorrow. I should be back in about ten days," Luke said. "Will you be all right?"

"I've lots to keep me occupied." She smiled. "I need to harvest some of those vegetables and start preserving them."

When night descended, so did the awkwardness. The cabin felt far too small for both of them. As soon as he could, Luke escaped to the barn. He couldn't spend another night in her company without taking her in his arms and—

He closed the barn door firmly.

*

Luke hitched the mules to the wagon and was ready to go in the early grey of dawn the next morning. He hadn't expected it, but Hope was waiting with a hot cup of coffee and a food parcel. Clearly, she'd been concerned about the possibility of his starving to death on the road as she'd packed enough food for three men, including an entire tin of the shortbread he liked.

Hope did nothing by halves.

They hardly spoke, their eyes saying all that was necessary. As he drove out, he looked back from the end of the yard. She was standing at the cabin door watching. As she lifted a hand in a brief wave, Luke realised it was going to be a long ten days away from her.

But when he did return, he'd have a dozen smelly chickens - and the preacher.

CHAPTER THIRTY-TWO

B ROTHER Gareth?"

The tall, angelic looking man wearing the dog collar glanced up. The old man was waiting for an answer.

"Sorry, Reverend Drago. I was just marvelling at how God works. My first mission here and it's a wedding! Between Mr Harcourt and...Hope Booker, is it? It couldn't be better."

Reverend Drago's chubby, weathered face split in a grin.

"You are so right. It is indeed a pleasure and an honour. I wish I could go myself, but with this gout I'd never make it." A heavily bandaged foot resting on a small stool bore testimony to the old man's plight. "It is a miracle you turning up when you did."

Luke was disappointed. He liked the old man and had looked forward to having the humorous, and often mildly scandalous, stories of his life before becoming a man of God enlivening the trip home.

This new preacher, there was something about him that didn't ring true. Luke had an overwhelming desire to cancel the whole thing and go straight back to Hope. He'd much rather wait till Reverend Drago was well enough.

"How long does your gout attack usually last, Reverend Drago?" he enquired.

"Oh, well, it depends. It comes and goes. I'm delighted that you are wanting to put this right, Luke. I've never been convinced of the legality of Mr Butler's scheme. Seems to me, a man can't buy a wife. He has to marry one." He shifted in his seat, trying to ease the pain in his foot. "Now, don't you worry, my boy, Brother Gareth Harper here comes highly recommended. You don't want to put off your wedding because of me, do you? Think of your lovely bride waiting at home for you," he chuckled richly.

What could Luke say? "No, I suppose not. Will you be ready to leave first thing in the morning, Brother Gareth?"

"Certainly. Do I need to hire a horse? I believe the livery stable here is an excellent one."

"Yes. I came in the wagon. I have to get some supplies. There'd probably still be room, but you'll need a way to get back to town."

"Excellent," the young pastor exclaimed. The seemingly forced enthusiasm grated on Luke's nerves. He really disliked the man.

"I'll meet you here tomorrow then, about six in the morning?"

"Six! Oh, yes, of course. It's always best to get an early start I say."

Really? thought Luke. I'd have said you're more used to getting in at six, after a night of drunken debauchery. How'd you ever get that dog collar?

"Fine. Goodbye, Reverend Drago, I hope your foot gets better soon."

When he shook hands with both of them the old man returned a hearty, solid clasp, whereas Brother Gareth's soft hand made Luke's skin crawl.

Luke was glad he'd told the man to hire a horse. It gave him some space. Harper tried to make conversation. Luke was polite, but his gut instinct told him something wasn't adding up. It was a long five days to get home. The chickens didn't help.

It was when they arrived at the cabin that the future Luke planned and dreamed of disintegrated before him.

*

Hope heard the wagon rumble in and raced out of the barn, Wolf at her heels. Luke pulled up and leapt out of the wagon. Striding over he swept her up in his arms, swinging her around with a laugh and kissing her passionately, Wolf jumping up around them.

"Luke!" she gasped.

His delight at seeing her, his strong arms around her and she was laughing up at him in unaffected joy. "Hope. I've brought you a surprise. One that means that we can be together, really together. Forever."

"What are you talking about?" she laughed.

"I've brought a preacher. He can marry us now. Today. This is Brother Gareth, by the way." Luke nodded over his shoulder. "Do you want to put on that pretty yellow dress I got you? We'll wait, but not too long." He grinned, pulled her back in his arms and kissed her, hard.

Wolf growled.

Hope stilled in his hands, her eyes filled with confusion, searching his face. Marry him? But...he hadn't said he loved her. She knew without a shadow of doubt he wanted to sleep with her, that he desired her, but there was more to being married than that. She looked over Luke's shoulder and with a sharp intake of breath, fainted away in his arms.

When she came to, she was lying on the bed in the cabin. Luke was sitting on the edge of the bed, holding a cool, damp cloth on her forehead. "How are you feeling?"

"A little dizzy. What happened?" Her hand drifted to her head.

"You took one look at the preacher and fainted."

"The preacher?" She sat up quickly, pulling the cloth away, "Where is he?"

"Outside. He went for a walk down to the river."

"Luke. He's not a preacher."

"What? Yes, he is. Reverend Drago vouches for him. Drago couldn't come, so he asked Harper to come—"

"No, no, you don't understand." She scrambled up, pushing past him, her hands twisting together. "His name's not Harper, it's Gabriel Hunter. The man I told you about."

"Hunter? The one that asked you to marry him? The day, you think—"

"Yes. He can't have changed that much. He can't marry us!"

"Hope is correct." Harper...Hunter stood at the door. Luke got to his feet. The image of two dogs circling each other flashed through Hope's mind.

"My name was Gabriel Hunter. We knew each other in Savannah. But I have changed, Hope. I changed my name when I changed my way of life." He turned back to Luke. "But the one thing she is right about, I can't marry the two of you."

Luke stepped slightly in front of Hope. "What are you talking about, Hunter?" His voice was dangerously quiet.

A smile twitched at Hunter's mouth. "She's engaged to me."

Time slammed to a halt. Hope swallowed hard. This couldn't be happening. She'd recognised Gabriel, but she still couldn't remember those lost hours. She'd regained nearly all her lost memory, but nothing except snatches from that afternoon of the church picnic and waking up on the boat.

"No, I'm not, Gabriel." Her voice wavered.

"Are you going back on your word, Hope? That's not like you. You always had such...integrity." A slightly mocking smile flickering at the corner of Gabriel's mouth.

"She never said yes." Luke's face was hard.

"Not to you, Harcourt."

"No, Gabriel. I never agreed to marry *you*," said Hope staring wide eyed at Hunter.

"I'm afraid you did."

"I wouldn't have, Gabriel. I never loved you. That's why my mother was so angry."

He smiled slightly. "Your mother was always upset with you, Hope. You never could please her. This unladylike behaviour won't surprise her in the least." He glanced around the cabin. The fact that there was only one bed seemed more obvious now than it ever had. It felt huge, overwhelming in the small cabin.

Luke's clenched fist curled tighter.

"Imagine how disappointed your father will be," Hunter continued, "when he finds out you've been living here as Harcourt's wife. Which you're not."

Hope sank slowly onto the bed. "We haven't—"

Luke stepped in. "How we live is none of your business, Hunter. It's time for you to leave."

"Not without Hope."

"She's not going anywhere with you. Get out."

Hunter turned to her. "Hope, the way you've been living is...wrong. You know that. As a man's wife, without being married to him? No one will ever believe you haven't slept with him." He pressed his point harder, "It'll destroy your father, if it doesn't kill him. Not to mention your family's reputation. You know how happy your mother will be about *that*. Your family will be ruined. Charles will never succeed as a doctor with this scandal hanging over him. He'd have to leave Savannah. Even then, you know how scandal follows a man." He paused. "You can prevent all of this."

"How?" she whispered.

"By coming back with me. That way no one need know about this...rather sordid arrangement." He waved his pale hand disdainfully around the room. His face gave the distinct impression he'd walked into a bawdyhouse.

Hope's face was white. Luke stared at her, stunned. It was everything Hope feared the most. "Hope, don't listen to him. You know we've done nothing wrong. He's talking nonsense. Your family will never know."

"Really?" smirked Harper. "You expect me not to tell them? They think she's dead. It would be cruel not to let them know she's still alive." He spread his hands and shrugged. "Of course, I'd have to tell how I found her and how she's been living."

"Luke?" Hope's voice was no more than a whisper.

"You're not seriously listening to this, Hope?"

"My father. Charlie." Her voice broke. "My mother. She'll be so angry. Oh, Luke, what should I do?"

Luke went cold. He could feel Hope slipping away. He turned to her, put his hands on her shoulders. Hunter coughed. Luke frowned. Somehow Hunter made even this feel dirty. He stepped back. His hands falling away. "Hope, is this what you want?"

"No! Oh, Luke, I don't know what to do. I can't let my family think...what should I do? Tell me. What do you...I'm so confused." She stretched out a hand towards him, but he didn't respond.

There was a long silence. Hope stared at Luke. His face was grim, his lips a thin, hard line, his eyes like ice. The fact that she hadn't instantly refused to go with Hunter staggered him. Why was she even thinking about this? Deep inside he knew. This went far back, further than the day he'd bought her off the ship. He couldn't fight her history, her fears. They'd been ingrained since childhood. How could she even contemplate leaving? What about everything they'd been through? What about how they felt about each other? Did his love mean so little to her? Did she really not feel the same about him?

"Tell me what to do, Luke. Do you want me..." Her voice trailed off in despair. The moment stretched out, it tightened, a garrotte around their hearts.

"It's your choice, Hope." Luke's voice was cold, stony. He walked straight up to Hunter, so fast the man had to lean back. "This is my cabin. Get out." Hunter bowed his head and walked out.

*

Hope moved mechanically. She felt numb. The pain in her heart was mercifully deadened by the blankness of her mind. She was unwanted. Luke...

She'd been wrong. He only wanted to sleep with her. He didn't love her. He never had. She wanted to get away from him as quickly as possible. To go as far as she could and never see him again.

He'd given her a carpetbag to pack her few belongings in. She took only what Lee-Ming had given her, nothing Luke had bought. The skirts, blouses, the dress, even the hairbrush, she left in the cupboard.

She still didn't remember what'd happened after Gabriel proposed to her that day at the picnic, but she knew he'd never taken her in his arms as Luke had. He'd never kissed her as Luke had. She was only going with him to get away from Luke.

She wanted to stay with Luke, if he'd only asked her. Instead, he'd given her the choice. She didn't want a choice, she wanted him to take her into his arms and tell her he loved her, tell her to stay. Demand she stay. But he hadn't.

Hope's heart was in pieces. As soon as she was packed, Luke brought round the wagon. He'd tossed the chickens into the coop and put down food and water while she was packing. His face told her nothing. It was a cold, hard mask. He didn't even look at her. He swung her bag into the back of the wagon and held out a hand to help her in. When she hesitated, he spun away, leaving her standing in the yard.

Gabriel extended his white, long fingered hand towards her. It was almost flaccid to her touch. A shiver ran up her arm. She climbed up as quickly as she could and folded her hands tightly in her lap.

Luke shoved open the cabin door, ripped the quilts off the bed, scattering pillows, her nightgown, messing the sheets. He tossed the quilts in the back of the wagon and climbed up beside Hope.

They headed higher into the mountain. There'd be nobody at the cabin while they were in town. Luke would have to ask Daniel to look after the animals. Hopefully, he'd forgiven him for the last 'disagreement'. When they pulled into the Nlaka'pamux village Luke handed the reins to Hope and jumped down. Adam and Daniel were inspecting the string of horses on the edge of the camp.

"Adam, Daniel." He greeted them in their own tongue, unaware the astonishingly bleak look in his eyes had shocked both Daniel and Adam. Especially Adam. The old despair in Luke's face had faded months ago, but now it was back, deeper than ever. Hope's sorrow and the smugness of the man on the horse were obvious. He wore the disgusted, pained expression Adam had seen before, on men, and women, who thought of his people as savages, dirt, vermin. Adam's eyes narrowed. A muscle in his jaw twitched.

"Be careful, Luke. He is not a man to be trusted."

"I know. Daniel, will you look after the animals at the cabin for me?"

Daniel frowned and gave a brusque nod.

"Thank you."

Luke pushed the mules as hard as he dared. He wanted it over as soon as possible. He spoke only when necessary.

It was a nightmare journey. The days were arduous. The rains had carved deep ruts in the road and Hope was constantly flung against him. Luke made no attempt to make the journey easier for her. Eventually, she insisted on walking over the roughest bits. Of course, Gabriel dismounted to assist her out, then stayed to walk with her. He bent his head so Luke couldn't hear and talked quietly and earnestly to Hope. Luke had no choice but to stay in the wagon.

But there was more than that worrying Luke. Every now and then, he'd catch a disturbing, calculating look on Hunter's face, especially when he thought no one was looking. Luke's mood blackened. He brooded over ways he could kill the reptile. And how much he'd enjoy doing it. When they made camp for the night, he sat staring into the fire long after the other two retired, Gabriel to his bedroll and Hope to curl up tightly under the quilts in the wagon.

With the cold dawn of every morning, Luke's misery increased. He could see Hope wasn't getting much sleep. Her eyes were filled with despair, dark shadows thickly smudged beneath them. Her unhappiness made him so angry the metallic taste of it filled his mouth. He'd never believed he could be this enraged at her. If she didn't want to go, all she had to do was say so.

But she was leaving. And it was her choice.

He kept going over and over it in his tortured mind. How could she want to? He'd lost Tess and survived, but this... this twisting knife, this losing Hope, plunged him into a deeper, bitterer darkness than he'd ever known. He hated that tall snake of a so-called preacher who was taking her from him. Luke longed to feel the bones of the weasel's face, his ribs, crunch under his fist.

When they arrived in town, they took separate rooms at the hotel. All three, for very different reasons, were relieved to finally be alone.

CHAPTER THIRTY-THREE

WITH a hard smack that left the saloon doors swinging Luke stalked up to the counter.

"Whiskey. The bottle."

The noise in the room had faded when he strode in but picked up again almost immediately as he surveyed the place in the cheap, fly-dotted mirror above the bar. Stephen Butler was playing a quiet game of poker with some patrons in a dark corner. A movement caught Luke's eye. A brassy blonde in an extremely tight bodice was staring at him. She was draped over a tipsy, but shy miner, her hand rested on his flabby stomach, not far, Luke noticed from a fat purse tucked into the man's belt. The idiot still had the dirt from the mine all over him. Luke guessed that since arriving in town he'd probably been boasting about his strike to anyone who'd listen. Gold was like that. It made a man feel invincible. It made a man stupid.

The blonde smiled at Luke's reflection and said to no one in particular. "Look who finally succumbed to our charms."

Luke knew exactly what she was thinking. It was written all over her face. She eased her way to the counter and watched him, clearly trying to calculate the right time to make her move.

Luke took the black bottle and glass and made his way to the end of the counter, as far away from the rest of the room, and the slut, as possible. He finished the bottle almost without stopping for breath. "Another."

A second bottle replaced the first. Luke poured the gold liquid into the small glass and tossed it down. He was aware of the blonde's smile and her gravitation towards him, hips swinging. He looked up slowly. He made no attempt to hide the contempt he felt. It sat in rigid lines on his face. Since Hope had left him, he'd felt nothing but cold, hard, uncompromising rage. The whore froze. Fear swept across her face. She stepped back. Luke's eyes dropped down to the empty glass. He could almost smell her relief. His scorn deepened as she turned back to the miner, the safer prospect.

Another drink disappeared down Luke's throat. He picked up the bottle and looked at it. Nameless. No saying where it came from. Whatever it was, it burned as went down. It was strong. It wouldn't take too much to reach oblivion. He shouldn't have started this. It'd been hard to stop the last time. It was always women that got him drinking. First Tess and now… he'd never imagined it would have been Hope as well.

Many hours and bottles of whisky later, he deliberately picked a fight with the shy miner. It didn't take long before he was flat on his face, blood seeping from a cut over his eye. He dragged himself up and took another sloppy swing at the miner. The tough, old man simply sidestepped and then shoved him through the swing doors. Luke staggered. His feet weren't working properly. As he stepped off the sidewalk he tripped, collapsing in an untidy heap in the street.

He sighed, coughing in the dirt. It was quieter down here, but the dirt tasted bad. He rolled sluggishly onto his back and lay there, hurting. Dark forms peeled themselves from the shadows of the alley and made their way towards him. He swore. His arms were like lead. He wasn't sure if his hands were still attached to his wrists. He was going to get robbed, probably hurt, again. There wasn't a damn thing he could do about it. He laughed. He didn't care. He'd actually welcome the pain of another beating.

Four oddly shaped and distorted faces peered down at him, swimming, blurring and melting into each other. He sighed and let his head drop onto the street.

"Ow," he muttered.

*

Gabriel Hunter, lying on the bed in the hotel was, for once in his life, thinking through a plan before putting it into motion. He'd have to disembark at San Francisco. He had no intention of enduring that Panamanian railway again, and he couldn't go back to Savannah. Neither jail, nor the men he owed money to, were an enticing prospect. Besides, he was broke.

Silver Birch Landing was meant to be a chance to start over. A new name, a new life. Fate clearly had other ideas. Money and Hope, they always seemed to be intertwined, a tightly clinging vine threatening to choke him. When he'd proposed to her the day of the church picnic, he'd been desperate. His gambling debts had been enormous.

Money seemed to trickle through his fingers like melting jelly, sticking just long enough to give the impression he had some. It had all started when his father had refused to meet any more of his gambling debts. A month later, he'd met Stephen Butler at that poker game in Savannah. He shouldn't have lost so much money to him. It wasn't possible. He was convinced the man had cheated. When Butler had refused to wait more than a week for the money, he'd hatched what then seemed like a fool-proof plan – marry Hope Booker.

Her family was rich; her mother liked him. Her mother was a snob and would never allow even the breath of scandal to touch her family. She'd make sure his debts were paid.

When they met in public, he paid just enough attention to Hope's mother to flatter her. It took more effort than he'd imagined. She expected adoration and could command it with merely the lifting of a neat eyebrow. For a moment, he considered blackmail, but she was as impregnable as a fortress. She enjoyed men at her feet, but she had no intention of allowing him into her bed. He quickly changed tack and played up to her desire to reign socially.

Being connected by marriage to his family would open that door for her, especially as his own mother had died many years before. As his mother-in-law, she would become one of the most important women in the town, the gracious hostess at every function his father threw. And there were many, all attended by the cream of Savannah high society. It was the glittering *haut monde* her heart craved. His father was, after all, the Episcopalian Bishop of the city.

They hadn't considered Hope. Neither of them could believe it when she refused him. He tried pleading, flattery, but she still didn't accept him. He took her back to the one person she was most afraid of— her mother.

He stood just outside the door and eavesdropped on the conversation. He struggled not to laugh. It was a masterful piece of destruction. Hope was humiliated, torn to pieces. When her mother was finished, Hope left the loveless, elegant room, carefully shutting the door behind her. He waited until she mounted the first step on the iron-framed staircase twisting its way up the wall.

"Hope? My poor child. You look terrible. Let me help you. Please. Come, some fresh air will do you good."

It was unlikely she even heard what he'd said, but she turned and walked out of the house with him. He drove her along the seashore. The crisp, salty tang to the air brought some colour back to her pale cheeks. She was utterly silent the whole time, staring ahead, a lost, blank look on her face.

As they were bowling along in the carriage, Stephen Butler, on a high-spirited chestnut trotted towards them.

Just as they were about to pass each other, Butler pulled up and grabbed the reins, effectively stopping Gabriel's horses.

"Are you able to meet your commitments yet, Hunter?"

"Not yet, I'm working on it." Gabriel saw Butler's eyes slide towards Hope.

"Are you confident of a prosperous outcome?"

"I think so."

"Don't think. Be sure. You're running out of time. If you fail, you may want to consider exchanging your current merchandise for your obligations. As I'm sure you know, I have a number of establishments that require," he glanced again at Hope, "that particular type of commodity."

"I'll find the money."

"You have until six this evening, Hunter. My ship sails at seven with the tide. If you don't have the money and you don't want to part with the goods in question, there's always debtor's prison or I could ask your father." He smirked, touched the rim of his hat and dug his heels into the horse. The beast carried him away at a brisk trot.

Taking a deep, shaky breath, Hunter turned the carriage to face out to sea. He had some idea it would be more romantic. Perhaps that's what was called for - a romantic gesture.

"Hope," he began, "I know I said I wouldn't mention it again. But I can't help myself. I feel for your situation. Let me take care of you. Marry me." He leaned in and tried to kiss her. A look of horrified shock surged across her face. Her eyes wide with - was it surprise or disgust? He pulled her into his arms. His anger flared as she struggled.

Even thinking about it now made him grind his teeth. She'd actually cringed away from him. Him! As if he was a leper. If there hadn't been other people promenading and riding along the seafront, he would have gladly taught her a lesson.

He had no choice now, and it was all Hope's fault. His life was on the line. He managed to 'get lost' on their way home.

In fact, they'd never been too far from the dockyards despite the tortuous twists and turns he'd taken.

Pulling up in front of a seedy, dilapidated inn, he jumped down and taking her hand solicitously said, "Why don't you go inside, Hope, and have some tea while I ask for directions."

Pulling her hand free, she climbed down on her own. As she stepped past him, he pulled out the short, rubber cosh he kept for protection and hit her hard on the back of the head. Catching her as she fell and slipping the cosh back into one of his voluminous coat pockets was the work of a few seconds. At first, he worried he'd hit her too hard. It was with relief that he saw she was still breathing. He tossed her unceremoniously into the carriage and drove as quickly as he could for the wharf.

Butler was leaning on the taffrail of the ship when Gabriel drove up. He issued a brief command to a sailor who sauntered down the gangplank, pulled Hope roughly out of the carriage and tossed her over his shoulder like a sack of grain. He carried her onto the ship disappearing below decks with his burden.

"We square now, Butler?" Hunter shouted up.

Butler took a pull on the long, thin cheroot he was smoking, then gave a mocking salute.

It wouldn't have surprised anyone, except Gabriel Hunter, when two months later he discovered himself in debt again. Deeper debt than ever. This time, his creditors did go to his father. The bishop's rage knew no bounds. Hunter stood in stunned silence on the Persian carpet in his father's office.

"After all I said to you last time, I cannot believe that you would dare accumulate even greater debts than before! And then to have them brought to my attention, by those, those ruffians. Here, in my office! At the church! I cannot and will not pay any more. I cannot be seen to be sponsoring your disgusting lifestyle. You have gone too far this time. Get out.

Take your debts with you. Never set foot in my house again. I don't ever want to see your profligate face again. Ever! *Get out.*"

Hunter, desperate and reckless as ever, went straight home, packed his bags and then began a hunt for money, or anything he could easily sell. The desk in his father's study should have something. While searching the drawers, he came across a letter from Reverend Drago. Silver Birch Landing was growing; he needed help.

So many people live a few days out of town and cannot make it in for Sunday worship. If, Bishop Hunter, you could suggest a likely young man to assist with circuit preaching, I would be in your debt.

Hunter pocketed the letter, as well as some of the bishop's headed notepaper. Later that night, in a cheap hotel room, he wrote a very carefully worded reply, forging his father's signature with practised ease.

As far as he knew, Silver Birch Landing was a frontier town. Probably a gold town, despite its name. He'd be sure to find a number of poker games going on any night of the week. He'd stay only as long as it took him to win enough money, or gold, to put him back on his feet. And, more importantly, it was a long way from Savannah. A long way from his other creditors.

His shock at hearing Hope's name in his first week there had made him feel violently ill. On the five-day journey into the interior with Luke Harcourt, he'd turned over plan after plan in his mind. It was an uncomfortable journey, made worse by the fact that Harcourt had made no effort to hide his mistrust or disdain for him.

Gabriel grinned. How ironic that it should be honesty which put Hope into his hands. He could hardly believe how easy it had been. He laughed at the memory of the deep flush of embarrassment which flooded her face when he'd pointed out no one would believe she hadn't slept with Harcourt. What a prude.

Now all he had to do was make sure she never regained her memory. If she did, who knew what she might do? If she told anyone what he'd done, or even where he was, he'd be finished. The debt his father disowned him for was still outstanding. The men he owed it to were ruthless. If they had even an inkling of where he was, he was a dead man. He had to get rid of Hope as quickly as possible and this time she wasn't coming back.

He also needed to leave Silver Birch Landing.

CHAPTER THIRTY-FOUR

WHEN Luke awoke, his head was in two pieces and each piece was in a very bad mood. He groaned. His mouth tasted like a skunk had died in it. He sat up, slowly. But not slowly enough. His brain slid, banging into his skull. His stomach slid the other way.

Clutching his aching head, he groaned again. Even that hurt. His eyes felt like sandpaper and when he tried to open them, daylight jabbed its fingers viciously into his brain. He shut his eyes, rubbing hard at them, trying to clear the flashing lights. His neck was stiff and sore. His body felt bruised and battered. Had someone kicked him? He remembered nothing of the night before.

"Where am I? Hope?" There was no response but the pounding of his head.

His memory lurched back. That hurt his brain the most. Hope was leaving today. He was losing her. He felt sick. Really sick. There was a bucket near the bed. He fell to his knees and retched into it.

He pulled himself back onto the bed, wiping his mouth with the back of his hand. "What the hell?" He pulled at his underwear. "Where are my clothes?"

Lee-Chan stuck his head round the door. Seeing Luke was awake, he shouted over his shoulder in Mandarin. It bounced painfully around Luke's skull.

"Shh," he whispered.

Noise, and the pain in his head, erupted. Two young Chinese men ran in and grabbed him. They dragged him out the room and down the corridor. His head bounced between his shoulders sending violent waves of agony through his brain. They dropped him on the floor. Before he realised what they were doing, they lifted him and dumped him into a vat filled with ice cold water.

"*Aargh!*" He scrambled to get out. The young men shoved his head under. Spluttering, he pulled his head out, "What the—*No!*" Lee-Chan emptied another bucket of cold water over his head. He didn't get another chance to say anything for a while. He was thrust under the water again and again till he was choking.

"*Stop!* Stop. Please. I can't breathe." He was sober. Or at least well on the way to becoming so. If they didn't stop, he'd drown. They let him go.

"You get dressed now," Lee-Chan said crossly. "Then come to kitchen. My Ming make strong coffee. Stupid man." He hustled the young men out, slamming the door behind him.

Luke realised he did need to wake up properly. He had to think. Ducking his head under the water he tried to clear his mind and remember what had happened last night. Nothing, his head was still cotton-wool. He needed that coffee. He also needed to get out of the vat. He was blue with cold. His lungs hurt.

It wasn't much better out. A clean set of clothes was laid on a chair for him. They weren't his. Oh well, he couldn't go downstairs naked and it looked like they'd fit. Stripping off his wet underwear, he pulled the dry clothes on and ran his hands through his hair trying to neaten it. His body was still wracked with the occasional bone-cracking shiver. It didn't help his stomach. He made his way downstairs as quickly, albeit a little gingerly, as he could.

Ming and Chan were waiting for him. Both of them looked grim. The two young men stood quietly in the background.

"I'm sorry about last night," Luke said apologetically. "I think I probably gave you some trouble."

Ming rattled out a sharp sentence, banging her fist on the table. Luke winced.

"She wants to know where is Hope," Chan translated. His voice was just as tight as his wife's.

"She's gone," Luke said. "She's leaving today."

"What happened?" Chan asked.

A muscle twitched in Luke's jaw. "It's none of your business."

Ming slammed a huge cup of coffee in front of Luke. Coffee went everywhere.

"Drink," commanded Chan. "Then you tell us. Don't argue. I save your life. Your life my business."

"That was over a year—"

At the look on Chan's face, Luke stopped, embarrassed. He picked up the cup and took a swig. It scalded him all the way down. It was the hottest, blackest, thickest coffee he'd ever had. He could almost chew it. It was also worse than anything Hope had ever made. The only thing that made it palatable was knowing it would clear his head. The dead skunk in his mouth got another coating of fur.

Once he'd finished, he filled the cup with water from the jug standing in the middle of the table. He drank that down as well. He downed another. The skunk retreated, reluctantly.

He sighed, leaned back, his hands turning the cup round and round. He told them the whole miserable tale as dispassionately as he could.

The Lees stared at him. Ming asked a question. Chan didn't want to translate, although, Luke realised that for the first time since he'd known her, she'd needed no translation of his speech. Ming was insistent.

Chan harrumphed. "Ming wants to know what you said to Hope."

"I told you what happened."

"No. What you say to Hope when she say she go?"

Luke hunched over his empty cup. "It was her choice."

Ming interrupted, smacking her fist on the table again. "You tell her you love her? You tell her stay?"

Luke looked surprised, both at the question and the fact Ming was speaking English. "She knows I love her."

"You say so?" Ming demanded, her arms akimbo, her fists planted firmly on her ample hips. "You tell her to stay? You say, 'I love you Hope, please stay with me'?"

Luke looked down at his cup. "No."

A hard, sharp slap connected with the back of his head. Shocked, surprised pain ricocheted around his skull again.

She shook her finger in his face, "No wonder she leave you. Stupid, stupid man."

He rubbed the tender spot, cringing slightly away from her quickly lifted hand, clearly aching to give him another clout.

"How she know you love her, unless you say it? Why she stay if you not tell you want her to? When she leave?"

"High tide, I should imagine."

One of the young men stepped forward and whispered in Ming's ear. She leapt at Luke, her small hands tugging at him, pulling him out of the chair, shoving him towards the door. "You go now. Almost two o'clock. Hurry. Almost high tide. Go get Hope, tell her you love her. Tell her stay. Stupid man, hurry. Hurry!"

Out in the street, he could see the clock hanging on the front of the general store. Luke's mind suddenly cleared. He was more sober now than he'd ever been. He couldn't lose Hope. He ran for the livery stable first. There was something he had to get. He prayed he'd have time.

He weaved in and out of the crowd, forcing his way through. He could hear the whistle. The ship was about to leave. He had about ten minutes before it pulled away from the dock. He pushed harder, knocking people out of the way. Angry yells and shouts followed his desperate, determined progress.

He broke onto the wharf just as the final whistle blew. The gangplank was about to be raised. He raced along, yelling her name. A laden porter didn't see him. They collided, sliding along the floor, baggage flying. Luke ripped himself out of the chaos of man and luggage, and staggering, leaped for the gangplank.

He strode across the deck pulling women around to see if it was her.

At last. She was sitting on the far side of the deckhouse, squashed on a low bench crowded with other travellers. Hunter wasn't there. She'd been crying, her eyes were bright green, her face pale. Luke's heart jerked.

"Hope!"

She stared at him. Was it only shock in her eyes or was there, he dared to think, a glimmer of joy? Her hands were gripped tightly in her lap.

"Luke?" she whispered.

"Go away!" Luke's bark was harsh and uncompromising. The other passengers were only too glad to comply. They wanted nothing to do with this fierce looking man with the blazing eyes. The bench cleared in an instant. Passengers and sailors alike were staring in stunned silence, the business of the boat at a standstill.

Luke took a deep breath, trying to slow the dry hammering in his chest. She was wearing the old, pale grey dress he'd first seen her in, the one with the burnt hem and the torn petticoat.

He had to get this right. He wouldn't get another chance. "Hope." Now he was here, he wasn't sure what to say. God, help me get this right. Don't let me lose her now, he prayed.

"What are you doing here?" Gabriel Hunter stalked up.

Finally! Luke swung round and ploughed his rock-hard fist through the man's face. The crunch of his breaking nose was one of the most satisfying sounds Luke had ever heard.

Hope was on feet, her hand at her throat. "Luke?"

He turned back to her. "You are not leaving me!" His voice was still harsh. He cleared his throat. "I have something for you." He reached into his pocket and pulled out a small bag. It was heavy in her hands.

"What is it?"

"One hundred dollars in gold." He'd taken it from the secret hiding place under the seat in the wagon where he always kept it. One never knew when it might come in handy.

She didn't say anything, her eyes searching his face.

"It's what I paid for you. I figured you should have it. Now I don't own you anymore."

She blinked.

"I'll give you a receipt if you like." His mouth tipped in a quick attempt at humour. Her stillness worried him; he couldn't stand it anymore. "Dammit, Hope!" He swept her into his arms and kissed her, hard, ruthlessly. Hope dropped the bag of gold with a thunk onto the deck. She pushed against Luke. It made no difference. He simply pulled her closer, bent her backwards till she had no choice but to clutch his jacket tightly for fear of falling. His mouth possessed hers uncompromisingly.

As soon as he drew breath once more, he said, "Hope. I love you." He told her again. It was shockingly easy to say. Now it was out, he couldn't understand why it'd been so hard before. It was as simple as breathing. It gave him intense pleasure, indescribable joy to say it. "I love you. Marry me. Be my wife."

"No!" A hand clutched at his shoulder.

Luke smiled at Hope, stood her on her feet and turned fast, slamming his knee into Hunter's crotch. The reptile collapsed in agony.

Luke swept up the pouch of gold and shoved it back into his coat pocket. He swung round, crushed Hope against his chest again and kissed her passionately.

"You are *not* leaving. You hear me? I love you and you're coming home with me right now!" He tossed her over his shoulder, thrust his boot into Hunter's face, sending the man sprawling, and strode off the deck.

"Luke! Wait! Wait! Put me down!" Luke wasn't sure if Hope was laughing or crying.

"When we get off the ship!" He pushed a deckhand out of his way, ignoring Hope's pleas until he reached the wharf.

He dropped her back onto her feet. "Now, what was it you wanted to say?"

"Luke." She took his face into her hands. "Thank you. I thought you'd never come. Take me home."

"You mean—"

"I mean, yes, I'll marry you."

He'd never seen such a look of unadulterated love on a woman's face in his life. He put his hands on her waist carefully, afraid to break the magic.

She looked down. "But..."

He panicked, gripping her tightly. "But what?"

She smiled shyly. "Promise me something first?"

"Anything." It was reckless, but what the hell.

"Promise me... you'll marry me today."

He laughed and swept her into his arms, swinging her around and began to kiss her all over again. As they were walking back into town, arms wrapped lovingly around each other, oblivious to the stares of the townspeople, Hope stopped.

"What?" asked Luke.

"My family, my father, Charlie...Luke, I—"

"Don't worry, my love. I can't believe I didn't think of it before. If Hunter tells them where you are, he'll also have to explain what he was doing here and why he had a false name. Sounds to me like something's not right. A man only changes his name when he's in serious trouble. He won't say anything." He took her in his arms. "And now that we know where you're from, we can send them a letter ourselves, after we're married of course. No one's taking you away from me again!"

CHAPTER THIRTY-FIVE

I CAN'T believe this!" exclaimed Reverend Drago when they told him the truth about Gabriel Hunter. "I most sincerely apologise. I had no idea. Absolutely none, I do assure you."

"It's not your fault."

"Oh, but it is, I should have checked, I should have—"

"There is one way you can make it up to us." Luke's eyes twinkled. He grinned as Hope flushed.

"Anything, my dear man, anything."

"You can marry us. Now."

"Now?"

"Right now, this minute."

Reverend Drago laughed. "Delighted. Absolutely delighted to. But, if I may?"

Luke frowned slightly.

"You need a best man and dear Hope needs a bridesmaid."

"No, we don't, really!" Hope said quickly.

"Yes, we do," said Luke. "As witnesses, if nothing else."

"That's right. Any ideas whom you'd like to ask?"

Luke grinned. "Yes. I'll get Chan. The Lees would never forgive me if I didn't include them. Come on. Don't go anywhere, Reverend Drago! We'll be back shortly." He grabbed Hope's hand and dragged her along the aisle, down the church stairs and, practically at a run and to Hope's astonishment, into Miss Sylvie's Haberdashery and Ladies Emporium.

"*Miss Sylvie!*"

Miss Sylvie's thin china teacup rattled in surprise. "Mr Harcourt!"

"We're getting married. I mean, this is my wife, Hope. And we're getting married."

"I'm...not sure I understand."

"We're getting married, now. Hope needs a dress. A good one. I have to go. I'll be back, ten minutes. Hope will tell you everything." He went for the door, strode back, pulled Hope into his arms and kissed her full on the mouth.

"Well. I do hope you *are* going to tell me!" said Miss Sylvie as the bell tinkled in Luke's wake. "I'm Miss Sylvie, by the way."

"Hope, Hope Booker."

"Not Harcourt?"

Hope flushed. "It's a long story."

"And you're getting married, today?"

"Yes."

"Ah." Miss Sylvie ran her eyes quickly over the woman standing in front of her taking in the modest dress in subdued grey. "That explains the nightgowns."

"I'm sorry?"

Miss Sylvie shook her head; it wasn't important. "Come with me." She hustled Hope out into the street and down to the Chinese laundry, forgetting to lock the store in her excitement.

Lee-Ming crowed with delight at both the news and Miss Sylvie's plan.

"Bring her back as soon as she's ready," Miss Sylvie instructed.

A bath was quickly prepared for Hope. Laughing, she stripped off and hopped in. She wanted to wash away all the uncertainty and tears of the last few days. Luke loved her. It rang through her whole being like church bells, like the sound of waterfalls, like the breeze in the tops of the pines.

Unlike the last bath here at the laundry, Hope couldn't wait to get out. As she did, Ming and Sweet Jade reappeared, giggling and squabbling like children. They handed her a dark silk robe and some black felt slippers. Barely waiting for her to put them on they hustled her out the back door and down the alley back to Miss Sylvie's.

Miss Sylvie had been busy. She held up one of the most beautiful dresses Hope had ever seen against her. It was a cloud of light blue stuff with small white embroidered flowers scattered over the tight bodice. It was long enough, just. Miss Sylvie swirled away to hang the dress up and Hope found herself pushed down onto a stool. Ming and Sweet Jade began to rub sweet, jasmine scented oil into Hope's skin, while Miss Sylvie hunted for the perfect coloured ribbons and shoes.

The perfumed oil smelled heavenly. Hope's spirit, as well as her skin, soaked it in. Then the ladies addressed her hair. They made her bend her head over a basin and poured lovely lemony water over her hair, vigorously rubbed it with a towel and began to comb out the tangles.

Meanwhile, Mr Samson was, for once, speechless. He wiped his eyes which had teared up in delight at Luke's news and his request. Squaring his shoulders, Mr Samson said, "Mr Harcourt, I would be delighted. If I might..." He tugged Luke's shirt and waistcoat into order. Out of a small suitcase he pulled a clothes brush and furbished up Luke's coat.

"One moment." He hurried out the large open barn doors at the back. Luke was twitching with impatience. "Here we are," Mr Samson had a small wildflower and a short length of fern, which when he attached it to the lapel of Luke's jacket, served as a delicate and unobtrusive boutonnière.

"I believe we are ready, sir. Shall we go?"

The men stopped off at the Lees to pick up Chan, then made their way to the church. Luke had expected to wait for Hope. She did have to change clothes and maybe they couldn't find a dress to fit. After twenty minutes, he started to champ at the bit. After an hour, he was pacing the aisle. Mr Samson, Lee-Chan, Reverend Drago had made themselves at home on the pews and were enjoying a comfortable chat.

The door cracked open and Lee-Ming bustled down the aisle.

"Where is she?" demanded Luke.

Ming shushed him, flapping her hands at him, as she chirped at Chan. Her husband leapt to his feet, pulled Mr Samson with him and hustled the two of them back out the church.

A few minutes later, Chan, Ming, Sweet Jade and Miss Sylvie were hurrying towards the front of the church, broad smiles wreathed across their faces. Chan dragged Luke to the front of the church, nodding at the preacher who, after calling his wife from the back where she was bustling around setting up a hastily pulled together wedding tea, took his place on the shallow, wide step behind. The door opened and Hope, her hand tucked into Mr Samson's arm, stood framed in the doorway.

Luke almost didn't recognise her. The dainty, pretty shoes on her feet, the pale blue dress, the gleaming chocolate brown hair threaded with a wide blue ribbon, but most of all the glow on her face. Mr Samson gallantly kissed her hand and laid it in Luke's waiting one.

Hope's shyly smiling green eyes held an expression that took Luke's breath away. He wanted to say something, anything, but he was speechless.

Hope dropped her gaze for a moment, a blushing glow lighting her face. He squeezed her hand reassuringly. He felt as if he'd come to the top of a high mountain pass, where the air was clean and fresh. Where he could finally breathe. All he could see was her. She filled his vision with a smile that made his heart turn over. This moment had been worth waiting for.

Sunlight streamed in through the church windows and the open door. Tears were shed by the women. Even Mr Samson surreptitiously wiped a tear away.

As they took their vows, the church cat strolled in and sat between Luke and Hope, watching their every move, purring loudly. When the preacher asked if anyone knew of any just cause why they should not be married, the cat meowed. Everyone laughed. The cat, as if realising he'd made a faux pas began to clean his paw. He sauntered off again when Hope was pulled into Luke's arms and profoundly kissed by this man she loved so deeply, this man who was now truly her husband.

Later, after the small ceremony and some tea and cake, Mr Samson brought the wagon up from the livery stable. In his overflowing joy, Luke almost tossed Hope onto the seat in a flurry of petticoats and lace. As he laughed up at her a movement caught his eye. Standing in his shirtsleeves on the balcony of the Bright Star stood Stephen Butler, watching them through the drifting haze of his cheroot.

At that moment, Reverend Drago grabbed Luke's shoulder and spun him around pumping his hand up and down, making hilariously ribald remarks that seemed entirely inappropriate coming from a preacher. Luke swung himself up into the wagon and among laughter, hugs, kisses, good wishes and blessings Luke and Hope waved goodbye to their friends and began their journey home.

*

Luke and Hope retraced the trail they'd taken the first time they were 'married', the day they met, the day both of their lives had changed forever. But this journey was so very different.

Then, they'd been complete strangers who barely knew each other's names. Now, they not only knew each other, but loved each other deeply.

They stopped in the same field as before, on that first night so long ago. Only this time they were alone. And now, there was no embarrassment at being in the same wagon together, lying so close they breathed as one. Their quiet murmurs of love lifted into the night. Their skin, where it touched, was warmed with passion and desire.

On this, their first night together, Hope was very nervous and afraid. Not of Luke, but of what would happen between them. She didn't really know what to expect. She held her breath as Luke undid the buttons of her dress, carefully pulling the fabric off her shoulders and easing it over her hips. She was relieved when he left her in her shift; being naked wasn't something she was ready for yet. He kissed her with extreme gentleness and sweetness before lowering her to the bed of quilts.

It was only when her own desire took hold and she pulled at the buttons of his shirt that her shift joined her dress, along with his shirt and trousers.

He held her carefully, exploring her trembling body with soft kisses and gentle hands. Her wonder at the joy she felt when he touched her, grew into a breathless longing she'd never imagined. Hope never dreamed this kind of physical closeness with a man could be so sweet.

He placed a kiss in the soft centre of her palm and putting her hand on his chest, he drew it slowly down until it rested on his taut stomach, the muscles quivering at her touch.

Searching his eyes, she saw only deep, deep love. With a ragged breath, she moved her hand. His gentleness had taken away most of her fear. The rest of it soon dissolved in surprise and shared laughter. Their gentle lovemaking deepened into passion and desire.

Knowing the strength and power of him, Hope was grateful, thankful that he seemed in no rush, but instead, was slowly taking great delight in her. The feel of him against her took her breath away and she leaned into him, pulling him closer with a soft moan. Every moment with him was a new adventure. In the safety of his strong arms, she was willing to follow as he drew her along until she was ready to fall with him over the edge and into the night.

Much later, when velvet dark was deep and quiet, he stars turned slowly in their heavens and wolves howled on the mountain. Inside the confines of the covered wagon slept the two intertwined lovers whose lives and hearts had each found a new strength, a healing, a place of safety, and a home.

CHAPTER THIRTY-SIX

I T took over a week to travel back to the cabin this time. They woke late, went for walks, swam in the river, climbed into the forest and whenever their need for each other overwhelmed them, they made love. Needless to say, that was fairly often.

Luke was amazed at the way Hope gave herself to him. With no longer any fear or uncertainty. If he'd known, he would have taken her to town and married her sooner. He was filled with amused adoration at her shy attempts to initiate love making, and her desire, despite her inexperience, to please him.

It was a journey of discovery and he led her along slowly and gently. He wasn't a man with harsh or bizarre appetites. She was more than enough for him. She was all he'd ever wanted in a wife, in a woman, and in a lover. He simply revelled in her and in their new intimacy.

On the fourth day, they stopped at a forest pool to go swimming. She climbed onto the rocks and dived back into the water. As she surfaced, they heard a shouted greeting. She swam quickly to Luke and hid behind him. Just in time, for at that moment James Tyler, the neat, little doctor rode out of the forest. The twinkle in the old man's eye told Luke he'd seen the graceful dive his naked wife had taken.

"Morning folks," called the doctor.

"Morning, Doctor Tyler," replied Luke, a laugh fighting for possession of his face as his wife's soft body pressed against his back, her hands holding tightly to his chest.

"Nice day for a swim." The doctor grinned. "Be careful the turtles don't nip you. Luke. Ma'am." He tipped his hat and coaxed his mule back up the trail that led back into the forest chuckling to himself.

Luke meanwhile, was laughing. "I wouldn't worry, sweetheart. He is a doctor. It's not like he hasn't seen a naked woman before." He took her in his arms and kissed her wet neck. "Want to risk the turtles and stay in a bit longer?" She only half-heartedly tried to push him away.

They arrived back at the cabin late in the afternoon, three days later. An odd look of both pleasure and disappointment crossed Daniel's face when Luke told him their news, but he graciously wished them well, declined their dinner invitation, and rode out with a nod and a smile.

Both Wolf and Harriet were delirious with joy, Wolf practically turned cartwheels, the cat wound herself around their legs, purring loudly. Luke unhitched the mules, rubbed them down and saw to the other animals, while Hope made up the fire and the bed. She got the evening meal ready as quickly as she could.

It was a meal destined to be eaten many hours later, as more of a midnight snack. The moment Luke came into the cabin they were back in each other's arms, collapsing across the bed, making love late into the evening, eventually falling asleep in a thick blanket of joy only as the moon sank once more behind the mountain.

CHAPTER THIRTY-SEVEN

IT was a glorious day. It may have been the afternoon sunlight streaming in through the cabin's wide-open windows, the smell of new hay in the wagon outside, the sound of lazy bees or the fact that Luke was whistling as he split wood at the stump. It may have been the new-found joy Hope had, the delight in being loved as deeply and completely as she was by Luke. Whatever it was, Hope's contentment was as thick, clear and sweet as honey. Her world was complete. If she'd searched for him, she would never have found a man as perfect for her as Luke.

At first sight, it had been his quiet, calm strength, and his crooked smile that drew her to him. It was his steadfast honour, tenderness and depth of character that made her fall in love with him.

She was taking the sheets off the line, the whiteness snapping joyously in the crisp breeze around her. Luke's axe cracked through another log. In the vault of heaven, a pair of eagles rode the currents in easy circles above her. She was hoping that later this afternoon she could convince Luke to ride up to the high meadow and spend the rest of the day simply walking together through the long, yellow grass, although she had no doubt how that walk would end up. Thankfully there were no other people around for at least a day's journey and the grass was tall enough to hide them.

She was putting another sheet into the basket when she saw the carriage cross the bridge down below. "Luke?" She pointed at the river.

Laying down the axe, he took out a handkerchief and wiped the sweat off his hands. The carriage was coming towards them with a brisk trot. Stephen Butler and his daughter were inside it. Luke's eyes narrowed slightly, a frown creased his forehead.

They drew up and Butler jumped down. Miss Ida May, already exclaiming over how 'quaint' everything was, waited for assistance. Her father gallantly complied before turning to Luke and Hope.

With an exclamation of delight, as if he'd bumped into them at the park, rather than arriving announced, and uninvited, at their home, Butler said, "Mr and Mrs Harcourt! How do you do?" He shook Luke's hand, kissed Hope's and drew his daughter forward. "Allow me to introduce you to my daughter, Ida May. The sweetness of my heart."

Luke tried hard not to snort in derision. He knew just how 'sweet' she could be. Hope was torn between delight at having guests and the fact that one of them was Stephen Butler, the man who, if Luke hadn't rescued her, would have been more than happy to install her in his whorehouse.

"You must be thirsty," said Hope. "Would you like some apple juice?"

"Thank you, my dear," replied Butler. "That would be delightful. It's been a long ride."

"From where, exactly?" asked Luke. These two couldn't have come more than five miles. The horses hadn't even broken a sweat.

"We are on our way to Valley Town and were passing nearby and decided we couldn't come all this way and not stop and say hello," Butler said.

How absurd, thought Luke. Valley Town was the next town over the mountains from Silver Birch Landing, but it was a three-day journey out of their way to 'stop and say hello'. Stephen Butler was a fool.

"From Silver Birch Landing?" Luke pushed.

"Yes," Ida May exclaimed. "It's been quite an adventure. Father and I drive in the carriage while the men bring the wagons. It does take an awfully long time with wagons though, doesn't it? I much prefer racing along in the carriage." At the mention of the wagons Butler flashed her an annoyed look.

"Would you like to take off your bonnet and freshen up a little, Ida May? Come with me while the men see to the horses." Hope led the chattering girl towards the cabin.

The men looked at each other. Luke could see Butler was already struggling to maintain the pose. That's why he was such a bad poker player. Butler made no attempt to deal with his horses and although Luke didn't like the man, he wasn't going to let the animals suffer for it. He led them into the shade of the oak beside the barn. He put a bucket of water in front of them and left them to drink.

Wolf trotted over and sniffed at the horses, who moved nervously away from his questing nose. He worked his way down the length of the carriage.

"A wolf?" Butler raised an eyebrow as Luke shrugged. "A bit too mountain man for me," Butler said.

Luke just smiled. Less man than mountain, in his opinion. Men like Butler always drove flashier, newer, faster carriages than other men. Men like Luke Harcourt didn't need to.

"What do you want, Butler?" he asked bluntly.

"To the point, as always. I like that about you."

Like hell.

"I'm glad the ladies seem to get along," Butler commented, wisely ignoring the disbelieving expression on Luke's face, "I'm hoping they'll be neighbours soon."

"Unlikely."

"I'm hoping to build not far from here, in the valley just before the forest," said Butler. He tried hard not to make it sound like a question.

"Sorry, that's not going to happen."

"Why not?"

Luke just smiled.

"You can't stop me, Harcourt. You don't own the whole mountain."

"Actually, I do. You were at the poker game when I won it, if you remember. You've been trespassing for at least two or three days."

Hope and Ida May were on their way back across the yard. Hope carried the heavy jug and under her arm a rug, while a plate of sandwiches and four glasses clinked together on the tray in Ida May's hands.

"Why do you want my land, Butler?" asked Luke.

"Perhaps we can talk about it again later, let's not bore the ladies." Butler stepped forward and took the jug from Hope.

Luke made Ida May wait before he took the tray from her. When Hope raised a quizzical eyebrow at him, Luke just smiled blandly at her.

At Hope's suggestion, they went down to the river and sat on the rug under the willows on the soft mossy grass. Wolf tiptoed into the cold stream to snap at the swirling bubbles that formed along the edges of the rocks.

Talk was general. What else could it be? Ida May chattered away, flitting from one subject to another like dandelion fluff on a crisp breeze, weather, how the town was growing. One piece of news made Luke laugh. Mr Johnson of the general store had, it appeared, taken up permanently with Miss Sylvie of the Haberdashery and Ladies Emporium. Mrs Johnson, incensed, had booked a passage on the next boat back to Cape Cod, returning to the chilly and austere bosom of her family.

Hope caught a look between Luke and Ida May. If she didn't know better, she'd assume Luke was flirting with the girl. Ida May was definitely flirting with Luke. It was a hot day and they ran out of apple juice quite quickly. Luke volunteered to get some more.

"I think I'll go get my bonnet. It's rather warm." Ida May fluttered her hand in front of her face.

"Let me call Luke, he'll bring it." Hope turned to find Luke.

"Oh no, please don't call him. Really, I've been sitting all day and I need to stretch my legs." Her skirts rustled around her as she hurried off in Luke's wake.

Hope and Stephen Butler were left alone under the willow tree. Wolf had given up chasing elusive bubbles and was now nosing through the undergrowth.

"This is delightful," said Butler taking another sip of apple juice. "And how are you getting on here in your new life, Hope? I understand the two of you got married?" His tone had changed. There was a slightly more oily feel to it now. It made Hope uncomfortable. She certainly didn't like him being so familiar with her name.

"Speaking of which," she said tartly. She was pleased at the flash of surprise in his eyes. "At the auction that day, you said the sale was a legally binding marriage."

"So?"

"You knew perfectly well it was nothing of the kind."

"You seem upset about that."

"Of course I'm upset! I can read, but some people can't and they would have believed you and then they would have—" She broke off realising where this was taking her.

"And then they would have?" An amused and sardonic look slunk its way across his face.

"You know exactly what I mean. It was wrong of you. None of those people are really married. And any children they might have, well, they'd all be bastards! It's not right!"

"How quaint, as my daughter would say. Are you going to tell them?"

Hope stood up and brushed off her skirt. "If you would be so good as to bring the tray, the rug and the jug?" It wasn't so much a question as an instruction, albeit a polite one. It had the practised ease of someone who had grown up with servants.

She strode off towards the cabin. Behind her was the sound of a glass being banged down on the tray.

By the time she was halfway across the yard, Hope had regained her composure. She heard Luke laugh. There was a ringing slap and Ida May stormed out, almost knocking her over.

"Ida May! What on earth's wrong?"

"I feel very sorry for you, Hope Harcourt," exclaimed the young girl. "That, that barbarian!" She thrust out her hand in a gesture worthy of the stage. "He's the ugliest, most arrogant and stupidest man I've ever met! You wouldn't believe what he said to me!"

"But, what did—"

Ida May almost shoved her out of the way, striding towards her father. He had his hands full with the loaded tray but she failed to notice, raging at him even before he was within earshot.

"What on earth was that about?" asked Hope as she hurried into the cabin. "What did you say to her to make her so angry?" There was a distinct handprint on his cheek.

"I asked her if she'd grown up yet." Luke smiled at the question in Hope's face, poured himself a glass of water and took a long drink. The muscles in his throat pulled at the cold liquid. "It appears that Miss Ida May Butler doesn't take rejection too well, my dear." Luke set the empty glass on the table. "They both firmly believe they can take whatever they want, and when they don't get it, they behave rather badly."

"They behave badly anyway," she retorted.

"What happened?" Luke's voice took on an edge.

"Oh nothing, really. He thought I was being prudish when I said he'd deliberately misled people at the auction that day when you - that day on the ship."

She never liked talking about that day. She hated the fact that she'd been sold, that Luke had paid money for her, even now they were married. If it came up in conversation, which it did as point of reference, she talked about the ship, not the sale.

"It's getting late. Do you think they'll stay much longer?" she asked. Through the open door they could see Butler and his daughter engaged in a heated conversation. Butler shook his head. Luke laughed when Ida May stamped her foot. Butler ignored her and pushed past her.

"I think we're about to find out."

As Butler appeared in the doorway, Ida May stormed up behind him. "I must apologise. My daughter isn't feeling well," he said, putting the tray on the table. "I think it's the heat. Could we impose on your hospitality for a short time longer? If she could just sit indoors for a bit?"

The girl's beautiful, tempestuous face looked sulky rather than unwell.

"Of course," said Hope politely. "Would you like to come and lie down for a bit, Ida May? It is warm outside and often the cabin can be cooler. I'll get you some cold water to drink. You do look rather flushed."

Ida May's expression grew a new scowl.

CHAPTER THIRTY-EIGHT

A SMUDGE of purple was melting just above the horizon into the approaching night when Butler came out to the barn where Hope and Luke were finishing up the evening chores.

"How's your daughter?" asked Luke.

"Still unwell, I'm afraid. Even the slightest movement and she feels queasy." Luke raised an unbelieving eyebrow.

"Will she manage some dinner, do you think?" asked Hope. "Something simple, bread, cheese, some honey and warm milk? Luke makes excellent coffee, which might help settle her stomach."

Luke grinned. He doubted Ida May had ever eaten anything not prepared by a chef, and never anything as simple as this. It wouldn't improve her temper in any way.

"I'm sure that will be fine, thank you," said Butler.

"Hope and I will sleep in the barn and you two can have the cabin," said Luke.

"There's only one bed," said Butler without thinking.

Luke smirked. "If you push the two armchairs together it'll be almost the perfect size for Ida May. She's not exactly tall. Then you can have the bed. I'm sure she won't mind."

Butler's expression didn't change. It wouldn't be Ida May sleeping in the armchairs. He swung on his heel and left. Hope followed him and prepared the food, leaving it on the table for the Butlers and bringing some out to barn for themselves.

"You'd met the Butlers before, hadn't you?" asked Hope as she shook out the quilts after dinner. "I mean before..."

"Yes." He chose his words with care. "When I first arrived in Silver Birch Landing, I met them at the hotel. And then again the day before your ship arrived. He tried to talk me into selling my land to him then. Before that, he tried to win it in a poker game. He cheated."

Hope was shocked. "Did you catch him cheating?"

"If you mean, did I point out that he was, then, no. I just made sure he didn't win." Luke replied filling the animals' feed buckets.

"Did you cheat?"

Luke laughed. "No. I play better poker than he does. Then, he tried using his daughter." Hell. I shouldn't have said that, he thought.

Hope gave the quilt a vicious shake, then to Luke's amusement asked as nonchalantly as possible, "His daughter, Ida May?"

"Is a flirt."

"Is she a good one?" asked Hope.

Luke smiled at her lovingly. He knew Hope wouldn't deliberately flirt with anyone. Even when she teased him now it was almost unconsciously done, and then only because she knew herself safe and loved.

"She's not my type." He lifted the loose tendrils of hair off the back her neck and placed a warm kiss on her soft skin as he moved past her. His reward was slight giggle and a warm blush.

*

Luke was at the back seeing to the mules when there was a knock on the barn door. Hope opened it to find Ida May standing there with her arms crossed. She looked surprisingly well for someone with a bilious headache.

"There's no hot water."

"If you pop a kettle on the fire it shouldn't take too long to heat up," said Hope.

"A kettle? Oh honestly!" Ida May's chin thrust out, her eyes snapped. "I need lots of hot water. Do you expect me to go to bed without a proper bath?"

"There's always the river, Ida May," Hope suggested, knowing full well the spoilt girl wouldn't dream of using it. She couldn't help adding, "It's not too cold this time of year."

Ida May's eyes widened. "Are you serious? You expect me to bathe outside? In a river?"

"Oh no. I don't expect you to do anything you don't want to."

"Oh! How anyone can live like this I have no idea. In this… this… this dirt, this squalor. And the bugs! I'm quite sure your dog has been inside the cabin when you weren't there."

"All our animals are allowed inside the cabin." Hope smiled, knowing full well there were no bugs. "Well, all except the cow." She paused. "And the horse and the mules. Franklin does try to sneak in when we're not looking, so I expect you mean her, the goat, not the, er, dog."

Ida May's face had gone a soft shade of puce.

"But she's a very fastidious goat," Hope added quickly.

As Ida May flounced back to the cabin in a huff, Hope shut the barn door again. There was a splutter of laughter behind her.

"Hear that, Franklin? I bet you didn't know you're a 'very fastidious goat'." Luke grinned. The goat, unimpressed, just looked at him and carried on chewing.

"What is that girl's problem?" said Hope.

Luke smiled. "She's jealous."

Hope gave a small snort of derision. "Of what?"

"You have what she never could."

"I can't imagine what that could be," retorted Hope, giving a pillow a good thump before tossing it onto the makeshift bed.

Luke's arms came 'round her. He nuzzled her neck, breathing in her scent. She leaned back into him, her pulse leaping. She reached up and ran her fingers through his hair. Easing her shirt away from her sweet neck Luke kissed her soft, warm skin.

"You have me." His voice was thick with desire and her heart raced as he turned her to face him. He pulled out the pins in her hair and dug his fingers deep into the rich, silken, chocolate waves as it cascaded down. Cupping her head with one hand, his mouth hot against hers, he slid the other hand down her back and pulled her hips hard against his own. Her blood was on fire. Her arms went around him. As his tongue coaxed open her lips, she quivered, leaning into him. His grip on her tightened. His kiss deepened. He pulled at her blouse, dragging it free from the confines of her skirt. Her fingers fumbled with his buttons.

There was a knock at the barn door. A loud thumping. They broke apart, their breathing ragged. Whoever was there had apparently been knocking, impatiently, for a while.

Bang! Bang! Bang!

Luke strode towards the door and wrenched it open. It was Ida May, again.

"What?" He'd had enough of this girl, and her father.

"There's only one blanket," she said in an imperious tone. She seemed to notice his slightly dishevelled state and his quick breathing. She raised her pointy little chin higher.

"So?" Luke asked abruptly. "Stoke up the fire. By the way," his voice carried a slight hint of malice, "there are bears on this mountain. They roam around here at night, looking for an easy meal. So, if you don't want to get eaten, I suggest you stay inside the cabin till morning. Good night."

He shut the door firmly on her shocked face and dropped the bar across the door for good measure. He sighed and shook his head ruefully. He turned back to Hope who had her hand pressed against her mouth to stop herself laughing, but her eyes were brimming with delight.

"Bears?" Hope giggled.

He grinned back at her. "One or two."

Taking her into his arms once more he asked, among gentle kisses, "You don't mind sleeping in the barn, in this 'squalor', do you?"

"As long as I'm sleeping with you," she murmured and smiled as his arms tightened in response.

CHAPTER THIRTY-NINE

CLOSE on midnight, Luke stirred. He never tired of waking with Hope in his arms. He lay quietly, his hand resting on the dip of her waist, listening to her gentle breathing. Her soft body lay against his, her easy curves moulded to the muscle that ran through his own. Her arm lay across his chest, her fingers curled round the base of his neck. Her skin was warm and pale against the tan of his body.

He was tempted to kiss her awake so he could make love to her again. Since their first night as man and wife, she was growing more and more used to him and the intimacy two people can share. She was more spontaneous with him now. It was exhilarating. He breathed in the cinnamon scent of her skin, skin that grew hot under his fingers. Whenever she let her own fingers wander, tracing cool, delicate paths down his spine...

If he wasn't careful, he would be waking her.

A long, wavy lock of her hair lay across his stomach. He twined it round his fingers and brought it to his lips. Kissing it, he sighed with satisfaction and gazed out at the night sky through the barn's upper loading bay door.

When this barn had been Luke's home in the first few months of their life together, he'd gotten into the habit of opening this door and watching the stars, finding and naming all the ones he knew, going over all the nautical calculations he could think of in an attempt to take his mind of the woman in his cabin.

The night sky was one of the few things he did miss about the sea. The stars had been more than just a navigational tool. They'd become a comforting, familiar blanket, a glittering path home.

Sitting on one of the rafters far above was a large owl. Its ears twitching, its eyes shut, merely dark lines across its face, its feathers glowing in the silver cobweb of light that drifted in. Wolf was asleep near Augustus Brown's stall sighing gustily and whimpering in his dreams, his paws twitching.

In a heartbeat it changed. Both the owl and Wolf were awake and alert. The owl's head swivelled fast. The wolf stood up, tilted its head to one side, ears pricked.

Luke eased away from Hope and pulled on his trousers. He picked up his gun, checking it was loaded. Wolf pattered after him as he made his way past the stalls, to the back doors of the barn. He opened the Judas door just enough to slip through. Wolf followed like a shadow. Putting his hand over the wolf's nose, Luke breathed, "Shhh."

Wolf blinked; the end of his tail flicked once. The two of them slinked along the side of the barn. At the corner, Luke stopped. One of the lamps was on in the cabin, very low but the light slipped surreptitiously over the windowsill and lay across the yard.

Luke crept to the cabin wall and, keeping himself well hidden, peered in.

Butler and Ida May were turning the cabin over as quietly as they could. They'd pulled out every drawer, taken every book out of the bookcase, emptied the chest and, from the look of Ida May, had even been searching through the open sacks of flour and beans in the larder.

Whatever they were looking for, they weren't finding it. The only things of any value, of course, were the deed to his land and the confirmation of marriage from Rev. Drago. The corner of Luke's mouth tipped. They were wasting their time. The little chest with all his important papers was still in the barn, on the shelf in Augustus Brown's stall.

He tiptoed away again and eased himself back, next to the softness and warmth of his wife.

*

Butler had been relieved when his conversation with Luke had been interrupted this afternoon. He had no intention of telling Luke there was gold in the valley beyond Harcourt's mountain and therefore probably on the mountain. If he was right, Harcourt's mountain was the source of the gold. Lots of gold. It could be another Cariboo rush. Millions and millions of dollars just waiting to be unearthed.

At least, that's what the old miner had said. His ore samples had been incredible. Butler didn't want the word getting out just yet. Keeping the miner quiet had been easy. Amazing what a shallow grave could do.

And Butler had seen enough shallow graves. He'd dug a few himself. Nine of them in fact. The hardest one had been Katie. It was such a small grave. Her skin had looked so white against the black soil, so transparent he could almost see her tiny bones. There was no flesh to speak of, no fat bouncing baby. He'd buried skeletons. Starved to death by that repulsive slime which had eaten the potatoes before they could. Those bloody, fat, rich English had trotted past in their fine coach as he'd put the last lump of soil over her face. He'd patted down the earth and said a quick prayer. He never got to 'amen'. It made him sick to his stomach. He'd hawked up a thick glob of spit. It landed hard and he vowed it would be the last time he'd ever knock on God's door. He'd never go back to Ireland, not even in a box! He hated the place, the stink and the poverty.

Money, wealth— if that's what it took to survive, then he'd be the richest damn man on earth, no matter what it took. Harcourt's mountain could make him a billionaire. Butler didn't want a claim he could work, he wanted the whole fucking mountain and he wouldn't allow this man, or any man to stand in his way.

He knew there was a deed to the place. That ill-fated game had ended with Harcourt and the old man going to the bank to get it. He had to get his hands on that piece of paper. And the first place to look would be right here, even if it took all night, he was going to search every inch of this hovel. If it wasn't here, then it could only be at the bank. How he got it out of there, well, he'd only worry about that if he had to.

*

When Luke walked unceremoniously into the cabin the next morning, he was pleased to see the guests at least tried to hide traces of their search. Butler scowled at him.

Hope came in a few moments later with a heavy pail of fresh milk. Butler didn't offer to help, even though he was standing in her way. The social graces were only a veneer with him anyway. Breakfast of scrambled eggs, hot toast and coffee was a quiet, strained affair.

"We should be going," said Butler. "My men will have been wondering what happened to us."

"Really?" asked Luke, disbelief patent in his voice.

Butler wisely didn't reply. His daughter, however, was not so clever. "For your information, Luke Harcourt—"

"Be quiet!" Butler snapped.

"What? You're not going to let him talk to you like that?"

"One more word and you walk back!"

Luke tried hard not laugh. "I'll hitch your horses for you, then." He strode from the cabin and in minutes had the carriage at the door.

"You find what you were looking for last night?" Luke asked as they climbed into the carriage.

Butler shot him an angry look, one slightly tinged with fear round the edges. Luke's mouth twisted in his crooked smile and he stepped away from the horses.

"I hope you feel better soon, Ida May," said Hope solicitously.

Butler cracked the reins viciously.

"What was all that about?" wondered Hope as the carriage rolled briskly out of the yard. Luke just shrugged.

"The usual… land, gold, things they can't have. Come on, let's make more coffee."

CHAPTER FORTY

A LITTLE later, Luke saddled Augustus Brown. He rode to the far side of the mountain, checking to make sure Butler's men had left with him. Following the faint smell of wood-smoke, he soon heard the sound of stone chipping. He worked his way along the ridge.

As Augustus Brown delicately navigated the rocky bend, Luke saw three men at a small camp, two of them working away at the rock face. They looked more organised than the usual gold seekers. More like mining engineers conducting a survey.

Luke dismounted and leaving the big, black horse in the trees, draped the reins over a branch and pulled his carbine out of the saddle holster. Leaving the horse to browse, Luke made his way down towards the camp.

From a hidden vantage point, he assessed what, and who, he had to deal with. One young man, an old man who looked like the typical prospector, and a bald man whose clothes barely contained the bulk of fat that covered his body, made up the group.

"This is a bad idea," Luke heard the youngest one complain.

"Oh, shut up," growled the old, grizzled man, pushing his ancient, wide brimmed hat further back on his head. "You never stop bitching, you do? The boss sent us here and he expects results. So, we're not going back without any."

"What if there is no gold up here?" the youngster asked.

"There's gold," the bald man replied. "All the gold we've found so far is alluvial. So, it has to come from somewhere up-river, and this is as up-river as we can get. Now, do like Matthews says, shut up and make us something to eat."

"Yes, but what if Harcourt catches us?"

"He won't. He's too busy with that new wife of his."

"I'd rather be busy with her than up here with you lot. I hear she's real pretty."

"We can arrange for you to leave the mountain now, if you want," growled Matthews.

The bald man laughed. Luke watched as the younger man grumbled his way behind the chuck wagon and began to untie a large frying pan.

The slow, iron click in his ear stopped him. The young man froze.

"Want to go home alive?" Luke's voice was low, calm and the most threatening thing the kid had ever heard. The youngster nodded.

"Leave now and don't come back."

"But—"

"Changed your mind?"

The kid shook his head.

"Then go. Run fast and don't stop."

The youngster reached for his hat, turned, and found himself looking down the barrel of Luke's carbine. Carefully, he took a few steps to the left of Luke, snatched a quick glance over his shoulder at the two older men still crouched at the rock face and got foolish.

He took a deep breath to shout a warning. The hard, steel mouth of Luke's gun shoved his jaw shut. His eyes flickered at Luke, who simply shook his head. The youngster's courage broke. Luke stepped out of the way and the boy pelted straight down the mountain scattering small rocks and pebbles as he went.

"What the hell?" the bald man exclaimed when the kid disappeared over the ridge. A trail of dust billowed in his wake as he struggled to stay upright on his rapid scramble down. Matthews and Baldie watched him go.

"Wonder what spooked him?" said Matthews.

"Maybe he decided to go visit with Harcourt's missus."

They both laughed. It was cut short at the familiar sound of a gun asking to play. They turned, slowly.

Luke stood there, his carbine lifted to his shoulder. His face was hard, like the granite they stood on. "You're on my land."

The two men flicked a glance at each other.

"Who do you work for?" Luke asked.

Another silent exchange. This was not worth it. Even the way this man stood made every rumour they'd heard about him look true. Matthews shrugged. "Stephen Butler."

Luke looked at Baldie, who nodded.

"You prepared to die for Mr Butler?"

"Hell, no," said Matthews.

"Not a chance." Baldie spat a chewed-over tobacco chaw out of his mouth.

"Then it's time to leave, gentlemen. Toss your guns over here, carefully." The two men undid their gun belts. They landed in an untidy pile at Luke's feet.

"Good. Now, Matthews, I believe? Put all the rifles and shotguns you have on the pile as well."

The old man had no intention of dying on this mountain. He did exactly as he was told.

"Now," said Luke, "pack up and head out. You can pick up your friend along the trail. Don't come back." It was the cold, implacable look on his face that urged the men to hurry. In less than half an hour they had started off back down the trail.

*

"Do you really have to do this?" asked Hope as she packed food supplies for Luke, clearly unhappy about his proposed trip to town.

"If I don't sort this out now," replied Luke, shoving a shirt into his saddlebag. "I'll spend more time chasing miners off our mountain than harvesting apples. Loggers as well, I should imagine. I'd rather harvest apples." Luke was angry. If he had to, he'd go to Carter and lay charges against Butler. It was a drastic measure, but it might be the only way. Butler was a coward; perhaps the actual, real threat of law would deter him.

"Can I come with you?" Hope pleaded.

"No, Hope, I'm sorry. I'd love to take you, but I need to move fast, or we'll have more of these men here. We'd be too slow with the wagon."

He strongly suspected there was going to be trouble and he didn't want her anywhere near it. "I shouldn't be long. Six, seven days at the most and I'll be back. I promise."

Hope came up behind him, twined her arms around his chest and, pressing herself against his back, she nuzzled his neck and murmured, "Can't you at least go tomorrow? Those men won't reach town before you. It'll be dark soon and you'd still have to make camp for the night. It would be so much nicer to sleep here, with me, in our bed, together, don't you think?" Her hand drifted down his chest suggestively.

He laughed, took her hand, swung her round in front of him and down onto the table scattering clothing, saddle bags and cans. "You are a wicked, wanton woman, Hope Harcourt."

She laughed and he bent over her kissing the base of her throat.

When Luke rode out the next morning, Hope was still asleep with the sheets twined around her. He was glad he'd stayed. Leaving yesterday in such a rage would have been wrong, whereas leaving with the taste of Hope's sleepy, early morning kisses was infinitely better.

CHAPTER FORTY-ONE

GOING straight to see Constable Carter when he rode into town, Luke was irritated to discover the lawman was settling a mine claim dispute further up the coast. He wasn't expected back for at least a week. Luke wasn't prepared to wait that long. He wanted to sort this out and get back to Hope.

Leaving Augustus Brown with Mr Samson, Luke decided to check the hotel first. He hoped he wouldn't have to go to the Bright Star to find Butler. At the hotel, Luke learned the man was also out of town. He'd be back tomorrow. Luke had no choice but to wait. He took a room, left his saddle-bags there and paid a visit to the bank. He'd brought the land deed and the marriage confirmation letter with him to put into the bank's safe keeping. And while he was in town, he might as well buy some supplies.

Jonas Campbell, the big, bluff banker with the meticulously kept, squared off, curly beard, which always reminded Luke of drawings he'd once seen of King Nebuchadnezzar, was delighted to see Luke. One glance at the annoyed expression on the younger man's face and Jonas, who loved to gossip, dragged him into his office and dealt with the business side of the visit as quickly as possible.

"Now, Harcourt," he said, pouring Luke a generous glass of whiskey, "what's caused that black cloud hovering over your head?"

Luke told him about Butler's men.

"I'm going to have a conversation with their boss, just to remind him about the laws of trespassing."

Jonas frowned. "Be careful Luke, Stephen Butler may keep the bank's coffers full, but I for one, have never assumed any of it is honest gain. A man like that is unlikely to limit his 'conversation' to words."

"I hope he doesn't!" retorted Luke. "If it takes that kind of 'conversation' to keep him off my land, I'll gladly oblige."

The next day, Luke was annoyed to hear that Butler had gone straight to the lumberyard on his return. Luke collected Augustus Brown and turning left at the edge of town, rode out after him.

The forest had once stood like a dark wall against the ocean. When the town began to rise, the trees and the animals that lived among them retreated. Now, all that remained of the pines on the way to the lumberyard were stumps, drying and cracked, some with a jagged spear pointing accusingly through the brown, burnt ferns to the wasted barrenness above.

With the forest no longer providing shade and the ferns now dead, the soil had nothing to hold it in place. The heavy chains the loggers wrapped around the trunks to drag them to the mill had torn deep scars into the soil, ripping it up, gouging it down to the stones beneath. What the chains didn't get, the rain did, washing it away to be churned up in the road, eventually seeping into the harbour as silt. The land was raw, stripped of its flesh and silent as a grave.

Luke urged Augustus Brown through as quickly as he could.

A few hours later, he heard a heavy pulsing, like the heartbeat of some gigantic beast. It grew louder as he trotted into the lumberyard. The place was noisy, dusty and ugly. Naked, defeated giants stripped of their branches lay in neat piles, some of which had collapsed haphazardly. The astringent smell of pine mixed with the earthy smell of charcoal, the stink of mule dung and oily smoke clogged the throats of the men working there. The steam engine driving the saw was clattering loudly, retching black clouds out of its chimney. Four men, grimy with perspiration and charcoal dust, fed the voracious monster as it chewed coal and sliced trees into planks. Pine dust filled the air in a harsh, gritty cloud and stuck to everything, making sweaty skin itch.

Butler was berating a small group of men. He wasn't the wisest of bosses. He preferred the fear-and-humiliation strategy rather than mutual respect.

Luke nudged the horse forward until he was practically breathing down Butler's collar. The men on the receiving end of Butler's tongue lashing began to snigger. Augustus Brown gave a short, quick snort.

Butler nearly jumped out of his skin. He swung round. The surprise of seeing such a large, powerful animal a mere six inches away gave him a nasty shock. He stepped away in a hurry, a deep, annoyed frown embedded in his forehead.

Good manners dictated that Luke dismount. He stayed in the saddle. Butler was a tall man, so being on the horse gave Luke the height advantage.

"Mr Harcourt," cried Butler with fake geniality, stepping away once more from those large yellow teeth Augustus Brown was champing together in his direction. Grateful for the reprieve, the workmen slunk back to their various jobs in the mill.

"Butler." Luke was curt. Just seeing this piece of scum brought the anger back.

"What can I do for you? Looking for work or have you come to your senses and decided to sell me your land?"

"No man of sense would willingly do business with you, and my land is not for sale. It never will be. So, you can stop sending work parties onto the mountain. The next lot I find there, I'll have thrown in jail. Are we clear?"

Butler snorted. "Jail? Is that supposed to worry me?"

"Don't push me, Butler. I don't want to have to shoot someone for trespassing."

"Ha! You'd never kill a man, Harcourt. From what I hear, you don't have the balls to, even after they've played with your wife."

Luke's face turned to flint, his eyes narrowed, his mouth thinned into a hard line.

Butler laughed, flicking an imaginary piece of fluff off his jacket.

Luke murmured to Augustus Brown. His ears straight up and his gait aggressive, the horse walked fast and straight into Butler, pushing him until he fell against a pile of stripped and waiting logs.

"Stay off my land," growled Luke, "because you, I will kill."

*

As Luke rode out of the lumberyard, a man with a scarred face and a disturbing hollow where his left eye should have been, stepped from behind the stacked planks and strolled over to Butler, now fastidiously brushing the wood chips off his trousers.

"So, what do you want to do now?" he said, his voice curiously high pitched for a man.

Butler straightened up and tugged at his waistcoat.

"I can get rid of him for you, if you want. Then there's nothing to stop you taking his land," the weird voice continued.

Butler frowned at the man. He couldn't bear to be within ten feet of him, the stench was overpowering. But there were times when the bastard was useful. "What makes you think you could do it this time?" he sneered. "You failed spectacularly last time."

"I'll do it."

"Very well, how much is this going to cost me?"

"The usual, plus the wife."

"What?"

"I want his bitch."

Butler laughed. "She's all yours."

Tobias John giggled.

*

After his altercation with Butler, it didn't feel right to stay in the man's hotel. Luke paid his bill the moment he got back, collected his belongings and asked for lodging with Mr Samson.

"Of course, Mr Harcourt. I'd be delighted. There is more than enough room. I try to keep one of the stalls empty for anyone who needs it. Tonight, it's all yours. I hope you find it comfortable enough."

Considering where he'd been sleeping before he'd married Hope, Luke couldn't help a short bark of laughter. "Thanks Mr Samson. I'm much obliged. The Lees have invited us for dinner, by the way."

"How very kind of them. Unfortunately, I won't be able to join you. I am leading the prayer meeting tonight at the church. Please give them my best regards and my apologies."

Much later that night, Luke said goodbye to the Lees and made his way back to the livery stable. It didn't look like Mr Samson was back yet. The stable doors were closed. The place was in darkness. There was a bad smell in the air. Perhaps one of the horses was having stomach problems. He'd check it as soon as he was inside. He was still going over the 'discussion' he'd had with Butler earlier, debating whether to wait for Carter to get back. It was probably a good idea, but then, hell, getting back to Hope wouldn't happen for another week.

He wasn't paying attention.

Just as Luke reached the doors the smell hit him. It wasn't inside the stable, it was outside and behind him. He swung round, but too late. White pain exploded inside his head and he fell like a stone.

CHAPTER FORTY-TWO

HOPE woke to find Luke gone. She sighed. Being wakened by him would have been very enjoyable. She stretched luxuriously, with a feline grace, almost purring with the warm memory of their lovemaking the night before. She smiled sleepily and, pulling on her discarded nightgown, made her way down to the river for a bath. The water was cool, to say the least. She was definitely awake now.

Back at the cabin, she was scrambling eggs for her breakfast when a wave of nausea hit her, sending her running from the cabin. Stumbling to her knees she retched painfully. When it was over, she cleaned up and went back inside. She couldn't face the eggs now, even the thought of them made her queasy again. Wolf made short work of them for her. She managed a simple breakfast of toast, honey and tea.

Unsure if she had an upset stomach or if she'd eaten something that disagreed with her, she stayed close to the cabin that day. The nausea hung around, but thankfully, she managed not to throw up again.

The next day, it happened once more. And the next. And the day after that. Four days later she was exhausted. She could hardly face getting out of bed. She would much rather just lie there and groan quietly. But Pinkerton still had to be milked, the animals let out of the barn, fed, watered and the stalls cleaned out with fresh hay put in. Wood still needed to be chopped and water fetched from the river.

Day nine was bad. Not only had she'd thrown up a few times, but Luke should have been back three days ago. Concern, misery and that achy, dreadful feeling of illness drove her back to bed. She lay on top of the covers feeling very sorry for herself. Harriet came and joined her. The cat's gently purring was almost therapeutic and eventually Hope dozed off.

"I'm pregnant." The thought woke her. Her whole being flooded with joy. Delight captured her and laughter welled up until she was floating in a haze of happiness. She took the time to pray, to give thanks. It seemed the least she could do, considering she'd felt alone for so long and now she'd been given everything. A man who loved her, whom she loved in return. A man who made her feel safe, beautiful, precious and now, she was having his baby. Everything she'd gone through to get here meant nothing in comparison to this joy.

Eventually, she drifted off again, the nausea gone. A deep peace enveloped her.

When she stirred later, she still couldn't face real food. She was making herself some more toast, honey and tea, the only thing she'd been able to eat since Luke left, when Wolf, who'd been lying on the rug in front of the fireplace next to her, snapped to attention. His ears pricked, his eyes fixed on the doorway. He gave a low whine. Hope's heart started doing cartwheels, fireworks went off inside her.

Luke was home. She glanced out of the window.

It wasn't Luke. It was Stephen Butler and four men. Her mouth went dry. Tobias John was one of them.

"Stay, Wolf." She took the shotgun down from the wall, checked it was loaded, shut the door on Wolf and, praying she wouldn't throw up, went outside.

"Mrs Harcourt."

Hope didn't like the way Stephen Butler was smiling. "Mr Butler, what can I do for you?"

"I have some bad news."

Hope felt cold.

"Luke is dead." It was said so bluntly, her mind couldn't take it in.

"I don't believe you."

Butler pulled something out of his waistcoat pocket and flicked it over to her. The sun sparkled off it as it spun. Hope knew exactly what it was before she caught it. Luke's ring lay in her hand. His initials were almost black against the old gold. It was warm, as if it had just been taken off his hand. Vomit surged up in her throat.

"Where is he?" Hope whispered.

"His body?" The cruelty in Butler's voice was deliberate. "You don't want to see it. Believe me. He fell into the sea. The fish made quite a meal of him. In fact, it was only this ring that helped us identify him."

The ring cut into her hand she gripped it so hard. She knew she would vomit. Tobias John giggled. He shouldn't have done that. Hope slipped the ring into her apron pocket and swung the shotgun up.

"What do you want, Mr Butler?"

"The same thing I've always wanted; this land. Now would be a good time to sell it to me."

"No."

"I thought you'd say that, which is why I brought Tobias with me. As you know, he has a way with women that might help you change your mind. The boys and I will wait over there."

Hope whipped the gun up and fired at Tobias, but she was shaking so much it went wide. The men laughed. She was so frightened, so empty, she completely forgot about the second shell. She knew exactly what would happen, and this time there was no Luke to save her.

There was no Luke.

Luke was gone. Hope closed her eyes.

An answering explosion ripped through the air. The men swung round. Carter and Campbell thundered into the yard, dust spewing out from under their horses' hooves. They both had their shotguns out and ready to fire as they came to a scudding halt.

"You all right, Mrs Harcourt?" Carter barked, lifting his shotgun to his shoulder and aiming at Butler.

Hope nodded and lowered her gun.

"Seems everyone wants to visit the delightful Mrs Harcourt today," said Butler. "And here I'd always thought she was a lady." His men sniggered.

"Speaking of ladies," Carter said. "It was your daughter who mentioned you and your boys might be paying a call on Mrs Harcourt. It was an illuminating chat." He was pleased to see a shadow dart across Butler's face.

"Boasted about it in fact," said Jonas.

"Yep, got us interested. We thought we'd tag along and see you behaved yourselves."

"Now, Constable, would we dream of behaving in any way unbecoming to a gentleman?" asked Butler smoothly.

"He says Luke is dead. Is he?" Hope interjected.

"What proof have you got, Butler?"

Butler smiled and gestured towards Hope. She came over and put the ring into Carter's outstretched hand. Her fingers quivered. Carter turned the ring over and looked at it. He nodded at Jonas.

"It's his all right."

"So, he is dead?" Her voice cracked.

"Not necessarily. He could have been robbed."

"Then where is he?" Hope's momentary relief shattered at Butler's mocking voice.

Carter's eyes narrowed. If anyone knew where Harcourt was, Butler did. He turned back to Hope. Her face was white.

"We'll find him ma'am. Don't you worry about that. This fine 'gentleman' say anything else?"

"He wants me to sell him my land," she took a deep breath, "and he threatened to have Tobias John rape me to make sure I did." The white in her face was swiftly replaced by a painful red.

"No one mentioned any such thing, did they boys?" Butler interjected smoothly. "A brief conversation perhaps, but nothing more."

"Any sale of Harcourt property by anyone, including Mrs Harcourt, would be illegal at this point," Jonas' deep voice boomed out. "And will continue to be until her husband is declared legally dead and his Will is read by a lawyer. Before you ask, Butler, rest assured there is a Will and it's securely locked in the bank safe, along with the deed to the land."

Luke had never mentioned a Will. Hope wondered if the man was lying.

Butler's face went dark. His eyes narrowed to slits. His horse threw up its head and stepped back, rebelling against the sudden jerk on the reins.

"Unless you want to be arrested for trespassing," Carter said, "I suggest you leave. Now."

In the silence that followed, Hope could hear Wolf whining and scratching at the cabin door.

Butler kicked his horse's sides viciously and, without another word, rode out of the yard. His henchmen followed.

Tobias John stared down at Hope, his thick purple lips stretched out over his foul teeth in a smile that on his ruined face was nothing more than a grimace. Carter edged his horse forward.

"Next time then." Tobias John giggled slapped his own mount into a hiccupping trot after the others.

Once Butler and his gang were no longer in sight, Hope broke down. Dropping the shotgun, she buried her head in her hands and wept. Carter shifted in his saddle. Women in tears were not something he was comfortable with. Jonas Campbell, a man with four daughters of his own, swung himself off his horse, enveloped Hope in his arms and let her cry herself out.

They stayed at the cabin, sleeping in the barn for the night. Carter wanted to make sure Butler and his men, especially Tobias, weren't coming back.

*

Three days later, Butler and Tobias John were standing on the platform over the gigantically hungry, jagged edged, rotating saw.

Butler smirked. "If there's no body, how do I know you killed him?"

"I want my money now, Butler," Tobias John growled. Enveloped in clouds of hot steam, they were yelling at each other over the noise of the rattling logs being split into planks with monstrous efficiency by the thumping, smoky steam engine below them.

"Show me the body and I'll gladly pay you."

"I told you, I put him on that ship of yours. The captain knew him. He'd some old scores to pay back. He's gonna make him suffer just like he did to me."

"I don't care about your petty squabbles. I want Harcourt dead!"

"Petty! I lost an eye, he broke my jaw, and that wolf of his nearly killed me!"

"Sounds like you deserved it. I told you, show me the body and I'll pay you. Until then you're in the way." He pushed past the trapper.

"You owe me!" yelled Tobias John. The noise in the shed was too loud. Butler never heard him. But everyone heard Butler's splintering screams and the dreadful sound of the steam engine as it crashed to a shuddering, bloody halt.

Tobias John ran. Watching Butler's body be ripped apart like that had given him a thrill he'd never had before, even when he'd skinned alive the animals he'd caught in his traps. He was only sorry Butler died so quickly. Although he wasn't a bright man, he did realise he had to vanish as quickly as possible. He leapt off the platform and slipped behind the stripped bones of recently dismembered trees and ran, wiping the blood that had sprayed out of the slicer off his face.

By the time he'd made his way back to town on foot, hiding in what was left of the undergrowth, it was late afternoon. The lumberyard men had commandeered the company wagons, arriving long before him. They'd gathered in front the jail. Constable Carter, who'd only just ridden in himself, heard them out. He wasn't sorry to hear Stephen Butler was dead. And having a reason to introduce Tobias John to the noose was an added bonus.

"Which way was he headed?" he asked.

Everyone volunteered an opinion.

"One at a time!"

"He was headed this way, last we saw him," said a tall, dry man with a handlebar moustache.

"You gonna hang him, Constable?" yelled someone else.

"If he's guilty, yes."

"Oh, he's that for sure. We all saw him do it."

Carter took that with a pinch of salt. One or two maybe. Not all.

Tobias John crept back down the alley, behind the other buildings and slunk into the livery stable. Mr. Samson wasn't there. He could be back any moment though. Tobias John needed to get out of town fast. A good horse and he'd get a start on Carter. He couldn't believe his luck when he saw Augustus Brown. A hiccupping cackle broke out; his fingers were desperate as he saddled the big black.

Mr Samson was singing a hymn under his breath as he strolled back in through the open doors. A glint caught his eye. He scuffed at the loose straw with his foot. It was a button. It looked familiar. As he picked it up, the song in his mouth dissolved. It was off Luke's waistcoat. It was hard to mistake. Apart from the heavy coat he wore in winter, and the Navy Colt, the buttons were about the only thing Luke had kept from his time at sea.

Mr Samson had begun to feel a deep sense of unease. Even the horses were restless. Luke hadn't been seen for a few days. Now, rubbing the button in his fingers, he decided to speak to the Constable at once. A muffled grunt and curse sounded from one of the stalls. Mr Samson's head snapped up.

There was a sharp, angry animal snort. Hooves thudded against the wooden panels. Augustus Brown was trying to climb out of the confined space between the wooden partitions.

The stable door slammed back. The horse was out, twisting and rearing, his massive hooves carving the air. He came crashing down, whinnying in rage, and bolted for the barn doors, Tobias John clinging frantically to the reins and the saddle's pommel.

They banged into Mr Samson, sending him spinning as they raced into the street. They were past the mob and out of town before anyone could stop them. A few men made half-hearted attempts, but Augustus Brown was going too fast and no one had the courage to try to slow him down.

Carter turned to one of his deputies. "Scallion, get after him. Go!"

The young man leapt onto his horse and galloped off, scattering the crowd. The mob swung back to Carter, yelling and shouting.

"All right!" Carter yelled above the noise. "It'll be dark soon, if Scallion doesn't catch up with him, Frank and I are going to need some temporary deputies. Anyone here willing?"

"Reckon finding and catching him is your problem, Constable," one man shouted back. "What we want to know is, who's going to pay us now the boss is gone?"

"Sorry boys, 'not my problem'. Now, if you aren't going to help, stay out of our way."

"But what are we gonna do?" yelled one of the men. The mob rumbled angrily in agreement. "I mean, do we keep working the lumberyard?"

"Are we going to get paid?" Now all the men were shouting. Carter lifted his arms and tried to quieten them.

"All right, all right. Keep it down now. I have to inform his daughter of his death before I do anything anyway. I'll ask her who the lawyers are and you can talk to them."

The mob grumbled.

Carter left Deputy Frank keeping an eye on them and made his way to the hotel.

An hour or so later, Carter was back out on the sidewalk in front of the hotel trying to calm the now raging mob.

"Miss Butler says she'll make sure you all get paid. She has no money with her now, but she'll write to her father's lawyers about it first thing in the morning."

The sun had set and the men had gotten liquored up while Carter had been in the hotel, the only thing that would calm them was money. They'd never trusted Butler and they had no confidence whatsoever in his daughter.

"Why can't she pay us now?"

"Be reasonable men, she doesn't have that kind of cash on her."

"It'll take months for the lawyers to sort it out, what do we do until then?" shouted a short, fat man.

"Yeah!" chimed in someone else at the back. "That hotel belonged to Butler. Reckon it's got plenty of money in the safe. She can give us that!"

"S'right! We want our money. We want our money!"

The mob took up the chant. Carter was frustrated. The men had every right to be angry and concerned. If they'd been privy to the conversation he'd just had with Miss Ida May, they'd be livid. She wasn't interested in their plight at all. Her only concern was herself. She'd hardly shown any distress at her father's death. She'd seemed to view it more as an inconvenience than anything else.

Her life would be in danger if this mob got out of control, and it was heading that way fast. He was inordinately glad to see Deputy Scallion ride back in, albeit empty-handed, at that moment. The young man dismounted and pushed his way to the sidewalk. Carter pulled him aside and whispered some urgent and quiet instructions. Scallion nodded and slipped back through the mob and into the darkness behind them.

Ida May Butler was packing, ineffectually, fluttering between cupboards and trunks, driving her maid to distraction. Dresses were strewn over the bed and the chair like discarded, limp butterfly wings, shoes littered the floor, shawls cascaded from the white, iron bedstead, hat boxes stood mute, their lids half open, a testament to how easily Ida May could be distracted, even at a moment like this.

She was sure Constable Carter had exaggerated the sawmill workers' anxiety. After all, she'd said she'd speak to her father's lawyers as soon as she arrived back east. What more could they expect? Her father's death was unfortunate, but it did mean she could get out of this miserable town and go back to civilization.

The noise outside was growing. It had a rhythm now it hadn't had before. She glanced out the window. The shock hit her. It was a lynch mob! Constable Carter had been telling the truth. The men in the street were clearly drunk, rowdy and very angry. Some had lit torches, others were pulling out their guns, firing them off overhead into the night. She couldn't see the lawman. His office and the jail were on the same side of the street as the hotel. What were they shouting? She opened a window to hear better.

"Oh no, miss. Don't do that. They'll see you," begged her maid, terror making her voice, indeed her whole body, shake. She was all for leaving Silver Birch Landing with Miss Ida May, but she'd rather not do it in a coffin.

She was right. The men did see Ida May and immediately switched their attention from Carter to her.

"Give us our money, you silly bitch!" screamed one man.

"Open the hotel safe and pay us," yelled another.

The mob now had a real object for their rage, and they weren't backing down. Horrified at the eerie, torch-lit scene below her, the surging undercurrent of violence spilling out, splashing over anyone in the street, the truth of her situation smote her with stunning reality. She slammed the window.

It was a match to gunpowder. A savage roar erupted. The men surged towards the hotel doors. The deep, aggressive blast of four shotguns ricocheted between the buildings, echoing down the street. The mob lurched. The business-like way the four guns were cocked again made them pause. Carter, Deputy Frank, Michael O'Grady, the hotel manager and Jonas Campbell, who'd been eating in the hotel restaurant, all snapped their shotguns to their shoulders and took aim, the muzzles pointing directly at the front row of men. They couldn't have looked more deadly if they'd rehearsed it.

Carter was grateful. If the other two hadn't crashed out of the hotel and joined Frank and him right then, they would have been dead men.

It was a big mob, so the four men holding them at bay at the hotel entrance didn't see the small group slip away down a dark alley. From across the street, Scallion, just coming out of the Chinese laundry did. He took off at a run after them. Five of the laundry staff slipped into the other alley. They knew where the back entrance was. The men from the mob didn't.

ELAINE DODGE

*

The knock at her door almost made Ida May's heart stop. "Go away!" Hysteria made her voice shrill.

"Miss Butler, open up please. We come to help you. Hurry, men coming." It didn't sound like the lumbermen. It was a woman's voice. The maid hurried across the room.

"No!" shrieked Ida May. "Don't let them in!"

It was too late. Ida May wasn't sure whether to laugh with relief or start screaming at the sight of four young Chinese men and the girl who was with them.

"You hurry, quick, quick. Climb in basket, we take you safe out of hotel. Hurry, hurry." Sweet Jade was urgent. She didn't want to get caught in the middle of this. She despised Ida May Butler, but when Scallion had asked, her mother insisted they rescue her.

"Quick, quick, in basket," she demanded, grabbing hold of the spoilt girl's arm, pulling her out into the corridor.

"In a basket? You want me to climb in there?" Ida May exclaimed indignantly.

"Yes, yes, you hurry. In basket. We carry you out. No one stop laundry Chinamen. They not see us. *Quick.*"

Heavy feet could be heard stomping towards them.

"Where is the bitch?" a rough voice echoed in the corridor.

"What about my things?" wailed Ida May.

Sweet Jade banged the bedroom door shut. "No time, no time. In basket now or we leave you here. For them. You not our friend. We only help 'cause parents tell us to. You coming or not?"

The frightened maid was already scrambling into one of the two large, round wicker baskets that stood in the corridor. The footsteps were getting nearer. Ida May climbed as quickly as she could into the other basket. She gave a

303

muffled protest as a pile of dirty sheets was shoved on top of her.

"Quiet or we leave you," snapped Sweet Jade.

The Chinese men exchanged a quick look. They'd never seen Sweet Jade behave so aggressively. They quickly hoisted the baskets onto the backs of two of the men, pulling the straps across their foreheads. They had no choice but to head towards the angry voices. Six furious men stormed around the corner. The Chinese dropped their gazes and shuffled past them.

Sweet Jade had been right; the men paid no attention to them. Even when they crept out the hotel's alley door and made for the laundry, the mob was completely indifferent to the Orientals.

Back in the hotel, the lumbermen had found Ida May's bedroom. They were ransacking it, searching for anything valuable they could find, and if small enough stuffing it in their pockets, when Scallion arrived.

"Hands in the air. All of you."

As the men swung round to face the doorway, one lunged for his gun. Scallion moved fast. A bullet ripped out and tore through the back of the man's hand. He screamed, clasping it to his chest.

"Anyone else?" asked Scallion. No one moved. "Good. Now, hands behind your heads and kneel on the floor."

The men slowly lowered themselves to the carpet.

"Take their guns and search them for any other weapons," Scallion ordered the two hotel employees he'd grabbed on his way up the stairs. "Do it!"

CHAPTER FORTY-THREE

HOPE heard a horse huffing. Luke? She took the toast off the fire and hurried outside. In the yard, Augustus Brown snorted out an exhausted breath, Wolf sniffing anxiously at him.

Luke was nowhere to be seen.

"Luke, Luke?" she called. Was he playing a joke on her? If he was, it wasn't very funny.

"Luke?" He wasn't in the barn or the smokehouse. She ran down to the small wooden bridge across their river. He was nowhere to be seen. She kept calling, but there was no response. There was something wrong with the horse. Even from the river she could see he was worn out, depressed and injured.

"*Luke!*" she called once more, desperate anxiety straining her voice. The evening song of birds, the murmur of the river, the dying light and the perfume of early evening drifted around her, but nothing else. Unconsciously, her hand lay protectively over her stomach.

Wolf whined as she came back across the yard.

Where was Luke? She shoved the obvious answer away. It didn't mean he was—

She refused to even consider it. He could just as easily be lying injured somewhere. It was too dark to hunt for him now. Wherever he was, she hoped he'd be able to hang on until tomorrow. She'd leave at dawn and look for him. Perhaps Augustus Brown would be able to take her straight to him.

Her plan disintegrated when the horse limped heavily to her and blew into her outstretched hand, sighing gustily. He was badly lame; she wouldn't be able to take him anywhere. She'd have to ride one of the mules. There was no bedroll, no saddlebags, not even Luke's saddle holster on Augustus Brown, but there were deep gashes from spurs in the horse's side, the blood encrusted on his skin.

"Come on, boy. Let's get you sorted out." She led the big animal into the barn.

She searched for days, taking Wolf with her. They found no trace of him at all. Luke had vanished.

CHAPTER FORTY-FOUR

I T was the stench that woke him eventually. A sickly mix of grey-smelling salt, damp, rotting wood, slimy green mould, rusty iron, tar and filthy bilge water. It was everything bad about the sea. Luke had never noticed it until the war started. Then it became the taste of war.

The war turned what once was his greatest delight - being on the wide open ocean, the sharp white tang of the air, the thrumming sound of the wind singing in the rigging as the ship leaped gallantly through the waves - into a horror of broken limbs, starving crew, endless doubt and despair.

The smell was strong, like watery vomit on his tongue. It was a stench soaked in complete defeat and failure. It was the odour of Tess, broken under the wheels of the carriage, dead in the muddy street.

It permeated his skin, dug into his nostrils, his brain every day, until he'd left the sea behind, until he'd breathed in the clean air of the mountains.

There was something about this ship that gave an even darker undercurrent to the fetid stench. Slaves. It reeked of them. Foul, like the ship he'd taken Hope off.

Hope.

Luke groaned. The pain in his skull was excruciating. On the back of his head was a lump the size of an egg. He struggled to sit up and realised he was chained to a bulkhead. A thick, iron wrist-shackle prevented him from moving more than three feet from where he sat. He tugged fruitlessly at the chain, but there was no breaking it free from the plate in the wall. In the near darkness he made out the shapes of other chains hanging along the wooden partition.

Around him, packed tightly together, were wooden crates and metal-hooped barrels of different shapes and sizes. He was lying on sacks that covered the floor. They were fairly comfortable. Beaver pelts, probably.

The gentle slap of the water against the hull and the soft roll of the ship told Luke they weren't at sea, but in a harbour. Had they left Silver Birch Landing? He had no way of knowing; he didn't know how long he'd been unconscious. Either way, Luke needed to get out as quickly as possible. He yanked at the chain again. This was pointless. It would never come out. He leaned back against the wooden wall.

It was quiet. Too quiet.

It must be night, Luke thought. There was no point in shouting for help. No one who mattered would hear him. He'd simply have to wait until someone came down the companionway that stood a few feet away from him.

The last thing he remembered was the lumberyard, talking to Butler. He couldn't remember anything after that. His brain hurt. Why wasn't he dead? Why had they, whoever they were, tossed him down here? Beyond that cursory thought he didn't waste time trying to figure it out. He'd learn what he needed to know soon enough. He relaxed against the rough wood to wait.

He must have drifted off again because the next thing he knew the swell under the ship had increased, the sway of the boat deepening. He could hear feet running on deck, shouted orders and the heavy, rolling thud of canvas falling. Luke sat up straighter. As soon as the ship's under way someone will come down.

No one did. He could hear the crew working the sails and the ship picked up a predictable rhythm as it cleaved its way through the dark sea, a slice of moon drowning in its wake.

No one came near Luke for two days. Thirst was driving him crazy.

Eventually, the hatch cover lifted. Footsteps clattered down the stairs. Luke pulled on the chains, hauling himself upright and turned to face his captors.

Before him stood two good men, fine sailors who'd served under him during the Civil War. It was an odd reunion. The surprise on their faces mirrored his own.

"Captain Harcourt?" The two sailors stared at him.

"Alfonso? Hammond? How are you? It's good to see you again." Luke's response was one of genuine delight. He stepped forward automatically, his hand outstretched, only to be jerked to a halt by the short length of chain. The two men looked embarrassed.

Hammond stepped forward and shook his hand. "It's right sorry I am to see you here, Captain. I didn't know it was you he had holed up down here or I would have tried to get down here sooner."

"Whose 'he'?" asked Luke.

"You don't know? Well, I guess you're about to find out. He's sent us to bring you up on deck."

"I'm sorry about this, sir." Alfonso thrust the long iron key into the shackle's lock, twisting it hard against the rust inside.

"We hope you won't think too badly of us. We're just obeying orders, like." Hammond's embarrassment was uncomfortable. Luke nodded and the three made their way up onto the deck.

Hammond and Alfonso had reason to be embarrassed. Luke had been a good captain, his ship, impeccable. When they stood with him now, he knew they saw this vessel through his eyes. It was filthy, ropes left lying uncoiled on the deck, the deck itself unscrubbed and greasy, the brass was dirty green, the canvas frayed and torn, the rigging slack.

Luke didn't have time to do more than glance at his surroundings. He found it hard to believe any captain would let his ship get into this condition.

"Luke Harcourt." The voice dripped with amused mockery.

Luke swung around in surprise. One of the nastiest pieces of humanity he'd ever encountered, and had hoped never to see again, stood on the poop deck sneering down at him. The man was Jacob Cratchet.

Luke found it impossible to think of Cratchet as a captain in any sense of the word. He knew his time on the ship would either be short or brutal. Possibly both. Their roles had been reversed not so long ago, and as captain he'd had to flog Cratchet. The man had left him no choice.

Now, Cratchet was the one with the power. Luke suspected a flogging would be the least of his worries.

The only thing that kept Luke going was the thought of Hope. At night, she filled his dreams. There was one dream of her he hated, and it was happening more and more often. It was the one where he couldn't remember her face. Just as he caught a glimpse, she dissolved like smoke. He'd wake in a sweat, shaking with fear.

*

They'd been at sea for three months. He was put to work as a member of crew. The irony of finding himself in this position, under Cratchet's command, left a sour taste in his mouth.

Luke was given no opportunity to escape. Whenever they pulled into port he was chained up below decks. With San Francisco behind them, they were now on the long run down the coast of South America. At first, Luke tried to figure out when he'd be thrown overboard, and if Cratchet would even bother making it look like an accident. He doubted it.

Cratchet had two sidekicks. Gerard, the First Mate, was a ratty-faced creep with a sniggering laugh who enjoyed cruelty for its own sake. Murchesson, the mute, stood seven feet tall in his unwashed stockings, the scars of bad stitching crawled over his bald head and across one blind, white eye. Bulging with muscle, he did what he was told without question or hesitation. It was the only thing that kept the men in line.

At first, Luke was pleased to meet up with Alfonso and Hammond again, but after their initial meeting, he swiftly realised that friendship with him meant at best a reduction in water, or more importantly grog rations, and at worst, a flogging.

Unlike Luke, Cratchet enjoyed flogging his men. In the short time they'd been at sea, four men had been flogged for minor infractions and imagined insubordination.

For the most part, the crew were ordinary sailors who found themselves on a bad ship. And it was a very bad ship. Cratchet exulted at being captain. He made sure no one forgot it. What he didn't do was *be* the captain. Without a good leader, the men were lazy and undisciplined. Luke itched to be back in command. He hated to see a ship treated so badly and a crew rotting away with it. It was still a long haul to the tip of the continent, but if order wasn't brought back before then, Luke doubted anyone would make it around alive. Perhaps that's where he'd be 'lost at sea'. Cratchet certainly wasn't wasting rations on him. At each meal Luke was given less than half what the other men ate. Luke wasn't sure he really minded. The rations on board made Navy food look like a veritable feast, in retrospect.

Luke tried to keep his head down and stay out of trouble, but it wasn't easy. Cratchet had a new plaything and he toyed with Luke, pushing him to the limit, looking for any excuse to stretch him across the hatch and use the whip. It took all of Luke's Navy training and his own iron will not to react.

Cratchet read it as a sign of weakness. He mocked Luke every moment he could, making him stand double shifts one after the other till Luke was dropping with fatigue. The crew, well aware of Cratchet's hatred for him, stayed as far away from Luke as they could.

All except the cabin boy, Matt, a youngster of about ten. From the moment Luke took the blame for something Matt had done, the boy hero-worshipped him. That act had lost Luke his water ration for two days. After that, whenever he could, Matt sneaked Luke extra food or water claiming he didn't need it. He laughingly said he was too small for all the food the cook gave him anyway.

Matt was an unprepossessing kid. Small, skinny, with thick, thatch-like, ginger hair that stood up at all angles, hazel eyes and freckles spattered haphazardly over his too-thin face. He was all angles, knees and elbows and seemed to move only in explosive starts and spurts. He was continually covered in bruises and dirt and was terrified of Cratchet. He cringed if the man came near him. If he was summoned to Cratchet's cabin, Luke noticed the boy's face would suddenly go vacant, his body rigid.

CHAPTER FORTY-FIVE

The Pacific Ocean, The coast of North America

LATE one night while on watch, Luke was pacing the deck in an attempt to stay awake. As he turned away from the foremast to retrace his steps, he heard a muffled whimper. Matt was tightly huddled in the shadows of the short stairs of the fo'castle. His head buried into the crook of his bony arms wrapped around his skinny legs.

"Matt?"

"Go away," came the tearful reply.

Luke went across and sat down on the stairs near him without saying anything.

"I said, go away."

"I heard you."

They sat in silence for a while. Then Matt sniffed wetly and dragged his sleeve across his face, smearing tears, dirt and snot in its wake. He scrubbed at his face with the ends of his dirty shirt. It wasn't much of an improvement.

"Cratchet?" asked Luke.

The boy nodded once, blushing a painful red. His eyes filling with tears, his face bleak, Matt turned his head away. Luke's mouth set in a hard, thin line. So, the bastard is still at it. He felt wretched for the kid.

"Go to bed, Matt. It won't happen again."

He stared at Luke. What he saw in the man's face gave him the first bit of hope he'd had since he'd signed on as cabin boy six months ago. A small, nervous smile trembled at the corner of his wide mouth. An encouraging one pulled at Luke's mouth.

"Trust me," said Luke. "Wash your face, then go to bed."

The boy sat there for a moment longer watching Luke's face, his desperate eyes locked onto Luke's calm ones. He sniffed hard and dragged his poor, abused sleeve across his face again. He lurched awkwardly to his bare feet and made his way quietly below deck. Luke sighed. Matt was about the same age as David.

David. The other kid Cratchet had abused when he'd served under Luke in the war. The kid Luke had flogged him for. The kid who'd killed himself.

Luke's jaw clenched. Not this time.

Three nights later, Luke was once again keeping watch on deck. As he patrolled the length of the boat he paused, leaning on the bulwarks. It was a quiet night, and only the soft shush of the water could be heard as it ran past the ship's hull. The only other men on deck were those at the wheel and another sailor on watch at the bow of the ship. Below Luke was the Captain's cabin. The portholes were open. He could hear Cratchet belching.

"*Boy!*" Cratchet yelled. He belched again. The man had been drinking heavily, his voice was sodden with it. "*Boy! I said, 'boy'!*"

Luke thought he heard another, much quieter voice. The sound of a slap, a short yelp of pain and a thump of furniture. Luke leaned further over the rail. He strained to hear what was going on. The sound was muffled. Whoever was in there had moved away from the porthole.

He glanced around. There'd better be a damn good reason for a sailor to leave the deck while on watch. He could expect a flogging if there wasn't. Luke couldn't think of a better reason than keeping his promise to Matt. He slipped down the companionway and crept along the passage to the Captain's cabin. He pressed his ear to door and listened intently to the muffled voices behind it.

"No!" It was Matt.

"Do as you're told, boy."

A loud slap. Another drag of furniture.

"Please, no, not again." Matt was begging, crying.

Luke quietly opened the door. Matt was bent over the captain's table, his pants in a puddle around his bony ankles. Cratchet was hoisting up his shirt, his flabby, purple veined, pimply buttocks quivering with anticipation were exposed to the night air.

"Matt." Luke's voice was quiet. If he wasn't so angry he would have laughed at how fast Cratchet spun around, the incredulous surprise instantly wiping any trace of lust off his face. "Matt, go outside."

The kid didn't hesitate. He yanked up his pants, pushed Cratchet away and ran.

"How dare you!" Cratchet's voice squeaked with rage as he tried to shove his shirt back into his pants. He banged his fist on the table, made a grab for his pants as they slid back down. "You don't come in without knocking. Get out!"

Luke shut the door quietly and locked it.

The colour drained out of Cratchet's face. He took a breath to shout for Murchesson. It twisted into a distorted, desperate gasping for air. The frightening strength in Luke's fingers clenched around his throat was nothing compared to the cold look in Luke's eyes.

Cratchet tried to fight back but he didn't stand a chance. The moment Luke's fist connected with Cratchet's face, reason vanished, leaving Luke with nothing but incandescent fury.

There wasn't enough time to beat the man to death, something the darkness in Luke longed to do. The noise soon brought other sailors to the cabin. By that time, the cabin was wrecked, furniture broken, and Cratchet punished. He lay in a bloody, unconscious heap on the floor.

Luke wiped his brow with the back of his hand, smearing blood from his own torn knuckles across it. His breathing slowly returned to normal, along with the awareness of where he was. The banging on the door finally sank in. Someone was now trying to break it down. Luke unlocked it and, leaning back against the wall, breathing slowly, swung it open.

Murchesson stumbled inside the cabin. Other men were pushing behind him trying to get in. There was a stunned silence at the sight of Cratchet lying among the castrated remains of the room. Murchesson knelt and checked the body.

"Is he alive?" Gerard, the First Mate asked in a whisper. Murchesson nodded.

"Mr Harcourt, you're under arrest, for assault of a senior officer. Put him in the hold." If Gerard expected resistance, he was disappointed. Luke was blank. In the aftermath of the fight he was drained, empty. The dark violence had poured out of him. He barely remembered doing what, clearly, he had done. He was exhausted, in body and in spirit.

In the blackness of the hold Luke waited. He knew he'd signed his own death warrant. Luke wasn't sure if he cared. Cratchet had never planned to let him live anyway.

With nothing to do but sit in that dark, dank place, he sank into a deep depression. He'd lost Hope. He'd never see her again. His days were filled with despair. His nights, a sweat of bad dreams. On his first night back in chains, the nightmares had returned.

All of them.

Matt, the only one bringing him food and water, was worried about him. Luke ate less and less. Eventually, not knowing what else to do, Matt sought out Hammond on one of his night watches.

Hammond leaned against the railing amidships fixing up his pipe. He knocked the doddle out into the sea, opened his tobacco pouch and teased out some new strands to stuff into the pipe's cold bowl. He watched Matt pop up the companionway from under bushy, greying eyebrows. From the deep look of concern on his young face there was clearly something on the boy's mind, and he didn't think it was fishing, something Matt talked about whenever he got the chance.

"Mr Hammond?" Matt hopped nervously from one foot to the other, his thin shoulders twitching in the cool night air. Hammond carried on filling his pipe.

"What's going to happen to Mr Harcourt?"

"A flogging, I should think," replied the older man.

Matt shuffled his feet. The Scot waited patiently. He had all night. Eventually, with his eyes fixed firmly on the decking beneath his feet, Matt asked, "When you and Captain Cratchet served under Mr Harcourt, in the Navy, what did he flog Captain Cratchet for?"

Hammond's hands stilled. His eyes flicked over Matt. He struck a match and spent a few moments sucking away at the pipe's stem till he got the tobacco going to his satisfaction. Then he settled himself more comfortably against the railing and looked at the kid.

"What would you be wanting to know about that for, young Matt?"

Matt hopped as if his feet were on fire, his bottom lip caught under his crooked teeth. The story he finally began was jumbled and incoherent in his embarrassment.

"Stop," said Hammond. "I've a mind I know what you're trying to tell me. I've been at sea a long time boy, so nothing you can say will make me blush. Just tell me what's happened."

Matt nodded and swallowed hard. He forced himself to stand still, squared his skinny shoulders and began his tale again, staring out to sea as he rattled it off. Hammond's face didn't change. He puffed a little harder on his pipe at certain points. When Matt was finished, his usually ferocious gaze seemed even harsher. Hammond said nothing.

Matt was racked with a spasm of doubt. Maybe he'd just made it worse for the man in the hold. He shouldn't have said anything. He started back as Hammond stood up with a curt nod, knocked out his pipe again and shoved it into his pocket.

"Right fella-me-lad, you come with me and do as I say. We need to have ourselves a meeting." He marched Matt off to the companionway down to the crew's quarters.

CHAPTER FORTY-SIX

WHEN he was dragged out of the hold two weeks later, the bitter sun speared painfully into Luke's eyes. Cratchet was sitting in a chair facing the mainmast. The chair was about the only thing holding the man upright. He still bore the marks of Luke's fists and it was clear that broken ribs made every movement an agony of discomfort. Luke shot a glance at the mainmast. Tied to it was the hatch cover.

So, the flogging. At last. It was almost a relief.

The entire ship's company was assembled to watch. Just like in the Navy, discipline had to be seen to have its effect. Murchesson shoved Luke towards Cratchet.

"So, *Mr* Harcourt. Did you think you would get away with that?" Cratchet was dragging a cat o' nine tails through his fingers with a delicious sense of expectation. Luke didn't react.

"I've waited a long time for this. You thought you were so high and mighty when you were the Navy Captain, flogging me for nothing more than a little fun! Let's see how much you enjoy some 'discipline'. Do it, Murchesson!"

The big man turned Luke to face the mainmast, ripped his shirt off his back and shoved him into the hatch cover. Apart from a grunt as he hit the cover, Luke put up no resistance at all as he was tied to it. The ropes were so tight they cut into his wrists. He could hear Matt weeping. When Murchesson took the cat from Cratchet, Luke realised that today was the day he'd probably die.

He closed his eyes and thought of Hope. How she looked standing in the orchard with the sun in her hair, how she moved with such grace, how she felt in his arms, how much he loved her, how he longed to tell her that one more time—

A burning, searing scream of white-hot agony tore across his back. He grunted through clenched teeth. He was determined not to cry out, not to give Cratchet the satisfaction. He heard the whistle of the cat as it swung towards him again. He braced himself, his fingers clutching the trellis of the hatch cover as tightly as he could. The whip dug deeply into his flesh.

After the tenth lash, he was sweating, gasping for breath between each cut. The tight ropes around his wrists were all that were keeping him upright. He tasted the metallic edge of blood in his mouth. He must have bitten his tongue. He pushed himself to his feet with an effort, gripped the now slippery slat and waited. He didn't think he'd be able to keep quiet much longer. He tensed, the whip would land any moment.

But it didn't. He could hear the crew begin to murmur.

Luke shook his head to try and clear the sweat from his eyes and twisted round as far as he could, trying to see what was going on. Murchesson was standing in front of Cratchet. Hanging from the big man's fist, the cat twitched sharply, aggressively in the silence.

"What the hell are you doing, you big oaf?" spluttered Cratchet. "Get back to work. I want Harcourt skinned alive!"

Murchesson jerked the whip. It writhed behind him on the deck. "Come on. Do it. Kill him!"

Murchesson didn't move.

"*Kill him!*" Cratchet screamed. He struggled to his feet. "Give me the whip. Give it to me!" He lurched towards the Swede, who folded his arms and waited. "What's the matter with you? Give me the cat. Look what he did to me." He pointed to his face. "A sailor can't hit a superior officer, and I'm the captain of this ship! He must be punished."

Still Murchesson stood like a rock. Cratchet reached out to pull the whip out of the big man's hands. Murchesson shook his head.

"Captain?"

Cratchet turned. There stood Matt.

"A man *should* be punished for striking the captain," Matt said, his voice a little high with nervousness. "But, but he's been punished enough."

Cratchet was stunned into silence. Matt folded his arms just like Murchesson.

"Captain." Hammond stepped forward. "The ship no longer has need of your services."

Cratchet laughed. His voice had an edge of hysteria. "The ship? The ship! I'm the captain of this ship! You do what you're told, when you're told or you will get thrown off it!"

"Very well."

Cratchet swung round in surprise. The crew was just as astonished. The mute had spoken. A muscle twitched and a slow grin pulled hideously across his scarred face.

"You talk too much, but for once you say the right thing." Tossing aside the bloody cat, he picked the man up and strode toward the bulwarks. Cratchet fought desperately. The crew swarmed alongside.

Luke was stunned. He shook his head again to clear his vision. This wasn't mutiny; this was murder. He had to stop them. They could put Cratchet into his cabin or even the hold till they reached their destination or drop him off at one of the watering stops. Vigilante justice wasn't a good idea for many reasons.

"*No!*" he yelled, pulling desperately against his bonds. "Wait! Don't do this. Stop!"

Murchesson held the captain over the rail.

"Drop him!" yelled a sailor. It became a chant, one the crew picked up instantly.

"Drop him! Drop him! Drop him!"

Murchesson grinned at Hammond. The old man gave a short laugh but jerked his head back to the ship. Cratchet landed in a painful heap on the deck.

"As I said, Mr Cratchet," Hammond continued his prepared speech, "we no longer require your services. You're under arrest. You will be locked in your cabin for the remainder of the voyage. When we dock, you will be handed over to the authorities."

"Who's going to run the ship? Ha! You didn't think about that, did you?"

"We have a First Mate."

"Gerard! You're joking! Gerard! He doesn't know one end of the ship from another."

Murchesson pulled Cratchet to his feet, hoisting him up until his face was only inches away, his feet kicking in the air. "Perhaps, but he knows what we do to scum who fuck little boys."

The crew cheered in response. Murchesson nodded, then dropped the man back on his feet and shoved the man away.

"After you, sir." Hammond turned the captain around and marched him to the stairwell. The crew cheered again as the broken, disgraced captain made his way below deck.

"Cut the man down, Matt." Murchesson tossed the boy a knife.

CHAPTER FORTY-SEVEN

Harcourt's Mountain, British Columbia, Canada

B Y day, Hope scoured the mountain. She hadn't found Luke. She hadn't found anything. Neither had Adam White Knife. As soon as he heard about Luke's disappearance, he'd sent out search parties. Luke wasn't on the mountain; he wasn't within a day's ride from Silver Birch Landing either.

At night, Hope lay awake worrying about Luke, praying for him. She had to believe he hadn't left her. Why would he? Augustus Brown had come home, so whatever happened to Luke must have happened on the way back. Should she ride into Silver Birch Landing? Perhaps Constable Carter had found him. But if he had wouldn't he have come to tell her? Augustus Brown had been so lame, and his sides so badly ripped up. Luke would never have done that!

Each time she went out to search for Luke, she rode either Augustus Brown, Charles Dickens or William Shakespeare, trying to give them all some exercise. As a result, she explored more and more of Luke's craggy, tree-covered land.

One day, she rode up as high as she could. Looping Augustus Brown's reins over a rock, she climbed even higher and stumbled upon Luke's lookout point.

The view was breath-taking. Hope sat in the sun, resting her back against the rock. The smell of the pines and the breeze sighing through them tasted like honey. The peace teased at her. With the warmth seeping into her, she closed her eyes and let her mind drift, feeling Luke, his hands moving up her arms. Her skin started to heat up.

Putting her palms flat on the ground, she leaned out towards the sun, into her thoughts of Luke. Her fingers touched metal. The sharp, cold edge broke the spell. Slightly hidden beneath a lichen covered rock, she found a small knife. Luke had grumbled once about losing it. She coughed, the shock of finding it ripping through her. Leaning her head back against the rock, sobs tore at her, trying to burst out, to cripple her. She couldn't break down. Not now. She had to believe. If she started to cry it would mean she thought Luke was—

Clenching her fists, taking a few deep, gasping breaths, she forced the agony down, slipped the knife into her apron pocket and made her way back to the horse.

But the reaction had set in. No matter how much she refused to entertain the possibility Luke was dead, her body betrayed her. Even thinking his name and she began to shake, her whole body wracked in spasm. The harder she tried to stop it the worse it got.

When she got back to the cabin, she made herself some warm milk, curled up in front of the fire and sipped it slowly. Harriet came and perched on her lap, purring contentedly. Hope dug her hands into the cat's thick fur. She would not let this agony defeat her. She wasn't going to lie down and die. Luke was coming back. She just had to be patient. In the meantime, she would make sure that when he did, everything would be just as he left it.

And she'd be right here waiting for him.

She'd gone straight out into the orchard the next day and worked until she almost dropped, digging manure deeply in around each tree. Luke had done this. Hope didn't know if she was doing it right. She didn't care. She refused to believe Luke was dead.

He had found her, given her what her heart had always needed. She had a home, she was entirely loved, and now she was having his baby. He couldn't be dead.

The next morning, she was back amongst the apple trees. It was the one place, apart from their bed, where she could almost physically feel him near her. She swung the scythe from side to side through the alfalfa. Its soft whisper through the crop breathed around her. Wolf was lying in the shade of one of the apple trees having a snooze. Hope smiled. Her mind drifted back to the time when they had first found him. That night in the barn.

A yelp brought her thoughts back with snap. Wolf was on his feet staring in consternation at the ground where he'd been lying. A small apple glowed in the sunshine. Uh-oh. The apples on this tree were ripe. They needed picking. So did the apples in the next tree. And the one on the other side. The apples on every tree, all one hundred of them, needed to be picked.

The next morning, Hope rose long before dawn and whipped through the early morning chores leaving the whole day free to harvest apples. She had to get them all picked and stowed away. Then, when Luke came back, all he had to do was take them to town. This had to be done right. After all, without the apples they'd have nothing, no money, no food. Luke might lose everything.

First things first - a ladder. Those trees were nearly fifteen feet high. In the barn, she found four of them leaning against one wall. They had an odd shape, but they were definitely tall enough. She'd never really looked at the barn itself. It'd been merely the background to the most important thing in her life - Luke. When he was in front of her, nothing else existed.

Stacked so neatly that she hadn't realised until now that it wasn't the wall itself, were wooden crates. One had a very faded "Smith's Apples" in dark green on the side. Inside the trunk, under the stairs in the barn, Hope found some sacks with long handles. She tried one, slinging the long handle over her head so the sack hung in front of her. Could work. The ladders, the crates, the chest all stood together against the barn wall. Probably safe to assume they were all for the same job.

Just need to get it all down to the orchard now. It would take all day to carry all the boxes there. Filled with apples they'd probably be too heavy to carry back. There was only one thing to do; hitch the mules to the wagon, load everything up inside it and drive it all down there.

She studied the wagon and then taking down the halters she'd seen Luke use, laid them out on the barn floor. She scrutinized them carefully, comparing them to the wagon's shaft. Once she thought she had an idea of how they worked, she put it altogether and then hitched up the mules. Hope was extremely proud of herself when she was done. It had only taken three attempts to get it right.

She coaxed and pulled the mules until they'd manoeuvred the wagon as close to the crates as possible and then, standing on the chest, loaded the boxes inside the wagon. When the floor of the wagon was covered with crates she stopped. Getting one of the ladders in was a little more tricky, but she managed, eventually. Arming herself with a sack, she climbed into the wagon's seat and slapped up the mules.

With the ladder pushing its way through the tree branches, the wagon parked next to it, the sack slung across her shoulders and hanging on her hip, Hope got to work. She started at the top. As she tired, she would have less distance to travel every time her sack needed emptying. She was extremely careful with the apples. She didn't tumble them out of the sack but packed each one in a crate as gently as she could, putting a layer of hay between each layer of apples. Having no idea whether apples would bruise and then spoil, she wasn't taking any chances.

Before she realised it, it was late in the morning. To her delight, she already had a wagonload of full crates. She drove them back, unloaded them near the cabin and then began the arduous task of stacking them in the root cellar. It was exhausting. She'd never underestimate an apple again.

She plopped into a chair and with her feet up on another one, enjoyed a hot pot of tea, a brief lunch and some short-bread. It went down very well. In fact, tea had never tasted so good. Soon she was back in the barn loading more crates.

Her sense of accomplishment deflated when she realised she'd only picked one tree's worth of fruit. There were ninety-nine still to go.

She'd never get finished! The task suddenly became work. She managed to do only one more wagonload before dark. Collapsing into bed that night she dreamed of apples she'd already picked, appearing back on the tree each time she reached up for another one.

The next day, high on a ladder, her arms and shoulders already aching after only one hour, she was wiping her hot, damp brow when Adam White Knife, Rachel, their children, as well as a number of other Nlaka'pamux rode into the orchard.

"Good morning Hope," called Rachel.

"Rachel! Adam! How nice to see you."

"We've come to help."

Hope was never so glad to hear those words in her life.

"Oh, thank goodness," she exclaimed. "I'm so grateful. Thank you so much. You'll need some sacks. Let me go get some." As she climbed down, the Indians dismounted and hobbled their horses in the shade of the trees.

Adam's oldest son took Hope's sack from her and scrambled up the ladder. The young boy's first apple never made it into the sack. He sank his teeth into the crunchy, juicy fruit with delight.

"Jude." Adam frowned at his son. Tilting his head, Jude chewed with the considering air of a connoisseur, nodded his approval and began picking apples straight away. Everyone laughed; even Adam smiled indulgently.

"How did you know I'd need help?" asked Hope.

"We helped Luke last year and the old man, Josiah Smith, every year before that. It's a fair trade," replied Rachel. "You help us with the fish, and we help with the apple harvest. You get fish, we get fruit. Everyone benefits and—"

"We should get more crates," interrupted Adam, looking into the wagon. "Too much talking. Time to work." Two of the young men had already unloaded the empty crates from the back of the wagon.

"If you'll give me a hand, we can get them, Rachel," said Hope, glad to have a break from picking apples for a while.

Hope and Adam's calm-eyed wife climbed onto the wagon's seat and drove off at a brisk trot with the two young men perched on the backboard. The day didn't seem quite so 'work-like' anymore. Its suddenly more festive atmosphere lifted her spirits. They quickly set to work loading the wagon to the brim with the other three ladders, crates and sacks enough for everyone.

While they were loading the wagon Hope asked, "Who was Josiah Smith?"

"Josiah?" Rachel took another crate from the young man and stacked it in the back of the wagon. "He was the old man who owned this land before Luke. I've never known a grumpier old man. I don't know how Anna, his wife, put up with him. He was always polite to Adam, I think because he was afraid of him, but he was difficult with everyone else."

"How did Luke meet him?"

"Luke won the mountain from him in a poker game."

"What?"

"That's what I heard."

"But how? I mean..."

"Anna took ill and he drove her into town to Doctor Tyler, but she died before they got there. The old man got drunk and insisted on playing poker. Luke won, so the land was his."

Rachel caught and stacked another crate.

Hope didn't want to hear this. Not about Luke. Winning land off a grieving old man sounded so… ugly. Rachel caught the frown on Hope's face.

"You don't like that?" she asked.

"It doesn't sound right. The old man had just lost his wife. It seems almost like stealing."

"I can't see Luke doing that, can you?"

Hope looked away. The day has lost its lustre.

"Hope, Luke is a good man. You know that. Trust him."

Luke, Hope thought. Where are you? Please, please be all right. Soft, golden motes of dust that drifted aimlessly in the air around Hope. A silent tear slid unheeded down her cheek.

"Do you think he's still alive?"

Rachel's eyes filled with compassion. "Oh, Hope, I pray he is. Don't give up."

Hope sighed and stretched, her hand resting on her belly. Rachel's eyes widened and a smile leapt to her mouth.

"Hope? Are you—"

Hope glanced down, a soft smile on her lips.

"Yes. At least, I think so."

"Oh! That's wonderful." Rachel clapped her hands. "Come, let's get this wagon packed. The men can take it down to the orchard, and you and I, will have a chat."

CHAPTER FORTY-EIGHT

HOPE physically ached for Luke. His absence filled every moment, awake or asleep. She hadn't realised how alone she'd been until the Nlaka'pamux had stayed for a month. It was easier for them to remain rather than return to the village every night. They slept in the barn. A pile of thick blankets found in the barn's trunk came in very useful. They ate all their meals together. Hope's gratitude to them, not just for helping with the apple harvest, but their joy in her pregnancy, as well as their company, went a long way to helping her through this hard time.

Little Esther developed an obsession with Harriet. When she wasn't throwing a stray apple for Wolf to chase after or patting the mules, she would be lugging the cat around. Poor Harriet was very patient, stretched in the little girl's chubby arms until she was almost pulled out of her skin, the grey cat would wait until Esther stopped for breath, putting her down to get a better grip, before slipping out of her clutches and darting up a tree to hide among the fruit when she'd had enough.

At the end of the month, all the apples were harvested and stored in the root cellar, each crate's short legs lifting it above the apples in the one below. On the last day, Adam brought in a deer carcass. That night, with the meat crackling on a spit the men had rigged up in the yard, they feasted royally. Wolf chewed noisily on a bone, and Harriet took bits gently out of Esther's chubby little fingers. Roasted apples stuffed with nuts and honey and drenched in thick cream finished off the meal.

Rachel was glad they'd been able to help Hope. She was worried about her. Her pregnancy was advancing and, although she'd impulsively told the girl not to lose faith, she was afraid of what would happen if they did discover Luke's body. Every now and then Hope would turn from the top of the ladder and, shading her eyes, stare down the road as if Luke would appear at any moment. She refused to leave the cabin and move into the Nlaka'pamux winter quarters.

Autumn was at an end. It was already much colder than it should be. Rachel didn't want Hope on her own during hard weather, especially not as she was pregnant. Hope's chickens had already stopped laying because of the approaching cold. Before they left, the men moved the chicken coop into the barn so that at least the birds wouldn't freeze to death.

*

Luke, with a painful application of salt on his wounds healed quickly. He'd bear the scars for life but at least he was on his feet again, although he wasn't sure if he wanted to be. Incredibly, Gerard was a worse captain than Cratchet had been. He made no attempt to get the ship sorted out and was terrified to give an order. He'd seen what happened to Cratchet and was convinced the men wouldn't hesitate to put him under arrest as well - if not throw him overboard. He jumped nervously if the sailors passed by too closely. He was terrified of Matt and the sight of Murchesson made him want to throw up.

What worried Luke the most was his lack of seamanship. How did he ever get to be First Mate? Stupid question. He was a crony of Cratchet's which showed just how stupid Cratchet was.

It wasn't long before the ship had another man in charge.

The storm tore over the horizon straight towards the ship. A ferocious squall, terrifying in its intensity. The sails flapped, desperately trying to flee from their confines in the rigging. As soon as the shout rang out from the watch in the crow's nest, the men, who'd been sunning themselves on the deck, having no orders to the contrary, leapt to their feet. Gerard stared at the approaching horror, speechless.

"Orders, sir?" yelled Hammond.

Gerard didn't hear him.

"Sir! What are your orders?"

Luke was standing near Gerard. He took a step closer; the move startled the first mate. He cringed away.

"Sir, we should take the sails in," Luke asked. It was more a command than a suggestion.

"I give the orders!" snapped Gerard.

"Of course, sir, I was simply suggesting that, as time is of the essence, the sails should come down or the ship will go over when that hits." Luke pointed at the wall of violence that was tearing up the sea and approaching very fast.

"Don't tell me—"

"Sir!" roared Hammond. *"What are your orders?"*

"I don't— turn the ship around. We'll outrun it."

There was a stunned silence. No one could outrun this. Was the man mad?

"Hurry. Now. Go that way," Gerard screamed, pointing starboard.

"Sir, with all due respect," Luke had to shout to make himself heard above the roar of the wind. "We'll never outrun it."

"Yes, we will. Just do it! Go that way. Go, *Go!"* Bellowing at each other like this was impossible. Luke wondered if the men below could hear them.

"Get those sails down now! Cut them loose if you have to," he roared. The authority in his voice made the men jump into action.

"*Stop!* You do as I say, turn the ship around!" Gerard screamed.

The contradictory orders and the hysteria in the first mate's voice confounded the men. Some were trying to follow Luke's orders, others Gerard's.

It was too late for anything. The storm hit. A badly tethered boom ripped loose and swung out across the poop deck. It hit Gerard hard. Luke tried to grab him as he flew past, but the man was ripped from his grasp and flung into the churning sea. The boom was on its way back. Luke ducked but the edge of it caught him as the ship lurched. His head exploded with pain. Thick blood ran down his forehead, getting in his eyes. He shook his head, dragged his sleeve across his face and climbed unsteadily to his feet.

It was every man for himself. The ship was being tossed around so violently that simply holding on and staying alive was all anyone could do. Swinging booms, ripping sails, tons of hard, icy water beating down upon them, gigantic heaves and sudden, awful chasms in the waves beneath them were rapidly tearing the ship apart. Wood exploding under the pressure sent spear-like shards flying across the deck slicing open men's flesh and arteries.

Whenever he could, Luke grabbed a sailor and shouted an order into his ear, then pushed the man towards his objective. There wasn't much he could do now, but giving people sane, sensible and definite orders wouldn't hurt. Those who heard him grabbed others as they flew past and together, they tried to carry out Harcourt's commands.

The ship began to respond. Harcourt wasn't sure if they could ultimately save the ship or the crew, but he was damn sure going to try.

It seemed like hours later. A lifetime of hell. The storm had passed. The sea was calm again as if nothing more than the gentle swirl of dolphins ever disturbed its mirror-like surface. Even the sky seemed clean, polished.

Hammond, being the master, was now in charge, said, "Mr Harcourt, I believe there are wounded men that need attending to. We have no medical officer on board. Would you be so kind as to see what you could do?"

Luke was startled. He hadn't expected that. "I'll do my best, Mr Hammond."

"Thank you, Mr Harcourt. Please do. Simmons, you and Smith go with Harcourt and get the injured below deck, now. Get them patched up as soon as possible." The three men got to work. Hammond put work parties together quickly. He needed to know how badly damaged the ship itself was.

Luke worked like a demon, doing the best he could for the injured men, which wasn't much. He had no medical training whatsoever. Hammond had probably hoped his greater level of education made him a better prospect as a doctor. Two men died while he was trying to pull wooden shrapnel out of them. The utter futility of it all tasted like thick bile in his throat. He had to keep wiping his forehead, the blood and the sweat was blinding him. The screams of the injured ripped through the stench of gore and fear. It filled the small room as terrified, dying men, lost control of their bowels and then their souls. It was Luke's nightmare in the flesh. He was trapped.

"He's gone." The sailor holding the injured man down had to say it twice.

Harcourt shot a glance at the injured man's face. He'd been dead for a while.

Not another one. Dammit. He wasn't a doctor! He didn't know what he was doing here.

"Mr Harcourt." Luke turned. He wondered if his face was as grey as Hammond's.

"You've done all you can. This was the last one. Clean up, get someone to look at that cut of yours and then get some rest. I'll send Johnson down to help you with this," he said to the other sailor who nodded his thanks.

Harcourt just stood there. Exhaustion threatened to over-whelm him.

"Mr Harcourt. I believe I gave you an order."

Luke woke to a quiet ship. Peaceful, apart from the breathing and snores of the men swinging in hammocks around him. He lay still for a while letting the restfulness of it all seep into him. He let his mind drift, remembering, as he did every night, the quiet of the forest, lying with Hope under the quilt in the warmth of the cabin. Her soft skin, quiet laugh, green eyes.

Did she think he was dead? He gnawed his lower lip. Was she safe? He was thankful he'd taught her to use his guns. Was she coping at the cabin with the animals, the apples? Was she even still at the cabin or had she moved into town? He closed his eyes and imagined her cool fingers touching his face. He sighed, rolled out of the hammock and made his way up on deck.

Hammond, Alphonso and Murchesson were leaning on the port side railing.

"Mr Harcourt, would you join us?" Luke strolled over.

"You'd better stop calling me that, Mr Hammond," he said. "That's a politeness reserved for officers."

"I believe you were an officer once," said Murchesson.

"A long time ago."

"Not so long. I hear too you were a good one."

Harcourt snorted. "I did my job. A captain is only as good as the crew beneath him."

"No." The big man shifted to get more comfortable. "That is not so. The crew is only as good as the captain above them." The other two nodded. "And we have had a very bad captain. We have no first mate and Hammond here has no desire to command." He sighed lugubriously. "We are in a pickle."

The men laughed.

"Yes, I suppose we are." Luke grinned.

Hammond coughed. "Well?"

Luke realised the old man was talking to him. "Well what?" A sinking feeling began in the pit of his stomach.

"You can be our captain again, sir," Alphonso chimed in. He seemed delighted with the idea.

"What? No."

The three men looked shocked. Clearly, they'd expected him to jump at it.

"Look, I'm not employed by the company. I have no authority on board. I'm not in the chain of command. Hammond is. He's the master, that makes him next in line. I'm not even recorded as being here. As far as the ship's logs are concerned, I don't exist."

"No, but you're the only man on board with the experience to be the captain."

Luke frowned.

"It's not forever, son. Just get us safely back home."

"Where's that?" More damn responsibility, more time away from Hope.

"Well, as captain, that would be anywhere you like," said Hammond.

Luke looked up. It was the first glimmer of light he'd had. If he could go anywhere, he could turn around and go straight back to Hope. On the other hand, they were so close now to the tip of South America, if they continued on this route then he could go to Boston. He could see his family. He needed to see his lawyers. It could work. He'd be away from Hope for a little bit longer. A week. Two at the most, but at least...yes, this could work.

"What about the crew?"

"They're sheep," laughed Alphonso. "They listen to us."

"They'll do as they're told," growled Murchesson.

"Don't worry about them." Hammond chewed on the stem of his cold pipe. "They'll be glad to have a decent captain for a change. Besides, they followed your orders without question during the storm."

"If I have to discipline anyone? Will they do as they're told then?"

There was a pause.

"Only one way to find out," said Hammond, "but I don't think we'll have any problems. So, my lad, are you up for it?"

Luke's brows snapped together. "If I am the captain, there's one thing you'd better get straight. You address me as 'sir'. Not 'my lad'."

For a moment he worried that he'd gone too far, too quickly. He was relieved to see broad grins break out across the faces of the sailors before him.

"Yes sir!" they chorused heartily.

The next morning, Hammond assembled the crew on deck. Standing behind Hammond, looking down at them, Luke knew they'd be perfectly within their rights to insist Hammond take command. They might think this plan was his idea. He could very well find himself in even worse trouble than before.

"Men," shouted Hammond. "As you know, Captain Cratchet is under arrest. First Mate Gerard was swept overboard and lost at sea during the storm. As—"

The men cheered.

"As master of this vessel, I am the next in command." There was a half-hearted cheer from the back of the crowd.

"However, we do have a man on board who has experience at being a captain. A good one. I should know. Both Alphonso and I served under him during the war. He is a fair, honest man. None of us ever starved and he did his best to win every battle we fought and keep as many of us alive as possible while doing it."

Luke blinked. That wasn't how he remembered the war.

"I suggest we allow him to take command," continued Hammond. "Now, as you know, ships are not generally run on democratic lines,"

The men laughed.

"But in this case," Hammond continued, "I believe it would only be fair to let you decide. We either let Cratchet out and give him control of the ship again, or I take command, or we appoint a new captain. What say you?"

"Who's this captain you're talking about?" yelled a sailor.

"Mr Harcourt."

There was a stunned silence. Harcourt stepped forward. He stood there quietly. It was up to the men. It was their lives after all.

"Mr Harcourt!" a voice called out. Harcourt lifted his chin in response. "You like the cat?"

"Not especially."

The men cheered.

"But if you feel a desperate need to become reacquainted with her, I will oblige." Damn. He shouldn't have said that. He'd ruined Hammond's setup. That's all they'd remember now. What an idiot. There was a murmur of voices below him. Oh, well, what's done is done.

"Three cheers for the new captain! Hip hip—"

"Hooray!"

Harcourt was stunned. As the cheers rang out, he instinctively squared his shoulders. He was captain of a ship again. He grinned. He looked out at the sea. His first real love. There she was, bright, clean under the fresh, open sky. It reminded him of Hope.

Crap. His shoulders slumped a little. He was back at sea. He was captain of a ship again. Crap. Crap, hell and bloody damnation.

CHAPTER FORTY-NINE

Pacific Ocean, The coast of South America

H IS first order had been to clean up the ship. It had been carried out with surprising enthusiasm. The deck wasn't white yet, but it would be, woodwork glowed, brass was mirror-like again. The rigging was clean and freshly tarred. The old sails were still up. It seemed there were no better replacements in the locker. As soon as this assembly was over, Luke planned to meet with the purser to see where the ship's finances stood. He wasn't expecting good news.

The men in front of him had cleaned themselves up as best they could. Clothes washed, long hair retied, most of the men had shaved. He realised Hammond must have given the order for that. He appreciated it. Just as he'd appreciated Matt, after cleaning out the first mate's cabin for him to use, had brought hot water so he could shave this morning. Matt had also laundered Luke's clothes, inexpertly. They were hideously wrinkled, but at least they were clean.

The men were still waiting patiently. Luke cleared his throat. "Good morning gentlemen," he said. There was a rumble of response.

"In a matter of days, we will be at the Cape. Once we have navigated our way around, we will be making for Boston. We should be there by mid-January."

The men stared at him. One brave soul called out, "Why Boston?" There was a grunt. "Sorry. Why Boston, sir?"

Luke had agonised over this decision ever since he'd accepted the post. He could have turned the ship around that day and sailed home back to Hope. On the other hand, he hadn't seen his family in over two years. They didn't even know he was still alive. Apart from that, he had urgent business matters to deal with, especially now he had a wife—a new wife. His lawyers were in Boston.

He dragged his hand through his hair. Boston or not, he was still months away from Hope.

"Boston is where my lawyers are. Because of the inherent difficulties that will arise from Mr Cratchet's arrest and incarceration, I felt it would be prudent to hand the matter over to lawyers I know and trust. That way I can be assured you will get a fair hearing." He hadn't planned on saying that. It was inspired. The men accepted his reason with approval.

Later that day, he called Hammond, Alfonso and Murchesson into his cabin. To say it was cramped would have been an understatement. "As I'm sure you are aware, the crew, never mind the ship, is in no way ready to face what we surely will when we round the Cape.

Hammond, take Alphonso with you, I want a full and complete report on the state of the ship. I know you did it just after the storm, but please do it again. I want you to discover if, and how badly, that damage has deteriorated since then.

Murchesson, I may need your help with the men. They have grown lazy and slovenly. A group of schoolchildren could work the ship faster than they do. Tomorrow we will begin to fix that." He outlined his plan in detail.

The next morning, to the crew's astonishment, Luke stripped off until he stood barefoot in only his trousers, handing his clothes to Matt for safekeeping.

"Hammond, Alfonso, Murchesson, let's get that mis-sen-mast upper topsail in. Matt, you have my watch. Time us."

On Matt's go the four men raced off the fo'castle, across the waist, onto the poop deck, up the rigging, along the yard-arm and hauled up the sail, tying it off neatly and raced back down to the fo'castle as fast as they could. Luke snatched the watch from Matt and grinned at the time. Not as slow as he'd expected. That was a relief.

"Any four of you think you can do better?" he shouted. Almost as one the entire ship's company pushed forward clamouring for an opportunity. Within a short space of time teams of four were racing to finish whatever task Luke set the ship. Luke's team always went first. He was exhausted by the end of it. Muscles he'd forgotten he had ached, and his feet felt raw from the ropes, his skin hot and itchy from the sun.

The following day, Luke combined the teams, doubling the numbers and increasing the difficulty of each task until eventually the entire crew was divided into two.

The plan was a success. The men worked with a will. On day one it was simply the desire to beat the captain's team. After that, it may have been the prize of extra grog rations that spurred the men on. But in a short while, as Luke had hoped, they were competing for the sole sake of winning, of achieving better times than the other teams. The winners would earn ten points. The team with the most points at five o'clock would be counted as the day's winners. Work was judged, not just on speed, but also on performance. Fast but sloppy work lost points.

In a matter of days, the ship was completely transformed. It couldn't have happened sooner. The Cape of Storms greet-ed them with a vengeance.

One minute the sky had been clear, a vivid blue, the wind perfect. The ship was slicing through the waves the way ships are called to. There was a beauty and grace to her that she hadn't known for years. The ship herself seemed to sense it and responded gratefully, bounding through the waves with delight.

Luke was standing near the wheel with Hammond when he sensed a change in the air. He leaned forward and checked the horizon. It was clear. The ship hit a wave and bounced uncomfortably.

"Mr Hammond, would you be so kind as to call all hands on deck?" His tone was so curt, Hammond looked at him in surprise. He glanced at the horizon. There was nothing there.

"Immediately, if you don't mind," Luke said, the slightest tinge of sarcasm lent his voice an edge.

Hammond leapt forward and began yelling orders. Men ran. At first, they thought it was another competition, but in a matter of minutes they were fighting for their lives. The sky turned black with rain. Thick clouds boiled past obscuring the view to less than a few yards ahead of the ship. The massive sails billowed and slapped against the masts as men slipping on the tossing deck, struggled to lower them.

Matt battled his way up onto the deck to bring Luke a slicker and was almost swept overboard. Murchesson grabbed him at the last minute, then shoved him back below decks with a harsh order to stay there.

The storm lasted an hour and then disappeared as swiftly as it arrived. A quick count revealed they had lost no one. Luke ordered a hot meal prepared immediately. From now on they would have to catch meals as and when they could. The storms here were unpredictable. A fire, even as small a fire as the cook's was too much of a hazard in waters like these. He'd have to douse it immediately. The men would have to eat when they could.

As bad as that first storm had been, it was only a foretaste of what was to come. The temperature dropped continually as they approached the Cape and the storms grew in frequency and strength. In the end, they lost ten men. The sails were more than useless. One storm hit them so fast they couldn't take them all in on time and the old, rotten canvas ripped into a hundred flapping strands. For a moment, it seemed to Luke's imagination that the dreadful sound was ship's soul tearing in two.

It took two weeks to beat their way round the Cape and make the turn north. They were nearly out of water, food was low, and the men exhausted. Rationing supplies increased everyone's misery. Luke took his meals on deck, so the crew didn't think he was still enjoying full rations, as was the captain's privilege.

As soon as they could, they put in at a watering place on the coast of South America and bartered some of the cargo for supplies. They couldn't afford a whole new set of sails but managed to trade enough to replace the one the storm had claimed.

As they moved up the coast, the weather improved along with the men's spirits. That is until they left the Caribbean behind and sailed towards Boston. It was winter in the Northern Hemisphere and bitterly cold. Luke was grateful for the heavy coat Murchesson had 'borrowed' from Cratchet for him, even though it was just too tight for real comfort.

CHAPTER FIFTY

Harcourt's Mountain, British Columbia, Canada

IT was late. Hope should have been in bed ages ago, but she was so comfortable in the armchair, she was too lazy to move. Wolf was asleep, his head resting on her ankles, Harriet curled up on her lap. Hope was trying to read, but she kept dozing off. The knock on the cabin door broke in her sleepy thoughts. There was an instinctive lurch in her heart, but she knew it wasn't Luke.

He wouldn't knock.

She pulled herself out of the swathes of blankets she'd wrapped herself in, dislodging Harriet. The cat jumped down and stretched, then sauntered closer to the fireplace, still half asleep herself. She sat and stared at it for a moment and then curled up and promptly went back to sleep.

Wolf had lifted his head at the knock and also slowly stood up and stretched with a gigantic yawn. He followed Hope almost reluctantly as she went to answer the door.

Adam White Knife was outside, brushing snow off his shoulders.

"Adam! Come inside. Let me make you some coffee. You must be freezing. Come stand by the fire."

When Adam ran his eyes over her, Hope felt more ungainly than ever. Her belly was huge. As far as she could figure she had maybe another month before the baby came.

ELAINE DODGE

"Hope, will you come back with me this time? There's plenty of room and you know you're welcome."

She shook her head.

He took the coffee she'd poured him and drank it down almost in one gulp, grimacing as if he'd swallowed a large and very annoyed, old spider. "Rachel wants you to come stay with us. You are Luke's wife. You are family."

Hope was well aware that Rachel would be furious if he went home without her again, but she shook her head again.

"Then let me take you to town. You shouldn't be here on your own."

"No. I'm not leaving the cabin."

"If we don't go now, we'll never make it to town. As it is, the snow is getting deeper every day. This is a bad winter."

She hung her head; she knew he was right, but... "What if Luke comes back? He won't know where I am," she whispered.

"Hope," he said carefully. "It's been months now."

"No."

"Hope—"

"No! I won't leave Luke's home. I have to take care of it for him. I have to be here when he comes back." She was almost in tears.

The fire crackled in the silence that hung between them. "Luke is gone. You need to accept that."

"No, he can't be," she whispered.

He swore softly, "Women, you're all normally stubborn, but pregnant, you're impossible. There is a deer in the smoke house, as well as some dried salmon."

"Thank you for the food, Adam. I'm very grateful. You shouldn't worry about me. You have your own family to worry about."

He only scowled in response.

Adam stayed one more day and spent it chopping wood, seeing to the animals, clearing out their stalls and laying

345

clean hay. The pile of manure in the paddock was growing larger all the time. She was running short of hay as well but there was nothing to be done until the weather changed. He left before sunrise the next day.

When Hope went outside, she discovered a wood stack almost as high as the cabin door. If she was careful it should last quite a while. But it was frightening how much of it the fire chewed up in this incredible cold. If it weren't for the animals in the barn, she'd be tempted to stay in bed all the time.

Adam was a good friend. His offer to take her to town or to stay with his family had been more tempting than she would admit, even to herself. She'd never been so scared in her life, nor had she experienced cold as intense as that which had swept down the mountain these last few months.

She was well aware that if it weren't for the salmon and the deer Adam had brought she would have been in real trouble. The stores in the root cellar were running low as well, apart from apples. She had plenty of them. The apple picking season had been good in many respects. It had been a large crop. She had plenty of dried apples, not to mention bottles and bottles of stewed apples, apple curd, apple butter, applesauce and apple jam.

Without Luke, and being pregnant, she hadn't risked making the journey to town to sell any of the harvest. Now, she was glad, if everything else failed she at least had the fruit. She'd finally mastered fishing, and rainbow trout had fallen victim to her lures a number of times until it was too cold for even the fish to run.

CHAPTER FIFTY-ONE

Pacific Ocean, The coast of South America

THERE was a knock at the door.

"Come in," Luke called. Matt stuck his head round the door.

"They're ready for you sir," he said with a grin.

Luke smiled back. The kid's confidence had grown enormously. He loved being a part of the ship now and chattered incessantly, asking question after question until he drove whomever he was plaguing, insane. Even a cuff on the back of his head only silenced him for a few moments. Luke remembered what it was like, being a kid, sailing the high seas, that deep freedom that came with no real heavy responsibilities, the intense sense of adventure that permeated every day. Matt did his work well and enthusiastically. Luke had even heard him humming as he tidied up the cabin. Luke hoped he'd be able to find a good captain to take him under his wing when they docked in Boston.

"Thank you, Matt." He put the logbook back in the drawer, locked it and followed the lad up the companionway. He'd fallen back into the habits of the Navy very quickly once he took command. There was a sense of comfort in it. A rhythm that gave him something active to do, that kept his mind from brooding on being so far away from Hope. When paperwork failed, he looked for other things to do. He started to teach Matt to read. It was more difficult than he'd imagined. He'd also resolved to teach the boy some basic navigation, but the struggle to get him to memorize the alphabet had convinced him that navigation was beyond his limit of patience and had passed the task onto Hammond.

Now, Luke stood on the fo'castle and looked down at the men. They had become a completely different crew to the one he'd first encountered when he'd been 'press-ganged'. Today, wrapped up against the cold, they were at least clean and tidy. They'd made a real effort. Their hair washed and tied back, if required. Nearly all of them were clean shaven. Those with beards and moustaches had trimmed them neatly. They stood in orderly rows, their hands behind their backs, on the deck below him.

"We reach Boston Harbour tonight. In two days' time, I will visit my lawyers. I suggest we leave Mr Cratchet in his cabin until they have informed the authorities. There will, in all likelihood, be a hearing. If this were the Navy, there would be a court martial. All I can ask is that you tell the truth. I would suggest you remain with the ship until the hearings are over and you have received new instructions from the company or the lawyers. If you must leave the ship, please ensure Mr Hammond knows how to reach you. If he can't find you, he may have to send Murchesson to look for you."

The crew laughed.

"After the war, I'd vowed never to captain another ship. However, each of you has made this a good voyage and for that, I thank you. I wish you luck for the future." The men cheered as Luke, in Navy fashion, saluted them.

*

Early the next morning, Hammond, Alfonso, Murchesson and Matt, rowed Luke ashore. Even though they'd agreed it would be best if they all went to the lawyers together the next day, they also knew this was the last time they would have Luke as captain. They shook hands solemnly when they stood on the quay. Tears rolled unchecked down Matt's skinny face.

"Come on, my lad," said Hammond gruffly, "you stick with me. We'll make a good pair, you and I." And putting a large hand on the skinny boy's shoulders, marched him off to find warm, cheap lodgings for the night.

Luke watched the odd group as they made their way towards the town. The massive Murchesson who'd turned out to be one of the most eloquent men he'd ever met; Alfonso, who could sing like an angel; Hammond, whose fierce gaze, thick, bushy grey eyebrows and deep-barrelled chest hid a wise spirit. Luke had been relieved when Hammond came to him a few days ago to ask what he intended to do about Matt.

"If you haven't settled on any plans for the boy as yet, sir, I have a suggestion of my own. I'll take him. I always wanted a son and I've taken a liking to the lad. I think he'll be a good sailor one of these days, and I'll make sure he comes to no harm," the old man had said gruffly.

"Thank you, Mr Hammond, I would be most grateful, as I'm sure will Matt. I hadn't settled on anything as it happens. I had been thinking of sending him to school."

Hammond had given a hoarse bark of laughter that made Luke smile.

"I can't see him sitting still long enough to learn two plus two makes four, can you sir? No, no, he'll learn all he needs to from me, I'll see to that. We don't want anyone to break his spirit like, do we? Not after what Cratchet did. I think he's just coming right now wouldn't you?"

"Yes, I would. Thank you, Mr Hammond. Thank you very much."

CHAPTER FIFTY-TWO

Boston, United States of America

THE butler, his chin held at precisely the correct angle, his grey hair slicked back severely, his pace exactly right for the high position he held in the house, walked sedately to the front door of the large, high ceilinged, neatly appointed Georgian mansion.

The knock sounded again. The butler frowned. Impatience was not something he appreciated. No matter who the visitor was. He turned the handle and opened the door just wide enough for him to ascertain who was standing on the step outside. The man had his back turned and Jennings could see that his hair curled untidily over his collar. The coat itself announced the wearer to be a sailor.

"Tch," Jennings muttered in disgust. "All shipping business is conducted at the Harcourt Shipping offices in town. All deliveries are to be made at the kitchen entrance," he said austerely, and he closed the door just as the visitor swung round.

Immediately, another knock sounded. Jennings sighed and opened the door once more. "My good man—" he began, then stopped in astonishment.

"How about returning sons, where do they go? Jennings, you old buffer, let me in, it's freezing out here, or don't you recognise the heir apparent anymore?" Luke said with a laugh.

"Master Luke! I do beg your pardon. My most humble apologies."

"Don't give it a thought. I'd prefer if you bent your mind to allowing me in and finding my mother for me."

Jennings stepped back immediately so Luke could pass into the black and white tiled entrance hall. "Allow me to take you coat, Master Luke."

"I'll keep it for now, if you don't mind, I'm still rather cold."

"Of course, sir. I quite understand. The weather has turned a trifle chilly."

Luke laughed. "You could say that."

Anxious to make up for his earlier *faux pas*, Jennings said, "It is good to see you again. Master Luke. Would you like some tea?"

"Yes, please. But first, is my mother at home? I assume my father is at the office?"

"Yes, sir, he is. I will send—"

"Jennings, Jennings!" a light female voice called from the landing above them.

"Who is it? Who's arrived?"

Luke spun round and grinned up at the golden haired, young woman on the stairs. Her hand flew to her mouth in surprise. "Luke? *Luke!* Oh, it *is* you. You've come home. Mama! Mama, come quickly," she called, "Luke is home." With that she ran down the stairs and flung herself into his arms.

"Hello Hero, you're still as hurly burly as ever, I see," he mocked.

"Oh, hush and give me a kiss," she retorted.

He obliged and then swung her around, laughing. "It is good to see you again, little sister," he exclaimed, putting her back on her feet. "Do you always greet visitors with such enthusiasm? Or were you expecting someone in particular?"

She laughed, her eyes twinkling mischievously, but as she was about to reply a voice cried out in disbelief.

"Luke? Oh, my goodness, I thought the child was bluffing. My boy, my very dear boy." A lady, whose dark, toffee gold hair glittered with fine grey strands, swept elegantly down the stairs and took her son's face in her hands. Her fine eyes searched his. Gone was the intense bleakness and sorrow which had dominated his face when they'd stood together at that awful graveside. That had been the last time she'd seen him. He'd turned from Tess's grave, kissed her, shaken his father's hand and walked away. They hadn't heard from him since. There was a different look in her son's face now.

Before her stood a man she wasn't sure she knew, although his eyes had learnt to smile again, for which she was very grateful. She kissed him gently, almost as if she were afraid he would disappear. She turned to Jennings.

"Take his things up to his room, Jennings, order some tea and then send someone to the office for Mr Harcourt. No, do that first. Then order tea."

"There is no luggage, I'm afraid," Luke said, "Just what I'm standing in. But tea would be wonderful. What I'd like first though is a bath and a change of clothing."

Although she was desperate not to let him out of her sight for a moment, Mrs Harcourt nodded, "Of course, my dear. Off you go. Jennings, inform the cook that we'll be one more for dinner please?"

The butler bowed and went on his errands. Luke pulled his mother into his arms and hugged her tightly.

"I won't be long, I promise." With that he ran up the stairs to his old room.

It was nearly two hours later when Luke emerged a different man. Bathed, shaved and in a clean set of clothes, he was ready to face his family.

Jennings opened the door to the parlour for him. Seated around a brightly burning fire in the graceful, pale green and gold room he found his parents, his sister and a stocky young man he didn't know, who stood when he walked in. Luke frowned. He'd hoped to have his family to himself tonight. He didn't feel comfortable sharing what he had to say with complete strangers.

"Luke." His tall father stepped towards him, took him by the shoulders and then, uncharacteristically pulled him into his arms. He gave his son a brief, hard hug. "It's good to see you again. Very good. You look well. How are you?"

"Very well, sir. You're looking well yourself." In point of fact, he was a little shocked at how his father had aged since he'd been gone. A look of worry was etched into the neatly cut features. Luke had also forgotten how precisely his father spoke and found he was quickly slipping back into the habit himself.

"I imagine you've had many exciting adventures since you've been gone," exclaimed his sister. "I wish I was a man, women lead such boring lives."

"Well, if you were, I wouldn't be here!" retorted the young man standing near her. He turned to Luke and stuck out his hand, "We haven't been introduced sir, I'm David Wright. I'm betrothed to your sister."

Luke shook his hand. On closer inspection he liked what he saw but decided to reserve judgement until he knew him better.

"Do strive for a little more decorum, Hero," begged her mother indulgently. At that moment, Jennings came into the room to announce dinner was served.

During the meal, Luke gave his family a fairly sanitized version of events since he'd left home. How he'd spent a few weeks on the gold fields and hated it and how he'd discovered a talent for poker. At that, his father's brows twitched together, a look of even greater unease dug deeper creases on either side of his mouth.

"Don't be concerned Father, it's a talent, not an addiction." Luke smiled, but his father's look didn't change. When Luke recounted how he'd acquired the cabin and the apple orchard in a game of poker his father sighed deeply. It was only when Luke revealed that he had, in fact, persuaded the old man he'd won the land from to accept payment for it that his father's face finally cleared.

Relieved, Luke told his audience how he'd met and become friends with the Nlaka'pamux. He stopped before he got to the most important part of all.

CHAPTER FIFTY-THREE

LUKE waited until they were back in the parlour, coffee was handed around and Jennings retired, closing the doors behind him.

"There is one bit of rather important news I haven't mentioned yet."

They all looked at him expectantly. All of a sudden, he wasn't quite sure how to say it. He stirred his coffee and then said bluntly, "I have a wife."

There was a stunned silence. Mrs Harcourt broke it first, "You've got married again? Who on earth to?" Her voice was filled with concern and not a bit of dismay.

Luke frowned.

"My dear," said Luke's father sternly.

Hero, in her impetuous way, broke in, "Oh Luke, who is she? Where did you meet her?"

This was where things could get tricky and Luke knew it. "Her name is Hope, Hope Booker. Well, Harcourt now, and, well, the truth of the matter is that I bought her, off a bride ship."

His father's face drained of colour.

"Some little Irish slut!" cried Mrs Harcourt. "Oh no, Luke, how could you?" Bursting into tears, she crumpled where she sat. Hero's mouth fell open.

Even David Wright looked stunned. But, being the first to recover, he cleared his throat, "I feel sure there is more to it than that rather bald fact. Perhaps we should let Mr Harcourt tell us more?"

Luke was grateful. "Thank you, and please, call me Luke." He then took a deep breath and told the whole story. It took a while. He was peppered with questions from all sides. The only person who listened quietly was Hero's fiancé. For which Luke was grateful.

At the end of the recital Luke said, "I know it hasn't been conventional, or what you expected, but let me assure you, Hope is a lady in the truest sense of the word. I love her. I hope you can too."

"Where is she now?" his father asked quietly. His brows twitched together as his cup rattled in the saucer.

"She's at the cabin." Luke put his coffee cup on the side table at his elbow. "Let me tell you the rest."

"There's more?" Mrs Harcourt pressed her hand to her heart. "I don't think I can take it."

"Calm yourself, my dear," interjected her husband. "Allow Luke to tell us everything. Son?"

Luke took a deep breath and told his family the final instalment. When he reached the end David Wright said, "So your wife, Hope? She's been alone for over six months now?"

"Yes. But I know Adam will check up on her."

"The Indian?" asked the young man.

Luke nodded.

"Poor Hope," said Hero. "She has no idea where you are?"

"No. That's why I must go back as soon as I can."

"When do you plan to leave?" his father asked. His voice was quiet, strained.

"In a day or two, a week at the most."

"You've only just arrived!" Mrs Harcourt wailed.

"I know Mama, but Hope is alone, and the winters can be pretty brutal on the mountain. I have to get back. Father, may I have a word in private?" At his father's nod he turned to his mother, took her hand and kissed it. "Business, Mama. It can't wait. I'm sorry."

"The library, I think." Mr Harcourt stood stiffly, walked across the room and opened the door. "Please excuse us, my dear." He paused, at the look in his son's eye he continued, "Perhaps it would be best to say goodnight. I've a feeling this may take a while."

The two men didn't speak until they were comfortably ensconced in the dark panelled room. A small fire cast a flickering light over the room. In this quiet, masculine room Mr. Harcourt seemed more at ease. "Some brandy?"

"Thank you." Luke watched his father pour the golden liquid into the deep globes of the brandy glasses. His father's elegance never ceased to amaze him. He was a tall man with neatly brushed grey hair, grey eyes and long-fingered, well-manicured hands. Despite owning one of the larger shipping firms in Boston, he'd never been to sea.

It was his brother who had been the oceangoing member of the family, whose stories had filled Luke's boyhood imagination with fabulous tales of far flung adventures and rollicking, hilariously censored, sea shanties. Mr Harcourt handed his son a brandy and eased himself into his favourite Hepplewhite wing chair. Luke took the second one on the other side of the fireplace.

They sat in silence for a while.

"Hope," Mr Harcourt then said quietly, "It's a good name."

Luke smiled, his wife's loving face hung before him in his mind.

"Does your business pertain to her?" his father asked delicately.

"Well, I must make a new Will," said Luke. "I have to attend to that first thing tomorrow. There's something else you should know. I thought to engage our lawyers on behalf of the ship's crew."

"Indeed," his father raised an eyebrow. "For any particular reason?"

Luke rested his head back against the chair. He closed his eyes and told his father the full story of the ship. When he came to an end, he heard his father's glass clink as it was refilled with some more of that ambrosial liquid from the decanter. Luke opened his eyes.

"I am sorry to hear about that poor child's experiences. If our lawyers can help in any way to bring such a creature as Cratchet to justice, then we will, of course, pay whatever fees are required."

"Thank you, sir, I knew you'd understand."

"Now," said his father changing the subject. "Tell me about this mountain of yours."

Luke poured himself another glass of brandy. His father might have a strong sense of social responsibility, but he was a hard-headed businessman as well.

"I'm not sure you'll approve of this," Luke said quietly.

"I see. It sounds as if it may be a little late for my approval, although why you should feel you need it, I am at a loss to understand."

"I own the mountain, as you know, but I also don't own it."

His father raised an eloquent eyebrow.

"I have an arrangement with the Nlaka'pamux. I own and hold the mountain in trust for them. I, and my family, for as many generations as we survive, may live on the mountain if we choose to. When there are no more Harcourts, ownership of the mountain reverts to the Nlaka'pamux. As long as we live there, they also have the right to live there and nothing may be done on or to the mountain unless we all agree."

"I have heard that those mountains are worth a fortune."

"They are. There's lumber, salmon, gold, beaver pelts. It's a rich, beautiful country, Father."

"Yet you grow apples?"

"Do we really need the money? Besides, getting the wealth out of the mountain destroys it. You wouldn't believe the devastation that's left behind. After the war, the gold fields... I decided the mountain has more value as it stands."

"The Indians, what do they feel?"

Luke tossed back the best brandy he'd drunk in over two years. "They've lived there for centuries and have the same feeling for the land as I do. They'd take care of it as they always have. The other thing is, as long as I own the land, I can dictate who lives on the mountain and who doesn't. For them, that means they have less chance of being moved onto reservations."

"I see. Well, as you say, we don't really need any more money."

Before he went to sleep that night, Luke wrote to Hope. It was a long, passionate letter, assuring her of his love, devotion and imminent return.

CHAPTER FIFTY-FOUR

THE next few days were filled with meetings with lawyers and bankers. Being back in his family's comfortable and elegant home, Luke had realised that, although he'd made the cabin as comfortable as possible, a feat which had taken most of his first few months there, and despite the fact that it was much more sophisticated a dwelling than other homesteaders usually had, it was still rather rough and ready. He felt ashamed that he was making Hope live in a cabin when they were both used to far better surroundings.

He was in the parlour going over his ideas with his mother and sister, when Hero declared, "I think the cabin sounds cozy as it is."

"Really?" asked Luke sardonically. "Because we only have one room, and to be frank, it's not much bigger than this one. It's the bedroom, parlour, dining room and kitchen. I'd like us to have a separate bedroom."

"My dear," his mother interrupted, "I do hope you won't think I'm interfering, but I have been wondering about Hope. Didn't you say she arrived with nothing and that you have bought her, what was it now, a dress and two skirts?"

"Well, a bit more—" At the look on his mother's face, he mumbled, "Yes, that's about right."

"Well, for heaven's sake! Before you start thinking of adding new rooms, you should be thinking about your wife."

"But the new rooms—"

"Never mind the new rooms. Describe Hope. What does she look like, how tall is she?"

Luke laughed. His mother was behaving just like Miss Sylvie back in Silver Birch Landing. Once she'd recovered from the shock of his marriage and been reassured on numerous occasions that Hope wasn't some jumped up servant, or worse, her maternal heart had softened.

"Stand up, Hero," she demanded. "Now, is she anything like Hero?"

Luke stood next to his sister whose blue eyes brimmed with laughter.

"Yes." He smiled. "She's about the same height and size."

"So, anything that fits Hero would fit Hope?"

"Yes. I think it would."

"Excellent! What fun we shall have." She clapped her hands together excitedly. At that moment Jennings entered the room laden with a tea tray.

"Jennings! Order the carriage. We are going shopping as soon as we've had tea."

Jennings bowed and retired.

"Thank you, Mama." Luke took her hand and squeezed it. "I was hoping you would come to Hope's rescue."

The shopping expedition went off without a hitch. They spent most of the day at Jordan Marsh. The emporium had grown considerably since Luke had last seen it. It appeared to stock nearly everything one could imagine and was crowded with milling shoppers. Luke almost bolted at the sight of so many people, but his mother was ruthless and dragged him straight to the Ladies Clothing Department, as it was being called. As soon as she swept into the large room they were attended to immediately.

Taken to a viewing section, curtained off from the general public, they were seated on velvet covered chairs and given champagne and petit fours to consume while dressers and models rushed to find the garments Mrs Harcourt asked to see. Such attention was a relief to Luke, who'd expected to have to jostle with the crowds, being shoved around and having his feet stepped upon. When he commented on the individual courtesy they were receiving, his mother smiled indulgently at him. She wasn't one of the Boston Brahmins for nothing.

They returned, exhausted, much later in the day laden with parcels. Jennings served a large and scrumptious afternoon tea immediately. Luke silently vowed never to put himself through that again. Miss Sylvie's was quite enough for him. Looking forward to a quiet evening at home, he was disappointed to hear that he was expected to attend a ball that night.

"Must I, Mother? I'm rather out of society these days."

"What nonsense. Besides, you have to attend. It's Lilla Cabot's nineteenth birthday party. Although it appears the entire family has taken to farm life these days, like the proverbial ducks to water, it's a little thin on social occasions. Lilla apparently begged her parents to bring her back to Boston for her birthday."

"Lilla? But she's only..."

"Nineteen. And you know she was always fond of you. If she finds out you were in town and didn't attend, she'd be devastated."

Luke laughed. "It was just a child's infatuation, that's all. She probably doesn't even remember me now. Is she still sketching?"

"Rapaciously. She's very good."

"She always was. It would be good to see the sprout again."

"In that case, you'd better hurry up and get dressed. And for heaven's sake, whatever you do, don't call her the sprout!"

CHAPTER FIFTY-FIVE

BOSTON. To Ida May Butler even the name of the city rang of culture, breeding, the highest echelons of society. New York, by comparison seemed raw and brash, almost desperate in its chase after wealth. As for Silver Birch Landing, well, no matter how many whore houses and hotels her father could have built, he would never have given her an entrance to this kind of society. She was careful never to mention exactly how her father had made his money.

To her relief, she'd realised very quickly that Boston society may have vast amounts of wealth, but money was never spoken about. Simply the mention of it was considered extremely vulgar, such sordidly 'new money' behaviour. It was enough that one had it. Nothing could match the well-bred calm and composure that old money carried. So much so that the highest members of this exclusive society in Boston had earned for themselves the nickname, the Boston Brahmins.

Ida May had to keep on her toes so as not to put a foot wrong. It was hard work. But, to be accepted, she was prepared to do it. It was more difficult than she imagined. To Ida May's continued astonishment, wealth in Boston mattered less than character, perhaps because there was so much money already. Those with the deepest pockets, had the highest morals and calmly expected the same from everyone else. Those who didn't match up were ruthlessly excluded from their ranks. Politely, of course.

The little ditty some wit had composed summed it up rather well, she thought.

Here's to dear old Boston,
The land of the bean and the cod,
Where the Lowells talk only to Cabots,
And the Cabots talk only to God.

Here, if she played her cards right, Ida May could finally leave the frontier behind and have all the money and position her heart desired. She'd do whatever it took to be accepted.

She smiled at the man now sitting opposite her in the carriage. Francis Garrison was much older than Ida May and, she'd discovered, no fool. He'd deliberately let slip that he was well aware of her background. Without saying too much, he'd let her know he'd made it his business to find out everything about her, after they'd met on the boat from San Francisco. What she hadn't told him, the private investigators did.

At first, Ida May thought she had him wrapped around her little finger but had swiftly been brought to realise this was a deeper game than any she'd played before. He was prepared to give her everything her avaricious little soul desired, as long as she played by his rules.

Tonight was, she knew, her biggest test. Garrison had hinted that if she managed not to betray herself at this party, he might consider making her more than his mistress. If she didn't, he'd made it very clear he'd have to set her up in New York. A man of his standing in Boston couldn't be seen to have a mistress, especially not such a young one.

Her strategy was all worked out. Francis had promised to introduce her to the Cabots. If she passed muster with them, everyone else would follow suit. She didn't care whose birthday party it was, she planned to dazzle everyone. Tonight was hers!

The carriage pulled up at the front of the large house among the bustle of other carriages and people. Waiting footmen lowered the carriage step. Ida May hopped out, breathless excitement fluttering in her heart.

*

It was a glittering, crowded affair. All of the Boston elite filled the rooms. No one ever refused an invitation from the Cabots. Besides, Lilla was liked by everyone.

Luke was surprised at how much Lilla had grown up since he'd last seen her. Standing with her parents at the doorway to the ballroom welcoming the guests, Lilla's face lit up when she saw Hero Harcourt approaching on the arm of her betrothed, David Wright.

"Lilla," Hero teased. "I have the best birthday present that you could imagine!" She stepped aside to reveal Luke standing behind her, smiling down at the young girl.

"*Luke!*" Lilla squealed in delight. Heads nearby turned in her direction.

Luke laughed. "Happy birthday, Lilla." He gallantly kissed her hand, sending her into blushing giggles, which her younger brothers would tease her mercilessly about for weeks afterwards. "It's good to see you again, and in such beauty as well. I hear you're still sketching. My mother tells me your work is better than ever."

Lilla Cabot was so clearly thrown by having the object of her childhood infatuation hold her hand, she was almost incoherent in her reply. Her mother rolled her eyes.

"Luke," she said, patiently smiling at her daughter and taking her other hand. "I think you had best let Lilla greet her other guests now. It's wonderful to see you again. We've heard rumours of your adventures from Hero and I must admit, we are dying to hear more of them. Perhaps once all the guests have arrived?"

Luke gave a slight bow. "Until later then, Mrs Cabot, Lilla." He kissed her hand again. He couldn't resist; teasing young Lilla Cabot had formed a large part of his youth. He moved off to greet old friends, dance with their sisters and wives and indulge in the refreshments that covered the tables standing in the room next door. Despite the fact that it was still winter, the heat in the rooms rose as more and more people arrived. He didn't get a chance to talk to anyone for long.

He was turning away from the refreshment table when his heart skipped a beat.

Hope?

The woman turned around, laughing at something the man behind her had said. It wasn't Hope. Of course, it wasn't. How could it be? Luke's hand tightened on the glass he was holding. He wanted his wife. She filled his every waking thought. Every woman he'd danced with tonight had only made him long for her more. He realised he'd never danced with Hope. Would she enjoy a ball like this? He'd been in Boston now for a week. Far too long. He had to get back to Hope.

It was well after eleven when he heard a breathy little laugh he thought he recognised. Turning, he was surprised, and not a little shocked, to see Miss Ida May Butler.

Her hand rested on the arm of a man his father thoroughly distrusted and refused to do business with. Francis Garrison was smiling sardonically at the piquant little face gazing up at him.

Ida May laughed at something Garrison said, as he caught the arm of a passing waiter. She lifted her chin and looked around the room. Her eyes widened when she saw Luke. At her quick in-drawn breath, Garrison turned back.

"What's wrong?"

"Nothing," she fluttered, waving her fan. "Mr Harcourt, how nice to see you."

Garrison's eyes narrowed.

"Miss Butler." Luke gave a nod. "I didn't expect to see you here."

"Allow me to introduce you to Francis Garrison."

"I know Mr Garrison. How are you, sir?" The two men shook hands. At that moment, someone came up and claimed the older man's attention. Excusing himself reluctantly, he left Luke and Ida May together.

"How did you meet Francis Garrison?"

"Oh, on the ship." Ida May waved her hand vaguely.

Luke saw the large ruby ring that adorned it. It wasn't an engagement ring. He shot a look at Garrison's departing back.

"Is Hope here?" Ida May asked.

"No."

"So, here you are. A single man in Boston again," she purred, stepping closer to him. He gave short laugh. Perhaps Ida May and Garrison were perfect for each other.

"A married man in Boston, about to leave to rejoin his wife."

"Oh. So, you and Hope are still together?"

"Why would you assume otherwise?"

"She's not here. And besides, I should imagine any wife off a bride ship must pall eventually."

Luke raised an eyebrow. "Tire of Hope? A man would have to mad to do that."

"Then why isn't she with you? I'm sure it would be difficult to introduce her to the Lowells and the Cabots."

Luke laughed. "I wouldn't be embarrassed introducing Hope to the Queen of England. You, however, would be a different matter entirely. Don't throw a fit," he continued as she instantly bridled, "you'll only prove my point. Have you met the Cabots yet?"

"Not yet, apart from when we arrived, I mean. Dear Francis has promised to engineer a meeting. But it's not easy, the Cabots are such snobs."

Luke smiled. "Where's your father, by the way? Is he here tonight?" He sincerely hoped not.

"My father died." Ida May shook out her skirts. "I returned to the east coast immediately."

Luke's first reaction was one of relief. To know he wouldn't have to deal with the man who'd tried to have him murdered, was a reprieve he was grateful for. He felt a tap on his shoulder. Turning, he discovered Lilla Cabot, who had now recovered her composure. Well, almost. He grinned.

"Lilla, my dear." He put an arm around her waist and pulled her in close to his side. Her blushes were delightful. "Allow me to introduce you to Ida May Butler. Miss Butler, Lilla Cabot, the young ragamuffin this party is for."

"Oh, Luke, I'm not a ragamuffin!" declared Lilla. "Why, I'm positively a young lady now."

Luke laughed. "So you are. Forgive me."

Ida May cleared her throat in a ladylike fashion. "How do you know Lu—Mr Harcourt, Miss Cabot?"

"Know him!" Lilla exclaimed. "Why, his sister and I are the best of friends. We were in and out of each other's houses so much growing up that I often forgot whose mother was whose!"

"Underfoot, that's what you were!"

Lilla laughed. "You didn't really mind, did you?"

"No. Not at all."

"You are such a fibber, Luke Harcourt!"

"Never to you, Lilla. Well, almost never."

Lilla laughed up at him. "Father is looking for you. He wants an account of your adventures."

"Very well. Miss Butler, if you would excuse me."

"It was nice to meet you Miss Butler," said Lilla, "Thank you so much for coming to my party."

Luke tucked Lilla's hand into the crook of his arm and they walked off together leaving Ida May standing on her own staring after them. They hadn't gone far when Luke stopped.

"Wait a moment, Lilla."

In a few strides he was back in front of Ida May. Francis Garrison was wending his way to her side as well. Luke didn't have much time.

"Ida May," said Luke urgently, a slight frown on his face. "It's none of my business what kind of relationship you have with Francis Garrison but - a word of warning - be careful."

For once Ida May was speechless.

"I brought you some champagne, my dear." It was Garrison. She jumped. A flicker of fear showed in her eyes as Luke turned back to Lilla and disappeared into the crowd.

On the other side of the room the head of the leading family in Bostonian society greeted him like a long-lost son. Over the elderly man's shoulder, Luke could see the watchful, proprietary gleam on Garrison's face and the beginning of fear in Ida May's. Luke felt sorry for her. She was alone and out of her depth, but there was nothing he could do about it.

*

His family tried as hard as they could to get Luke to stay longer, but he was desperate to get back to Hope. He'd purchased a number of large items for the cabin, including a new bed, an enamel bathtub and a cast iron stove, and had them all stowed aboard the ship. By the end of the week he was back at sea. This time though, he was going home.

His father had purchased one of the new steam ships, testing the waters, like many other ship owners, with this advancement in engineering. *The Catherine*, named after Luke's mother, sailed off on her maiden voyage carrying Luke back to the only place he wanted to be - with Hope.

The vessel still had sails, but one large, smoky chimney butted its way out of the deck to belch thick, black smoke into the air.

Luke hated it, but he had to admit the ship was a lot faster than one with only sails. He intended to disembark at Aspinwall in Panama, take the train across the isthmus and then board another steamer to San Francisco. From there it would be only a few days to Silver Birch Landing. It would be the same route Hope had been dragged across over a year ago.

The Catherine would continue around the Cape and finally unload his purchases at Silver Birch Landing. The journey also gave his father an opportunity to compare how long it took a steam ship to do the journey as compared to one with only sails.

In a little over a month, he'd have Hope back in his arms. Luke couldn't wait.

CHAPTER FIFTY-SIX

Harcourt's Mountain, British Columbia, Canada

THE days and weeks wore on and now the snow lay in deep swathes around the cabin. Getting to the barn was a nightmare. Hope felt increasingly isolated and trapped. When she found herself pacing the cabin, she took herself in hand. Unable to get any exercise outside, apart from looking after the animals, and needing to work off the fidgets, she sat and wrote out a timetable, dividing up every day into sections, each with a task to be accomplished.

Without fail, she walked the length of the cabin five hundred times every day. That should take care of the fidgets.

To stop her mind from becoming fixated on the past or falling into despair over Luke, she determined to learn all the Psalms by heart. There were one hundred and fifty. At first, she thought about learning one a day until she remembered Psalm 119 with its twenty-two sections, each as long as some of the other Psalms.

She also set out to not just read Luke's books on agriculture and nautical history and tactics, but to become proficient in the subjects. Although, taking it beyond theory might be a little more tricky, especially naval tactics. And actually needing the knowledge, well, at least it gave her something to discuss with, with Luke when he came home.

For a change, and for something to do in the evenings, Hope turned her attention to Tess's kist. Opening it up, she took everything out and laid it down on the bed. If she was clever, she might be able to alter the clothes to fit her. It would mean a lot of careful unpicking, cutting some pieces to make extra sections for others, and although she might be able to get a few new outfits from the collection, she'd never done anything like this. Before she'd arrived in Silver Birch Landing, all her clothes had been made for her, but she needed something to do besides learning, and this would be a good challenge. Tess's sewing box, which she'd found in the bottom of the chest, had plenty of thread in it.

The first thing she tackled was the opera cloak. In a gratifyingly short space of time Hope had a comfortable, thick, warm, velvet skirt, that despite her increasing girth, made her feel very elegant.

There was a break in the weather. The sun came out and for a time it was warmer, much warmer. It was glorious. The sun danced on the snow. Melting ice dripped happily off the cedar shingles of the cabin roof. Everything looked bright and cheerful again. Even the animals seemed glad. Birds could be seen flitting through the sky at midday. Deep in their dens, hibernating creatures began to stir, rousing themselves from slumber.

Hope let all the animals out into the paddock, where the snow didn't seem as deep. They gambolled around, kicking out and racing up and down, relishing their freedom. Even Pinkerton was frisky. To be outside once more was wonderful.

When she put them back in the barn that night, Hope made sure they were well rubbed down and had their blankets neatly tucked over them.

Hope, warmly wrapped up, went outside each day and tried to catch up on all the chores that had been neglected. She spent as much time as she could splitting wood. She was running very low and she took advantage of this warm spell to replenish the supply. By the end of the week she could hardly move, her belly was getting so large.

As near as she could work out, she had about another two weeks before she gave birth, although she couldn't imagine getting any larger. She'd finally faced the fact that she'd have to leave with Adam White Knife next time he came around. The weather had made it impossible for him to visit for a while. The longing for the comfort and companionship of Rachel and their family, as well as the realisation that she couldn't give birth on her own had finally overridden her need to stay in Luke's cabin.

These days she was exhausted all the time and her back, which had been sore for a while, had ached almost continually now for a few days. No matter how she sat or lay down she couldn't get comfortable.

Today, she woke feeling more restless than usual. The cabin seemed to be closing in on her. Luke was filling her mind, every thought she had was about him. She could almost feel him; his presence seemed to fill the room. She dragged one of the armchairs close to the bookcase. She took all Luke's books off the shelves, stacking them in neat piles around the chair. She carefully wiped the bookcase down and dusted each volume, before replacing them on its shelves, one by one.

Over the months Luke had been gone, she'd read them all. She'd read every one of his Charles Dickens novels and the Bible from cover to cover at least twice. The books were like old friends now. Without them, she was sure she would have gone mad.

So far, Hope had managed not to cry too much over Luke's disappearance, but when the baby kicked, fear and loneliness flooded her heart. She struggled hard to stay in control, afraid that if she did allow herself to break down, she wouldn't be able to stop.

She picked up another book and gently wiped it down. It was a leather-bound copy of one of the volumes of *Jane Eyre*. It was one of her favourite novels. She'd planned to reread it as soon as she'd mastered Psalm 119. As she opened the cover a note slipped out onto her lap. Luke had obviously used it as a bookmark, although she couldn't ever remember seeing him read the novel. She almost tossed it onto the fire, but then opening it she saw Luke's handwriting and her own name. *Hope's List.*

It was the clothing he'd bought her.

After months of enforced stoicism, it was all that was needed to break her iron control. Her hand flew to her mouth, her whole body heaving with the pain in her chest. In one wretched, agonised sob the cries burst out of her. Wolf was on his feet in a second, hovering anxiously around her. Harriet leaped up onto the top of the closet and stayed there, her tail tightly wrapped around her paws.

Hope cried like she'd never cried before. Her face distorted with grief, her throat ripped raw with screams of despair. She raged, first at Luke for leaving and then at a nameless fate for taking him away, begging for him to come back.

Sweeping the closest piles of books aside, she beat the arms of the chair, kicking the furniture within reach. Wolf, whining, retreated nervously to the other side of the bed.

When she finally stopped, her head was pounding. She could talk in no more than a whisper; her eyes were almost swollen shut. Her back felt like it was breaking. She was exhausted.

She heaved herself onto the bed, pulled the covers over and holding her aching head in her hands eventually fell, hiccupping, into a deep sleep.

She was never sure what woke her, but the pain in her back forced her to her feet. Dull thumps still throbbed inside her skull. Perhaps if she made some coffee, she'd feel better. She shivered. The fire had gone out. Well, that was her own fault; if she would indulge in such hysterics, she'd only herself to blame. Thankfully, it wouldn't take too long to rectify.

She wrapped the quilt around her and ventured outside to get some wood.

The warm weather was lingering. Perhaps spring was finally on its way.

Perhaps not, the wind still had a crisp iciness that hurt. She gathered as much wood as she could carry and hurried back inside, kicking the door closed behind her. Within a matter of minutes, she had some thin slices of venison frying crisply in a pan, coffee bubbling and sliced apples simmering in a thick, sugary sauce to be popped into a pie casing as soon as they were ready.

She was straightening the bed when she heard it. A heavy shuffling, a clicking on the wooden porch, thick breathing and a deep huffing. It made her pause, turn her head and listen more closely. Whatever it was, at least the door was shut. She glanced over at it. Oh no! The latch was still up. Before she could get there, the door slowly swung open.

It stuck. A thump, it moved a little more.

Hope stepped back, not breathing, frozen with fear. A massive, heavily furred, dinner plate sized paw with long, curving four-inch nails, followed by a mobile snout, a huge head and high shoulders, wider than the door, pushed its way in. The grizzly's muzzle twitched at the smell of frying deer. He waved his head around to try and locate it. He drooled, the long strands of saliva stretched slowly onto the floor. He was enormous. At least a thousand pounds of muscle and fat covered in thick, rippling cinnamon and dark brown, grey tipped fur.

The cabin suddenly felt tiny around Hope. She glanced at the fireplace. That was where the bear was heading. That was where the shotgun was. She hesitated. Wolf was crouched, hair on end, black lips twisted back off his gums, long teeth bared, growling. His voice had a depth she hadn't heard before. Harriet flattened herself on top of the cabinet, hissing and lashing her tail sharply back and forth. The bear ignored them. He was ravenous. It had been a long, hard winter and now he needed food. He raised his head and sniffed wetly.

Hope moved very, very slowly. He didn't like that. Muttering under his breath, he shook his huge head. It rippled through his shoulders. She had to get to the shotgun. She hesitantly took another step, she was at the fireplace, between the bear and the sizzling food. The smell was driving the bear crazy. He took another step towards the fire. Hope had no intention of standing in his way. He could have the food. All she wanted was the gun, just in case. Hope reached up and ripped it off the wall.

But this bear had encountered guns before. As soon as she swung it towards him the animal hunched his shoulders higher and let out a bone-shaking, deep-throated roar. In the confines of the cabin the volume was deafening. He surged to his full height, but the roof was too low. He banged his head on the beams.

In this small space an angry bear was lethal.

Hope tried to slip around, out of his way. Her size made her clumsy, she caught her skirt on the arm of the chair. She tried to jerk it free as the bear continued to roar and rage. He swung a huge paw at her, trying to swat her away, smacked the chair instead, sending her flying. She hit the floor hard. Scrambling as fast as she could, she dragged herself out of his way. Terror made her feel slow. Her breath came in sobbing gasps.

A ghastly, hideous growling sounded in her ear. It was Wolf. He was only inches from her face. His black lips twisted terrifyingly with his snarl, his eyes savage. His stiff legged stance radiated sheer animal fury.

"No, Wolf!" She grabbed at his fur. He whipped his head round and snapped, tearing her hand, barely missing her face. She hardly noticed the pain. All that existed here was terror and the face of death.

The bear roared again, then turned his attention to the fireplace. He wanted that food and he meant to get it. As he tentatively pushed at the pan, Wolf sprang.

Blood, foam, gore flew across the room in a thunderous, ripping torrent of rage, anger and pain.

Hope screamed, struggling to the other side of the cabin, pushing herself up against the cupboard. The gun was unwieldy in her hands, she couldn't get a grip, couldn't lift it to her shoulder. Wolf and the bear were smashing the cabin to pieces.

Wolf yelped, flew across the room, over the bed and cracked against the wall, collapsing in a broken, bloody heap on the floor. The bear turned his head towards her, bloody drool hanging from his teeth.

"*No!*" Hope pulled both triggers. At that short distance, the shotgun couldn't miss. Half the bear's jaw exploded. Blood sprayed everywhere. The agony in his howl was more horrific than any sound he'd made so far. He lurched away from her, tried to push past the overturned furniture to get out, to get away from her.

Hope ran, ripped open the dresser drawer and dug around for more shells. She kept dropping them, sobbing, screaming at the bear to get out. She realised she was in his way again. Shoving the shells in, she shifted, keeping to the wall until she was behind the now stumbling bear. Blood was gushing from his face. He swayed backwards and forwards in excruciating agony. Hope turned the gun and beat him with the heavy stock.

"*Get out! Get out! Get out!*" she screamed.

The bear lumbered towards the door, his feet giving way beneath him. He was halfway across the yard when he dropped. Hope lifted the gun and emptied both barrels into him to make sure he never got up again. She slammed the door, ramming home the latch. She slid down, sobbing hysterically.

After a while she managed to get her breath back. Hauling herself to her feet she made her way to the window and peered out. The bear was still there. An unmoving lump. There was no sign of him breathing. He had to be dead. That wound was the most horrific thing she had ever seen. A wave of guilt swept over her.

The poor thing had only wanted some food. After such a hard winter, he must have been starving. Now he was dead. And she'd killed him. Tears rolled down her face.

"I'm sorry," she wept. "I'm so, so sorry." Wiping her eyes, she turned away from the window.

A thick twist of grey, blood-drenched fur sticking out from behind the bed caught her eye. *Wolf!* She made her way across the room to his side, her feet slipping in pools of thick, congealing blood. He was dead. She knelt and lifted his head onto her lap. His long tongue hung limply between his teeth, his eyes staring and empty. He was hollow, sunken, gone.

Cradling his body, she rocked back against the wall, letting the tears run unheeded and unchecked down her face.

The room stank of blood and carnage. She would have to clean it up, but first she was going to bury Wolf. She wrapped him in an old blanket and dragged him outside, making long smears of the blood as she went. It seemed so undignified to treat him this way. She paused when she got near the bear. You poor, poor thing. She wished—

The pain ripped through her belly. The baby! No! It can't be. Not now. It's too soon!

But it was coming, and she was all alone. She dropped the blanket and staggered back inside. She slammed the door shut and latched it. She couldn't risk another bear. Not now!

Driven to her knees by yet another contraction, she had to get to the bed as fast as she could. She couldn't give birth in the blood-smeared mess on the floor.

It was late in the afternoon. The contractions had been almost continuous for the last four hours. Hope was drenched in sweat, trembling with fatigue, weeping in fear and agony. She'd never experienced this amount of pain before. At first, she had crouched on the bed, but eventually, her thighs trembled so much she had to lie down. Now, leaning up against the bedstead, a pillow behind her back, her knees wide, she knew she couldn't do this much longer. The agony was tearing her in half. She had barely any strength left.

"Hope!" It was Adam's voice. The door rattled, a loud banging shaking it on its hinges.

"Hope!"

Rachel. Thank God!

"Rachel!" screamed Hope. "Help me!"

"Hope, can you open the door?" Rachel called.

"No!" She screamed as pain tore through her again.

The door splintered, the axe making short work of the wood. It was wrenched out again, smashed back in until the door gave way. Rachel and Adam flew through, stopping in horror at the carnage and destruction in the room. At Hope's anguished cry, Rachel flew to her side. She ran her hands over Hope's belly and turned to Adam.

"The baby's stuck."

Adam's face fell. "Can you help her?"

"I don't know. Boil some water, quickly. Put this in it." She tossed him a small pouch and turned again to Hope. "Hope, listen to me. You must do everything I say."

"I can't," sobbed Hope, "I'm so tired, I..."

The bleak, scared look on his wife's face worried Adam. "Hope!" he snapped, his aquiline face stern and hard. "Do as she says, or you *will* die."

CHAPTER FIFTY-SEVEN

Silver Birch, British Columbia, Canada

THE ship finally docked. It had been the longest journey of Luke's life. The enforced idleness hadn't suited him at all. He'd spent the days endlessly pacing the deck. At night, he'd forced himself to sit and play poker with some like-minded passengers, but even that couldn't hold his attention for very long. Being with Hope again had become a consuming passion.

Apart from the fact that he loved her, there was something nagging at him, a driving urge pushing him. He had to get back to her as soon as possible. He had to see her face again, to hold her in his arms and reassure himself that she was all right.

The ship slowly worked its way to the quay. Luke grabbed his bag, shoved on his hat and stood fidgeting on deck. The horn tooted with delight as the steamboat dropped anchor. Barely waiting for the gangplank to settle into place, Luke ran down to the quay.

He couldn't see Hope. He frowned. Surely, she'd received his letter? He'd been dreaming of spending the night with her in the comfort of the hotel. Perhaps she was waiting there for him. He gave hurried directions to the porter about his luggage. He pushed his way through the crowd.

The quay had changed during his absence. He hardly recognized it. There was a new building on either side along with a new sign. 'Silver Birch' it proclaimed. What happened to 'Landing'? Did they run out of paint or had they dropped it altogether?

He'd definitely been gone too long. He made his way to the hotel as quickly as he could. He didn't remember this many folk in Silver Birch Landing before. Make that Silver Birch, no Landing.

It was freezing, snow and slush lined the streets and lay heavily on the storefronts' wooden awnings. Icicles hung in long daggers off the edges. The mud in the street was thick and sticky. It didn't smell so good either. The cold and the snow meant the mule and horse droppings couldn't dry out. They were churned up in the already sticky mud under horses' hooves and wagon wheels. Luke stayed on the wooden sidewalk. He didn't want to come face to face with Hope in dirty boots. The hotel wouldn't be too pleased either.

Finally, he strode into the lobby of the Silver Forest Hotel. At least that still had the same name.

"Has Mrs Harcourt checked in?" he asked the clerk behind the desk. The man ran an elegant hand down the register.

"No sir, I'm afraid not."

"*Luke!*"

He turned at the shout. It was the banker, Jonas Campbell. Luke found himself crushed in a bear hug that drove the breath from his body.

"Luke, my good man, you're alive! Where have you been? How's your beautiful wife?"

The rapid-fire questions, each accompanied by a hard pounding on his back, made Luke cough.

"I'm not sure. I was expecting her to be here."

Jonas looked at him keenly. "Where have you been?" he asked seriously. "The last thing I knew, you were on your way to tell that rascal Butler to stay off your land. Haven't seen you since. He claimed you'd been eaten by the fishes."

He pointed to the scar running across Luke's forehead. "Did he do that?"

"No, you could say I was press-ganged. I've been at sea for the last six or seven months trying to get home. That's part of my wages." He rubbed the scar ruefully, remembering the pain it had caused it him at the time.

Jonas's jaw dropped. "Now that's a story I want to hear! And, my lad, you can tell me over lunch. They do a rather good steak here nowadays, lots of onions and gravy. Come on."

"Just a moment, I need to find out about Hope. I'd written her, suggesting she come into town with Doctor Tyler."

"The doctor hasn't been able to get out of town for months, Luke. The snow has been appalling this year. Reason the town's so full," said Jonas. "We've all been well and truly stuck here, indoors. Reckon there's going to be a flood of babies in a few months' time." He laughed. "She probably didn't even get your letter. I wouldn't worry."

He put his arm around Luke's shoulders and frog-marched him towards the dining room. He wasn't taking no for an answer. "You'll see her as soon as you get back. You can leave straight after lunch. One more hour won't make any difference and a good meal will set you up for the journey home. Now, come on, I want to hear about this press-ganging of yours."

Luke relented. He was hungry anyway and Jonas Campbell would be a good source of information on the happenings in Silver Birch over the last seven months.

It was more than an hour later when the men pushed their plates away and were enjoying a cup of coffee. It had been a good meal. Jonas Campbell was an excellent host and a good listener. He'd been amazed and appalled at the tale Luke told. Luke, for his part, was just as astounded at the news Jonas related.

He'd only heard a small fraction of the story from Ida May. The whole, unvarnished truth was incredible, especially Ida May's dramatic escape - he had to give the girl credit, she hadn't said a word of that to him in Boston. He couldn't say he was sorry to hear Tobias John was dead.

"Three days after Butler went into the saw," said Jonas leaning back in his chair, "Dr Tyler brings Tobias John back into town on a litter. The man couldn't have run if he wanted to. Saved Carter the effort of hunting him down. Tobias John was one tough bastard. He was lucky to still be alive. How he was, not even Dr Tyler could figure out. His face was smashed in, his shoulder nearly torn right off, his hip was cracked and three of his ribs and an ankle were broken. He'd been like that for three days. It must have been a hell of a journey being dragged on the doctor's litter like he was."

"Who did it?" asked Luke grimly. "I'd like to shake his hand." He poured himself some more wine.

"Well, I reckon you know him, bit hard to shake his hand though. Doesn't have one."

Luke's eyebrow shot up.

"Got a hoof," the banker continued, twirling his glass, watching the light sparkle through the heavy red liquid. His face was a study of innocence. "Got four of them last time I saw him."

"What?"

"It was that big black of yours. What's his name, Augustus Brown? Silly name for a horse, if you ask me." The banker gave a grunt of satisfied laughter at the look on Luke's face.

"What on earth happened?" Luke leaned forward in his chair, his eyes alight.

"As soon as Tobias John realised the mill workers could finger him for Butler's death, he ran. Went straight to the livery stable and took a horse. Yours."

"Mr Samson?" Luke interrupted. "Is he all right?"

"Yes, thankfully. He'd gone to one of his prayer meetings and was just coming back when Tobias John came charging out of the stable. Knocked the old man flying, but it was only the wind that got knocked out of him. He's still unhappy about that horse though. You might want to go talk to him about that. Figures it's his fault your horse was stolen."

Luke nodded. He had to go there anyway to hire mules, wagons and drivers for when *The Catherine* arrived. And a horse to get home now.

"Turns out, from what Tyler could get out of Tobias John, your horse is Satan personified. Seems it waited till they reached Thunder Creek. The bridge was out and he tried to cross a little further up. They got to the middle of the river and the horse went insane - for no apparent reason, he says. I say it was those vicious spurs he always wore. Why a trapper needs spurs is beyond me. Amazing what some men think makes them look big." He shook his head.

"What happened at the river?" Spurs on Augustus Brown. Bad idea.

"Threw him off, then started biting and smashing its hooves into him. Then it high-tailed it out of there. I assume it went back to your cabin."

Luke's laughter faded. If the horse had gone home, Hope would have assumed the worst. With no news of him for months, she must think he was dead. He had to get back to her now.

"I'm sorry Jonas, I must go. Many thanks for the meal. It was good. I have some calls to make before I leave town and I'm anxious to get back to Hope." Luke dropped his napkin back on the snowy white tablecloth and pushing his chair back, stood up, holding out his hand.

"I'm sure you are, son," laughed the banker, rising and shaking his hand. "Let me know if there's anything you need."

"I will, thank you."

The sun was out, and the street began to steam a little. The smell was, if anything, worse. Luke hurried to the livery stable. Mr. Samson almost burst into tears at the sight of him. Luke gave him a very short summary of the last few months. Mr Samson offered up thankful prayers to the Almighty that Luke was safe, patting Luke's arm and nodding his head.

"It's a wonder to see you, Mr Harcourt. I knew you could not be dead. And I knew you would never leave that pretty wife of yours. I have been praying and praying for you, sir, and I am mighty relieved the good Lord has kept you safe. It's a miracle. A miracle. But, that fine horse of yours—"

He had to reassure the old man over and over again that the loss of Augustus Brown was not his fault. "I need your help, Mr Samson."

The old man stood up straighter. "You have but to ask, sir. How can I be of assistance?"

Any feelings of remorse over Augustus Brown were quickly wiped away when he heard Luke's request. "Well, Mr Harcourt, I can certainly rent you four mules and two wagons, but if I might be so bold, you'll never get them home. The snow outside of town is still very deep, although now that the thaw has set in, it may be possible in a week or two, but the mud may then be a concern."

"I see." Luke had suspected as much. "If that is the case when they arrive, may I store my goods here until we can get them up the mountain more easily? This is the safest place in town I know of, barring the bank." It was the perfect thing to say.

"I am honoured Mr Harcourt, I will personally watch over your belongings."

"Thank you, Mr Samson. May I ask you to supervise their transfer from the dockyard to here? I will leave a letter of authorisation for you at the hotel. Now, if you do have a horse I can buy, I would like to start for home straight away." He'd wanted to call in on the Lees but his need to see Hope was becoming more than he could bear.

"Of course, I have one right here. He's not the calibre of Augustus Brown naturally, but Horatio is a good, strong horse. A fine mountain pony. He's used to this kind of weather. But I will not accept payment. Your horse was in my care and I—"

"That's kind of you, Mr Samson, but I insist."

The old man, seeing the determination his Luke's eyes, bowed his acceptance. "You'll be needing a saddle and a bed roll. I'll put in an extra blanket for you. Do you have supplies, sir? Allow me to put some together for you. I have a small store here for just such emergencies."

The transaction was quickly done. Luke mounted up. "May I ask you one more thing? Could you see the Lees for me? Let them know I'm back and that I'm sorry I can't see them today, but I will be back in town soon. Right now, I must get home."

"I know they will understand Mr Harcourt," said the old man, patting the shaggy brown horse's nose. "Have a safe journey and please give my compliments to Mrs Harcourt."

"I will." Luke smiled. He never left Mr Samson without feeling enriched somehow. The old man's stately dignity imbued the barn with the atmosphere of a palace and being the owner of a livery stable, as the most important job on earth.

Luke slapped the reins and left the stable at a trot. He itched to urge Horatio to a gallop. As soon as they passed the last building on the edge of town, they were off, flying like the wind up the road towards the mountain.

CHAPTER FIFTY-EIGHT

A S much as Luke wanted to gallop the entire way from the town to the cabin, he knew it wasn't possible. To start with the horse would collapse, mountain pony or not, and the weather wouldn't allow it. The sky was clear, but snow did indeed lie thick on the ground. So deep in some places he had to get off and walk, pushing a way through for the horse to follow. He behaved like a sensible man for about half an hour. He crested the small rise and before him lay the open field where they'd spent their first night after he'd bought her.

He laughed out loud at the memory of the moment both of them suddenly realized what they'd done. They'd each married a complete stranger and every night from then on would be shared with that unknown person. He remembered how the colour had drained from her face. Even after his promise not to touch her, she'd been as skittish as a frightened colt.

The memory of their last night together washed over him. Luke's body flooded with heat. Kicking the horse into action, they plunged across the field, the cold air whipping at him. It was exhilarating. A grin stretched across his face as he reigned in at the tree line and stroked the horse's neck. The horse shook his head making the harness jingle and they headed up the track into the forest.

He pushed the horse as hard as he dared each day, pausing to rest only as long as necessary. Each night was an exercise in frustration. Sleep eluded him. He tossed and turned restlessly thinking about Hope. He ached to have her back in his arms, to feel her pulse jump when he kissed her throat, her trembling as his hands moved down her body. He was also desperate to know that she was alright, that this nagging feeling in his gut was just nerves.

Eventually, with only one day's ride ahead of him he fell into an exhausted sleep. He was wakened late in the morning with the horse's mobile lips nuzzling his face.

The sun was high in the sky when he arrived at the cabin. He'd pictured this moment a thousand times. His heart pounded and tears sprang to his eyes.

I must be tired, he thought, rubbing his face. A mob of ravens swirled up from the cabin roof protesting loudly and flapped off into the trees. The horse danced uneasily, an icy apprehension dripped into the hollow of Luke's stomach. Something wasn't right. He pulled the horse up, dismounted and looked around.

"Hope?"

Was she in the barn? A wooden shutter creaked on its hinges. He took a swift step towards the cabin. Then he saw the door. Someone had taken an axe to it. A cold sweat broke out on his forehead. He ran.

"*Hope!* Hope! Where are you? Hope!" He almost fell into the cabin. It was empty of life. Snow lay in a light powder at the door. The fireplace was dead, cold, the ashes scattered by the wind. Furniture was overturned and broken. The bed was unmade, the sheets rumpled and tossed in a heap. And there were bloodstains.

They were everywhere, the bed, the floor, sprayed over the walls. He was standing in it. Vomit rose in his throat. Luke stumbled out of the cabin, leant over to catch his breath and realised he was standing where a large amount of blood had soaked itself into the soil. He stepped back quickly, spun round and threw up in the yard. Wiping his mouth with the back of his hand, he sucked in a deep, ragged gasp of air.

He retched over and over again. Hardly drawing breath.

It was much later before he could move without the bile rising in his stomach.

Opening the barn door, he saw all the animals were gone. Wolf wasn't around either. The barn was deserted; even his small box that had stood on the shelf in the horse stall was missing. The absence of life, the silence, twisted at his gut.

There was a small frisson of movement. A grey shadow crept from behind the remnants of a hay bale and wrapped itself round his ankles, weaving in and out, rubbing its head against him.

"Harriet." Luke picked her up. The heavy purring reverberated against his chest. The cat, making small bird like chirps of delight, began to need its claws into his arm. "Harriet." He rubbed the cat's head. "What happened here? Where is she?" The cat pushed its way beneath his jacket. He did up the buttons to hold her in.

He walked back outside and looked around. The vegetable garden was a mess. Despite the fact that it was half buried under the snow, it looked like bears had plundered it. There was a skunk rooting around in it now. That's when he saw the mound under the oak.

It looked like a grave. He stopped breathing. The blood stilled in his veins. His heart seemed to be pounding dry, constricting tighter and tighter every moment. He forced his legs to move. They buckled beneath him and he landed with a jolt. The cat struggled out of his jacket and fled back to the safety of the barn.

He was almost afraid to touch it. The muscles in his arm cramped under the strain when Luke pushed out his hand towards the mound and with rigid jerks brushed away the snow.

It *was* a grave. It looked shallow - whoever had buried her must have been in a hurry.

His eyes burned. The pain in his chest grew. His hands kneaded the cold, barren soil over and over as he fought the truth of her death. From deep within him an agonized groan, an incoherent cry of rage and desperate loss, a primeval animal howl tried to rip its way out of him, tried to batter through his clenched teeth.

He lurched to his feet, turning away he stumbled towards the cabin. The vomit was rising once again, clutching his stomach he bent over, coughing. The axe was lying on the porch. His hand locked around the handle; his knuckles white.

The fury and anguish tore out of him when he smashed the sharp blade into what remained of the cabin door. Again and again the sound of the axe and his torment were twisted tightly together, tearing each other to pieces.

When he stopped, his breathing rasped in his chest. For a brief moment, he hefted the axe in his hands, then swung it back and now silently and methodically, began to destroy everything.

He only stopped when he found the whiskey. He drank until the rage exhausted itself. The axe fell from his hand and he tripped over it as he stumbled back towards the larder. He pulled another whiskey bottle off the shelf. His fingers seemed numb and the bottle slid from his grasp, smashing on the floor. The warm fumes flooded the room. It reminded him of Christmas pudding, his family, home, Hope. He swore viciously, kicking the broken glass out of his way and grabbed another bottle, opening it and drinking deeply before he staggered back outside.

Evening was flowing slowly down the mountain, seeping across the yard. Cold mist drifted before it, but Luke was too drunk to notice. He had to get away from here, away from that grave. Away from the memories of love. The horse was standing quietly, small shivers rippling his skin. Luke hauled himself into the saddle and headed out the yard, up the mountain, meandering deep into the forest, dragging the whisky down his throat as he went.

He had no idea how much time had passed before he finally reached the Indian winter quarters, but he'd finished the whiskey long before.

Night had fallen. The dark was welcoming. He cradled the empty bottle against himself, tears rolling down his cheeks as he sobbed drunkenly, swaying in the saddle.

The horse came to a halt on the edge of the camp and Luke slid off, unceremoniously landing in a pathetic heap on the ground with a thud. He was conscious of hands pulling at the bottle, but he clung on as he faded in and out. All too soon, oblivion beckoned, and he accepted the invitation gratefully.

It was an unconsciousness mingled with swimming dreams of Hope. He could almost feel her lying beside him. Her face sliding in and out of his vision. He groaned and tried to swat it away. He craved the promise of the black, deep void and the thought of Hope, dead, cold under that icy mound made his stomach lurch. He rolled over and curled up tightly into himself and slid back into his drunken stupor.

The thumping pain in his head woke him. Now he really felt ill. Even opening his eyes hurt. There wasn't much light in the lodge but still it stabbed the back of his eyeballs painfully. He groaned and rubbed his face. He heard a soft sigh and turning his head saw little Esther sitting close beside him. He had no idea how long he'd been out, but clearly it was daytime.

He pushed himself upright, moaning as his brain banged against his skull. It felt like something had been chewing on it. His stomach lurched dangerously. He staggered to his feet, pushed his way past the hide that covered the entrance and stumbled as far as he could before falling to his knees and retching violently.

When the spasm had passed a raging thirst possessed him. He felt disgusting; his throat thick, his mouth dry as gravel. He spat but it didn't seem to help. He needed a bath and a strong cup of coffee. He was glad he was on the outskirts of the village. He didn't really want anyone to see him like this.

Esther had straightened the blanket he'd been sleeping under and was just patting it back into place when he came back into the lodge. She sighed again, heavily, when she saw him. Luke's mouth twitched. Clearly, she wasn't very impressed with him. He pulled some clean clothes and his shaving kit out of his saddlebags and made his way down to the river.

The camp was almost empty, only a few old folk were pottering around doing daily chores. The women must be out foraging for roots, the men folk hunting. Well, at least he could sober up properly before meeting them again. He felt foolish. He must have been a mess when he'd arrived.

A very cold and quick bath was enough to clear his head if not sober him up completely. He was desperate for a cup of coffee. But a shave was called for first.

Luke forced himself to concentrate on the blade against his skin. With a blade this sharp, he wasn't as sober as he'd like to be. A movement in the mirror caught his eye. Esther was approaching with that studied concentration children have when they're carrying something very carefully. The edge of her dress was hiked up and wrapped around the cup in her hands. She reminded him of Hope. His heart lurched and his eyes swam with sudden, hot tears. He cut himself.

Shit.

One thing at a time. Shaving, a simple task. Concentrate on this. Don't think about anything else.

Luke washed the soap off his fingers, rubbed his eyes, moved the mirror so it reflected only the river and began shaving again. By the time he was finished Esther was stand-ing nearby and handed Luke a hot cup of steaming coffee. Smoothing her dress, she watched him in silence as he drank. It was good. It smothered the last of the fumes floating around his brain and made him feel a little bit stronger.

Luke cleared his throat. "Thank you." He gave her back the cup.

Esther dipped her head with a brief, shy smile. When he had gathered his kit and dirty clothes, she took Luke's hand and stood solemnly beside him, looking up at him with her huge, brown eyes. He could see Hope as she used to look standing in front of him. Everything brought her back. Luke's heart shrank tightly in on itself. His hand jerked. He probably hurt Esther, but apart from a blink she said nothing. She simply held on tight and walked back to the lodge with him, giving a little skip every now and then to match his strides.

Luke wasn't really paying attention; his mind was still blank. All he could see was that grave back at the cabin. The only thing he was truly conscious of was that little hand inside his. As small as it was, it was an anchor. He focused on that.

CHAPTER FIFTY-NINE

A S he reached the lodge an ancient, very wrinkled woman came up to him. She gave his arm a squeeze. Looking down at her he was surprised to see a mischievous grin. She threw her skinny arms around him, hugging him as tightly as she could, laughing up at him. He didn't move. His face set like flint. He wanted to be polite, but his head had started to pound again. She pushed him, as if annoyed with him and flapped her hands. "Go, go."

He stepped past her, letting go of Esther and pulled the hide covering down behind him. He wanted to be left alone. There was a woman in the lodge. A wave of irritation swept over him. She was kneeling beside a pile of blankets, her back turned towards him. Had he come into the wrong lodge? He couldn't have, that was his saddle.

She had the same colour hair as Hope. His heart tightened again. She reached out, fussing with the blankets. He frowned. Her skin was pale, almost alabaster white. She wasn't an Indian. She heard him and turned around.

The world lurched. His heart stopped. He stumbled to his knees. "Hope?" his voice was a ragged whisper. "Hope?"

Her eyes were huge, smiling and filled with joy. He shook his head to clear his mind. This couldn't be real. He must be hallucinating. Had he drunk that much? But it was real and in the space of a breath, Luke's arms were full of his living, breathing, loving wife. He crushed her hard to his chest. He breathed in the wonder of her. "Hope."

"Luke. Oh, Luke!"

Kisses damped by tears, hands on each other's faces, in each other's hair, more tight hugs and hard desperate kisses.

Light burst through the darkness that had been a part of their souls for so long and tore it into tatters.

They managed, eventually, to ease back and take stock of each other. He simply drank her in, almost afraid she wasn't real.

With her fingertips, she gently explored the new scar on his forehead. "Oh, Luke. I have missed you so much. I thought you were dead," she whispered.

"I nearly did die a couple of times. The thought of coming home to you was all that kept me going." He kissed her gently. "But I saw your grave!" She looked confused.

"Under the tree, by the barn."

Her eyes filled with tears and she gently cupped his face with her hands. He closed his eyes, revelling in her touch.

"Oh Luke. I'm so sorry. That's Wolf. Adam buried him there." She told him about the bear. He shuddered at the horror of the danger she'd been in, pulling her back into his arms.

"Poor Wolf. He was a good friend."

"I have something to show you." She eased herself out of his arms and fussed among the blankets behind her. When she turned back, her eyes were alight with a glow he'd never seen before, not even after they had lain together as man and wife. She was lit from the inside. He couldn't take his eyes off her face.

"Hold out your arms," she said quietly. She put a small bundle into his hands.

It was a child. The smallest, tiniest, little baby he'd ever seen. An irrational terror that he might crush it swept over him. His hands were huge. He looked up at Hope with concern.

She smiled with such love it almost scared him. "Luke, this is your daughter, Faith."

He adjusted his hold and cradled the tiny bundle in his arms closer against his chest. "Faith," he whispered. "She's... beautiful." He lifted the baby's hand and kissed it. "She's perfect." He pulled back a little and squinted down at his daughter. "Perhaps we should change her name though."

Hope looked startled.

"I was thinking...Cornelius." He struggled to smother a grin.

Hope gave a soft laugh and shook her head. "I think you should stick to naming the animals and I'll name the children." She kissed him gently and leaned against his shoulder.

Luke's eyes filled with tears. He'd ridden into the village with only ashes in his soul. And now, now in one moment, he had more than he'd ever dreamed possible. The baby yawned, waving her fist in the air, then opened sleepy eyes and blinked at him. A fierce love he'd never imagined possible overwhelmed him. The power of it blew away the final rags of darkness littering his soul.

After a while, Hope put Faith back among the blankets. Luke's face was filled with a look of wonder and love that made her heart swell. She leaned towards him and kissed him gently. His eyes closed. He was almost afraid to move in case he broke the spell. Terrified that if he even breathed too hard, he would wake up and find it was only a dream. But her lips were so real. Soft and warm. His fingers traced their outline; the back of his hand brushed her cheek, his eyes shone as he sank into the dark green depths of hers.

"Luke," she whispered, her voice husky. "I'm so glad you're home."

He reached for her then and kissed her with extraordinary gentleness. Gazing deep into her eyes he said, his whole heart in his voice, "I will always come home to you. Nothing could ever keep me away. You are my home."

He laid her gently down among the blankets and moved over her.

The night deepened as man and wife made love, as lover and beloved entwined themselves together and drew each other into the circle of peace and desire that only they inhabited.

THE END

HEART OF THE
Mountain

Love saved them once, will it be enough to save them now?

ELAINE DODGE

CHAPTER 1 OF BOOK 2
IN 'THE HARCOURTS OF CANADA' SERIES

CHAPTER ONE

1866

Pinkerton National Detective Agency,
Chicago, Illinois, United States of America

ZEBEDIAH Harrigan was an imposing presence. An angry six feet three, muscle in the shoulders, a face which had smiled often when he was younger, with devastating effect on women.

He wasn't smiling now, and the result was as profound.

"I need you here in the office, Zeb. This strike is going to happen. Jackson Cole is one man, and he isn't going to come in without a fight. I'd prefer to send a couple of the younger men—"

"They're city born and all of them have strike-breaking experience," interrupted Harrigan. "Matthews is good. Put him in charge. Hunting Cole is going to take time. He's not as stupid as other criminals. Most of the Agency's younger men don't have the enthusiasm for being on the trail for a long time. And as far as the older ones go, you can't ask married men to be away from their families indefinitely."

True enough, thought Pinkerton. He didn't know how Harrigan did it. There were times when the other agents couldn't keep up with the older man's remarkable stamina.

Allan Pinkerton sighed. "I'm not happy about this, Zeb."
Few could negotiate with angry, violent mobs like Zeb Harrigan. Union men tended to back down faster when

Harrigan was on what the Agency euphemistically called 'the debate society'.

For the last few months, Zeb Harrigan's eyes had been dark with a smouldering rage. Whatever was eating him perhaps time hunting a killer would help him work it out.

Pinkerton sighed. He knew he'd lost the argument.

So did Harrigan. The dimples in both of his cheeks deepened, the slight smile hidden under a neatly trimmed, heavy, dark moustache. Despite his age, his still thick hair was only lightly salted with grey.

Unstoppable and incorruptible, as a detective he was second to none. If anyone could bring Jackson Cole in, Pinkerton knew it was Zeb. Despite being in his late sixties, or even older, no one knew for sure, he didn't behave like an old man. Moving with a fluid, if heavy tread, he had the air of a cowboy who could both rough it and live in comfort with equal ease.

"Apart from the fact we know Cole's left town heading west, we have no leads. How are you going to find him?"

"I'll find him," said Harrigan. "Trust me." The dampened anger in his eyes flared again.

The Scotsman shook his head. "Fine." He opened a drawer in his desk and pulled out the list of agents. "Who do you want assigned with—"

"No one. I told you, I'm doing this on my own."

Pinkerton scowled, and shut the drawer with a snap. "Now, Harrigan, see sense, man. You know the company rules. It's not how we work, and Cole is a dangerous criminal. He took the lives of those five strike breakers himself!"

"I know," said the detective. "But his big mistake was taking something else." He picked up his saddlebags and slung them over his shoulder. "I'll send you progress reports." He opened the door.

"Harrigan, wait man, what did he take that's got you so riled?"

Harrigan turned in the doorway and put on his hat. "My granddaughter."

ELAINE DODGE

After many years in design, advertising, broadcast television, and content creation, Elaine Dodge's first novel, 'Harcourt's Mountain' was published in August, 2013, the first in the historical romance, family-saga, adventure series, 'The Harcourts of Canada'.

'The Man with a House on His Back' A short story which reached the semi-finals of the international Screencraft Cinematic Short Story competition was also featured in the SA Horrorfest Anthology, 'Blue Honey and the Valley of Shadow' available here:

https://www.amazon.com/Elaine-Dodge/e/B00H2EK45S

"The Man with the House on his Back, by Elaine Dodge, has the taste of old legends told to children before bed; the kind of stories that provoke nightmares." – Ana de Belen

Other books by Elaine Dodge:

Heart of the Mountain
Book 2 of The Harcourts of Canada

L.E.T.H.A.L.
A short story anthology

Blue Honey and the Valley of Shadow
- A multi-author anthology

(Including Elaine Dodge's story, 'The Man with a House on His Back'.

Out soon:

The Device Hunter – a speculative adventure thriller.
The Queen's Executioner – a contemporary thriller

ELAINE DODGE

Social Media Links:

Website – www.elainedodge.com
Facebook: https://www.facebook.com/ElaineRosemaryD
Instagram: elainerdodge
Pinterest: https://za.pinterest.com/edodgesa/
Twitter: ElaineRosemaryD
Goodreads:
https://www.goodreads.com/author/
show/7222320.Elaine_Dodge

Read Me Ink

htpps://facebook.com/readmeinkbooks
www.readmeinkbooks.com

read ME ink
www.readmeinkbooks.com.
BOOKS FOR EVERYONE

Made in the USA
Middletown, DE
20 November 2023

43077707R00243